Watch Me

A. J. Holt

First published in Great Britain in 1995
by HEADLINE BOOK PUBLISHING

First published in paperback in 1996
by HEADLINE BOOK PUBLISHING

A HEADLINE FEATURE paperback

10 9 8 7 6 5 4 3 2

ISBN 0 7472 4933 4

Typeset by Keyboard Services, Luton, Beds

Printed and bound in Great Britain by
Mackays of Chatham PLC, Chatham, Kent

HEADLINE BOOK PUBLISHING
A division of Hodder Headline PLC
338 Euston Road
London NW1 3BH

For
You Know Who,
with love,
and for my agent,
Helen Heller – truly a great criminal mind

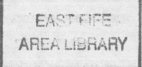

'*Man, though successful biologically, is in many ways an unsatisfactory species.*'

—Anthony Storr, *Human Aggression*

CHAPTER ONE

'Your name?'

Clarice Starling.

'Janet Louise Fletcher.'

'I believe your friends call you Jay, is that right?'

'Yes.'

'Jay, you're a female Special Agent employed by the Federal Bureau of Investigation, is that correct?'

'Yes.'

'You have a degree in psychology from the University of Ohio?'

'Yes.'

'A master's degree in criminology from Columbia University in New York?'

'Yes.'

'And a degree in computer science and statistics from George Washington University in Washington, D.C.?'

'That's correct.'

The defendant's exquisitely dressed attorney rose to her feet. She looked more like a fashion model than a Hollywood/Beverly Hills lawyer and had a reputation for getting her clientele out of impossible situations, ranging from patricide to date rapes of the rich and famous. Her name was Samantha Rhodes, and rumors circulating around the L.A. Criminal Courts Building maintained that she occasionally took on stinkers like this one just to keep her name in circulation.

According to Barney Silkwood, the Deputy District Attorney prosecuting the case, her client, Dennis Lloyd Shaw, had first tortured eleven flight attendants, then raped them vaginally, orally, and anally, and finally decapitated them, at which point he masturbated into the newly created orifice. Shaw had been staring at Janet Fletcher ever since she had been called to the stand. Staring and smiling.

'Your Honor.' Samantha Rhodes spoke up.

'Miss Rhodes.' The judge's name was Rose Alexander, a tiny, wizened black woman.

'The defense has already stipulated as to Special Agent Fletcher's qualifications as an expert witness in this case. Do we really have to go through her entire résumé?'

'Mr Silkwood?'

'Your Honor, I feel that it is important that the jury know something about Special Agent Fletcher's background.'

'I'll go along with that.' Judge Alexander nodded.

'Just so long as he doesn't bore the jury to death,' muttered Shaw's attorney as she sat down. The judge let the comment go with nothing more than a nasty look.

'How long have you worked for the FBI, Jay?'

'Since 1985. I went through the Academy just after getting my master's from Columbia. I took summer semesters and night classes to get my degree in computers.'

'Why computer science?'

'I saw it as a fundamental tool in law enforcement. I wanted to keep up with the technology.'

'What exactly do you do at the Bureau?'

The jury looked interested. Jay frowned and tried to look like an expert witness.

'I work for CART. The Computer Analysis and Response Team, in the Laboratory Division.'

'What do you do there?'

'I analyze evidence that involves computers. Decryption, unlocking files, programming for various groups within the Bureau. The Identification Section in particular.'

'You were asked to help the LAPD Task Force in their investigation of the flight attendant murders, is that correct?'

'Yes.'

'Why?'

'Because of my familiarity with the C-Bix program.'

'What exactly is C-Bix?'

'It stands for Criminal Behavior Index. It's a template of several hundred indices of criminal behavior, particularly as it relates to crimes of violence.'

'You developed this program for the Bureau yourself?'

'Yes.'

'How does it work, Jay?'

'A database of suspects is filtered through C-Bix. On the basis of a scoring curve, the list of suspects is reduced.'

'In this case how was the database of suspects formed?'

'The victims all worked for domestic airlines flying into Los Angeles International Airport. They all flew regular routes. We asked the airlines for access to their reservation records going back for a year.'

Not exactly true. Getting into the SABRE Reservation Computer was as easy as picking the lock on a teenager's diary. After we got what we wanted, we went back and asked for permission.

'What was the result of your investigation?'

'We had a total of eleven million passengers booked in and out of L.A.X. for the last twelve months. C-Bix was programmed to delete any name that didn't appear on flight manifests for all the airlines concerned. That gave us 1,136 names. We ran those names through the National Crime Information Center computer in Washington to see how many showed a criminal record on file. That reduced the list to 382. We compared that list to the VICAP database.'

'VICAP?'

'Violent Criminal Apprehension Program.'

'What was the result?'

'We came down to a list of 32 possible suspects.'

'What happened then?'

'We used C-Bix to select the most likely suspect on the

basis of scores against the baseline indices for multiple homicide.'

'Did Mr Shaw's name appear on this list?'

'Yes.'

Samantha Rhodes was on her feet again. 'Objection, Your Honor. If the initial list prepared by Agent Fletcher contained eleven million names, the possibility of mistaken identity or computer error is overwhelming. Defense has done its own computer test here. There are two hundred and sixty-one "D. Shaws" listed in the Los Angeles County telephone directory alone. This is presuming that the so-called Fly Me killer lived in Los Angeles, which hasn't been proven so far. By our count there are more than three thousand "D. Shaws" living in the various cities from which the flights in question originated.'

'Mr Silkwood?'

'Perhaps Agent Fletcher would be so kind as to educate my colleague as to her methods in this regard.'

'We were aware of the possibility of mistaken identity. Most of the names on the list used credit cards to place their reservations. Mr Shaw was no exception. He used a Citibank Visa in the name of Dennis Lloyd Shaw.'

'Objection overruled.' Samantha Rhodes sat down.

'We were discussing Mr Shaw's appearance on your list.'

'Yes.'

'How did he score?'

'High.'

'How high?'

This was all part of the script. Time to put the icing on the cake.

'To some extent our scoring parameters are based on previous, well-documented crimes. Up until now Ted Bundy was on the high end of the curve followed by Jeffrey Dahmer and David Berkowitz.'

'The so-called Son of Sam?'

'Yes.'

'And now?'

'Dennis Lloyd Shaw beat out Ted Bundy by almost 20 per cent. We've never had a higher score.' Silkwood glanced in Samantha Rhodes' direction, smiled briefly, then turned his attention back to Jay.

'Was there anyone else on your shortlist?'

'Yes. We had seven possibles.'

'What did you do at this point?'

'The LAPD Task Force put them all under surveillance. By that time Mr Shaw was no longer living in Los Angeles.'

'Where had he gone?'

'Florida. His company had transferred him there.'

'He was arrested in Miami?'

'Yes.'

'This was shortly after the murder of the eleventh stewardess, Miss Cynthia Goode?'

Samantha Rhodes was on her feet again. 'Objection, Your Honor. Mr Silkwood is leading the witness. There has been no connection established between my client and the murder of Miss Goode.'

'She was on the flight to Miami when he moved there.'

'So were two hundred other people.'

'Not with a score like his.' Silkwood levered himself off the edge of the table and returned to his seat. He began leafing through his notes. The session was over.

'Objection sustained.'

'No further questions.'

Samantha Rhodes declined to cross-examine and Jay was excused. Climbing down from the witness box, she noticed a small movement at the defense table. His eyes still locked on her, Dennis Lloyd Shaw's hands moved together on the table, the index finger of his left hand sliding into the curled fist of his right. The gesture was obscene, unmistakable, and meant for her alone. She felt like a bug in a killing jar and she shivered. Barney Silkwood shuffled some papers on his desk. Samantha Rhodes looked up at the ceiling. Someone coughed and a chair creaked, the sounds echoing moodily. Dennis Lloyd Shaw looked pleased with himself and continued to smile at Jay, the stiffened index finger rotating slowly in its tight enclosure. The son of a bitch was mocking her.

Fuck you.

She went back to her seat and sat down. Two days later the trial ended and the jury began its deliberations. All she could do was pray that Justice wasn't deaf and dumb as well as blind.

CHAPTER TWO

Jay Fletcher and Lt Mike Stearns of the LAPD sat in the observation-deck bar of Los Angeles International Airport, waiting for Jay's flight to be called. The bar was almost empty, and beyond the bar's floor-to-ceiling window, L.A.X. was a surreal wasteland of sulfurous arc lights and huge, empty aircraft stranded on the asphalt taxiways like massive whales stranded on a midnight beach.

Stearns was in his early forties, a few years older than Jay, his blond good looks seamed and roughened by almost twenty years of being a cop. The two had flirted seriously during Jay's stay in Los Angeles, but nothing had come of it. Both of them were interested, but neither wanted the complications that an involvement would have presented. A homicide investigation like the one they'd just completed wasn't the best environment for an affair, even a fleeting one; still, it was nice to know that the juices were still flowing.

Jay was nursing a virgin Caesar and Stearns was working his way through his fourth beer. They were both exhausted by the Shaw investigation, but they were also sharing a feeling of triumph at a job well done. From the looks of things, the jury was well beyond the guilty or not-guilty stage – now they were trying to figure out just how hard Shaw could be punished. For Stearns it wasn't enough.

'It's like chipping at a mountain with a hammer,' said Stearns. He took another swallow of beer. 'Shaw gets put away, but there's a dozen others standing in line to take his place.'

'So what do you do?' asked Jay. 'Give up? Let guys like him get away with it?'

'Ask the D.A.,' snorted Stearns. 'He did a costing on the Fly Me Task Force. Two point five mil, Jay. To lock up one guy. Jesus!' He shook his head. 'They're still trying to figure out the bill on the O.J. thing.'

'That's different.' Jay smiled. 'Think of all the jobs it created. Trickle-down criminal economics. CNN reporters, T-shirt salesmen, publishers, TV producers.'

'Bronco dealers.' Stearns grinned.

'There you go.' Jay nodded. 'What would Larry King have done without him?' She ran a finger around the rim of her glass and sucked her salt-covered finger. 'Maybe we should start thinking of ourselves as researchers for the next Movie of the Week. Casting directors.'

Somewhere out in the darkness a Jumbo was spooling up its engines. Jay glanced at her watch. Another forty minutes and she'd be on her way.

'Sometimes I wonder why we do this shit,' Stearns

said finally, staring down into his bottle. 'Sometimes I think I've pissed away the whole first half of my life.'

'It could be worse.' Jay shrugged. But she knew exactly what he meant. After almost a decade with the Bureau, her batting average was pitiful. Of a hundred cases, no more than a dozen had resulted in convictions. If it was all a game, the good guys were losing. 'At least Dennis Lloyd is going down for the count. Score one for us.'

'Don't count on it,' Stearns grunted. 'I've seen bigger fish than him swim out of the net.'

'Well, at least I'm not Kelly Mountjoy,' said Jay.

'Who?'

'Mount Kelly with Joy,' she replied with a smile. 'Girl in my class at F.D.R. Consolidated High School in Tomahawk, Wisconsin.'

'What about her? asked Stearns.

'She was the first girl in our class to give up her virginity. We all spent two weeks planning it out with her.'

'Girls did that?'

'Of course. What to wear, what to say, what to do, and when. Kind of like alternative home ec. Somewhere between bran muffins and the baby shower.'

'It was different for guys,' Stearns said wistfully. 'We just fumbled around and hoped for the best.' He laughed. 'I think it's still that way.'

'Well, anyway, for some reason I went to a class reunion a few years back, and there was Kelly. Married to a Baptist minister. Four kids. My old pal

11

Margie Watson was pregnant with twins and Selena McKendrick, the pot-smoking hippie, was a nun. I think they all thought I was a closet lesbian or something, just because I wasn't married.'

'Are you?' Stearns smiled. 'A closet lesbian?'

Jay lit a cigarette and let out a histrionic sigh. 'I'm just a dedicated cop, married to her work. A martyr to social conscience. A clam.'

'A what?' Stearns asked.

'That's what they call them at the Bureau. When I was at school, a recruiter came up from Quantico and made it sound like it was my feminist duty to join. I was in one of those commonsense, be-mature stages and I swallowed the bait. It took me a couple of years to figure out the recruiter had orders to rake in a token quota for that year's Equal Opportunity program.'

'Well,' said the policeman. 'I never thought I'd say it about a Bureau Feeb, but I'm going to miss you, Jay.'

'It's mutual,' she answered. He put his hand out and she ran her fingers lightly across his palm. Not hard to imagine the hand pressed to her cheek. Her own hand touching him.

A monotone voice on the PA system announced her flight. They both stood.

Diplomatically, Stearns tried to kiss her on the cheek, but Jay turned slightly, bringing her mouth to his. The man's lips were surprisingly full and soft against her own. She brought one hand to the back of his neck, gently urging him forward. She let her lips part, enjoying the beer taste of his breath.

The world's full of might-have-beens.

She gave him a light squeeze on the arm. He picked up her suitcase from beside the table and they left the bar. A few minutes later, she boarded the red-eye to Washington, D.C. She watched the starfield twinkle of L.A. vanish below her, then leaned back against her pillow and closed her eyes. The dull hum of the engines should have put her out like a light, but her mind was filled with the cold dead eyes and secret smile of Dennis Lloyd Shaw.

And that, she thought, right there that was the problem. The men in her life were killers and cops. Killers and cops and no one else. No loving touches, no cup-of-coffee in bed, no steady date on New Year's Eve. No softness anywhere.

CHAPTER THREE

The morning rush hour was beginning to wind down as the man in the rented car turned off Broadway and moved into Denver's Curtis Park district, a neighborhood of narrow, tree-lined streets and well-maintained Victorian houses dating back to the gold boom days of the 1860s. After the Depression, Curtis Park had fallen on hard times, but the Yuppie hordes moving back into the inner city during the seventies had made the area into one of Denver's most desirable residential areas. It was still on an upward cycle.

At a stop sign, the man flipped down the visor in front of him and glanced at the folded page from the classified section of the *Denver Post*. He'd circled one of the advertisements in the Apartments to Rent, Furnished section and tracked it down two days before. His new home.

Six month lease
Available immediately to Dec. 1st. Large one-bedroom base. apt. Curtis Park. Close to Downtown. $550 per mo. N.S. pref. Call 892–1112 eve.

He'd found several other possibles in the paper, but this one was easily the most suitable. The apartment itself was more than adequate, but even better, the owner of the house filled all his basic criteria. The recently separated Mrs Ellen Putnam and her teenage daughter, Tina, were just what the doctor ordered. He smiled at his little private joke and drove through the intersection, gliding slowly down the street. It had been almost three months since Phoenix, and it was time for a change. New blood. He smiled again.

The man found the house, pulled in to the curb, and parked. Like all the others on the street, Mrs Putnam's house was large and well looked after. It was painted in discreet shades of charcoal and white and surrounded by a low, wrought-iron fence. The lawn was neatly trimmed and there were pots of flowers hanging from the eaves of the old-fashioned front porch. There was no car in the driveway; his timing was perfect. Ellen Putnam had already left for work and Tina would be in school. Two weeks until the summer holidays began. More than enough time.

Pulling up the toggle switch beside his seat, the man popped the trunk of the car and then stepped out into the bright, early-morning sunlight. If anyone was watching from one of the other houses, they would have seen a medium height, very fit-looking man in his mid-forties wearing dark green jogging sweats and black Nikes. His hair was dark brown, flecked at the temples with a frosting of gray and his eyes were hidden behind an expensive pair of Serengeti Driver sunglasses. He wore

16

a full beard that was closely trimmed and as dark as his hair except for the faint gray stripe running down the chin.

He walked around to the rear of the car and pushed up the trunk lid. Inside there were two black, hard-shell suitcases. He took out the suitcases and closed the trunk, pausing for a moment to look around. Anyone seeing him at close range would probably have described him as being handsome, although they might have wondered why he was wearing tightly fitting surgical gloves over his hands. He knew that from a distance the gloves were invisible.

Gripping the suitcases the man walked casually down the driveway to the side entrance of the house. He put down the suitcases, fished the key Ellen Putnam had given to him out of his pocket, slipped it into the lock, and twisted. He picked up the suitcases again, pushed open the door with the toe of his sneaker, and went inside. Using his shoulder he nudged the light switch on the wall to his left and went down the short flight of steps into the apartment, leaving the door open behind him. Dropping the suitcases again, he went back up the stairs and closed the door, throwing the deadbolt and putting on the night chain as well. Satisfied that he wasn't going to be disturbed, he went back down to the apartment.

It was large, just as Ellen Putnam had described it in the advertisement, brightly lit with recessed spots in the low ceiling. The suite was divided into four areas,

17

living room, bedroom, bathroom, and kitchen. Except for the bathroom, the floor was covered in ash-gray wall-to-wall industrial carpeting. From the feel of it under his feet, the man assumed that the carpet was laid over bare concrete. The walls were painted white and the modern, uniformly beige furniture was a quickly assembled, midprice ensemble that had probably been ordered out of a catalog.

The day before, when he'd come to pay his first month's rent and damage deposit, Ellen Putnam had taken him on a quick tour. He knew that the door at the far end of the modern kitchen led to the laundry room, which he would be sharing with the woman and her daughter. A flight of stairs led from the laundry room up into the Putnam kitchen on the floor above. Yesterday he'd noted that the upper door was also fitted with a deadbolt, but he doubted that either Ellen or Tina bothered to use it. Even if they did, it wouldn't present much of a problem for him.

He carried the smaller of the two suitcases to his kitchen, placed it on the table, and opened it. Inside, a variety of equipment was nestled in custom-designed expanded foam niches. He took out the small Nikon with its wide-angle lens and a plastic bag containing four cigarette pack-sized FM intercom modules he'd manufactured himself, stripping down commercially available Radio Shack units. Looping the camera strap around his neck and carrying the bag, he pushed back the small bolt on the door to the laundry room and opened it.

18

The room, dimly lit by a small, dusty window set high on the far wall, smelled of laundry detergent and bleach. It was equipped with a relatively new Maytag washer and dryer and a large, old-fashioned porcelain laundry tub. There was a roughed-in cubicle under the open stairway with an electrical box. Half a dozen sheet-metal ducts spread out from the cubicle and disappeared into the ceiling. The furnace. To one side, also under the stairs, there was a dark blue, enameled hot water heater.

Stepping forward he pulled open the electrical box door and glanced inside: two rows of breakers with the locations of various circuits written on to a diagram pasted to the inside of the door. Nothing out of the ordinary. No alarm system. The upper floors and the basement apartment were on separate meters for the appliances, but the baseboard circuits were joined. He closed the box door. Above the box he could see the characteristic wires used by the telephone company. Two separate lines, one for the house, one for the apartment. He nodded to himself, pleased. With his splitter he could keep his computer line open all the time and still have the use of the telephone, although he knew he wouldn't need it much. Satisfied with the arrangements, he turned away from the electrical box and climbed the stairs to the main floor.

At the top of the stairs, he put his ear to the door and listened. The faint sound of a radio. Classical, Schubert to be precise, which meant KVOD. It had been playing in the upstairs kitchen when he'd signed the lease. She left it on to keep Archimedes company when she was away at work. Archimedes was a cockatiel. Smiling, he made a silent wager with himself and put one hand on the doorknob. It turned easily. No bet. With the laundry room in regular use, he'd known it was unlikely that either Ellen or Tina would remember to lock the door each time or, even if they did remember, to bother. He opened the door.

The kitchen was lavish and only two or three years old. Jenn-Air range, huge double-door refrigerator, gourmet preparation island in the center of the room, rows of copper-bottomed pots hanging from an overhead rail, black Formica counters with an expensive, hand-painted *faux* marble finish. All of it done in better days, when her marriage was still a going concern. Ellen had told him all about it: the recent separation from her husband, Bob, who now lived in Vail with his new and younger girlfriend; the fact that the divorce was still pending, which prevented her from selling the house for at least another six months, which in turn meant that she really needed the money from the basement apartment. The man had found her openness immediately attractive. Her softness. The slightly pleading, honest innocence that would make the agony so exquisite.

There was a telephone with a pad and pencil on the counter near the archway leading into the living room. Ellen Putnam had taken down the name he'd given her, and the phone number for his hotel. Dr Henry B. Saunders. You could always trust a doctor.

20

Still holding the plastic bag, he lifted the Nikon and took some exposures before moving into the living room. A long couch and several upholstered chairs grouped around a brick fireplace. Earth tones to match the scattering of off-white, roughly knotted Berber rugs. Large framed prints on the white walls advertising art shows in distant cities neither Ellen Putnam nor her husband had ever visited.

A pale, birch monk's table under the large front window that looked out over the front lawn and the street. In the window itself a hanging oval of stained glass that left a bloody stain of sunlight in the center of the table. The window faced west and by his calculations, the stain of light would shift into the middle of the floor at sunset. A suitable marker. If he'd been a superstitious man, he might have taken it as an omen.

There was a large lamp on a table beside one of the upholstered chairs. Crossing the room he saw that the lamp was plugged into a double wall socket almost hidden by the table. Bending down he ran his finger along the baseboard and then stood up. The gloved finger was coated with a fine layer of dust. By all appearances Ellen wasn't particularly finicky about vacuuming. He opened the plastic bag, took out one of the intercom modules, plugged it in, and slid the small box under the chair. Invisible. You'd have to get down on your hands and knees just to see the cord running into the plug.

He took another set of exposures with the Nikon and

moved out into the front hall. Nothing of interest there. An old hat stand, a tall Chinese garden vase growing a crop of umbrellas, and a wide mirror framed in bamboo above a rustic-looking bench. Through an open doorway he could see into the only other room on the main floor – the den, bare of furniture except for a half-empty bookcase and a filing cabinet. Several cardboard boxes overflowing with office equipment. Bob's room before he'd run off to Vail. Smart Bob. Better not to know. Better not to see.

Ignoring the den he climbed the stairs to the second floor. Three bedrooms and a bathroom here, the master bedroom overlooking the street, the bathroom in between the master bedroom and Tina's room. He knew it was Tina's room because of the rap group posters on the wall and the inevitable canopy bed with the equally inevitable pink chenille spread. At the far end of the hall, there was a small room that might have been a nursery once, but which was now a guest room. Sterile and unused. Turning away for the moment, he went forward to the master bedroom and paused in the doorway. He sniffed. Two or three different perfumes, as though she couldn't make up her mind. Equivocal, which fit the analysis of her he'd already made. Another scent. Something like cinnamon and cloves. Probably a potpourri in one of the bureau drawers, or even – so sweet – under the pillow.

He photographed the room from the doorway, catching the way the sun spilled through the trees outside and dappled over the puffy, overstuffed duvet on the bed. Plain rectangular side tables in black lacquer, each with its own high-intensity lamp, each with its own telephone, both dark green.

The walls were light blue, the ceiling two or three shades darker, and looking upward he could see a scattering of small spiky shapes. He'd seen them in stores. Stickers in the shape of stars. At night they would glow in the dark. It was hard to tell in the early-morning light, but he was sure she'd gone to a lot of trouble to make the constellations accurate. It was the sort of just-too-perfect romanticism that would have driven poor Bob out of his mind. Foolish man. Women with that sort of gentleness were getting harder and harder to find.

The man dropped down on his hands and knees beside the bed and flipped up the edge of the duvet. There was another twin outlet hidden at the head of the bed. There was a power bar plugged into one of the sockets with longer cords that traced back to the bedside lamps. There was a third, thinner cord plugged into the bar, and following it with his eyes he saw that it led up under the mattress. He climbed to his feet and turned back the duvet fully, then levered up the near corner of the mattress. A small hand-held vibrator with a knobby, red-rubber tip was hidden between the mattress and the box spring. Bob's replacement. Not as romantic as the sticker stars but probably a more practical solution in the absence of real love. He checked under the pillow on Ellen's side of the bed, just for fun, and much to his delight, found the potpourri exactly where he'd imagined it.

Pleased with himself, he let the mattress fall back into place and got down on to his knees again. He opened the plastic bag and quickly installed another intercom module, tucking it up out of the way between the head-board and the wall. Invisible. Sure not to be noticed. Standing, he took a few more photographs, moving slowly around the room to make sure he caught every angle, finally taking three separate shots of the bed itself. Through the viewfinder he could almost see Ellen there. On a Sunday afternoon not so long ago, Tina had gone off with one of her friends and Bob and Ellen had made love here. Bob had lain above Ellen, thinking about his new girlfriend while Ellen had thought about ... what? The sticker stars in her ceiling sky? It didn't matter. The man let his eyes roam around the room one last time and then turned away, making sure he'd left everything as he found it.

He spent much more time in Tina's room. Of the two she was more important. He had to know her almost as well as he'd know his own child. He went through all the drawers in her bureau, letting his fingers trail over the soft, silky underwear, the folded T-shirts, the balled, much-washed sweat socks, the pajamas. There was no vibrator under Tina's mattress, but there was a diary, red as a Valentine heart and unlocked. He sat down on the edge of the bed and leafed through the pages.

Vince Gannett is a dork ... If I don't see Tabby ever again it's going to be way too soon ... Mom won't get MTV, she says we can't afford it ... I met Terry again, I think he sort of likes me ... Terry and I went to IMAX for the Stones flick. I think he wanted to make out but ... Terry & Tina ... Tina & Terry. I want T. to be the first, make that FIRST, but ... Andrea told me that ... It was kind of nice but maybe we shouldn't ... God! It was so embarrassing! Why does your P. have to be so messy???!!!

He closed the diary and put it back under the mattress. Lots of cards and notes and scraps of paper pinned to the bulletin board over the small pink desk. A young man in a rented, electric blue tuxedo standing in front of the fireplace downstairs. Terry? Another photograph. Tina, younger, hips and breasts still a year or two away, standing in front of a pitched tent at a campsite with a man in his early thirties, dressed from head to toe in L.L. Bean. Dad. Bob. Mr Putnam.

The shadow of the person taking the photograph had fallen across the lower half of Bob's face, obscuring the mouth and chin. Ellen? Better days, but the storm clouds would have begun to gather, like her shadow. Bob's eyes were blank in the picture, trying to hide the truth from the camera. I love my daughter, but my wife bores me to tears. I'm trapped, I can't get away. I want, I want, I want.

'Soon,' the man said quietly, standing in the silent room. 'Very soon now.'

He found a plug behind Tina's bureau, plugged in another intercom module, then took half a dozen photographs, finishing the roll. There was a photo store down the block from his hotel that could give him eight-by-tens by midafternoon. Glancing at his watch, he saw that he'd been in the house for almost half an hour. It was enough, at least for now. He left the room and went back down to the basement, satisfied with the progress he'd made. Tomorrow he would officially move into the apartment, and then it could begin.

CHAPTER FOUR

Jay Fletcher arrived at Dulles shortly after nine. She took a cab to her apartment, told the driver to wait, then dropped off her luggage. On the way back into work, she wondered if she should have taken time for a shower; in late June, Washington was like August everywhere else and by the time the cab reached the Pennsylvania Avenue entrance to the Hoover Building, she felt like a soiled, slightly damp dishrag.

The FBI Headquarters building in Washington was a massive concrete bunker shaped like a slightly skewed tetrahedron filling the entire block from 10th to 9th Street and back to E Street. Since its completion shortly before its namesake's death in 1975, the huge and obscenely expensive monument to J. Edgar Hoover had been described as a giant toaster with two slices of bread on top, an alien cheese grater, and a 2.5-million-square-foot example of how not to design a government building. Almost everyone agreed that it was a monstrosity. Conforming to the height restrictions on Pennsylvania Avenue, it climbed to only seven floors on that side, but

four more stories had been added at the rear of the
building, creating a vertigo-inducing overhang on the
northern face that gave the illusion it was about to
topple over on to the street below. From the outside
the rough-concrete aggregate façade was a brutally
designed, impenetrable fortress. From the inside it was
a confusing maze of beige-walled corridors and anonymous charcoal-colored doors used by its 7,500
employees.

The small entrance used by Special Agents and
expected visitors was located on Pennsylvania Avenue,
as far as possible from the larger E Street entrance used
by the hourly tour groups. Jay stepped into the welcome, air-conditioned coolness of the reception lobby, a
small area furnished like a comfortable living room,
complete with couches, coffee tables, and cozy stuffed
chairs. A glass wall looked out on to a small brick
courtyard with a fountain and park benches. There was
no door leading out to the court and in all the years she'd
been coming to the building, Jay had never seen anyone
out there, or even figured out how you reached it.
Presumably, like a lot of other things about the Bureau,
it was there for show.

Facing the entrance door was a sign-in desk with a
large mirror behind it. The mirror, Jay knew, was
actually one-way glass to let security personnel peer at
visitors. There were also framed portraits of Hoover, the
President, and the presiding Attorney General of the
moment. The Hoover portrait was screwed to the wall,
while the portraits of the President and the Attorney

General were hung on wire. Two elevators were set into the left-hand wall. As Jay entered she noted that the lobby was empty except for the plain-clothes guard at the desk. She presented herself at the desk, flipped open the small leather case holding her plastic-coated ID card and badge, and then signed in. The guard gave her the nod and pushed a hidden button under the desk; one of the elevator doors swished open. Jay climbed in and rode down to the first basement level.

The Laboratory Division of the FBI took up 145,000 square feet of space in the building, most of it on the third floor. The third-floor scientists and technicians called it the Fish Bowl, since the entire section was enclosed by a glass wall so the endless string of tourists could watch the crime fighters at work. Less interesting units like CART were relegated to the rabbit warren of tile-floored offices in the basement.

Leaving the elevator, Jay made a beeline for the windowless lounge, smoked a quick cigarette, then poured herself a muddy cup of coffee from the machine. She took the Styrofoam container down several dog-leg corridors and eventually reached her destination. The CART unit was a low-ceilinged, fluorescent-lit compound of a dozen cinder-block cubicles arranged around the larger room containing the mainframe computers.

The terminals in each office were connected to the CART mainframes as well as the VICAP and National Crime Information mainframes at Quantico and the even more exotic equipment at the brand-new Engineering Division building nearby. CART was buried in the basement, but Jay knew it contained some of the most sophisticated technology available to the Bureau. Contrary to popular perception, the FBI was ludicrously backward when it came to computerization.

Upstairs in the Identification and Administration Division, most files were still hard copy and most of the field offices were still terribly underequipped, but from her own terminal Jay sometimes felt as though she could reach out and touch the world. The decor was nonexistent, the fluorescents gave her a headache, and the coffee was ghastly, but there was no place she'd rather be.

As usual the mainframe office was a mess. Stacks of magnetic tape were piled on dollies; shelves overflowed with thick, spiral-bound manuals for a thousand different systems and programs, and the metal desks around the perimeter of the room were buried under endless reams of fan-fold printouts.

Jack Prine, CART's Aging Specialist, was seated at the big, double-size graphics monitor in the outer room, working with a light pen to add years to a blurred photograph of a girl who appeared to be eight or nine years old. A milk-carton kid, probably abducted years ago. Prine would bring her picture up to date, but Jay knew the chances of finding the child were statistically very low.

Prine glanced up as she entered the room. He grinned. 'You look like shit, Fletcher. Welcome back.'

'You should talk.'

In J. Edgar's day, Special Agents like Prine would

have been fired on the spot. His streaked blond hair hung over his collar, the lab coat he wore over his rumpled suit was awash in coffee stains, and he refused to wear anything but bolo ties. If ever there was an Agent to Embarrass the Bureau, it was Prine, but as long as he stayed hidden in the basement, nobody minded, since he was far and away the best graphics man on staff. His computerized aging techniques were uncannily accurate and he'd been instrumental in putting together extrapolated enhancements that had solved at least half a dozen murders.

'Langford's looking for you,' Prine added. 'Either his ulcer's acting up again or somebody seriously pissed in his cornflakes.'

'Oh?' Charles Langford was Deputy Director of the Computer Analysis Response Team and Jay Fletcher's direct superior. A grizzled, gray-haired widower in his late fifties with two grown daughters, Langford had given most of his adult life to the Bureau and it showed. He'd come up the hard way, from Special Agent to Special Agent in Charge, and finally to his present rank as a Deputy Director, collecting a fistful of citations and an ulcer along the way.

Langford knew barely a thing about computers in any real sense, but in the early seventies he'd been one of the first administrators at the Bureau to recognize the significance of microprocessor technology and its potential within the sphere of law enforcement. Heading up CART was the direct result of that recognition and he was now regarded as the grand old man of computers at the Bureau. There was also a rumor that he'd put his money where his mouth was and invested early in the Microsoft Corporation, which explained his predilection for expensive suits and his big house in Chevy Chase. Either that or he knew where J. Edgar's secret files were stashed.

'He wants to see you as soon as you come in,' said Prine. He grimaced. 'Hell of a way to start the week, Jay. Sorry.'

Jay shrugged. 'Probably wants a debrief on the Fly Me case.'

Prine shook his head. 'Uh-uh. He's got blood in his eye, my dear. Something's about to hit the fan.'

'He's in his office?'

'He is indeed.' Prine grinned again. 'And definitely in a mood.'

Charles Langford's office was at the end of a short hall that ran off the far end of the main room. A year or so ago, some anonymous Bureau wit had mocked up a copy of a Bureau Wanted poster and taped it to his door. There were three faces on it – Anthony Hopkins, Jodie Foster, and Jimmy Hoffa. Langford had left the poster on the door instead of ripping it down, surprising for a man known to have no sense of humor at all. She rapped lightly on the door.

'Yes.' A bark, and his bite was equally bad.

She opened the door and stepped into the office. Langford's cubicle was just as messy as the main computer room. The desk was piled with printouts, there were stacks of government reports on the filing cabinets, and the bulletin board behind his chair was tacked three-deep in departmental memos. Jay's boss was scribbling something on a legal pad. He looked up as she came into the room.

'You wanted to see me, sir?'

Langford stared at her coldly. 'You fucked up,' he said without any preamble.

'Sir?' She was startled. She hadn't thought the word was even in his vocabulary.

'The Fly Me case. Whatshisname.'

'Dennis Lloyd Shaw.'

'I spent twenty minutes on the phone with Barney Silkwood late last night. He's had notification from Shaw's lawyer. She wants the presiding judge to rule a mistrial.'

'On what grounds?' asked Jay, shocked, and suddenly nervous.

'Who was your liaison with the LAPD Task Force?'

'A guy named Stearns. A lieutenant. Homicide.'

'He know anything about computers?'

'No. That's why they called me in.'

'So you were the one who accessed the reservation computer in Tulsa?'

'That's right. SABRE.'

'And you did all the paperwork, right? Permissions, entry passwords?'

'Yes.' Jay swallowed.

'According to Shaw's lawyer, you first accessed the SABRE computer at two-fifteen p.m., May twenty-ninth. A Sunday.'

'I don't remember exactly.'

How did she know that?

'I'll bet you don't,' snorted Langford. 'Apparently your friend Lieutenant Stearns has a better memory.'

'Oh?'

'Shaw's lawyer leaned on him and he rolled over. Told her the whole story, chapter and verse.'

Shit.

'Maybe you should tell me exactly what the problem is,' Jay bluffed.

As if I didn't know.

'The problem is that you didn't get official confirmation from the people in Tulsa until Tuesday, May thirty-first. The fact that you went on an unauthorized trolling mission two days before compromises the evidence you found later. It's fruit of the poisonous tree, Fletcher. Inadmissible.'

'Does Shaw's lawyer have any concrete proof other than Stearns?'

'You bet your ass she does.'

'I don't believe it,' Jay answered flatly. She'd used a blind back door to get into the SABRE computer and followed it up with an exotic little worm program to sweep away any evidence of her presence. There was no way Samantha Rhodes could have found out that she'd been inside the computer without the proper authorization.

Unless Mike Stearns kept a record to cover his ass.

'Do you deny accessing the computer without notifying the people in Tulsa?'

Jay stared down at Langford. He stared back, lips drawn down into a thin, angry frown. She was in deep enough. It was time to bail out and take whatever was coming to her. If Stearns wasn't going to back her up, she was screwed anyway.

'No. I don't deny it.'

'Jesus!'

'I still don't believe there's any hard evidence.'

'Do you think that really matters?' said Langford. 'Shaw's lawyer knows, for Christ sake! Evidence or not, the judge is going to ask for a deposition from you. To get out of it, you'd have to lie under oath. Perjury. You willing to do that, Fletcher?'

Jay shook her head. Langford was right. Somehow the Rhodes woman had found out about Jay's snooping and now she was baying to the moon. If Jay stonewalled and it came out later that Rhodes really *did* have evidence, it would be a disaster.

'Unauthorized entry into the computer is a felony all on its own,' said Langford. 'A perjury charge would make things even worse.'

'So what are the options?' asked Jay. 'Or is Shaw's lawyer going to play hardball?'

'Silkwood's already had a preliminary conference. Miami PD has Shaw dead bang for the last woman – bloodstains, semen, and fibers. She wants a guarantee of diminished capacity for that one and a walk on all the others. He'll do time, but he won't go away forever.'

'There's no other way?'

'No.' There was a long, agonizing silence.

35

'Shit,' she said finally. He'd get twenty to life and be out in eight.

'Exactly.' Langford dropped his pen on to the pad in front of him. 'Like I said, Fletcher, you fucked up. At least this way we can sweep it under the rug.'

'I'm sorry.' She knew it was a lame response, but what else was there to say?

'Not good enough, Jay.' Langford's tone softened slightly. 'We almost got into the same situation when you wanted to do a trial operation with C-Bix, remember?'

'That was different,' she insisted.

'No, it wasn't. It was exactly the same thing. You wanted to run your program through a medium-sized urban center and sift through all the relevant databases – local sex crimes, firebugs, credit bureau, IRS, adoption records, mental institution committals, sealed juvenile records, the works. Anything that fit the profiling indices. A wholesale data sweep.'

'I still think it makes sense,' Jay answered. 'We could cull a list of potential suspects before the crimes took place. We could save some lives.'

'And diddle the constitutional rights of each and every suspect on the list.'

'I thought we were supposed to be fighting crime.'

'We're supposed to do it playing by the rules. Ted Bundy's civil rights were under constitutional protection right up until we fried his ass in the electric chair. You either buy into that or you get the hell out of the Bureau, Jay.'

'It's a game, then.' She felt her shoulders sagging. Without the Job, there was nothing. She might as well be dead. 'Just a game.'

'No. It's the law,' said Langford. He let out a long sigh. 'How long have you been with the Division, Jay?'

'Six years this September.'

'Maybe it's time you had a rest.' He let it sink in. Jay paled, finally seeing where all of this was heading.

'You want me to resign?' she asked tightly. She bit her lip, furiously holding back the tears welling up in her eyes. No matter what, she wasn't going to cry.

'No, nothing like that,' Langford answered after a long moment. 'But this Shaw thing isn't going to go away. There's going to be some heat. I can deal with it, but I don't want you in the line of fire.'

'What does that mean?'

'A transfer. Detached duty.'

Detached? She felt as though she was going to sink through the floor. 'Detached where?' she asked finally.

'Santa Fe, New Mexico. You'll be working with a guy named Cruz.'

'We don't even have a field office there. Just a resident agency.'

'I told you, it's detached duty. Cruz is setting up an arson investigation unit. He asked us for some help with the computer side of things.'

'Arson?' breathed Jay. 'This guy is with the Fire Department?' She stared at Langford. 'I'm a cop, not a fireman. I can't do this.'

'They profile firebugs just the way they do serial

killers, Jay. It's not so different.' He frowned again, sitting forward in his chair. 'It's important work, it falls under the Bureau's mandate, and right now it's the best I can do.'

'Unless I resign.' That was bullshit and they both knew it. Langford sighed again.

'Do that and you're a private citizen, Agent Fletcher. I won't be able to cover your ass.' He paused. 'Or protect you from people like Shaw's lawyer. At least this way...' He let it dangle, watching her. The bet was down. Hold or fold, just like the song said.

At least this way the Bureau doesn't get embarrassed, even if it means I get sent to the boonies.

'When?' she asked, her voice dull.

'I told Cruz you'd be there a week from today, but I want you out of here now. This afternoon.'

'Preemptive surgery?'

'If that's the way you want to look at it.'

She took a deep breath, then let it out slowly. She realized suddenly that she was still holding the Styrofoam cup of coffee in her hand. She had a brief fantasy of throwing it in Langford's face, but then she nodded, accepting the inevitable.

'All right.' She turned away. Langford's voice stopped her.

'Jay?'

'Sir?'

'It's not forever, Jay. You've done a lot for the Division. We'll keep a light burning in the window for you.'

'Thanks,' she muttered, turning away again. She left the office, closing the door softly behind her.

She went home. Since coming to work at Headquarters, that had been a second-floor apartment in a roomy old brownstone on 13th Street at East Capitol, overlooking Lincoln Park. She hadn't invested in Microsoft like Langford, but the rent-controlled apartment was almost as good an investment. The district, only a mile or so from Capitol Hill, had once been predominantly poor and black, but times had changed, pushing the black population farther out toward RFK Stadium and the Beltway, turning the area around the brownstone into a haven for white-faced and white-collared professionals. Now Lincoln Park was full of crack dealers, instead of muggers and purse snatchers, servicing Congressional aides and office workers.

There were five rooms in the apartment, all painted in varying shades of yellow, her favorite color. From the living-room window, she could look out over the chestnuts and magnolias to the life-size statue of Lincoln holding the Emancipation Proclamation, and beyond to the distant dome of the Capitol.

Like the rest of the apartment, she'd furnished the living room one piece at a time, from the seventies-style maroon Naugahyde couch she'd picked up at a garage sale just after moving in to the ultra-modern Nakamichi stereo system she'd given herself for Christmas the year before. In between there was a comfortable collection of chairs, small Oriental carpets, and bookcases.

There were two bedrooms, both simply furnished, the smaller one for sleeping, the larger for her computer equipment and more bookcases. A short, narrow hallway led to the back of the apartment and the side-by-side bathroom and kitchen. Except for a framed print by a Canadian Eskimo artist her sister had given her, the art on the walls was entirely of the movie poster school.

The apartment was cloyingly hot, the air stale after being closed up for more than a month. Nadine, her downstairs neighbor and jogging buddy, had forgotten to water the plants, but she'd expected that. Nadine was a surgical nurse at the nearby Capitol Hill Hospital and when she wasn't trying to pull double-shift time to pay for her brand-new Miata, she was downstairs entertaining an endless stream of boyfriends in an admittedly crass quest for a doctor husband.

Jay dropped a Pachabel tape into the Nakamichi, cranked up the volume, and then spent five minutes going around the apartment opening all the windows. That done, she went to the bedroom and stripped off her clothes, then padded down the hall to the bathroom. She adjusted the shower to a luke-warm spray, climbed into the tub, and proceeded to cry loudly and hammer her fists against the walls of the fiberglass enclosure. It didn't do the slightest bit of good, so she gave up and washed her hair instead. By the time she turned off the shower, the tape on the stereo had ended.

She toweled off in front of the full-length mirror on the back of the bathroom door and examined herself critically. Average height, average weight, average hair. Her chest was too small, her hips were too narrow, and her legs were too skinny. The only things she had too much of were pubic hair and crow's feet.

She frowned at her reflection for a moment, then tossed the damp towel into the hamper and went back to the living room. It was still hot, but at least now there was a bit of a cross draft. She glanced out the window. If there was some freak out there with a pair of binoculars, he was welcome to the view. She crossed to the bookcase beside the silent stereo and looked at the titles.

'What the hell do I know about New Mexico?' she said aloud. Only what she'd read in a bunch of Tony Hillerman novels, and she doubted that the exploits of Jim Chee and Joe Leaphorn would offer her any insights into her new job. After more than a decade with the Bureau, her long-time passion for detective stories was beginning to wane. For her, murder was no longer a mystery; it was a banal, day-to-day horror and the root cause of a growing cynicism that was beginning to frighten her. Maybe Charlie Langford was right, maybe she needed a change after all.

She found a battered paperback copy of *The Story of the Amulet* by E. Nesbit, a Victorian children's fantasy she'd read dozens of times. After taking it down from the shelf, she went to her bedroom and dropped on to the bed, letting the faint breeze waft across her still damp skin. She started up the big fan on the table beside the bed, then settled back to read. The book, which concerned the time-traveling exploits of a London family of children, a magic charm, and a monkeylike creature

41

called a Psammead (you didn't pronounce the *P*) failed to distract her. After a few minutes, she let it fall to the floor and sagged back against the pillows, staring up at the ceiling, listening to the humming fan.

They always catch the breaks, she thought. The rapists, the killers, the scum. There's always a loophole or a procedural mistake. Most cases never even get that far.

In her mind's eye she saw the face of Dennis Lloyd Shaw, just one link on a grisly chain that stretched through the years all the way back to Robby Robson – Tomahawk's golden boy. He could have had anybody, so why did he need to rape skinny little Janet Louise? The whole thing was ridiculous. The cop she'd called could hardly keep a straight face. And neither could Robby. The whole town laughed – everyone except Janet. Somehow she never saw the funny side of it.

She remembered herself, small, thin, plain, victimized. And there was no one out there who would listen to her. No one to get her through that night. Well, they listened to her now, at least most of the time. No little girl was going to sit shivering in a bare room while some scumbag rapist laughed and got away with it. Maybe that's why it had been so easy for the recruiter to rake her in all those years ago. 'Fuck.' She laughed weakly and put one hand flat over her stomach, pressing hard.

Now there's a thought.

The fan hummed. For a moment she resisted and then gave in. She rolled over on the bed, pulled open the drawer of the table beside her, and reached inside.

42

CHAPTER FIVE

The man calling himself Dr Henry B. Saunders sat
behind the desk in the 'instant office' he'd rented, using
a magnifying glass to examine the photographs he'd
taken on the first and second floors of the Curtis Park
house owned by Ellen Putnam. He'd used an automatic
setting on the Nikon and the pictures were far from
being professional quality, but they were more than
adequate for his purposes.

The noxious little man at the photo store had rudely
asked him why he wanted so many photographs of
an empty house, and biting back an angry retort,
Saunders had mildly explained that he needed them
for insurance purposes. It seemed to be a satisfac-
tory answer. Twenty years ago, back in the days
when Saunders was just beginning his career, the
clerk in the photo store would have been fatally marked
for his nosy interest, but Saunders had much more
control now, and knew how to focus his energies
properly. At least his therapy had given him that
much.

A. J. HOLT

Saunders turned his attention away from the photographs and swiveled around in his chair. The tiny, fully furnished office was on the tenth floor of a building on East Colfax Avenue with a pleasant view of the State Capitol and the greenery around the Civic Center complex. The office was close to the corner of the building and by craning his neck he could even see the mountains rising to the west. It was a perfect, downtown center of operations for his activities away from the Curtis Park house, and when his work was finished in Denver, it would be the ideal place to begin a new cycle.

This morning he'd brought in one of his two Double Hardcase units, unplugged the telephone line, and set up the Texas Instruments Travelmate computer. With it, he could begin searching for a new target identity. A fresh suit of clothes so to speak, necessary now, since Dr Saunders was beginning to fray a little at collar and cuffs. He would leave this computer on all the time, using an identical unit at the basement apartment when he was away from the office.

That was another reason for having a base away from Curtis Park, of course; fate and the mathematics of statistical probability would eventually provide him with a pursuer more efficient than those he'd dealt with in the past, one who would have sense enough to check the telephone records of Ellen Putnam's basement tenant with a cold and fishy eye. With the two computers in place, those records would show nothing but a list of calls to the instant office main switchboard, since the TI portable here was fitted with a drop-out that would erase his modem links with Internet and the other E-mail lines. A blank page and a dead end. Confusion to his enemies.

He smiled, looking down at the tiny figures of the tourists strolling around in front of the Capitol. *A blank page.* His therapist had used that phrase a lot. When was that? Just after Vietnam? He'd been a medical orderly then, at Tan Son Hut Air Base in Saigon, using the name Jackson, culled from the dog tags of a dead man, black in life and blacker still after riding a flaming helicopter gunship into the ground. Life had been good then. Death and its attendant pleasures were as convenient to him as a Square Meal Deal at McDonald's.

In the end it had been too easy, and he'd transformed himself again, returning home with a modest chestful of medals and a psychiatric discharge. Therapy had been the price he'd paid for a quick release. In the beginning, it had rankled, but eventually he began learning from it, making the best of an irritating situation. He smiled again. So long ago. Saunders couldn't even remember the therapist's name, let alone where he'd buried the man. He shook his head, still smiling, and turned his attention back to the photographs. What was that quotation – someone's dying words? So much to do, so little time to do it.

Jay Fletcher sat in the psychiatrist's office at Capitol Hill Hospital, mentally kicking herself for taking

Nadine's advice. She was in the middle of packing up for the Santa Fe move and didn't have time for this, but after the two-hour crying jag and the dish-breaking orgy she'd gone through on Monday evening, her friend had insisted. According to Nadine it couldn't do any harm and at the very least she'd wind up with a Prozac prescription.

The shrink was the epitome of political correctness. Thirty pounds overweight, in retro-Woodstock/New Age skirt and shawl, waist-length graying hair. In the first five minutes, Jay had learned that the woman didn't call herself a psychiatrist; instead she was a 'healer' and a 'mental health facilitator.' Jay wondered if she referred to raging psychotics as 'sanity challenged.'

The office was a perfect match for the woman's looks. Soothing earth tones, a few large, impenetrable macramé hangings, and a forest of plants in the window looking out over Constitution Avenue. Instead of a desk, she had a roughly stripped and finished Shaker table, and instead of a couch, she had a huge wicker basket chair that creaked and rustled every time Jay shifted her weight. Half a dozen brightly colored Mexican throw rugs were littered across the dull green, institutional linoleum that covered the floor.

They'd been talking for the better part of an hour and Jay still had no idea where any of it was going. The shrink's voice was like a priest giving extreme unction and Jay could feel her eyelids beginning to droop. She jerked upright in the chair, suddenly realizing that there had been a long silence. The psychiatrist had asked a question.

'Sorry?'

It didn't seem to bother the woman that Jay had lapsed into a bored doze. 'I was just saying that I'm surprised you came to me. I would have thought the FBI had its own psychiatric staff.'

'They do. I didn't want to see anyone at the Bureau.'

'Why?'

'I'm in enough hot water as it is. I don't need to give them any more ammunition.' And by going to a shrink of her own choosing, she could fend off a departmental order telling her to visit one of the Bureau's own people. If she was going to go crazy, she preferred to do it on her own time. Surprisingly, she was also beginning to enjoy her visit, New Age woo-woo or not. At least it was someone to talk to.

'You mentioned before that you were worried about being forced to resign.'

'It would solve a lot of problems for everyone.'

'Except you.'

'Yes. Except me.' She caught the woman's tone. 'And I'm not paranoid, Doctor; the Bureau is. It's a cardinal rule: Don't embarrass the Bureau. Someone even wrote a book about it.'

'How does the thought of resigning from the Bureau make you feel?'

'Terrified. I wouldn't know what to do with my life. I don't *have* any other life.'

'Perhaps that's the problem. You've become too focused on your work.'

'I'm not going to stop feeling this way just because I go out and get a boyfriend, Doctor; believe me.'

'I didn't say anything about a boyfriend.' The psychiatrist paused and looked down at the notepad in front of her for a few seconds. 'You seem to think this reassignment to New Mexico is some sort of punishment. Maybe you should think about it more positively. A lifestyle change, a chance to reevaluate things.' Maybe the shrink had a point, but it still felt as though she was being sent into exile.

'Things? There's only one thing getting to me, Doctor. My job is to catch the bad guys. I do that, and then the system sets them free. A couple of years ago we nailed a guy who liked to sodomize little boys with Coke bottles. He brought in a shrink who said he did it because he'd been abused as a child himself. He got one to five, six months served, and probation. How do I fight that, Doctor? Christ, how do I live with that?'

'You're talking about control.'

'That's right. I'm afraid of losing it.'

'What do you think would happen if you did lose control, Jay?' Soothing. Caring. Better than nothing.

'That's just the problem, Doctor. I don't know what would happen.'

'That frightens you? Not knowing?'

'Yes.'

Jesus, Doctor, you have no idea!

48

'Have you thought about what you could do to change that fear? Change how you feel?'

Multiple choice. Yin yang. Black white. Yes no. Just like a computer. Take a gun and blow out my own brains or walk into the nearest Dunkin' Donuts and start blasting.

'Yes. That frightens me, too.'

'Why? What conclusions have you reached?'

'None. I don't see any future for myself. Nothing but a big black hole I'm standing on the edge of.' She smiled weakly at the doctor. 'Emotional fear of falling.'

'But you can still make jokes about it.' The psychiatrist smiled back.

'Laughter in the face of...' There was a short, crackling silence. Jay resisted the urge to jump out of the stupid, whispering chair and run out of the office.

'What?' the shrink prompted cautiously. 'Laughter in the face of what?'

'I'm not sure.'

Liar.

'There's something else you should consider, of course.'

'What?'

'Your age.'

'I'm not even forty yet, Doctor. It's a bit early for a midlife crisis, don't you think?'

'I was thinking along more ... physical lines.'

Jay laughed, the sound harsh in the quiet room. 'I'm a bit young for menopause, don't you think?'

'It's something to think about. Intense stress some-times presents the same pathology.'

'My periods have been regular as clockwork since I was thirteen, Doctor. They still are.' She leaned forward and rubbed one finger across her upper lip. 'See? No mustache either. And no hot flushes.'

No marriage, no kids, no boyfriend. A Judas kiss from Stearns at the airport. No wonder I'm depressed.

The psychiatrist had an old-fashioned man's pocket watch dangling on a leather thong around her neck. She glanced at it, then looked across the table at Jay.

'Our time's just about up.' She frowned. 'Since we won't be able to establish a long-term course of therapy, there's not a lot I can really do, I'm afraid.' She paused. 'I could write you a prescription for an antidepressant if you think...'

Jay interrupted quickly, before she changed her mind. 'No thanks, Doctor. My boss has put me out to pasture for a while, but I still carry a gun. Firearms and drugs don't mix very well.'

'Yes, I see what you mean,' the psychiatrist said, offering one of her best shaman-style nods. She didn't see at all, of course, except she had a mildly frightened look on her face as her eyes scanned Jay, wondering where she kept the weapon hidden. The woman stood up and offered her hand. Jay shook it.

'Thanks again, Doctor. Believe it or not, you've been a help.'

A little. Don't send me out there all by myself, Doc. Not yet. Maybe I should take the pills after all.

'I hope so. Good luck, Jay. Feel free to call me ... anytime. You have my card.'

'Thanks. I'll be okay.'

Liar, liar, pants on fire.

She left the office, the heavy feel of the holstered, Bureau-issue, 9 mm. Browning like an ice-cold dead-weight against her spine.

Charles Langford piloted his Saab through the late-afternoon traffic, heading for the main gates of George-town University. In Bureau terminology the Saab was a POV, or Personally Owned Vehicle, rather than a 'Bucar' from the FBI motor pool. The use of personal automobiles was frowned on by the Bureau's upper management, but Langford would do anything to avoid the hard-sprung Bucar tanks. He'd long ago given up putting in at work for gas and mileage but what he spent on it was more than covered by what he saved in visits to the chiropractor.

Waiting for the light to change at N Street and Wisconsin Avenue, he glanced down at the thick manila envelope on the seat beside him. It had arrived today from the Phoenix Field Office and even before going through the grisly contents, Langford had known exactly what the envelope contained. There was a neatly typed address sticker centered perfectly in the middle of the envelope:

William DeMille Hawkins,
Department of Criminology, Georgetown University,

c/o Special Agent in Charge,
Federal Bureau of Investigation Field Office,
Phoenix Arizona

The light changed and Langford drove through the intersection, thinking about the envelope, and thinking about the man it had been addressed to.

Bill Hawkins had begun his law enforcement career as an MP in Saigon during the late sixties. Returning to the States, he'd opted to stay in the Army and joined the Criminal Investigation Division, eventually dead-ending in a desk job at CID Headquarters in Falls Church, Virginia. Along the way he managed to get a master's degree in criminology, and with that in hand he switched from military to civilian life, joining the Federal Bureau of Investigation in 1976.

He was immediately attached to the fledgling Behavioral Sciences Unit as an interviewer and spent the next three years hopscotching across the country, talking to a cross-section of the nation's most infamous serial killers, rapists, mass murderers, and child killers, assembling the information that would become the foundation for the BSU's profiling program and the baseline data for the National Center for the Analysis of Violent Crime – NCAVC. It was during this time that he first met and became friends with Charlie Langford, a friendship that had endured ever since.

In 1979, he was rotated to regular duties as a Field Agent and for the next nine years he worked out of a number of field offices, eventually becoming Deputy

SAC of the Washington Metropolitan Field Office. In 1988, at the age of thirty-nine, his career in the FBI came to an abrupt end and he retired on a partial-disability pension.

Like Langford and every other FBI Special Agent, Bill Hawkins was fully aware of the dangers involved in his chosen profession, but he wasn't prepared for the idiot irony of a faulty valve on the propane tank of his gas barbecue. The device exploded in his face, blinding him in the left eye. Unable to pass the standard physical examination for Field Agent, he was offered a variety of bureaucratic posts both at the WMFO and Head-quarters. He declined, opting for early retirement instead. A year later, backed by the enthusiastic recom-mendations of Langford and other friends at the Bureau, Hawkins accepted a post as a lecturer in the history of criminology at Georgetown University.

He continued to maintain close ties with the Bureau, acting as a consultant to the VICAP program and the profilers at the Behavioral Sciences Unit, as well as expanding his teaching program to include a course in crime literature. During his time at Georgetown, he'd also managed to write four books, three of them academic texts, the fourth a popular history of Scotland Yard, which had actually drifted around in the bottom third of the *New York Times* best-seller list for a few weeks.

A fifth book, this one telling the story of the Pinkerton Detective Agency, was due to be published later in the year, and the last time Langford had spoken to his friend, there had been vague talk about a film deal. All of which was just fine, according to Hawkins, but it still wasn't a replacement for real police work. Even with all his new successes, he still yearned for it, sometimes even dreamed about it.

Langford turned right on to 37th Street, then left through the main gates at the O Street intersection. He drove slowly through the confusion of narrow roadways that meandered around the collection of neo-Gothic buildings, eventually reaching Hawkins' office on the southwestern edge of the campus and overlooking the dense greenery of Archbold Park. Langford parked the Saab in one of the visitor slots, then reached across and picked up the envelope.

'You asked for it,' he muttered, climbing out of the car.

Hawkins was studying a large map of the United States pinned to the wall as Langford stepped into the office. The retired FBI man was medium height with a middle-aged pot belly and dark blond hair thinning into a widow's peak over a broad, weather-beaten forehead. There was an outsize patch over his left eye and upper cheek. He was wearing a blue chambray shirt without a tie, faded blue jeans, and an ancient pair of battered Topsiders. Hawkins called it his 'overweight pirate/cowboy' look.

'Afternoon, Charlie.' He gestured to the large, red-leather captain's chair that stood to one side of his desk, then sat down himself. Langford glanced around. Not much had changed since his last visit, except there seemed to be even more books than before. Along with the desk there were several tables in the small, high-ceilinged room, all of them buried under drifts of paperbacks and hardcovers. Two walls were fitted with floor-to-ceiling bookcases, all fully loaded. The wall behind the desk was taken up with a pair of curving, deeply recessed Gothic-style windows that looked out over the campus, and the fourth wall was papered with maps, including the big one of the U.S.A., which was dotted with large, red-tipped drawing pins.

'This place looks worse every time I see it,' said Langford.

Hawkins smiled, tipping back in his chair and putting up his feet on the desk. 'Creative chaos,' he answered. 'Comes with the academic life, no extra charge.'

'Horseshit,' said Langford.

'I think better in a messy room.'

'More horseshit. You're a slob, Bill, and you know it.'

Hawkins looked at the envelope in Langford's lap. 'Presumably this is about the Iceman.'

Langford smiled wearily. 'You must have known that already. I saw you looking at the map.'

'Another one?'

'Phoenix.' Langford nodded.

Hawkins tilted his chair forward, opened a desk drawer, and extracted a box of drawing pins. He opened the box, took out a pin, and stood up. Crossing to the map, he poked the crimson-tipped pin into the appropriate spot.

'Arizona,' he said quietly, stepping back from the map

and staring at the new location. The other pins were scattered randomly from Seattle to Boston, Cleveland to Miami. Fourteen in all. 'Fresh territory.'

Langford shrugged. 'As far as we know.'

Hawkins went back to his chair behind the desk. 'So tell me.'

Langford took a small notebook out of the inside pocket of his jacket hanging on the chair and began flipping through the pages.

'A man named John Fuscianna rented an apartment in Phoenix. Paid three months in advance, including utilities. Cash. When he didn't show up with the fourth month's rent, the landlord went in to check out the apartment. There was no sign that Fuscianna had ever moved in. Place was empty.'

'Except for the refrigerator.' Hawkins predicted. 'Or a freezer.'

'Freezer this time. Luckily they hadn't turned off the power. At least the Phoenix PD didn't have *that* to deal with.' Langford blew out a long, frustrated breath and then went on. 'So, no surprise, there's a body in the freezer. Man in his early forties, dark hair, blue eyes. Naked. No ID, no clothes, nothing. One bullet in the back of the head. Twenty-two caliber. The medical officer couldn't fix much in the way of time of death. Two, two and a half months. He was frozen solid.'

'Did the Phoenix PD run the Fuscianna name or did the Bureau?'

'We did,' said Langford.

'Because of the pictures?'

56

'That's right.' Langford let his fingers trace across the envelope in his lap. 'They were underneath the corpse. The envelope was sealed inside a Ziploc bag. When the Phoenix cops opened the outer envelope, they saw your name and turned the package over to our field office.'

'What did you get on the name?'

'Fuscianna was listed as a missing person in Des Moines with wants and warrants. A real estate agent. He didn't pay his monthly alimony and his ex-wife went looking. All his accounts had been cleared out, including a trust account with about sixty grand of deposits on houses he was selling. He was one of those guys who had about a dozen credit cards. They'd all been cash-advanced right up to the limit. The Des Moines police figured he'd split.'

'VICAP?' asked Hawkins.

'Yeah. Ten weeks later the Little Rock Field Office put out a bulletin on him for a triple murder and rape. Mother, teenage daughter, and a seven-year-old son. The Petrie family.'

'Divorced?'

'No. Father was in the Air Force. Posted to the Middle East.'

'It all fits the Iceman.'

'Yeah. Except no one put it together until this Phoenix thing. If we had a cross-link between VICAP and the Missing Persons Index, it might have shown up sooner.'

'Has the real Fuscianna surfaced yet?'

'Nothing positive. As soon as we had the name, we got

in touch with Des Moines and asked them if they had any John Does lying around. Turns out they did. One of those dead storage places. Another freezer. A fuse blew and the locker started to stink. They've got Fuscianna's dentist making an ID. We should know in a day or two.'

'So I can add Little Rock to the map?'

'It looks that way. Des Moines too, maybe. They've got a rape-murder there that fits the timeframe.'

'Too bad you can't get a name for the body in Phoenix. There might be time to stop the next one.'

'Phoenix is like a rest stop between Here and There,' Langford answered. 'What do they call them – Snowbirds? We're trying to get a match with Missing Persons, but I don't think we'll come up with anything.'

'So you brought it to me?'

'You and the freezer man go back a long way. Wasn't it you who gave him the name?'

Hawkins nodded. 'The Iceman was better than most. These days he'd probably be called Ice-T.'

Langford smiled. 'According to the last *Law Enforcement Bulletin* I read, the Bureau adds eight hundred thousand files a year. One code name is as good as another, I guess.' The older man leaned forward and carefully placed the envelope on Hawkins' desk. Hawkins barely glanced at it. 'Or maybe it's an omen,' Langford added.

'Don't try that *mano a mano* crap on me, Charlie. I'm a teacher now, not a cop.'

Langford shrugged. 'Just thought you might be interested.' He stood up. 'Especially with school shut down for the summer.' The older man paused. 'The Iceman sends his dirty pictures to you, not me.' He paused. 'You ever wonder why he chose you?'

'He needed an audience. There was no secret about me digging into old cases. I fit the bill for him. Every artist needs his critic.'

'You think it's that simple?'

'Maybe not. There's probably a psychiatric reasoning behind it.' He shrugged. 'But does it really matter?'

'What matters is you answering my question. Are you going to take this on?'

'I'm working on a new book, Charlie.'

'Really? From what I can figure, your old pal is working on a new victim.'

'What am I supposed to do, track the crazy son of a bitch all on my own?'

'We can't do anything with it, Bill. It's the same old story. There are seven or eight thousand unsolved murders every year. BSU handles maybe fifty or sixty. They turn down stuff all the time. The Iceman moves around all over the country and we wind up with jurisdictional problems up the wazoo. No one's going to bring down the Iceman by going through due process; you know that as well as I do. And like I said, for some reason he's chosen you as his connection to the real world. Without you he has no game. The hunter can't hunt without being hunted himself.'

'What kind of official status would I have?'

'None.'

'Unofficial?'

'I'll see what I can do.'

'This isn't like you, Charlie. End runs aren't your style. You could wind up with your ass in a sling just for talking to me about this. And I'm no assassin.'

Langford frowned. 'Yesterday I had to burn someone who was just trying to do her job. Strictly speaking, I probably should have fired her. When this stuff on the Iceman came in, I started thinking about her, and about the way the system works. Everybody talks a good line about civil rights and the Constitution, me included, but then it occurred to me that the Ted Bundys and the Mansons and the Icemen always get the edge. I thought maybe it was time we evened up the odds a little, that's all. I don't want an assassin, Bill; I want a bloodhound. Just find him. Any way you can.'

Hawkins looked up at his friend for a long moment. 'Okay,' he said finally. 'I'll think about it.'

'Thanks,' said Langford. He nodded briefly, then turned and left the office. Hawkins listened to his footsteps receding down the stone stairs. Sighing, he reached forward and picked up the envelope. Maybe Charlie was right; the game had gone on long enough between him and the Iceman. It was time to bring it to an end.

CHAPTER SIX

The fireman from Santa Fe was waiting for her at the passenger pickup curb, just outside the baggage-claim level of Albuquerque International Airport. He was short and muscular with jet-black hair, a drooping black mustache, and large, intelligent-looking black eyes. He was wearing black cowboy boots, black jeans, and a snow-white shirt, and he was sitting perched on the right front fender of a dusty, dark green Jeep Cherokee. There was an ornate seal on the door of the Cherokee identifying it as an official vehicle of the New Mexico State Fire Investigation Office. The man was holding up a small sign that said FLETCHER in his left hand.

'Lieutenant Cruz?' Jay approached him. She put down her suitcases, ignoring the streams of people moving around her as they exited the airport concourse. She was dead tired. Of course there was no smoking allowed on the plane, plus the air-conditioning had broken down in midflight, and the sudden change to Albuquerque's six-thousand-foot elevation was leaving

61

her short of breath. It was just past noon and the air was baking hot.

Smiling, Cruz dropped down from the fender of the Cherokee. 'Special Agent Fletcher.'

'Jay,' she said, trying to be friendly. She noticed that Cruz was almost exactly the same height as she was, or perhaps just a little taller. 'I'm not feeling much like a Special Agent these days.'

Cruz frowned. 'Jay like the initial, or Jay like the bird?'

'Like the initial, but spelled like the bird. Why?'

'It's the same as mine. J. M. Cruz. Everyone calls me Jay.'

'What's the J. M. stand for?'

'Jesus Maria. Bit of a burden, even in New Mexico.'

'Mine's Janet. I hate it.'

'You call me Cruz, I'll call you Fletcher, how's that?'

'It's a deal.'

Cruz loaded Jay's suitcases into the back of the Cherokee while she climbed into the passenger seat. He got behind the wheel and they drove away from the airport. Directly ahead Jay could see a highrise city skyline backed by a brilliant blue sky with a range of low, rugged mountains to the right. At the end of the airport road, he turned left, then right on to the I-25 Freeway ramp. As Cruz maneuvered into the middle lane, Jay scanned the dashboard. There was a package of Marlboro Lights tucked up close to the windshield and the ashtray was open and overflowing.

'You smoke,' she said, relieved.

Cruz nodded. 'Like a chimney.'

'Thank God!' Jay fished around in her purse and brought out a package of Camel Filters and her lighter. 'Sometimes I think the whole world has quit on me.'

'Maybe you'd better wait for a while,' Cruz suggested, glancing at her. 'Elevation can get to you for the first few hours. Santa Fe is even higher.'

'I can handle it,' Jay answered. She lit up and took a drag, regretting it almost instantly. Cruz was right. For a second she thought she was going to pass out.

'Told you.' Cruz grinned. 'Maybe you should butt it.'

'Not on your life,' Jay said, gritting her teeth. 'I've been waiting hours for this.'

Cruz drove on and Jay continued to smoke – cautiously. The freeway rose upward, cutting through almost the exact center of the city. Jay looked out the window. Except for the mountains, it could have been any midsize city in North America. Strip malls, suburban tract houses, and a defiant core of gleaming office towers. The predominant color appeared to be brown, about two shades darker than the dusty-looking ground. There didn't seem to be much smog.

'It gets prettier,' said Cruz, watching her. He was right. Fifteen minutes later they'd left the city behind them. The northern suburbs faded and then they were into open countryside. The mountains were closer now, giant, piled oblongs and rough rectangles of striated, sand-colored stone, the lower levels shrouded with stands of alder and pine, the lower foothills dotted with scrub juniper. To the left was a broad band of blue.

'The Rio Grande,' Cruz explained. 'Sandia Indian Reservation on the right. The trees up there are part of Cibola National Forest. It's mesas and flatlands like this all the way up to Santa Fe.'

'How long will it take us to get there?' asked Jay. Cruz seemed nice enough, but all she really wanted to do was sleep.

'Forty-five minutes, an hour.' Cruz threw her a quick smile, reading her mind. 'Take a nap if you want. I don't mind. You look beat.'

'Thanks,' Jay answered gratefully. 'Maybe if I close my eyes for five minutes.'

'Sure, whatever.' Cruz nodded. Jay let her head fall back against the seat. Cruz began to hum quietly, an eerie, almost hypnotic tune. Thirty seconds later she was fast asleep.

When she woke up, they were on the outskirts of Santa Fe. 'Sorry.' Jay muttered, sitting up. 'I guess I dozed off.'

Cruz laughed. 'You've been sleeping for an hour and a half. I even stopped off to get something to eat in Lamy. There's still some left if you're hungry.'

Jay sniffed. The inside of the Cherokee smelled like a Taco Bell and there was a litter of paper wrappings and foam containers on the dashboard.

Jay blinked, then yawned. 'No, thanks.'

Cruz took one hand off the wheel and rummaged around in the mess. He found his cigarettes and lit one.

Jay looked out through the windshield. With the exception of its church steeples, Santa Fe was two stories high and fifty different shades of brown. Even the architecture of the light industrial section they were traveling through had a faintly prehistoric look. The mountains here were smaller than those outside Albuquerque, but much closer to the town, looming over it. According to the little she'd read in the few days before she'd left Washington, Santa Fe had a population edging up to 75,000, much of it wealthy.

'All of this is adobe?' Jay asked.

'Some,' said Cruz. 'Most of it's actually stucco over concrete block. Real adobe is clay and sand and straw.' He made a small, snorting sound under his breath. 'When I was a kid, having a house made out of adobe meant you were poor. Now it's all handmade by some old hippies and the only people who can afford it are rich Anglos.'

'All that concrete block, there can't be too many fires,' Jay commented.

Cruz looked at her, lifting an eyebrow. 'You'd be surprised, Fletcher.'

'So surprise me.'

'Santa Fe has gone through a lot of changes in the past ten years. It's a lot bigger for one thing – housing developments going up everywhere. Ten years ago there were a few Indians here, lots of Hispanics, and a few Anglos. That's all been turned on its head. The population's mostly Anglo now and the Hispanics are being forced out by the real estate prices. There are half a dozen Indian tribes, and they all hate each other. The Indians hate the Hispanics, and the Hispanics hate the Anglos. That's friction, and friction causes fires.'

'You've given this speech before.' Jay smiled.

'Once or twice,' Cruz answered, smiling back. 'But it's true.'

'With a name like Cruz, you must be Hispanic.'

'I'm a mongrel. J. and M. are just the first two initials.'

'What's the rest of it?'

'Jesus Maria San Ildefonso Standing Heart Cruz.'

Beyond the clustered buildings of the Deaf School, the arson investigator swung off on to Guadalupe Street. Once upon a time, it had literally been on the wrong side of the tracks, but the old warehouses and one-time used-car lots had been transformed into a tourist-oriented honey trap of boutique esplanades, antique arcades, and hole-in-the-wall art galleries. It was only mid-June, but the sidewalks were already filled with browsers in Hawaiian shirts and camera-toting Japanese tour groups.

They crossed the narrow bridge over the dry, grass-covered ditch of the Santa Fe River and Cruz guided the Cherokee through a twisting collection of narrow streets above a thin strip of parkland. The little area was filled with more 'adobe' buildings and small, wood-frame houses, but at least half of them had been turned into restaurants, art galleries, and jewelry stores.

Striking even farther west, Cruz finally turned on to a block-long street that dead-ended above a broad ravine. The houses here were tiny, but each one had its own small front yard. Cruz pulled to a stop at the last house on the street, a minuscule, stucco-sided cottage. The front of the house was shaded by a pair of gnarled apple trees. There was an aging Ford Escort parked in the laneway, painted the same green as the Cherokee and also sporting an official seal on the door.

'Car's yours for the duration,' said Cruz, switching off the engine. 'I sprung it from Highways. Your boss in Washington is paying gas and maintenance.' They got out of the Jeep and Cruz helped Jay into the house with her luggage. 'We got a good deal on the house,' explained Cruz, unlocking the door. 'Some guy at the Capitol who's gone to Europe on sabbatical until September. Any longer than that and we'll have to find someplace else to put you.'

Any longer than that and I'll kill myself.

She followed Cruz and the suitcases into the house. 'I don't think it'll be that long.'

There were four rooms in the compact house, a living room, a kitchen-dining room, a bedroom, and the bathroom. The furniture was rustic, the rugs on the floor were Mexican, and the art on the walls and hanging from the open beams in the living room was Indian. The living-room window looked out over the ravine and out to the hills. It was just beginning to sink in how far she really was from D.C. and the familiar surroundings of her own apartment.

I've been banished. It was an old-fashioned word, but it fit.

'Why don't you spend a little time getting settled?' said Cruz, heading for the door. 'I'll come back in a couple of hours and take you on the tour.'

'I wouldn't mind seeing where I'll be working,' said Jay.

'Okay.' Cruz nodded. 'I'll show you the shop and then we can go check out my latest project.' He gave her a little wave and left the house, closing the door behind him. Jay sighed, lit a cigarette, and started to unpack.

Cruz's 'shop' turned out to be a second-floor suite of offices above the main branch of the Santa Fe Public Library. The low, concrete building was on the corner of Washington Avenue and West Marcy Street, just outside the downtown core and the Plaza. According to Cruz it had once been the Municipal Building, housing the fire station, mayor's office, county courthouse, and jail. From the down-at-heel look of the office furniture and equipment, Cruz was operating on a minimal budget.

There were a couple of relatively new-looking computer terminals and a metal storage cabinet full of video gear, but everything else had a thirties look. The floors were bare wood and the plastic cover over the secretary's old IBM Electric looked as though it hadn't been touched in years.

Jay dropped down into a wooden swivel chair and

looked around. The chair squeaked every time she moved. 'This is it?'

'This is it.' Cruz nodded, sitting down behind a scarred metal desk piled high with papers.

'Would I be wrong in concluding that your office doesn't entirely have the confidence of the State of New Mexico?'

Cruz smiled broadly and lit a cigarette. 'Gee, whatever gave you that idea?'

'Cops notice these things,' said Jay. 'The subtle nuances.'

'Let's just say there's a certain hesitation on the part of the powers that be.'

'Why is that?' asked Jay.

'You're a Fed; you must know all about government bureaucracy, Fletcher.'

'Some,' she agreed, nodding.

'It's like walking on eggs,' Cruz explained. 'Everyone thinks I'm going to step on people's toes.'

'What people?'

'State Police, local cops, local fire departments. You name it. Albuquerque has its own Fire Marshal's Office and so does Las Cruces. Then you've got the volunteer FDs, and on top of it all the Reservation Departments. They all have their own turf.'

'You're supposed to coordinate?'

'Yeah, as well as give advice and expert assistance, liaison with the military types at White Sands, that kind of thing.'

'Why you?'

Cruz shrugged. 'I was a fireman until my knees went and then I was a cop.' He laughed briefly. 'And I was stupid enough to volunteer for the job.'

'And now I come along to make it even worse.'

'The success of this whole thing hinges on computers, I'm positive about that. Without some kind of coherent system linking everyone together, it's going to be impossible. You're the big city expert ... and you're not costing me much.'

'I don't know anything about fires, Cruz.'

'And I don't know anything about computers.' He smiled. 'You teach me about bytes, I'll teach you about burns.'

'Fair enough.'

Jay spent an hour at one of the terminals in the Fire Investigation Office, quickly establishing the short-comings of the system Cruz had been saddled with. Basically, both terminals in the office were standard IBM-clone PCs, linked by a dedicated phone line to whatever mainframe was being used by the State Government Offices at the Plaza a few blocks away.

From what Jay could tell at first glance, the FIO computers had a very low priority on the mainframe and whatever access Cruz had was further hampered by the mainframe's own basic programs, most of which were several years out of date. Digging a little deeper, she also noted that there was no way for Cruz to link up with either the local Santa Fe Police Department, the State Police, or any other law enforcement agency. The terminals were equipped with internal modems, but

Cruz hadn't figured out how to use them. For the most part, the FIO was deaf, dumb, and blind.

After her first look at the computers, Cruz suggested that they go and check the site of the most recent fire he was investigating. Jay agreed, even though she was still feeling a little fuzzy-brained by her trip and the oxygen-depriving effects of the high altitude. The house in question was located in the eastern foothills, high at the far end of Hyde Park Road.

The sprawling, one-story, ultra-modern building had been totally gutted, leaving nothing but the soot-stained concrete walls and portions of the roof. Before the fire it had obviously been a beautiful residence, with huge windows and a large flagstone deck offering a panoramic view of Santa Fe and backed by a rising stand of alders, the nearest of which were nothing more than charred skeletons.

The cleared area around the ruins of the house was a rutted, oozing quagmire. Cruz reached into the back of the Cherokee and handed Jay a heavy-soled pair of rubber boots. 'Put these on,' he instructed, getting another pair for himself. 'A fire site can be a dangerous place unless you're careful, not to mention the mud.'

Jay did as she was told and then followed Cruz to the patio. There was broken glass everywhere and the plastic lawn chairs and table had melted into a surreal white-and-yellow puddle across the stone. There were also strewn fragments of charred fabric. The air reeked with the sour-sweet stench of burnt wood and wet ash. He continued looking at the house. 'Quick and hot,' he said finally. 'Air heated up so quickly it blew the windows out within a few minutes.'

'Was it an accident?' Jay asked.

'Not a chance,' Cruz answered, shaking his head. He bent down and picked up one of the small pieces of pale white cloth that lay among the shards of glass. There appeared to be a small length of duct tape attached to it. 'The person who started this didn't want anyone detecting the fire too soon. He taped up the edges of the drapes so nothing would show until it was too late.' He dropped the piece of cloth back on to the ground. 'Come on.'

He crunched across the patio and stepped into the house through what was left of a sliding-glass door. Jay followed close behind. The interior of the living room was a disaster. Part of the roof had collapsed and Jay could see sections of the exposed beams that were burnt almost completely through. The floor was ankle-deep in rubble and the incinerated remains of the room's furniture. Cruz found what looked like a sodden pillow and examined it for a moment. He tossed it across to Jay.

'What does that look like?' he asked.

'The pillow from a couch.'

'Notice anything?'

'The top is burnt more than the bottom, and it's ripped. The stuffing is coming out.'

'Not ripped. Slashed. Our guy wanted to make sure everything burned.' He smiled. 'I thought you were the one who noticed subtle nuances?'

Jay smiled back. She sniffed. 'Gasoline?' She sniffed again. 'Not quite. Gasoline and something else, right?'

'Half and half. Pure gasoline would probably have exploded, maybe even snuffed itself out. The other smell is kerosene – keeps the fire going.' He nodded appreciatively. 'You've got a pretty good nose, Fletcher; stick around.'

They moved to the center of the room. Directly above them was nothing but open sky. Several sections of roof beam had burnt through completely and the roof had collapsed into the interior. Cruz took a bone-handled clasp knife out of his pocket, snapped open the blade, and dug into a section of roof beam directly in front of them. The blade went in more than an inch before it stopped.

'Is this where it started?' Jay asked.

'Five points.' Cruz nodded. 'If you want to find out where a fire started, find the place where the burn is deepest.' He used the knife to point at an area three or four feet along the beam. 'See that?'

Jay nodded. The wood was crazed into dozens of black, shiny, tile-sized rectangles. 'Looks like coal.'

'That's called "alligatoring,"' Cruz explained. 'The more intense the fire is, the smaller the little squares, until you get right back to the origin of the fire.' He pulled his knife out of the beam. 'Then you get charcoal.' He stood up. 'Notice anything else?'

Jay glanced around the room. There seemed to be several distinct areas of heavy burning that ran back toward the rear of the house. She edged around the pile of rubble from the collapsed portion of the roof and used her boots to push aside the mess on the floor.

Before the fire the floor had been covered with wall-to-wall carpeting installed over a plywood subfloor that had in turn been bonded to a concrete slab. Where she had detected the areas of heavier burning, the carpeting and the subfloor had been burned right down to the concrete. He might as well have left road signs.

This is too easy.

'He used his gas-kerosene mixture to lay down trails to the rest of the house.'

'Bingo,' said Cruz.

'He must have been crazy,' Jay said. 'He could have been burned himself.'

'This guy isn't a freak,' Cruz answered, shaking his head. 'This is a revenge fire. And he was long gone before the fire started.'

'How did he manage that?'

'A condom,' said Cruz. 'When we go over the beam here, we'll find what's left of a tack or a drawing pin.'

'How do you use a condom to start a fire?' Jay asked.

'Red phosphorous and water,' said Cruz. 'Red phosphorous ignites when it comes into contact with air. He tacked a condom full of the stuff on to the beam directly over a pool of the gasoline-kerosene mixture and then he put a pinhole into the bottom of the condom. The water dripped out until the phosphorous was exposed. It ignited, then dropped down into the pool of accelerant.'

'You've seen this before.'

'This is his fourth in the last two months. The bastard's driving me crazy.'

'What makes you say it's revenge?' asked Jay.

'Basically there are two kinds of arson,' said Cruz. 'Arson with a motive, and arson without a motive. Real firebugs and pyros, the crazy ones, usually don't go to all this trouble and they almost never use a delayed-action igniter.' Cruz folded up his knife and slipped it back into the pocket of his jeans. 'So if you rule out a psycho, that means there has to be a motive, and I can't figure one for any of the four fires.' They headed back out to the patio.

'The victims have anything in common?'

'Not that I can see.' Cruz shrugged. 'The man who owned this place works at Los Alamos.'

'The atom bomb place?'

'Right. He's head of one of the research divisions. The first victim works for Los Alamos Labs too, but in a completely different department. The second victim is a lawyer in Albuquerque with a summer place here, and the third one is an artist, does set design for the Santa Fe Opera.'

'They don't know each other?'

'No.'

'Was anyone hurt in any of the fires?'

'No. He made sure the houses would be empty.'

'So he's not a killer,' said Jay.

'Not yet,' Cruz answered. 'Accidents happen, though.'

They went back to the Cherokee. Jay opened the passenger-side door, sat down on the rocker panel, and began toeing off the heavy boots. 'You're sure all the fires were set by the same person?'

'Positive. The MO is identical and we never released any information about the condom thing to the press.' Cruz pulled his cowboy boots on again and tossed the muddied rubber ones into the back of the Cherokee. Jay followed suit. Cruz started the vehicle's engine and hauled the wheel around.

'You missed something,' said Jay as they reached Hyde Park Road and headed back down into Santa Fe.

'Obviously,' Cruz agreed flatly. 'But what?'

'You're sure it's the same guy, you're sure the motive is revenge?'

'I'm sure.'

'Then there has to be some common element between the victims. Something that ties them together, even if you can't see it.'

'So how do we find out what that common element is?' asked Cruz.

Jay held up both hands and wiggled her fingers. 'We consult the magic keyboard, that's how.'

CHAPTER SEVEN

Leaning on one of the white-painted wooden posts supporting the wisteria arbor, Bill Hawkins smoked his pipe and watched the sun go down over the steep wooded cliffs of Potomac Palisades and the dark, winding course of the river itself, a hundred feet below him. Here, forced through the ancient gorge, the stream was narrow, deep, and treacherous; two miles downstream at Chain Bridge on the district line, the river met the tidewater surge from Chesapeake Bay and became fat and sluggish.

The rambling old colonial farmhouse on the bluffs had been one of Hawkins' few personal indulgences after leaving the Bureau. Built on the site of the old High View Hotel, the house had once belonged to William Doak, Herbert Hoover's Secretary of Labor who named it Notre Nid. Hawkins, who'd purchased it from the estate of Doak's son with his insurance settlement after the accident, jokingly renamed it Goldeneye. Five years later the pun had become even more appropriate as Washington's relentless outward sprawl drove real estate values skyward. Now it was worth almost twice what he'd paid for it.

Not that he had any intention of selling it. Goldeneye was home, his first and last after a nomadic life that had begun in childhood as an Army brat moving from base to base and that had continued throughout his adult years. These days he traveled as little as possible, and if he had any say in the matter he'd prefer to die right where he was standing, smoking his pipe, watching the sun give birth to the moon, perhaps with a glass of Glenfiddich in his hand. He smiled at that; drinking had never been a particular vice of his, but he liked the image. Better than the can of Pepsi going flat beside the computer in his study.

He turned away from the darkening view and went back into the house, closing the door and locking it behind him. Time to get back to work. He went down the long, cherry-floored hallway and turned into the study. It was a big room with tall French doors at the far end opening on to the overgrown rose garden. Once it had been the library, complete with built-in oak bookcases covering the walls, heavy, dark green carpeting on the floor, and half a century's worth of nicotine stains on the ornately molded plaster ceiling. When he'd first seen it, the room had been furnished with dark upholstered club chairs; a massive, thickly varnished partners' desk; and an assortment of small tables and lamps from somebody's dimly realized dream of what the smoking room in a men's club should look like.

Hawkins had changed all that. The carpeting had been ripped up and the hardwood floor sanded and varnished with urethane. The ceiling had been cleaned, repaired, and repainted a crisp white and the furniture was now clean and very modern, the partners' desk replaced by a black lacquer computer workstation. All that remained from the original room were the bookcases, stripped and varnished like the floors. His books, thousands of them, virtually all relating to criminology and crime, were neatly arranged, spines flush, each one bearing a small bar code that interfaced with his computerized bibliographic catalog.

The study, meticulously tidy, was the antithesis of his office at Georgetown University. When people asked him why the two environments were so different, he explained it away by telling them that his office at the university was for abstract thought, while the study at Goldeneye was for things more concrete and logical. He wasn't sure that his explanation was entirely accurate, but he did know that he felt more comfortable here than there. This was home; the Georgetown office was something else – almost like a different version of himself, showing only that part he wanted to reveal.

He sat down at the workstation, relit his pipe, and began scrolling slowly through the file on the large color screen of his computer. There were thirty-seven Iceman files in the hard drive, secured from prying eyes with a double-depth, six-character password. This document, while not the first he had assembled relating to the Iceman, was the one tagged with the earliest date: 27

July 1968. What a year that had been for him. Twenty-two years old, scared shitless, and an MP in Saigon. He'd assumed his fresh-as-a-daisy degree in journalism would have landed him a job with *Stars and Stripes* or that being able to type sixty-five words a minute would have been worth a clerk's billet filling out requisitions at MACV, but true to form he'd been given a white helmet, a Sam Browne belt, and a baton.

He spent that whole summer hauling drunk and occasionally violent officers out of the Pink Nightclub at the Hotel Catinat and riding a jeep up and down Tu Do Street, from the docks to the basilica, looking for suspicious bicycles that might be bombs, listening to Aretha Franklin singing 'Chain of Fools' over and over again. Twenty-five years later, hearing that song could still bring back the spice and rotting-fish scent of Saigon to his nostrils.

When he wasn't on patrol, he'd been in his bunk, reading Carlos Castenada, looking for answers. He hadn't found any and for some reason which he still couldn't quite fathom, he'd stayed on in the Army, even after his tour was up, transferring into CID. From bicycle bombs to heroin smuggling, black-market antibiotics, and illegal gold trading.

Meanwhile, back home, there were Bobby Kennedy and Martin Luther King being assassinated, the Democratic Convention in Chicago, Black Panthers, campus sit-ins, the Gathering of the Tribes, and the presidential election of Richard Milhous Nixon. Somewhere in there, a single tree invisible in a forest of more newsworthy violence, there had also been a murder in Berkeley, California.

Her name was Carol Prentice, an eighteen-year-old self-styled free spirit from Rochester, New York, with long, dark brown hair, a tiny blue-and-red yin-yang tattoo just below her navel, and an apartment in an old house on Dana Street, around the corner from Mary Beck High School and less than a block from the Harmon Gymnasium entrance to the Berkeley campus. Her father worked for Kodak and her mother sold cosmetics to her friends. Her brother, ten years older, was a Catholic priest.

Carol Prentice had been killed by a single golf-style swing from a Louisville Slugger baseball bat while she was lying, presumably asleep, on the foam slab she used as a mattress. According to the autopsy report, she had died instantly, the blow crushing her temple and shattering her skull. From the direction of the swing, it was presumed that the killer had batted left-handed and from the point of impact it was further presumed that he was between five foot ten and six feet tall. The autopsy also indicated that Carol Prentice had engaged in sexual intercourse with at least two separate partners within twelve hours of her death. There was no indication of rape ... and pubic hair samples taken at the scene suggested that one of her partners was black.

The young woman had been enrolled in the theater arts program at Berkeley and was a member of Berkeley Agit-Prop, a political theater group, as well as being an apprentice with the San Francisco Mime Troupe. As it turned out, the Louisville Slugger was one of the bats used by the SFMT team for their regular Saturday pickup games at the Mary Beck diamond next door. Carol Prentice had been clean-up batter and also played left field. Several members of the SFMT and Berkeley Agit-Prop admitted to having sexual relations with the girl at one time or another, but all had alibis for the period around the time of her murder.

There had been an incredible amount of physical evidence at the crime scene and even now Hawkins was astounded that so little had come of the investigation. As well as the murder weapon, pubic hairs, and semen, there was an entire outfit of blood-spattered men's clothing and huge quantities of recently cut hair in the kitchen sink. The clothing included a pair of worn blue jeans, a pair of sneakers, heavy woolen sweat socks, and a UC Berkeley sweatshirt.

Hair samples from the sweatshirt and the jeans matched the Caucasoid pubic hair samples taken from Carol Prentice's body. The head hair from the kitchen sink was medium brown and very long. There was also a quantity of facial hair in the sink as well as a recently used Gillette safety razor on the kitchen counter. The facial and head hair were a perfect match.

Friends of the victim told investigators that Carol Prentice had recently become involved with a young man known only as Wheels. From what they knew of him, Wheels had drifted in from somewhere in the East a few months before and had been living in the Haight-Ashbury district. His nickname apparently stemmed from the fact that he rode a motorcycle. There was no evidence that Wheels was enrolled at Berkeley. Witnesses agreed that Wheels had a flat, Midwestern accent and seemed to be quite intelligent. Wheels had long, medium brown hair and a scraggly medium brown beard. By the looks of things, the man, in an effort to disguise himself, had changed his clothing, cut his hair, and shaved his beard shortly after killing Carol Prentice.

After a week and a half of investigation, the Berkeley Police hadn't come up with any substantial leads even though the file listed more than twenty separate interviews. There were only two other small fragments of information that interested Hawkins. A shrewd Berkeley cop named Goddard had suggested that, given the time of the month in which the murder took place, Carol would have been getting ready to pay her rent. According to her landlord, Carol always paid in cash and on time, yet there was no cash in evidence at the apartment. Because of this, Goddard had concluded that the most likely motive for the girl's murder had simply been greed. To Hawkins that seemed pretty thin, especially in light of the fact that relatively large quantities of marijuana and hashish had been found in the apartment.

Two other witnesses, both young adolescents from Mary Beck High School who had been cutting class, mentioned that they had seen a man wearing the uniform of an Army corporal exiting Carol Prentice's building at around the time the murder had taken place. The witnesses had been surprised, since people in military uniform were a rare sight in Berkeley then. Their description of the corporal, with added hair and beard, matched that of Wheels. If their description of the man and the time of his appearance was accurate, there was clear evidence of premeditation on the part of the killer. He'd come to Carol Prentice's apartment with his disguise, knowing that he would need it after the murder.

A month after the killing of Carol Prentice, the decaying body of a young man eventually identified as Lance Follett was discovered, buried in a shallow grave in Charles Lee Tilden Regional Park, a few miles east of Berkeley. Follett, a corporal in the United States Army, had been on a week-long furlough immediately prior to being shipped off to Vietnam. His furlough had been due to end on June 29, two days after the murder of Carol Prentice. No one had made the connection between the two deaths until several months later, but the report on Follett's killing had one curious anomaly.

After reporting the young corporal's murder to the proper military authorities, it was presumed that Follett would have been listed as AWOL. Oddly, this was not the case; according to the records, Corporal Lance Follett had left for Vietnam precisely according to his orders, traveling on Pan Am to Manila, and from the Philippines to Saigon via a regular Military Airlift Command flight. At this point, CID in Saigon was advised that there might be an impostor in their midst and they put out a trace on the man calling himself

Lance Follett. Their investigation showed that Follett
had never presented himself at MACV headquarters
for his assignment. Somewhere between Manila and
Saigon, he had simply vanished into thin air.

Hawkins leaned back in his chair and stared at the
computer screen. At the time he'd been completely
unaware of both the Prentice and Follett murders; his
involvement hadn't come until years after the fact,
leaving him with a trail that was cold and stale, but
after backtracking the early Iceman killings, he'd been
led inexorably into the past, finally coming to what was
literally a dead end in Berkeley on that day in June so
many years ago. Every now and again over the years,
tracking the Iceman's terrible odyssey, he found himself
wondering if he might have crossed paths with the
killer in Vietnam, hunter and hunted passing in the
night, long before the chase was joined. The thought
haunted him, the faceless man sometimes appearing
wraithlike in his dreams, always turning a corner just
ahead, always unidentifiable except for a bloody baseball bat perched nonchalantly across his shoulder.

As far as the Bureau was concerned, the linkages
were too vague to justify a full-scale investigation, but
Hawkins was positive that the murders of Corporal
Lance Follett and the young Carol Prentice had been
the Iceman's preliminary foray into the netherworld of
serial killing, and marked the beginning of a dark and
horrifying career that had lasted for the better part of
thirty years. It was a career the Iceman was clearly
proud of; like most serial killers, he needed an audience

and after an ill-advised interview with a reporter at the *Washington Post* in which Hawkins mentioned one of the Iceman killings, the relationship between hunter and hunted had begun. The Iceman had been taunting him with evidence of his crimes for almost fifteen years now, usually in the form of photographs like the ones Langford had brought him. Frustrated by the serial killer's studied arrogance, Hawkins' search for the Iceman had become almost an obsession. The fact that the killer had chosen him to play the role of father-confessor without leaving him any choice in the matter made it even worse, each death and its consequent, grotesque correspondence with the killer serving to increase Hawkins' anger.

Hawkins used the stem of his pipe to scratch thoughtfully along the line of his jaw. He took a thin file folder out of the drawer on his right and opened it. Langford was right; Hawkins had known there'd been another killing even before the FBI man had called him. There were almost a dozen single-page letters in the file folder. The most recent one had been delivered to him at his University office just three days before. Without picking up the sheet of paper, he read the single typed word in the center of the page and the line of text below it:

PHOENIX
Maybe next time you'll write a book about me.

The message was signed, in fountain-pen ink, with the letter *K*. K for 'Killer? K for 'Krazy? K for 'Katch me? It didn't really matter. What mattered was the implied challenge.

'All right, you sick son of a bitch,' Hawkins said quietly. 'It's time to bring you down.'

Like most hospitals, the morgue at Denver Presbyterian was located in the basement. It was a large room, high ceilinged, well lit, white walls. The floor was concrete, painted with a gray, nonslip vinyl compound. The floor also had large, chrome-ringed drains set under each of the seven permanent autopsy tables. Two walls were filled with floor-to-ceiling stacks of brushed-steel compartments while the wall closest to the door was fitted with a number of supply cabinets and refrigerator units. The fourth wall, at the opposite end of the room, was sheet glass and had originally been used as a viewing area for bodies. The glass wall had since been spray painted and the viewing chamber turned into an office for the morgue supervisor.

The compartments for the bodies were kept at a constant thirty-seven degrees while the rest of the morgue was at room temperature. Electronically controlled deodorizer units had been installed behind the ceiling vents and the whole room smelled vaguely of a pine forest. On first encountering the obviously artificial scent, the Iceman had been amused. Perhaps he'd spray some air freshener around the Putnam residence after the job was done, Herb and Spice maybe, or would Lavender Bouquet be more appropriate? He glanced at his watch. Just after ten.

The Iceman had been going through the filing cabinets in the glass-walled office for the past quarter of an hour, occasionally removing a folder and photocopying its contents using the small 3M machine beside the desk. When the copying was completed, he returned the folder to its appropriate place. The copies were fastened to his clipboard. Like the slightly rumpled white jacket he'd taken from a laundry cart, the clipboard was a useful prop; with it and the jacket, he became invisible, just another faceless member of the hospital staff.

He worked slowly and methodically; the morgues in most hospitals came under the aegis of the Department of Pathology and generally worked on nine-to-five business hours. If some sort of special autopsy had been scheduled there would have been a table prepared in the outer room and even if a real member of the staff suddenly appeared, the Iceman could justify his presence in the office with any number of plausible explanations.

Ten minutes later his task had been accomplished; he had the vital statistics of six possibles, including their dates of birth, addresses, and Social Security numbers. Within seventy-two hours, he could easily assemble birth certificates, passports, and valid driver's licenses for all six names. With a little more work and another forty-eight hours, he could have replacement credit cards for them as well. Rabbit holes for him to leap into should the need arise. He picked up the clipboard and left the office, switching off the light and closing the door behind him. Time for a light meal, an hour or so with the computer, and then a few minutes monitoring the intercoms. He wondered if Ellen Putnam would use her vibrator again tonight. He smiled; the woman was incredibly vocal when she climaxed. It was almost embarrassing. He smiled again. He liked the word *climax*. It was so much more final than *orgasm*.

The Iceman left the morgue and took the elevator up to the main floor. As he walked out of the building, he found himself thinking about Ellen Putnam and the photographs he'd taken. He smiled again. Hawkins was going to love this one.

CHAPTER EIGHT

The day following Jay Fletcher's arrival in Santa Fe, Cruz was scheduled to give an all-day seminar in Albuquerque to a group of visiting Mexican firemen from Chihuahua. He invited her to come along, but since the seminar would be conducted entirely in Spanish, she didn't see the point. Cruz took an early-morning shuttle from the little municipal airport on the southern edge of town. After a mouth-burning breakfast at the Plaza Cafe, Jay drove the loaner Ford Escort to the office over the library. The breakfast, recommended by Cruz, was something called Christmas Huevos Rancheros. Beans and eggs she'd heard about, but *Christmas* referred to the fact that it was served swimming in a pool of red *and* green chili sauce. It had taken three huge glasses of iced tea to stop her eyes from watering and bring peace back to her digestive system.

By nine-thirty she had the coffee machine brewing and the computers booted up. By ten she'd read through the entire file that Cruz had put together on what he

called the Safe Sex Bug. He was right; at first glance
there was nothing in the file that seemed to join the
fires, except for the arsonist's *modus operandi* – the use
of a condom as a delay mechanism.

The first victim was a man named George Bingham, a
deputy director at the Los Alamos National Laboratory
Historical Museum, about thirty-five miles northwest
of Santa Fe. He had been on vacation in Europe with his
wife when his house was destroyed. The second victim
was a bachelor lawyer from Albuquerque named Brian
MacDonald, while the third fire had partially destroyed
the home and studio of the Santa Fe Opera set designer
Rand Symington. The fourth, and most recent, victim
was Dr Julius Lowenthal, a Los Alamos Lab project
director.

Bingham, MacDonald, and Lowenthal all had full
replacement insurance on their properties, while
Symington had only enough insurance to satisfy the
Bank of Santa Fe, which held his mortgage. From the
looks of things, none of the four had made any profit
from the fires and Cruz had ruled out personal gain
as a motive. The fires were far too orderly and well
executed to be the work of an out and out random
pyromaniac, so maybe Cruz was right: they were
revenge fires.

She worked her way through an entire pot of coffee
and half a dozen reference books on arson that Cruz kept
in the office. By noon Jay had half-filled a yellow legal
pad with notes and come up with a general profile on
revenge arsonists. Not good enough for a masters thesis,

but adequate for the time being. Remembering breakfast, she decided to forget about lunch and spent another hour putting together the notes before she got down to work at the keyboard.

Like the vast majority of arsonists, the one setting a revenge fire was most likely male – statistically there were almost no women arsonists. On the other hand, while most arson fires were set by relatively young people – fourteen to twenty-five – there were no age restrictions for the revenge arsonist. The predominant feature of revenge fires was a serious desire to kill, maim, or cause irreparable damage; there was nothing spur of the moment about such fires; they were often the result of a serious, usually long-standing grudge, and were generally well planned.

The rationale for the fires was usually just as specific, the result of some real or imagined action on the part of the victim. From what Jay could gather, the Safe Sex pyro was in the most dangerous subgroup among revenge arsonists, since he was setting fire to residences rather than places of business. A residence fire was much more likely to have murderous consequences and the failure of the arsonist to consider the possibility of physical harm to his victims was often the result of low intelligence, senility, intoxication, or a variety of psychological disorders.

The revenge arsonist, like almost all fire setters, was also likely to require some sort of 'release factor' precipitating the incident. The most common were emotional disturbances within the home, a recent trauma such as unemployment, a number of sexual problems including impotence, spousal and incestuous abuse and arousal of previously suppressed sexual behavior, and excessive use of alcohol resulting in the loss of inhibition. Often release factors were combined in the revenge arsonist.

None of the information was very specific, but assuming that the Safe Sex Bug was local, using the general profile would probably cut the number of potential suspects in half. Of course there was also the possibility that Cruz had erred in his diagnosis; according to the books she'd skimmed through, there were a lot of similarities between revenge fires and those set for racial and religious reasons. On the basis of what Cruz had casually mentioned about the multiple racial tensions in the Santa Fe area, it was something that would have to be investigated – very discreetly.

Using the access code Cruz had given her, Jay began the process of getting into the mainframe at the State Capitol. As she worked her way into the system and began setting up her search program, she suddenly realized that she was enjoying herself; tracking down the Safe Sex firebug wasn't up there with Ted Bundy or the Green River Killer, but it was a lot more interesting than she'd expected and at least here, alone in the musty old office above the Santa Fe Public Library, she wasn't surrounded by ten thousand Fibbie bureaucrats or buried under an avalanche of memoranda. It was a refreshing change.

Operating on the assumption that Cruz was right

about the fires being motivated by revenge, she decided to forget the arsonist, at least for the moment, and concentrate on the victims instead. Using a broad-based template with nothing more than the four names, she ran it through virtually every major database in the mainframe, from the Department of Motor Vehicles and the New Mexico State Police files to the Santa Fe Chamber of Commerce and the information held by the library downstairs. She switched on the old-fashioned dot-matrix printer, watched as the search program began chugging its way slowly through the mainframe, and went out for a walk.

She returned to the office forty minutes later and found a disappointingly short tongue of paper drooping out of the printer. Beyond the standard appearances on the DMV and City Hall lists, the four victims had reasonably clean slates. Lowenthal, the Los Alamos project director, drove a Mercedes and paid the highest property taxes, which probably meant he made the most money; Rand Symington, from the Santa Fe Opera, drove an Izuzu Trooper; MacDonald, the Albuquerque lawyer, drove a Porsche; and Bingham, the Los Alamos museum employee, drove a late-model Chrysler. The only items of interest were several recent DUI notations on the lawyer's sheet with Motor Vehicles and a cross-reference blip on Symington's file indicating that there was more information to be had on him from the Business Licencing Division in Los Angeles.

With nothing else to go on, Jay dumped out of the

mainframe and spent the next fifteen minutes finding out how to get into the L.A. computer. After two false starts, she made the electronic link to California, ID'd herself with her FBI/NCAVC code, and requested whatever information the L.A. Business Licensing Division had on the set designer. The file appeared on her screen in Santa Fe almost instantly.

'I'll be damned,' she murmured, scanning the file. She lit a cigarette and read through it again.

> Symington, Randall Andrew/020456-37
> rsp/corp.div.:
>   ---PYROTECH INC.--
> Cal. Explosives Lic.[Class A]#237-12-83

'He's got an explosives license?' said Cruz, biting into the fast-food chiliburger he'd picked up on Guadalupe Street. It was early evening. He'd arrived back from the seminar in Albuquerque an hour before and he and Jay were sitting at a picnic table in Santa Fe River Park, watching the sun go down. Twenty yards away a light breeze waved through the sawgrass in the dry riverbed.

'Class A. He's had it for the last nine years.' Jay nodded. 'I called some people I know at LAPD and they did some digging for me. Pyrotech did special effects for movies, specializing in fires and explosions.'

'And Symington was sole proprietor of the company?'

'It was a one-man operation,' said Jay. Cruz used his teeth to rip open a plastic package of green chili sauce, which he proceeded to squeeze over the last few bites of his hamburger. The half-eaten remains of Jay's own burger lay in front of her on the picnic table. She sipped at a carton of chocolate milk and watched her colleague eat.

'Okay,' said Cruz, swallowing. 'He has means and opportunity; what about motive? And why would he burn his own place, especially if he was underinsured?'

'Doesn't make much sense, does it?'

'And what happened to Pyrotech? Designing sets for the Santa Fe Opera is a long way from being a Hollywood special effects expert.'

'He screwed up,' Jay answered. She took a last swallow of her milk.

'How?' Cruz motioned toward the remains of her chiliburger and she nodded. He pulled it over to his side of the table.

'Blowing up a house in one of those martial arts movies. According to my contact at the LAPD, he'd been drinking the night before and laid the charges wrong. A lighting man was killed and the star was pretty badly burned. Symington was blacklisted.'

'That still doesn't explain why he's running around town torching people's houses,' said Cruz. He finished off Jay's burger and lit a cigarette.

'Maybe we should ask him,' said Jay. The air was cooling and she shivered.

'Cold?' asked Cruz.

'A little.'

'Santa Fe can fool you. Hundred degrees at noon and

you're freezing by midnight. Not what you're used to, I guess.'

'No.' She smiled. 'During the summer Washington is like a sauna twenty-four hours a day.'

There was a long silence. Cruz finally spoke. 'So what exactly are you doing here, Fletcher?'

'My job,' she answered. 'Catching crooks.'

'I'm serious.'

'So am I.'

'Bullshit,' Cruz said bluntly. In the fading light, Jay couldn't read the man's expression. 'For someone like you, Santa Fe is a punishment detail. Your boss handed you over like a hot potato. I'd like to know why.' He paused. 'Did you screw up, too? Like Symington?'

'Not quite as badly as that,' Jay answered. 'But yeah, I screwed up.'

'Booze? Drugs? What?'

'Bad judgment.'

'How bad?'

'Too much enthusiasm. I compromised a case. Langford decided I should lie low for a little while.'

'And here you are.'

'That's it.'

There was another silence. Cruz broke it again. 'I'm glad,' he said quietly.

'Glad I screwed up?'

'No. Glad you're here.' The tip of his cigarette glowed brightly in the gathering gloom. The sky had gone purple and the distant hills were black.

'Can I ask you a favor, Cruz?'

'Sure.'

'The next time we eat, can we get something that doesn't have chili in it?'

Jay was back at the J. Edgar Hoover Building, sitting with Prine and trying to put together a digitized picture of a murder victim. Prine kept talking about Stephen Hawking and black holes, and every time they tried to work up the victim's picture, it was Dennis Lloyd Shaw staring back at her from the computer screen. The picture smiled and the lips moved. Shaw speaking to her, his voice hollow and distant. *You don't know a fucking thing, Special Agent Janet Fletcher. Not a fucking thing.*

The phone buzzed. Jay opened her eyes and rolled over in bed. She blinked and came fully back to consciousness, the dream fading. The little travel clock on the bedside table said that it was twenty past two. The phone rang again. She reached out and grabbed it.

'Hello?'

'Fletcher? It's Cruz.'

'What?'

'Get your ass in gear. Twenty minutes, the airport off Cerrillos Road. There's a State Police chopper waiting for us.'

'What's going on?'

'A burn. In Albuquerque. A bad one.'

The helicopter flight took less than half an hour, the breakneck drive from the heliport at the Albuquerque airport twenty minutes more. They arrived at the fire scene barely an hour after Cruz's call. The building was a fifties vintage apartment building on the north end of Edmunds Street, a block from Chavez Park and jammed in close to the I-25 Freeway. The building was surrounded by half a dozen others just like it, the spaces between them littered with rusted-out cars, rotting mattresses, and an assortment of broken, abandoned furniture. In daylight the neighborhood would have been a depressing tenement ghetto; in the raging firelight it was a nightmare.

By the time they reached the fire, the building was fully involved, towering tongues of vivid flame rising up from the flat roof into the night sky, coiling billows of thick black-and-gray smoke vomiting out of a score of shattered windows. Bright yellow sparks and red hot, flaming cinders flew around like an incendiary plague of deadly locusts and waves of blast-furnace heat spread out in all directions. There were fire trucks everywhere, at least a dozen of them and hundreds of gaping spectators were pressed up against a line of police barricades, watching as the firemen worked to extinguish the blaze before it spread to the surrounding buildings.

Lights flashing, Cruz bullied the borrowed AFD Fire Marshal's Office car as close as he could to the flaming building, aiming for a group of uniformed fire chiefs and Albuquerque PD officers standing beside a blood-red Pumper. A dozen bloated canvas hoses ran away from the truck, nozzle ends manned by a squad of firemen dressed in full turnout, boots and helmets. They were training their high-pressure flumes of spray on the lower levels of the seven-story building. The street was already ankle-deep in water and the noise was incredible, battering madly at Jay's ears in an insane symphony of crackling, roaring flames, furiously gushing water and the groaning, tortured creaking of the building as it disintegrated in front of her.

'Stay close.' Cruz reached into the backseat and hauled out the gym bag he'd carried with him from Santa Fe. He climbed out of the car and walked quickly over to the waiting group of men, Jay hard on his heels.

'Cruz, FIO. Which one of you is Teale?'

A stocky, bald-headed man in a beige windbreaker extended a hand. 'I'm Teale. Albuquerque Fire Marshal's Office.' Cruz shook the hand briefly. Teale glanced at Jay. 'Who's your friend?'

'His friend is an FBI agent. Jay Fletcher.' Jay put out her hand. Teale ignored it. A hundred feet away, the blazing pyre that had once been an apartment building continued to burn furiously. The heat was overwhelming and for a split second Jay seriously considered turning tail and running like hell. Instead she gritted her teeth and stood her ground.

'I called you because S.O.P. and the fucking Commissioner's Office says I have to in any case of suspected arson. So I called.' Teale made a small snorting sound. 'Far as I'm concerned, that's it.' The bald man turned away.

'That's not it as far as I'm concerned, Teale,' Cruz said harshly.

'I've got a fucking job to do, Mr Cruz. I don't have time for this shit.'

'Neither do I,' said Cruz. 'So why don't you just give me your report and we'll get out of your hair.'

'All right,' Teale answered. 'Three alarms, full exposure. Place has been burning for an hour and a half. We've kept it to the top three floors so far. Looks like the plant was in a fifth-floor apartment. First Due saw heavy flame involvement and a lot of black smoke from that part of the building. He sent out the ten-forty-one. I picked up the call.'

'That's it?' asked Cruz.

'No, man, that's not it,' said Teale. 'So far we've got three Code Twos and eleven Code Ones. Good enough for you?'

'Christ!' whispered Cruz. 'Eleven dead?'

'So far.'

'Why so many?'

'Because there was a fucking wetback crib on the sixth floor,' said Teale. 'One of those illegal overnight day cares.'

'Kids?'

'Babies. One adult female, probably the woman who ran the place. And an unidentified male in the stairwell. Toasted and roasted.'

'What about pictures?'

'Give me a break, Cruz. Like I said, I don't have time for this shit.' Teale turned away again and this time

Cruz made no attempt to stop him. Cruz walked back to the car, stepping over the web of hoses running away from the trucks. Jay followed him.

'I didn't get much of the jargon,' she said, raising her voice over the sound of the flames. 'Sounds like cop-talk.'

'Pretty close.' Cruz nodded. '*Plant* means the place the bug started the fire. *First Due* is the first engine company on site. *Ten-forty-one* is a radio code for a suspicious fire.'

'*Code One* means a dead body?'

'Right. *Code Two* is someone seriously injured.' Cruz set the gym bag on the hood of the car and pulled back the zipper. 'The fact that the First Due crew saw large flames and a lot of black smoke from the fire site means that whoever set the fire probably used gasoline.'

'You can tell that from the smoke color?'

'If you catch it early enough. Black means petroleum products. White means some kind of humid material, like hay.' He pulled a matched pair of palm-sized video recorders from the bag. 'Gray smoke usually comes from a phosphorous igniter and you sometimes get a real garlicky smell to it. Red, or reddish brown, means some kind of acid, hydrochloric, sulfuric, or nitric.' He handed a camera to Jay. 'You know how to use one of these?'

'Sure.'

'Then start shooting,' Cruz answered, zipping up the bag again. 'There's a two-hour tape in there. When you run out, I've got more in the bag.'

'What am I looking for?'

'Anything out of the ordinary.' He looked back at the burning building. 'You cover the crowd; I'll do the fire.'

By the time the fire had been put out, dawn was leaking up over the eastern hills and Jay was exhausted. She'd gone back for new tapes twice, scanning the slowly diminishing crowds around the fire scene, not really sure if she was accomplishing anything or not. By six the tenement on Edmunds Street was a charred hulk and the crowds had drifted away; there was nothing particularly exciting about watching firemen poking around in a burnt-out building or rolling up hoses.

She was dozing in the borrowed AFD car when Cruz reappeared. Stripping off the canvas firefighter's suit he was wearing, he dropped it in the trunk, then climbed into the car and slid in behind the wheel.

'Done?' asked Jay. He looked worn out.

'For the time being,' Cruz answered. He turned on the ignition and put the car in gear. He backed and filled until they were facing up the street.

'Where to now?' Jay sat up, yawning. 'Breakfast?' she added hopefully.

'Not yet,' said Cruz, shaking his head. He headed for the expressway. 'Because of the deaths, there's a homicide debriefing downtown. We should be there.'

Albuquerque Police Headquarters was located in the Law Enforcement Building on northwest Roma Avenue, tucked in behind the courthouse, which discreetly screened it from the Civic Plaza half a block away. The debriefing was held in a large conference room in the Homicide Department on the fifth floor of the building, and it took Jay all of thirty seconds to realize that there was no point in her being there. Cruz was barely welcome himself and she knew a kibitzing FBI agent, and a woman at that, was just going to be more of an embarrassment. She excused herself quickly and went off in search of a coffee machine.

The Homicide Department was a maze of narrow hallways, office cubicles, and interrogation rooms decorated in cop casual, a style that was as universal as the lobby of a Holiday Inn, combining scarred furniture, pale green walls, and bulletin boards plastered with three-sheet memos and union notices. This early, Homicide was quiet; the night's body count was still being tallied and it was a bit too early for the day shift.

Jay found what she was looking for in a medium-sized meeting room with a window that looked out on to the parking lot between the Law Enforcement Building and the back of the courthouse. There was a hand-lettered sign on the door: HAND JOB. Filling the empty pot in the adjoining bathroom, she began making some fresh brew. While the coffee dripped, she dropped into a chair and looked blearily around the room. It was obviously in regular use. The big table taking up most of the space was littered with empty cups, overflowing ashtrays, and lined, yellow memo pads. Overhead a trio of fluorescents flickered and crackled. The far wall was taken up by a large chalkboard, its surface covered by a black felt curtain sagging along a length of wire. She had a

105

sneaking suspicion she knew what the room was being used for; it looked like the temporary task force office they'd had for the LAPD Fly Me case.

Curious, Jay filched a steaming cup from the still-filling pot, threw in some whitener, and went down to the other end of the room. She put her cup on the table, lit a cigarette, then pushed back the curtain.

'Christ!' she murmured, staring. '*Déjà vu* time.'

Half the chalkboard was covered in various overlapping charts of names, places, and times, interconnected with color-coded lines. The other half was wallpapered with eight-by-ten photographs in black and white as well as color. Even without the grisly subject matter, Jay would have recognized the harsh, almost surreal lighting of crime scene pictures taken by the Coroner's Office.

The majority of the photographs were of hands, each one mutilated in the same way: someone had taken an extremely sharp instrument like a meat cleaver and slashed down between the second and third fingers, cutting deeply into the palm, and in some cases almost splitting the hand in two. The rest of the pictures were head and torso shots of the victims, all women and of varying ages, but most seemed to be in their late twenties or early thirties. Their breasts and stomachs had been mutilated with deep puncture wounds and their throats had been slashed. Jay counted nine different faces. The pictures were neatly numbered and labeled. Three of the victims were from Albuquerque, the other six were from out of state: Virginia Beach,

Virginia; Rome, Georgia; St Petersburg, Florida; San Diego, California; Rochester, New York; and Detroit, Michigan.

As far as Jay could see, there was no obvious connection between the nine women. Even in black and white she could see that some were blonde, others dark, and two were clearly redheaded. Two were on the pudgy side, one looked very young, no more then seventeen or eighteen, and another could have passed for someone's grandmother. One was black, another Oriental. It was odd, since every serial killer she'd ever heard of went after a particular race, physical type, or age group. This one seemed to be playing the field. At least now she knew what the sign on the door meant.

'Mind telling me what you're doing in here?'

Startled, Jay turned and found herself facing a large, balding man in his fifties wearing a rumpled gray suit and a white shirt. His cheeks, chin, and neck were heavily pockmarked and he had very bushy eyebrows. He was frowning, his eyes fixed on the visitor's badge clipped to her lapel.

'I was making a fresh pot of coffee.'

'Yeah. I smelled it,' said the man. 'That's why I looked in. No one's supposed to be in here this time of the morning.'

'Sorry.'

'So who are you?'

'My name's Fletcher. I'm supposed to be at a debriefing down the hall.'

'The crispy critters thing? The barrio fire?'

'Yes.'

'My name's Sladky. What's your connection to the barbecue?'

'I'm with Cruz, State Fire Investigation Office.'

'What do you mean, "with"?'

'I'm working with him.'

'You're not from around here.'

'Washington. Detached duty from the FBI.'

'A Feeb?'

'Yes.' Jay nodded her head at the photographs. 'This your case?'

'Hand Job? Yeah. He's mine.'

'Six out of towners.'

'Yeah, all with the same MO. He seems to like it here. I wish the fucker'd go somewhere else.'

'How long has he been around?' Jay asked.

Sladky went to the coffee machine, poured himself a cup, and joined Jay at the chalkboard. He sipped his coffee and stared at the photographs. 'He did the first one almost two years ago.'

'In Albuquerque?'

'Yeah. From the timing it looks like he pops one every two months or so.' He glanced at Jay. 'You handled this kind of thing before?'

'Yes.'

'You one of those *Silence of the Lambs* hotshots? Bureau of Behavioral Blush?'

'No. Computers.'

'I hate the fucking things. Can't figure them out.'

Jay grinned. 'Me too, sometimes.' She paused, looking

at the photographs again. 'Does he sexually assault the victims?'

'Naw. Not unless he's jerking off into a cocksafe or something. Scene's always clean as a whistle. Coroner's reports say he ties them down to a chair with duct tape. He does the tits and stomachs first, then the throat. The hand thing is last, postmortem.'

'The victims all look different.'

'Yeah, that's the bitch. No clear pattern. Age spread is off the fucking profile, too. Seventeen to fifty-nine. Big, small, short, tall, black, white – the fucker doesn't seem to care.'

'The only real signature is the hand-mutilation thing?' asked Jay.

'Yeah. And the notes.'

'He leaves notes?'

'Yeah, I guess you could call them that.' Sladky went to the chalkboard and took down a blown-up photocopy.

'What the hell is this?' said Jay. The notes were neatly typed and totally incomprehensible. She read one aloud, stumbling over each syllable, 'qaStaHvlS wa'ram LoS SaD Hugh SlijlaH qetbogh loD.'

'Beats the hell out of me,' said Sladky. 'We ran all the notes by the Linguistics Department at UNM and they couldn't figure it out either. Nobody knows what it is. Notes are done on a laser printer, Hewlett Packard IIP or so they tell me, but there's a million of the fucking things around. Not much help.'

'A code?' Jay suggested.

Sladky shook his head. 'Naw, we tried that, too. Zip.'

He shrugged. 'We think it must be gobbledygook. Some kind of secret language only he knows, or a freak religious thing. Doer thinks he's the fucking reincarnation of David Koresh maybe. Task force was set up eight months ago. We don't have shit.'

'Weird,' said Jay.

Sladky made a grumbling sound deep in his throat. 'Yeah. That's one word for it.' He snorted. 'But aren't they all?'

CHAPTER NINE

Arriving at Sky Harbor Airport in Phoenix, William Hawkins rented himself a Lincoln Town Car and drove to the Sheraton, a block from Civic Plaza in the downtown core. After a quick lunch in the hotel restaurant, he called the FBI field office, made an appointment, then took the Lincoln north up the Black Canyon Freeway. Half an hour and two missed exits later, he finally found the field office on East Indianola Avenue. The building was a medium-sized block of poured concrete squatting within earshot of the freeway. It was built like a fortress. After getting into the featureless lobby, it took him another fifteen minutes to transcend the involved identification and clearance procedure that included everything short of a retinal scan and a strip search. Hawkins wasn't surprised. After a terrorist attack in Atlanta a few years before, during which a dozen FBI agents and support staff were held hostage, getting access to your neighborhood Fed was no longer easy. In the Dallas office, they really did use retinal scanners; even the men's room had a combination lock. God help the average citizen who came in to report a crime. Hawkins' eye patch and his casual clothing didn't help the security procedure, either.

Rodney Jones' office was on the fourth floor of the building. As Special Agent in Charge of the field office, Jones rated a corner suite with a view of the cars streaming up and down the freeway. He stood up from his desk and took Hawkins' extended hand as though it belonged to a spitting cobra. The SAC was tall, at least six foot three inches, stocky, ruddy-haired, and balding. He wore heavy, dark-rimmed glasses perched on a broad nose and had a weary, time-worn expression on his face. He looked more like a university football coach than an FBI agent. He offered Hawkins a chair, then sat down behind his desk again.

'I've been asked to give you my full cooperation,' said Jones. The voice was intelligent and low on the register with just the barest hint of a western drawl and a sour edge.

'Asked?' Hawkins smiled. 'Or told?'

'*Told* would be a better word.'

'Tact isn't a strong suit at Headquarters,' said Hawkins. 'It wasn't in my time, either.'

'Just so long as this isn't some goddamn sting from OPR.'

'It's not,' said Hawkins, shaking his head. The Office of Professional Responsibility was the FBI version of a regular police force's Internal Affairs Division. Officially OPR was supposed to check auditing procedures, interview employees, and generally evaluate how well each field office did its job. From time to time, though, they'd been known to employ less overt measures. Within the Bureau OPR operatives were known as Goons.

'So what exactly do you want to know?' Jones said. He leaned back in his chair, putting his hands behind his head. The gesture was designed to make him look relaxed and at ease, but it had the opposite effect. His turf was being violated and he resented it.

'Whatever you can tell me.'

'From what I hear, you know more about this guy than anyone else already. I doubt if we can add much.'

'They're all different,' said Hawkins. 'How did you catch the case in the first place?'

'The envelope addressed to you. Phoenix PD found it underneath Mr Freezee. It was an excuse to hand it to us, get it off their files.' Jones laughed briefly. 'They were tickled pink. Last thing the locals want is a murder like that hanging around their necks like some kind of albatross. Not that I blame them. Their chances of putting it away are zero and they know it.'

'What about the Bureau?' asked Hawkins. 'How do you rate your chances?'

'About the same.'

'Any progress?'

'None to speak of. There's not much to go on.' He shrugged. 'We're following procedure. VICAP, that kind of thing. I guess you know the drill.'

Hawkins nodded. Jones sounded as though he couldn't

have cared less, but when you got right down to it, he was right: there wasn't a hell of a lot he could do. The Iceman never fouled the same nest twice; to Jones, and to the Phoenix PD, it was a single murder and had to be treated that way. For a concerted investigative effort, you'd need the cooperation and coordination of police forces and Bureau field offices all over the country, and that just wasn't going to happen. Phoenix was a jurisdictional nightmare all on its own. There were twenty-three different local forces, the State Police, and half a dozen County Sheriff offices to deal with in the area, not to mention the language problems. Hawkins sighed. Law enforcement in the United States was being bureaucratized into near impotence. They were already listing basic computer skills as an entrance qualification at most police academies these days.

'You mind if I take a look at the files?' he asked. It was his main reason for the chat with Jones, that and to get a feel for what he might be up against from the Good Guy side.

The SAC shrugged and nodded. 'Sure. Be my guest.' He smiled, but behind the heavy glasses his eyes were humorless. 'Who knows, maybe you'll get a book out of it.'

Hawkins took the Xeroxes of the files back to his hotel room and got down to work. For a back-burner homicide without any real ongoing leads, the Iceman had generated an enormous amount of paper: the 911 transcript from the first call, the first crime scene report from the uniforms who responded to the 911, the preliminary

interview with the landlord who'd discovered the body
in the freezer, the detectives' preliminary report, the
medical officer's on-site report, the transcript of the
autopsy protocol, forensic test results, transfer documents from Phoenix Homicide to the FBI field office, a
preliminary evaluation of the case by one of Jones'
Special Agents, and memos to Jones as the case was
streamed into VICAP.

And it didn't amount to a hill of beans. There was still
no ID on the body and nothing at all on the Iceman. Once
again it looked as though the son of a bitch was getting
away with murder. Hawkins kept digging, using a legal
pad to build up a timeline on the case. By midafternoon
he had a general grasp of things. Taking his notes to
the telephone beside his bed, he placed a call to Bo
Stevenson, the detective sergeant at Phoenix PD who'd
been the original investigating officer. Hawkins
explained who he was and arranged to meet Stevenson
at the crime scene.

The body had been discovered in a three-story apartment complex in the southwestern section of the city.
The building was cinderblock anonymous, twenty-odd
units built around a pool courtyard and looking more
like a weatherbeaten motel for traveling salesmen than
anyplace you'd call home. The surrounding neighborhood was a wilderness of strip malls, taco stands, and
all-night liquor stores.

Det. Sgt Bo Stevenson was waiting for him at the
apartment unit when Hawkins arrived. He was a tall,
heavily built man in his forties with a boxer's battered

face and a shaved head. He greeted Hawkins at the door of the apartment with a perfunctory handshake, then took him on a guided tour. There wasn't much to see.

'Pretty standard,' said Stevenson. 'Bedroom, bathroom, kitchen, breakfast nook, and living room.'

Hawkins nodded. White walls turned beige with nicotine, cheap parquet floors with pieces of wood veneer missing here and there, a coil of cable coming out of the wall on one corner of the living room, and not a stick of furniture. The only thing that stood out was the midsized freezer unit in the breakfast nook. It was still covered with a layer of sooty fingerprint powder.

'Not much to go on,' he commented.

'Nothing.' Stevenson shrugged.

Hawkins stood in the middle of the living room and turned in a slow circle. Over the years the Iceman had refined his technique and this was the result. A perfectly clean, anonymous room in an anonymous location in an anonymous part of the city. The perfect killing ground for an anonymous victim. 'Shit,' said Hawkins, succinctly.

The detective smiled broadly. 'That's what I said when I saw this place the first go round.' He waved a large hand around the empty room. 'I've been in Homicide for eight years. You expect just about anything under the sun. But not boring.'

'You got a few minutes?' Hawkins asked.

Stevenson shrugged. 'Sure.'

'Let's get a coffee somewhere.'

They found a McDonald's a block away and settled

into a corner booth. Stevenson took a notebook out of his sports jacket and spent five minutes giving Hawkins a blow-by-blow of the initial investigation. Except for the envelope found with the frozen corpse, there was nothing out of the ordinary.

'You turned the case over to the Bureau as soon as you found the envelope?'

'Yup.' Stevenson smiled. 'Seemed like the thing to do.'

'But you checked the pictures first.'

'Wouldn't you?'

'What did you think?'

'There didn't seem to be any connection. The photographs looked like something from a slaughterhouse. The body in the freezer looked like a mob hit. One crazed, the other surgical. Didn't make any sense.'

'So you handed it off.'

Stevenson bristled slightly. 'We didn't just hand it off, Mr Hawkins. We followed procedure. There was an obvious connection between the Feebs and the body in the freezer. We get a sniff that a homicide has federal connections, we follow the rules.'

'But it was a relief.'

'Sure. We've got lots of murders to keep us busy; we don't need any extras.' The detective frowned. 'I didn't like it, though. Not a hundred percent.'

'What do you mean?'

'Whoever the perp is, he knew we'd hand the case over as soon as we found the envelope.'

'So?'

Stevenson grunted. 'So I don't like being played like

a fish on a hook.' He scowled. 'I don't like being manipulated.'

'You think the killer knew what he was doing?'

'Yeah. I think he knew exactly what he was doing. Phoenix PD scrubs the case and hands it over to the Bureau field office. The field office hands it over to the elves in Santa's workshop at Quantico. All of a sudden it's not a local case anymore; it's this hypothetical situation a couple of thousand miles away. Instead of a concentrated investigation, it all gets thrown into a filing cabinet. Pissed me off.'

'I can see that.' It was the essence of Langford's argument and the reason Hawkins was in Phoenix. The Iceman, whether by design or otherwise, was using the bureaucracy to cover his tracks.

Stevenson took a sip of his coffee and looked across the plastic table at Hawkins. 'Frankly, I'm surprised you showed up. According to you, this isn't even an official visit. I can't figure out your angle.'

'I just want to catch the guy,' Hawkins answered.

'How?' Stevenson asked bluntly. 'We don't even know who the fucking victim is, let alone the killer. To catch him you're going to have to trip him up, and from what I can tell, he doesn't make any mistakes. He got away clean.'

'We all make mistakes,' said Hawkins. 'Believe me.'

In the basement apartment of the Putnam house in Denver, the Iceman sat listening to the tapes from the night before. He was naked except for the headphones over his ears and the apartment was dark, the venetian blinds shut tightly. The only light came from the little red digital read-out on the cassette machine. Ellen Putnam had gone out to dinner and a movie with a girlfriend last night, leaving her daughter alone in the house. Tina hadn't been alone for very long; five minutes after her mother left, the girl had called her boyfriend and fifteen minutes later Terry had arrived.

The Iceman sat in the dark, listening, stroking himself gently.

A clicking sound, the door of Tina's bedroom closing. A little nervous laughter, rustling clothing, the tinkle of a bracelet. Silence. Soft wet sounds. Kissing. Giggles and padding footsteps. The creak of the bed, the whisper of sheets.

'I wonder what the neighbors would think?' A boy's voice. Terry.

'I wonder what my mother would think?'

A longer silence. A small groan. More rustling.

'Would you ... ?'

'Sure, okay ... No, don't move.' More rustling, then the engulfing sound of her mouth.

His voice. *'Mmm. Just like I remember it.'*

Wet. Licking. Panting. Mewling, kitten sounds. Shifting on the bed. Little groans and whispers, rising into something deeper in her throat, almost a growl.

Her voice. *'Here ... let me. Oh!'*

'I've got it.'

'You're sure it's on?' Her voice.

'Yeah.'

'*Okay.*'

'*What we wanted last night.*' His voice.

Quick creaking, pants and groans.

Her voice, ragged, excited. '*Do you want to put it in from the back?*'

Pause. '*I didn't make it.*' His voice, chagrined, embarrassed.

'*Oh.*' Her voice, surprised.

'*I was thinking about the fun we were going to have all afternoon, I guess . . .*'

'*It doesn't matter.*'

'*Sorry.*'

'*No. It's okay. Really.*' Pause. '*How long does it take?*'

'*It just did.*'

'*No. I mean . . .*'

'*I don't know. I don't think about it.*'

'*Oh. Okay.*' Pause. '*No. Don't move. Oh! That's nice.*' Pause. '*Nice and squishy.*' Another pause, then her stuttering breath and the sound of his quick movements. A final storm of movement and moaning breath, rising. Collapse and laughter.

'*Oh great!*' His voice.

'*Did it stay on?*'

'*Yeah.*'

Pause. Wet snap of rubber. Her voice. '*Neat.*'

The Iceman slipped off the headphones, then stopped the tape. He sat in the darkness, naked, staring up at the ceiling. No more than ten or fifteen minutes. All she would ever have or know. Safe sex? He smiled invisibly.

It would have to last her a lifetime.

Jay Fletcher sat in the dark office above the Santa Fe Public Library and stared at the glowing screen of the computer, blank except for the steady electronic pulse of the cursor in the upper-left-hand corner. They'd returned from Albuquerque in midafternoon, but after a couple of hours, Cruz booked off, pleading exhaustion, and went home to bed. Jay knew she should have done the same thing, but she was too hyped on coffee for sleep. Coffee and the glimpse she'd had of the Hand Job killer's work.

What she was contemplating was madness, of course, the very thing that had landed her in Santa Fe. Hand Job was the Albuquerque PD's problem, not hers. If she meddled, then got caught in the act, it would land her in very hot water indeed. If that happened, it would mean more than just a transfer. She'd be fired, perhaps even arrested.

But it sure was tempting. She glanced at the stack of floppy discs beside the computer. The C-Bix program. Her brief tour around the Santa Fe mainframe for Cruz had shown her that the Local Area Network for the State Capitol computers was virtually devoid of any kind of security system and it was doubtful that the city computers in Albuquerque would be any different. With Cruz's access codes, she could travel the networks at will and with what she knew about computers, she was sure she could cover her tracks. Hand Job was the perfect proving ground for the C-Bix Master Program.

Instead of waiting around for more forensic information to accumulate as the killer continued his spree, Jay could use the program for what it had been designed to do – track down the murderer blind, using existing databases.

The only problem was that without a deskful of warrants and authorizations, using C-Bix was illegal and unconstitutional and would violate the civil rights of any individual it scanned as it sniffed its way through the mainframe databanks. It was generally accepted that a lesser law could be broken in defense of a greater one, but C-Bix went at it wholesale. It was Big Brother at work on a grand scale.

Except she wasn't Big Brother; she was just a cop trying to track down a killer, a patrol car cruising up and down on the President's electronic superhighway. Jay snorted under her breath and lit a cigarette. During her five years working with the Computer Analysis and Response Team, she'd noticed a steady increase in computer-related crime, from bank fraud to a computer hotline for pedophiles. By using a modem to plug yourself into Internet, the enormous, invisible, and completely unregulated system of networks that spanned the nation, you could find anything from kinky sex to chat lines discussing ways and means of tampering with your college records. The White House was promoting the expanding use of nationwide computer networks as though it was some kind of go-west-young-man new frontier. They forgot to mention that as well as honest settlers and explorers, the frontier also had its fair share of virtual reality gunslingers, data rustlers, and marauding gangs of hacker outlaws.

So why not a cyberspace Robin Hood?

'Who are you trying to kid, sweetheart?' she said aloud. She butted her cigarette into the ashtray beside the computer and frowned at the pile of floppy disks. The unauthorized use of C-Bix was against the law, pure and simple. On the other hand, so was murdering people and hacking away at their hands with a meat cleaver. The chances of catching Hand Job through normal procedure were almost nil, and the chances of Jay getting caught using C-Bix were about the same. In the end it came down to a black-and-white moral decision. Yes or No, Plus or Minus, On or Off, Vigilante Justice or Due Process? Elegant and simple, just like a computer ... or a John Wayne movie.

I say we hang the bastard, Sheriff!

She lit another cigarette and began loading the disks into the hard drive.

CHAPTER TEN

At ten o'clock the following morning, Hawkins found himself at the Phoenix Medical Examiner's Office at Sixth and Jefferson, a few blocks west of Civic Plaza. The doctor who had performed the autopsy on the unidentified corpse in the freezer was a squirrel-faced little man named Simpkins. He checked his computer file, then took Hawkins down to the morgue. A few minutes later, the retired FBI man got his first real look at the victim.

Lying on the stainless steel examining table, the corpse looked like a clay model. The skin was gray and loose over the flesh and the features seemed sunken into themselves, almost as though the man had gone on some kind of afterlife diet. Hawkins commented on it.

'He spent a couple of months in that freezer.' Simpkins shrugged. 'Lot of water leached out of the tissues. A year like that and he would have been freeze-dried. Like a mummy.'

The killing wound was obvious – a neat hole in the

back of the skull, made even more visible by the patch of scalp shaved by the medical examiner. There was no exit wound; the twenty-two-caliber bullet had tumbled around in the man's brain, turning it into oatmeal. Hawkins visualized the apartment. The sound of the gun firing would have been no louder than someone popping a paper bag.

'Any other wounds?' he asked.

Simpkins shook his head. 'Nope. Just like I said in the report.'

'Anything you *didn't* mention in the report?' Hawkins asked. Simpkins thought for a moment, then shook his head again. 'Not that I can remember.' He shrugged. 'Pretty cut and dried. Standard mob hit.'

'Who told you it was a mob hit?'

'No one. But it fits the profile.'

'The freezer?'

'Smart. Meant no one would find the body for a while.'

'You've seen it before?'

'No.'

'So it doesn't fit the profile, then.'

'I suppose not.' Simpkins was starting to look uncomfortable. He dragged one hand through his shock of carroty-red hair.

'So give me something else that doesn't fit the profile,' pressed Hawkins. Simpkins flipped through the sheaf of papers on his clipboard. He nodded to himself, put the clipboard down on the table, then lifted the dead man's right arm.

'There,' he said, pointing.

'I can't see anything,' said Hawkins, bending down.

'Inside of the elbow,' Simpkins instructed. 'Puncture.'

Hawkins saw it, or thought he did – a faint discoloration of the skin on the inside of the elbow joint. 'What is it?'

'Needle,' said Simpkins. 'Pretty heavy gauge.'

'Why didn't you mention it in the report?'

Simpkins shrugged again. 'Guy wasn't a hype. It's one puncture, not a set of tracks. Too healthy to be a user anyway.' The Assistant Medical Examiner gave a little braying laugh. 'As healthy as a dead person can be.'

'So what caused the puncture?' asked Hawkins.

'Could have been a lot of things.'

'Like what?'

'Heavy-gauge needle like that, it could have been an IV tube, but I don't think so. IV would have gone into the wrist or the back of the hand.'

'Why don't you tell me what you do think?' Hawkins sighed. 'Give me an informed opinion.'

'I'm not supposed to have opinions,' Simpkins answered. 'I'm supposed to analyze physical evidence. I'm a pathologist, not a homicide detective.'

A world full of specialists, each with his or her own turf. No one taking responsibility for anything. 'The guy's got a hole in his elbow,' said Hawkins. 'You say he's not an addict. What's in between?'

'Blood donor,' said Simpkins. 'Maybe.'

'He goes to a blood-donor clinic, gives a pint, and then has his brains blown out?'

'Ridiculous, isn't it?'

Hawkins grinned. 'Just a little, yeah.'

'Which is why I don't give out opinions.' Simpkins stared at Hawkins across the gray lump of the cadaver. 'I know what the police want, Mr Hawkins. I know what the District Attorney wants, and most important, I know what my boss here wants. They all want the same thing – simple answers to complicated questions. They want a mob hit. The guy fits the profile, I give them a mob hit. Keep it simple. No Sherlock Holmes, no weird clues, no anomalies, no conundrums. The guy gives blood before he gets shot. So what?'

'And now the Phoenix PD isn't handling the case at all, so nobody wants anything, right?' File it under *F* for Forget It.

'Right.' Simpkins nodded.

'You said the puncture could have been caused by lots of things. Like what?'

'He could have been a first-time junkie, but there was no dope in his system. He could have gone to a clinic for an HIV test, except the needle gauge is wrong. He could have been a freak who liked to stick triple-O needles into his arm. Maybe his girlfriend was a vampire or he was on some kind of intravenous medication that didn't show up on the scans.'

'But you say blood donor.'

'Yes.'

'Why?'

'Because he was AB-Negative.'

'I don't understand.'

'When I tested his blood, he showed AB-Negative. It's

a rare blood type. The Red Cross and the commercial blood banks are always short.'

'But you didn't say anything about that in your autopsy report.'

'Sure I did,' Simpkins answered, bristling. 'I listed him as AB-Negative.'

'But you didn't connect that to the puncture wound in his arm.'

'I didn't mention that he was probably left-handed or that he was a prime candidate for male pattern baldness, either. Or that he probably put his pants on one leg at a time just like the rest of us. It didn't seem important at the time. It still doesn't.'

'How rare is AB-Negative?'

Simpkins thought for a moment. 'About fifteen percent of the general population. Something like that.'

'Does the Red Cross or the commercial banks keep lists of rare blood donors? Names and addresses?'

'I don't have the faintest idea,' said Simpkins. 'I've never given blood myself.' He smiled thinly. 'Needles give me the creeps.'

Rand Symington, the set designer for the Santa Fe Opera, lived in the wooded foothills just west of the city. The house, a renovated and retrofitted adobe Indian school, was set in a small clearing just off Buckman Road.

'Very artsy-craftsy,' said Jay Fletcher, climbing down from the Cherokee. The main building was painted bright blue and the clearing was littered with piles of old opera flats – everything from Italian *palazzos* to Norman castles, in every color of the rainbow. There was a large, slope-roofed building made out of sheet metal off to one side, its corrugated walls marred with long, sooty stains from the recent fire. Parts of the roof were buckled and half of a huge, multipaned window was blanked out with sheets of plywood.

'He told me he'd be in the studio building,' said Cruz, pointing to the sheet metal structure.

Symington was a good-looking man in his late thirties, narrow-hipped and lean, wearing jeans, a T-shirt, and cowboy boots. His hair was dirty blond and long, tied back in a ponytail. As they stepped into the studio, he was hard at work with a plasma torch, eyes obscured by heavy goggles, welding two long strips of angle iron together. The large, high-ceilinged room around him was racked with a dizzying array of supplies and equipment arranged neatly on metal shelves and stacked on worktables. More opera flats were leaning up against the walls and at the far end of the room, underneath a lofted second level, Jay could see something that looked like a gigantic waffle iron, thick cables snaking across the cement floor to a homemade electrical panel.

Symington snapped off the torch and pulled the goggles down around his neck. Approaching him Jay saw that the man's eyes were a peculiar, turquoise shade of blue green. He smiled and waved a hand.

'Lieutenant Cruz. Nice to see you again.' He grinned at Fletcher. 'You I haven't met before.'

'Jay Fletcher.'

'You working with the lieutenant?'

'She's helping me out for a little while,' Cruz explained.

'Get you some coffee?' asked Symington. 'Fresh pot in the house.'

'No, thanks,' said Cruz.

'Interesting place,' said Jay, looking around. 'Everything but the kitchen sink.'

'I'm a pack rat,' Symington said. The grin on his face seemed to be a permanent fixture. 'Never throw anything out.'

'Much damage from the fire?' asked Jay. The interior walls were sheetrock and appeared to have been recently painted.

'No,' Symington answered, shaking his head. 'I was lucky. I was setting up for *Don Giovanni* the week it happened. Most of my equipment was out at the Opera House.' He followed her glance. 'I've fixed most of the structural damage. Repainted.'

'Expensive,' Cruz commented. 'As I recall you didn't have a whole lot of insurance coverage.'

The grin finally vanished. 'No,' said Symington. 'I didn't.' He paused. 'I do have friends, though. Everyone at work gave me a hand. The Opera threw in the new sheetrock and the paint.'

'Nice of them,' said Jay.

'Why do I get the feeling this isn't a friendly visit?' the set designer asked. 'Not so long ago I was an arson victim; now it feels like I'm a suspect.'

131

'Not really.' Cruz shrugged. 'We're just following up on a few leads, that's all.'

'Such as your explosives license,' said Jay. 'From what I gather, you never mentioned it to the lieutenant during his preliminary investigation.'

Symington looked startled for a moment. 'What does me having an explosives ticket have to do with anything?'

'Maybe nothing,' said Cruz. 'But you should have mentioned it, along with the accident you had on that movie set.'

'Christ! Not that again.' Symington shook his head, then peeled off his welding goggles. He threw them down on the table behind him.

'People died,' Cruz said flatly. 'You make enemies that way.'

'People in the business knew it wasn't my fault. I was a scapegoat. The producers had to pin it on somebody.'

'You weren't at fault?'

'No. The sons of bitches wanted big-buck effects on a chicken-shit budget. One-take wonders,' he snorted angrily. 'Why don't you ask them about insurance?'

'You were blacklisted,' said Cruz.

'How do you know that?' Symington was beginning to look uncomfortable .

'We did a little digging,' said Jay. 'You were born in Kansas. Your father had a business fixing farm equipment. A welder. You left Kansas in the mid seventies, went to Berkeley, got into theater there. Started doing sets. You got lucky and wound up working for Lucasfilm on the original *Star Wars*. That led to the *Star Trek* films, all of them, right up until number six.'

'That was in 'eighty-three,' said Cruz, picking it up from Jay. 'Then things started to go downhill. Quickly. No more big productions. From A pictures you went down to the Bs. Eventually you wound up doing chopsueys out of Hong Kong.' He paused. 'What was it, Mr Symington? Booze or coke?'

The set designer had gone pale and Jay could see a muscle twitching in the corner of his right eye. 'Why are you doing this to me?' he said. His voice was fluttering. Jay couldn't tell if it was anger or fear. She casually undid the button of her jacket and moved her shoulders, feeling the weight of the holstered weapon in the small of her back. Half the equipment in Symington's shop was potentially lethal.

'We've had four fires, all connected,' Cruz said quietly. 'So far no one has been hurt, Mr Symington. I want to keep it that way.'

'Are you accusing me of something?'

'Not yet.'

'Means and opportunity,' said Jay. She glanced around the shop. 'You've got both.'

'What about motive?' said Symington. 'Why would I go around burning down people's houses? Including my own.'

'Give us time,' said Cruz bluntly. 'We'll come up with something. I guarantee it.'

'I think you'd better leave,' said Symington. 'Before I call a lawyer.'

'Not a bad idea,' said Cruz. 'You may be needing one.'

The arson investigator nodded to Jay and then both of them turned away and left the shop.

'Think we accomplished anything?' asked Jay as they headed back to the Cherokee.

Cruz shrugged his shoulders. 'Maybe. Hard to tell. Never hurts to stir things up a little. He didn't like us digging around in his past; that's for sure.' He tugged the car keys out of his jeans and climbed into the 4 x 4. Jay got in beside him.

'So maybe we should dig a little deeper,' she said.

By five o'clock that afternoon, William Hawkins was back at the field office on Indianola Avenue. Rodney Jones, the Special Agent in Charge, didn't look particularly pleased to see him again so soon.

'You're sure about this?' asked the heavyset man, tapping the handwritten report Hawkins had dropped on his desk a few moments before.

'His name is Henry Saunders,' said Hawkins, settling into a chair across from the SAC. 'Until three months ago, he was on the staff of the Sports Medicine Clinic at Arizona State University in Tempe.'

'You figured all this out within twenty-four hours?'

'A lot less than that.'

'I'm impressed,' said Jones.

'I'm not,' Hawkins answered. 'It wasn't that difficult.' If Jones or the Phoenix PD had been on the ball, they could have identified the body in the freezer weeks ago. More bureaucratic fumbling.

'Do tell,' said Jones.

'Like it says in the report – Saunders was AB-Negative. According to Simpkins, the Assistant M.E., there was evidence that he'd given blood recently.'

'That wasn't in the autopsy report,' said Jones defensively.

'It should have been,' said Hawkins. 'Anyway, I checked with the Red Cross. They have sixty-two AB-Negative donors on file. Twenty-six of those fell within the right age group. Seventeen of those have given blood within the last three weeks.'

'That leaves nine,' said Jones.

'Seven of whom are still alive and kicking. I checked.'

'You're down to two.'

'Dr Henry B. Saunders and a guy named Lincoln Jeffries. Jeffries last gave blood on the same day as Saunders. Two days later he was killed in a car accident. He was also black.'

'Which leaves Saunders.'

'That's right. I went out to the university and checked with the Sports Medicine Clinic. They had a photograph of him in their files. It's a match.'

'Shit,' said Jones wearily. Hawkins tried not to smile. His identification of Saunders wasn't going to look good on Jones' monthly update sheet.

'According to the university, Saunders was single, no listed next of kin.'

'They didn't report him missing?'

'No. Three months ago he resigned his position at the clinic. He'd been offered a research job in Denver.'

'And?'

'He never showed up there.'

'Shit,' said Jones a second time.

'I'm booked on a flight out of here in two hours,' said Hawkins. 'I'd appreciate some backup.'

Under the circumstances Jones could hardly refuse, and Hawkins knew it. 'Like what?' asked the SAC.

'Smooth the way with the Bureau people in Denver, same with the local police. Check with TRW and see if you can get me a paper trail on Saunders' plastic.' TRW was the largest credit reporting agency in the country – if the Iceman was using Saunders' credit cards, they'd have a record of it, or they could access the credit card company files and find the information he needed.

'I can do that,' said Jones. 'I suppose you want this ASAP?'

'I'd appreciate it.' Hawkins nodded. 'I'd like to get this bastard before he deep-freezes someone else.'

It was just past midnight in Denver. The Iceman stood at the bottom of the stairs leading up to the main floor of the Putnam house and listened carefully. Above him was nothing but silence. Behind him in the dark basement apartment, his suitcases were already packed and waiting by the side entrance. The computer and the intercom master unit had been disconnected and were packed away as well. He was ready.

The lightweight autopsy suit he'd stolen from the mortuary at the hospital rustled as he shifted his weight slightly. It was made of Mylar and came complete with a hood and a clear plastic faceplate. Usually the suits were used for autopsies of AIDS victims or people who had died of infectious diseases, but tonight the Iceman had a better use for it. Dropping one surgically gloved hand, he checked the bulging pocket. His Nikon.

The rest of his equipment was loaded into the WalMart carpenter's utility belt around his waist: two cleavers he'd purchased at a Vietnamese kitchen shop on Alameda Avenue, a portable bone saw stolen from the hospital along with the suit, half a dozen preknotted loops of nonslip, insulated wire, three different-sized pairs of needle nose pliers for the teeth, and a folded, drawstring dry-cleaning bag from the Holiday Inn. He'd put everything in the bag when he was done, including the suit itself.

His heart was beating rapidly and his mouth had gone dry. Sweat was beading on his forehead and he realized that if he didn't do something to control his breathing, he was going to fog up the faceplate of the suit. Between his legs he could feel the familiar heaviness of his engorged genitalia; he was excited, but wasn't that the whole point?

The Iceman took a deep breath and let it out slowly. Still no sound except the faint rustling of the suit. It was time. He hadn't felt this good since Phoenix and he could hardly wait to spread the news: life was good, but death was even better. Smiling happily, he headed up the stairs, letting his mind fill with thoughts of Ellen Putnam and her young daughter, his heart swelling with joy at what was to come.

CHAPTER ELEVEN

It was almost noon by the time Hawkins reached Ellen Putnam's house in Curtis Park. Yellow crime-scene ribbons were strung around the house and grounds like tinsel on a Christmas tree; the driveway was choked with official vehicles. Hawkins could see a black unmarked stationwagon from the Denver Coroner's Office, but no ambulance. Police, uniformed and plainclothes, were everywhere.

Hawkins climbed out of his rental car and stood for a moment, taking in the scene. The call had come in less than three hours before. The mailman had noticed spatters and streaks of red across the picture window at the front of the house, and standing on tiptoes he'd looked through the glass door insert and seen more blood in the hallway. After ringing the doorbell several times without any answer, he'd gone to the house next door and called 911. According to the police logs, there had been another call from the same neighborhood made shortly after midnight. Someone had called in complaining about a noise like a cat being strangled.

The disturbance hadn't been repeated and no car had been dispatched.

Hawkins made his way up the front walk. A uniformed cop blocked his way. Hawkins flashed the bogus ID he'd been given by Langford and was directed to the man heading up the preliminary investigation, a detective sergeant named Prokop. The homicide detective was in conversation with a morgue attendant in a white coat as Hawkins climbed the steps to the front porch. The morgue attendant was carrying a bulging, heavy-duty garbage bag in one hand. Hawkins introduced himself.

'They told me you'd be coming out for a look.' Prokop was in his early thirties, dark-haired, and expensively dressed. 'Something to do with VICAP, right?'

'Not exactly,' said Hawkins. He watched as the morgue attendant went down the steps, lugging the garbage bag. 'The victims?'

'What's left of them,' said Prokop sourly. 'Nothing in there bigger than a bread box.' He looked at Hawkins curiously. 'You don't seem very surprised.'

'I've seen it before,' said Hawkins.

'Oh yeah?'

Hawkins handed over the envelope of photographs left behind with the newly identified body in the Phoenix freezer. Prokop flipped through them quickly.

'Christ!' Prokop glanced over his shoulder and through the open door leading into the house behind him. Hawkins could faintly smell the odor of hot copper and human waste. 'Where did these come from?'

'Des Moines,' said Hawkins. 'A family named Petrie. Mother and two kids, boy and a girl. Same MO.'

'I had the ex-husband here marked for this one,' said Prokop. 'High school teacher in Vail. According to the neighbors, they'd been split up for about a year and a half.' He shrugged. 'Supposedly there was a tenant in the basement apartment, but no one knows anything about him.'

'Forget about the ex-husband,' Hawkins advised. 'You look in the basement apartment?'

'Yeah.' Prokop nodded. 'Clean. Doesn't look like anyone's been living there for a while.'

'You have a name for the tenant?'

'Not yet. We're working on it.'

'Try Saunders,' Hawkins suggested. 'Dr Henry Saunders.'

'The guy was a doctor?'

'It's a cover name. Saunders was a Phoenix John Doe up until yesterday.'

'Homicide?'

'Afraid so.'

Prokop frowned. 'You want to tell me just what the fuck is going on, or is this some kind of Feeb cloak-and-dagger thing?' There was a dull, angry undertone to the Denver policeman's voice. Hawkins sighed wearily. More of the same crap he'd been given in Phoenix. The Bureau was doing just fine as far as Hollywood was concerned, but in the down and dirty world of local police, he might as well have been a leper.

'No cloak and dagger, Sergeant. I'm stringing pearls here, trying to put some things together.'

'Easier than trying to put Mrs Putnam and her daughter together.'

Prokop paused. 'You going to be taking this off our hands?'

'No,' said Hawkins, shaking his head. 'The Bureau doesn't have any official interest in this.'

'I don't have to give an advisory to your field office?'

'Not if you don't want to,' said Hawkins. 'But it probably wouldn't hurt. You're going to come up empty here. Saunders, or whatever he's calling himself now, is long gone. Out of the city. Probably out of the state. That's how he works.'

'So we get to mop up and that's it?'

Hawkins lifted his shoulders. 'Set up a task force if you want to. It's none of my business; I'm just telling you what I know.'

'So what do you want from me?' asked Prokop.

'A look in the basement, if you don't mind. Then I'll be out of your hair.'

'Suit yourself,' said the Denver cop. 'Entrance is around the side.' He poked a thumb over his shoulder. 'Sure you don't want a peek in here?'

'No, thanks,' said Hawkins. 'I'd like to hang on to my breakfast for the time being.'

Prokop was right, the basement apartment was sterile. The refrigerator was empty except for a box of baking soda probably left there by the Putnam woman herself. There was no grease on the stove and no residue in the oven. The cupboards were bare and the bathroom was spotless. He'd remind the detective to check the sink, bathtub, and toilet traps for hair or anything else that might be useful, but that was probably a dead end, too. For the Iceman the basement apartment hadn't been a place to live; it had been a duck blind to shoot from.

Except he hadn't been shooting. Hawkins glanced up at the ceiling, picturing what lay just over his head. Asleep, the Putnam woman and her daughter didn't have a chance. The Iceman would have done the daughter first, slipping into her bedroom and using a razor knife or perhaps a scalpel to slash the child's Achilles tendons, effectively hobbling her. The girl's screams would have awakened the mother, who would then have been beaten into unconsciousness. A quick, surgical stroke to the girl's larynx would have muted her, and then, with the girl watching, he would have methodically raped the mother in every possible orifice before killing her. After that he would have turned his attention to the girl again. When both mother and daughter were dead, the Iceman would have spent a further period of time moving the bodies from room to room, eviscerating, dismembering, and butchering until, as Prokop had put it, there was nothing left larger than a bread box.

The rooms upstairs would be a slaughterhouse, blood sprayed and splashed on to floors and walls, pools of it soaked into carpets, smears of it across hardwood, spatters and streaks staining furniture; fist-sized chunks

A. J. HOLT

of meat in the sinks, the dishwasher, and the bathtub; bones and tissue choking the garbage disposal unit; brains and skulls cleavered into glistening wet splinters and muck on the kitchen cutting boards, teeth, individually extracted, tossed across the floor like strewn pebbles on a beach.

And when it was done, the photographs.

Swallowing the sour taste rising in the back of his throat, Hawkins looked away. The worst of it was the knowledge that the Iceman took the photographs for Hawkins' benefit. With each blinding flash in the middle of the night, his own name would have been uppermost in the madman's thoughts. He shivered, trying to force away the fear.

That was part of the game, of course, making him think that way, being forced to fight off the terror, to stop himself from believing in the hideous magic of it. Somehow, Hawkins was sure, the Iceman saw himself as Death itself, not just its mortal instrument, and no one was safe from his inevitable touch, least of all William Demille Hawkins, one-time Special Agent for the FBI. To reinforce that frightful fact, in two months, or perhaps three, there would be another frozen corpse in another freezer waiting for him and another plastic sealed envelope of photographs. For the moment Hawkins could avoid walking through the horror scene upstairs, but eventually he would be forced to look, to see, to know, and to be afraid.

Cruz had been called back to Albuquerque for another

144

meeting about the tenement fire and Jay Fletcher had the offices above the library to herself. After seeing Cruz off, she booted the terminal she'd left on-line the night before and dumped the catch of the day out of the C-Bix net and into the hard drive.

Normally C-Bix ran like any other template program, searching through a particular database for information, putting square pegs into square holes, and round pegs into round ones. Although she'd never mentioned it to Langford or anyone else at the Bureau, her pet project also had a 'worm' capability.

Worms, like computer viruses, were usually associated with the anarchic activities of hackers hell bent on screwing up computer systems just for the fun of it. Computer viruses infected databases and overwhelmed them by replicating themselves like a spreading cancer, logic bombs destroyed files en masse, and worms simply roamed around databases, searching out and destroying key pieces of information. The worm in C-Bix was something else again, and was an offshoot of work being done at MIT and CalTech on so-called combots, robot programs that cruised through a database collecting information relevant to its parameters, then carrying that information back to the originating program at the home terminal.

Since the databases Jay was interested in were all connected through various networks, and since she had the official entry codes provided by Cruz, the C-Bix worm had simply moved electronically over the telephone lines from mainframe to mainframe, comparing data to its own logic base, either keeping or rejecting it. During the night C-Bix had invaded the privacy of virtually everyone in the state of New Mexico, scouring state adoption records, criminal records, both adult and juvenile, records of admissions to hospitals and mental institutions, the state firearms registry, both Democratic Party and Republican voter registrations and the Department of Motor Vehicles. One of the new breed of forensic accountants used by the Bureau to track money laundering might have been able to track the C-Bix worm given enough time, but Jay doubted that anyone would notice her electronic intrusions.

After a full night of meandering, the C-Bix worm had come up with an astonishing 478 possibles culled from the New Mexico state computers. These were primary-level 'hits' – people on one file or another who fit a minimum of 20 per cent of the C-Bix parameters designed for the basic profiles of both 'organized' and 'disorganized' serial killers developed by the BSU at Quantico. It was far too vague, of course, much like assuming that you were a potential sniper simply because you owned a rifle.

Jay spent an hour resetting the C-Bix parameters based on what she knew about Hand Job, including the fact that he was definitely one of the organized type. She ran the program again and the number dropped to a much more manageable 136 possibles. The age range of the 136 people was between 14 and 75, of those 40 were female. Since women, juveniles, and the elderly were unlikely prospects, she readjusted the parameters of the program for a second time. The result was 11 names. She tagged the names on the computer, then ordered a total search and file merge for them, assembling the available material for each subject. It took all of a minute and a half. When it was done, she printed out everything, winding up with an impressive 85 pages of documentation. By then it was shortly after noon.

At that point Jay realized that she was hungry, but rather than endure yet another meal dosed with chili peppers, she stuffed the 85 pages into a manila folder and drove back to the house Cruz had rented for her. She put together a stomach-soothing lunch of soft-boiled eggs and dry toast, made herself a cup of tea, and settled down in front of the television set with the envelope and her cigarettes. She was pleased at how efficiently the program had worked, even if the use of it was a clear violation of civil rights, not to mention being an indictable offense under federal law. Still, though she'd worked the list down to eleven names, it remained an intimidating number of suspects to work through.

The television was tuned to KOAT, the ABC affiliate in Albuquerque. After watching a brief update on the tenement fire, she opened the envelope and began going through the printouts. During a commercial break the announcer mentioned that the afternoon matinee was the first *Star Trek* film. Jay lit a cigarette and wondered if Rand Symington would be watching, reliving his past glory in Hollywood.

The C-Bix subprogram for serial killers was based on

a sliding scale of profile elements that ranged from personality traits common to some serial killers, to traits shared by all of them. The mean average score was five hundred, the highest possible being one thousand. Of the eleven names on her list, seven were below five hundred, one was on the median line, and three ranged between six hundred and fifty and eight hundred. For the moment she assumed that she could set aside anyone below the median, which left her with four names.

The highest score belonged to a man named Mark Abzug, a thirty-eight-year-old old plumbing contractor from Raymac Park in the southern area of Albuquerque. He was adopted, had a long history of juvenile arrests, mostly for minor arson and petty theft, and had a psychiatric discharge from the United States Air Force. His adult criminal record showed a string of Driving Under the Influence arrests, two assault arrests without conviction, and a sexual assault on a young woman that looked like a plea-bargained rape, since there was a codicil to his suspended sentence requiring psychiatric counseling. The picture on his driver's license facsimile showed him as thin and nervous. Smalltime.

The second highest score went to a forty-year-old unemployed draftsman named Emil Francis Dinnerstein, but his criminal sheet showed nothing except pedophile crimes; it was unlikely that he'd switched from boys to girls.

Number three was Timothy Hershaut. Like Abzug, the twenty-nine-year-old hospital orderly was adopted.

His juvenile record included a stay in a New Mexico Youth Correctional Facility for the violent assault and rape of his adopted mother at the age of fifteen, a second tour at the same facility for substance abuse within six months of his first release at the age of seventeen and a driver's license suspension for dangerous driving a year after that. He'd gone into a retraining program shortly thereafter and his record had been clean ever since. His driver's license was the capper, though – Hershault was black. C-Bix and every other method of tracking serial killers had long ago proved that multiples like Hand Job rarely went outside their own race for victims.

The man on the median line was someone named George Gaddis. According to the record, he hadn't been adopted, but had been put into a variety of foster homes between the ages of six and thirteen. At fourteen he'd been a prime suspect in a series of animal mutilations, but nothing had been proved. At fifteen he'd been returned to state care after being withdrawn from the foster program, and at sixteen he had been arrested for and convicted of indecent exposure. Gaddis was thirty-nine and worked as a part-time driver for an Albuquerque courier company, but on the Republican voters' list, he called himself an actor. The picture on his license showed a man with a remarkable resemblance to a young Leonard Nimoy from *Star Trek*. Only missing were the points on his ears.

So which, if any, of the four was Hand Job? Somewhere, hopefully, there was a thread tying everything together, leading to the killer. But what were the links?

She dropped the bulky file into her lap and stared at the television. As well as running C-Bix, she'd also asked the computer to retrieve everything listed in the Albuquerque Homicide files that related to the Hand Job killings. She'd take the suspect file back to the office and see if she could find any connections.

The *Star Trek* movie on television was well underway. The film was about fifteen years old and Jay had only the vaguest recollection of the plot. Something about an old Voyager satellite that returned to Earth surrounded by a weird energy cloud that was threatening the entire planet. The story had reached the point where Mr Spock was about to be invested in some bizarre Vulcan secret society.

Jay watched as Spock climbed the steps up to the altar guarded by T'Pring, his longtime mentor and High Priestess of the pure logic cult. Spock gave T'Pring his split-fingered Live Long and Prosper salute, then bowed low to receive the old woman's blessing and some sort of medallion signifying his total abstention from emotion. Jay stubbed out her cigarette and gathered up the file, pushing it back into the envelope. Enough fantasy; she had reality to cope with, including the fact that Cruz would be back the following day and he'd want to know what she'd been doing with her time.

She half stood, then sagged back into her chair again, realizing what she'd just seen on the television.

'Jesus!' she whispered. The scene had cut back to the newly refitted *Enterprise* and William Shatner welcoming his old pal Dr McCoy back on board.

Live long and prosper.

She jumped out of the chair and ran for the door.

Back at the office, a quick call to the Albuquerque office of the Screen Actors Guild confirmed that George Andrew Gaddis really was an actor. According to SAG he wasn't represented by an agent in New Mexico, but he did have representation in Los Angeles. According to them he was listed with a company there called X-Tra Helpings. They were registered with SAG as a casting company for extras, stunt and body doubles, stand-ins, and crowd scenes. Jay called the number the SAG representative gave her and found herself speaking to a brassy-voiced woman named Sharon Shellsley. From the sound of it, X-Tra Helpings was a one-man, or rather one-woman, operation.

'Sure, we represent Gaddis,' said Shellsley, after Jay introduced herself. 'Why are you interested in him?'

'Just a routine check,' offered Jay.

'Yeah, right,' Shellsley answered. She didn't sound convinced.

Jay ignored the skeptical tone. 'Does Gaddis get a lot of work?'

'Some.'

'Could you be more specific?'

'We get him conventions and stuff. That's what he specializes in.'

'Has he had any major roles recently?'

'No. Last feature we've got him down for was in 'seventy-nine. Paramount.'

'What was the film?' asked Jay, almost sure that she knew the answer.

'*Star Trek*,' Shellsley answered. 'The first one.'

Bingo.

'What part did he play?'

'He didn't have a part. He was a make-up stand-in. He'd get made up, then stand there while the shot was set up and lit.'

'Who was he a stand-in for?'

'Leonard Nimoy,' said Shellsley. 'Spock.'

Of course!

'And since then?'

'Like I said. Conventions. Science fiction stuff. You know, Trekkies.'

'Do you have a list of his bookings for the past year or so?'

'Sure.'

'Fax them to me, please.'

'Sure thing.'

Five minutes later Jay had the list in her hand as well as a blurry copy of X-Tra Helpings file picture of Gaddis. She could see why he'd been used as a stand-in for Nimoy. Except for the ears, he was the spitting image of Mr Spock. She pulled up on her computer screen the Albuquerque Hand Job file, found the chronology of deaths, and compared them to the faxed list from the casting company.

Creation Convention, Sheraton Hotel, Virginia Beach, Virginia

Legends, Riverside Mall, Rome, Georgia
Vulkon, St Petersburg Hilton & Towers,
St Petersburg, Florida
Con-Dor, Town and Country Hotel, San Diego,
California
Astronomicon IV, Radisson Inn, Rochester,
New York
Wintercon, Lincoln Park Kennedy Recreation
Center, Detroit, Michigan

The dates and cities were a perfect match.

Jay held up her right hand and tried to re-create the classic gesture Nimoy had used as far back as the original television series. She hadn't been able to do it then and she still couldn't. At a guess it was probably something that Nimoy had shown the rest of the cast on the set of the TV show and that the writers had incorporated into the Spock character. Using her left hand, she spread the second and third fingers of her right, forming an open *V*. She tried to imagine Hand Job slicing down through his victims' hands and winced.

There was only one thing left to check, just to be sure. She found an Albuquerque Yellow Pages on a shelf behind the desk Cruz used and flipped through it until she found the bookstore listings. There were half a dozen that seemed to specialize in science fiction. She dialed one at random.

'Fantasy West. Can I help you?'

Jay took a deep breath. 'Hi. I've got a weird question.'

'You wouldn't be the first.'

'If I wanted to learn how to write Vulcan, what would I do?'

'Forget it.'

'There's no book on Vulcan?'

'Uh-uh. So far there's only a Klingon dictionary.'

'Really?'

'Yup. You might find a fanzine or a computer bulletin board that does Vulcan, but the only official dictionary is *Star Trek: The Klingon Dictionary*. Marc Okrand, Pocket Books. Ten bucks. *Q'os.*' The last word was a cross between a grunt, a dog bark, and someone gathering a mouthful of spit.

'Excuse me?'

'*Q'os,*' repeated the voice on the telephone. 'Klingon for "sorry."'

'Oh,' said Jay. 'Me too.'

'*Qo' Q'ay,*' said the voice. 'No problem.' He hung up. Jay sat back in her chair. It made an insane kind of sense. If you were a Vulcan serial killer, how would you send the cops on a wild goose chase? You'd leave your messages in Klingon, of course.

It was the only logical thing to do.

CHAPTER TWELVE

The Iceman used Dr Henry Saunders' Mastercard for the last time at 4:30 a.m., forty minutes after leaving the Putnam house in Curtis Park. He dropped his Hertz rental at the compound just off Martin Luther King Boulevard at the edge of the airport complex, paying for it with the card. Then he walked to the Avis lot a hundred yards farther down the boulevard, stuffing the Saunders credit cards and other identification into a waste bin along the way.

Using a completely new set of ID, he rented another car at Avis, then drove back along Martin Luther King Boulevard to Quebec Street and Interstate 70. Five minutes later he reached the freeway and headed due west toward Lakewood and the Rocky Mountains. By sunrise he was slightly west of the Copper Mountain Ski Resort, and by the time Bill Hawkins arrived at the murder scene in Denver, the Iceman was through the mountains and three-quarters of the way to Las Vegas, traveling along Interstate 15.

The Iceman reached the glittering city in the desert

shortly after four o'clock in the afternoon. He drove the
rental to McCarran Airport, dropped it off, then picked
up his own nondescript Toyota from the long-term level
of the airport parking garage. With the air-conditioning
turned up high against the mind-numbing 100 degree
heat, he left the airport and made his way down the
Strip, traveling through the seemingly endless canyon
of casinos and hotels. Ignoring the overwhelming bulk
of the MGM Grand, he turned right on to Flamingo
Road and drove toward Paradise Valley. A few minutes
later, he turned into the driveway of a modest stucco
rancher on Caliente Street and switched off the engine.
He was home.

It took Jay Fletcher two hours to make the impulsive
trip from Santa Fe to Albuquerque and another hour
and a half to find the address Gaddis had on file with X-
Tra Helpings. It turned out to be a tan-colored postwar
shoebox in what had probably once been the southern
suburbs – a Dick and Jane neighborhood from the fifties
gone to seed, its pastel shades faded like old dreams,
surrounded by strip malls, in and out hotsheet motels
and by a neon-lit array of transmission shops, Minit-
Lubes, and family restaurants where no family in its
right mind would go.

The little house was a blank page. Off-white curtains
covered the front window, there was no visible movement, and the driveway and carport were empty. The
grass on the postage-stamp lawn was short enough,
but most of it was burnt yellow and there weren't

any signs of a green thumb at work, or any thumb at all for that matter. No flowers, no shrubs, not even some whitewashed rocks or a set of plaster dwarves.

The concrete driveway was cracked, stained in the middle with a large patch of motor oil. Patches of asphalt shingle were missing from the roof, the eaves troughs looked rusty, and there was a pile of junk in the carport, stacked up against the side wall of the house and covered with a large, orange plastic dropsheet. No dreams here, faded or otherwise; nothing but dull, down-at-heels reality.

Jay spent twenty minutes watching the house, parked half a block away, next to a weed-infested vacant lot marked with a FOR SALE sign so old the real estate company name had faded away. After three cigarettes she drove off, found a 7-Eleven and looked up Gaddis in the White Pages. She called, ready to hang up instantly when he answered. On the sixth ring a machine cut in with a commercially recorded message backed up by the *Star Trek* theme. She hung up before the beep. Gaddis wasn't home. She bought herself a raspberry Snapple and another package of cigarettes, then drove back to her vacant lot.

Okay, Ms Sherlock, what would good old Jodie do now?

Sucking up her flavored iced tea through a straw, Jay stared at the house down the street. Clarice Starling, wunderkind neophyte BSU hotshot, would go charging in, regulation sidearm at the ready, protected by truth, justice, and the American Way, not to mention the sage advice of Anthony Hopkins.

Jay put the bottle of Snapple on the dashboard and lit a cigarette, grinning nervously at her unintentional pun. Sage advice and ten cents might get you an order of well-seasoned fava beans, but that was about it. Common sense, on the other hand, suggested that at the very least she should call both the Albuquerque Field Office of the FBI as well as Detective Sladky and the Hand Job Task Force.

Which was out of the question. The Albuquerque SAC and Sladky would both want to know how she'd found out about Gaddis, and thirty seconds after she told them, the cuffs would be snapped on for a variety of illegal actions on her part. She'd wind up in a federal woman's prison, and Gaddis would vanish like a puff of smoke. Running C-Bix without any warrants or authority had taken her across the faint line between right and wrong, and parking outside Hand Job's door was just making things worse. Somehow she'd thought that the whole process would have taken a lot longer; she hadn't been prepared for this.

So drive away, stupid. Forget about the whole thing. You can still go back.

She couldn't do that, either; if she did, the whole thing would have been for nothing – the work, the risk, everything. And there was also that line she'd crossed. She dragged on her cigarette and stared out through the windshield, thinking. Maybe she'd crossed it a long time ago, when she first had the idea for C-Bix. Even then she'd known that a program like that could be used only covertly, at least if you really wanted to get the most out of it. Or maybe the crossing had taken place when she'd gone into the SABRE reservation computer without authority. Or had it been when that son of a bitch, Mr Dennis Lloyd Shaw, made his secret gesture in the L.A. courtroom? She stubbed out her cigarette in the ashtray and finished off her Snapple, the straw gurgling harshly as she drained the last of the liquid. Her mouth was still dry; it tasted like old tin cans.

Six minutes. I'll give myself six minutes, no more.

Jay Fletcher climbed out of the car, touched the comforting bulge of the gun against her spine, and checked her watch. Thirty seconds to the door, another sixty with the pick set in her jacket pocket, and she'd be in. Four and a half minutes inside, that was her window. Enough time to make sure, enough time to make it worthwhile.

Trying not to wave her fear like a flag, she crossed the street and approached the house. She made it through the door with ten seconds to spare and closed it softly behind her. The place was gloomy dark and smelled like a pine forest. Air freshener.

What'd you expect? A slaughterhouse? This guy's not Jeffrey Dahmer, he's Mr Spock, cool and logical.

Everything was on one floor. No stairs, no basement. Short corridor leading back to a small kitchen, living room and dining room on the left, bedroom and bathroom to the right. The floors were covered in thin, dark green carpeting, low-pile indoor-outdoor, not broadloom, and not original. It felt like artificial turf through her thin-soled flats.

The bedroom door was open and enough of the dusky daylight leaked through the window for her to see the interior. More like a cell than anything else. An iron bedstead, dark blue chenille cover, two pillows, and a cheap clamplight attached to the plain head-board. A chest of drawers and a bedside table loaded with books. Jay checked her watch. Two minutes, four left.

She approached the bedside table and scanned the titles of the books. All paperback, all well worn, all *Star Trek* adventures. At least twenty of them. Gaddis was a fan. She stood up. There were five or six expensively framed movie posters on the walls around the room: *Kid Monk Baroni*, *Francis Goes to West Point*, *Zombies of the Stratosphere*, *The Brain Eaters*, *The Alpha Caper*, *Invasion of the Body Snatchers*, the remake. They all had one thing in common – Leonard Nimoy was on the credit list of each of them. More than a fan.

Jay checked the armoire on the other side of the bed. Some shirts, a hanger loaded with ties and belts, a suit and a sports jacket. There was also a dark brown, bulky-looking suitbag pushed to the end of the hanger pole. She unzipped it hesitantly and glanced inside. A full-tilt *Star Trek* officer's uniform, the old-fashioned design with the Indian arrowhead patch on the chest of the buttonless velour shirt. There was also a pair of cuban-heeled boots in the bottom of the bag. Working clothes for a killer. She zipped up the bag and left the bedroom.

From the size of the clothes, Gaddis appeared to be of medium height with a twenty-eight- or thirty-inch waist. It could have been worse. She crossed the hall, heading for the living room, and checked her watch again. Another minute gone. Three left.

Couch, coffee table, large, elaborate TV and VCR in a tall entertainment center with a bottom shelf filled with boxed tapes. She didn't bother checking the titles. More posters. All the *Star Treks*, I through VI, *The Good Mother*, *Three Men and a Baby*, which Nimoy had directed, *Funny About Love*, also directed by Nimoy, and a promotion poster for his TV documentary series, *In Search of . . .*

There were also dozens of production stills and PR photos on the walls, filling almost every square foot of space. Spock on the set of the original TV series, Spock in action, Spock with Kirk, Spock with McCoy, Spock with Scott, Spock with Chekov, Spock with Sulu. No pictures of Spock with any of the female characters in the series like Uhuru or Yeoman Rand. Spock the misogynist? A kindred spirit.

Several of the framed pictures were obviously taken by an amateur. One showed an older Nimoy on a film set with a slightly shorter man dressed identically in *Star Trek* uniforms of the kind she'd seen on television earlier that day. Jay examined the photograph carefully, squinting in the half-light. Both Nimoy and the other man were smiling, but the expression on Nimoy's face was fixed, a practiced beam for the camera. The other man was genuinely grinning. There was an inscription: 'Best Wishes, Leonard Nimoy'. The photograph beside it was a simple shot of a relatively modest Beverly Hills estate. A window on the second floor had been circled with red marker. The picture looked as though it had been clipped from a magazine. Nimoy's house in Los Angeles?

Jay shuddered and moved on to the dining room. The pictures were the kind of thing that would give a public figure like Leonard Nimoy a lifetime of nightmares. Gaddis was obsessed, consumed by the actor as intensely as Mark David Chapman had been with John Lennon, or John Hinckley Jr had been with Jodie Foster and Ronald Reagan. Celebrities used like a burning glass to focus the deadly rays of murderous intent, the ultimate, obscene invasion of privacy that went far beyond anything Jay had ever contemplated. Ninety seconds.

She paused in the archway leading to the dining room. The windowless ten-by-twelve area had been turned into a computer freak's paradise. There were only two pieces of furniture – an enormous U-shaped workstation, homemade from unfinished plywood, and an old-fashioned wooden office chair on casters.

No wonder he lives in such a dump; he spends all his money on hardware.

There were three Dell 486s arranged around the workstation, two of them blank-screened with blinking cursors, the third hard at work, steadily moving lines of text scrolling up the screen. Gaddis was on-line with the machine, collecting E-mail. All three computers were strung with cables connecting them to stacks of hard drives; switchboxes; modem units; exterior disk drives; two printers, one dot matrix, the other laser; and at least four separate CD-ROM units, and a flatbed scanner. From a quick glance, Jay could see machinery going back several years; Gaddis had created his little empire over a long period of time.

A shelf unit behind the three Dells was stuffed with neatly labeled log books and a library of software packages, everything from the newest Delrina Communications software to an ancient version of Microsoft Word. At least half a dozen of the boxes were game packages bearing the classic *Star Trek* logotype. She took a closer look at the labels on the spines of the log books. Gaddis was spending a lot of time hooked up to the Internet with something called Special K.

She pulled one of the log books off the shelf and flipped through the pages. Line after line in tight, exceptionally neat printing, moves and countermoves, intricate strategies, tactics identified with obscure initials. Special K was a MUSE, a Multi-user Simulation Environment, also known as a MUD, for Multi-user Dungeons and Dragons. Technically they were role-playing games, but some became so addictive that they'd been banned because the players became utterly involved, sometimes to the point where jobs were lost, and in one reported case at Yale, to the point of mental collapse and eventual suicide. Then Jay found a playlog for a game sequence, saw the player names listed, and understood.

'Oh shit,' she whispered. She dropped down into the wooden armchair.

Abel

Axeman

Berkowitz, the Son of Sam

Chikatilo, the Wetback killer

All the way through to *Sutcliffe* and *Zodiac*, the L.A. astrology murderer. All infamous, well-publicized serial killers. *Special K* – a cereal. S.K. – Serial Killer. George Gaddis, Hand Job – Serial Killer.

'Christ, it can't be.'

Why not?

Two years ago the Bureau had discovered three different pedophile electronic bulletin boards using Internet to discuss their youthful conquests, complete with visuals, and with the widespread use of CD-ROMs there was a steadily growing market for digital pornography. Hackers and crackers had been using networks to post illegal access numbers for years. At last count there were roughly four and a half million personal computers traveling on the Internet in the United States alone, and for the most part no one had the slightest idea who they were. The real world had serial killers. Why not the virtual universe as well? In the real world, killers like Bundy and Dahmer liked nothing better than to talk about their exploits, usually with policemen and psychiatrists. In the virtual world, with a dime-store modem and Internet, protected by a pseudonym...

They can talk to each other.

Jay's toe stubbed something under the desk. She bent down and retrieved a worn United Airlines flight bag.

She lifted it on to her lap, then checked her watch. Fifteen seconds. She held her breath and listened. Nothing but the click and whir of the hard drives. Dully, the muted snoring grumble of distant traffic.

To hell with it.

She unzipped the bag.

Hand Job's tool kit. A roll of heavy-duty duct tape; a needle-sharp leather punch with a plastic handle; a package of disposable surgical gloves, half empty; an unopened box of Trojan large condoms; and a Rambo-sized assault knife in a leather sheath. Enough evidence to send George Gaddis away forever, as long as it wasn't tainted by her own presence. Jay looked at her watch again. She was a minute over. She tucked the bag back under the desk. A conversation with Sladky from the Albuquerque PD, on some neutral turf and maybe they could figure out a way to make it work.

The right-hand computer made a loud beeping noise and Jay almost leapt out of the chair. She took a deep breath and put a hand on her chest, trying to slow down her racing heart. The E-mail on the screen had cleared, replaced by a prompt command.

n.talk. sk.Wiz. req.irc. II.irc.2.1. 5a.

IRC was the acronym for Internet Relay Chat, a real-time back-and-forth conversation that simulated CB radio talkback. Someone called Wiz wanted to talk and was announcing himself.

Well?

She decided to risk it. She pulled out the flight bag again, swallowed hard, and reached in. She slipped on a pair of the surgical gloves and turned to the keyboard. So far she hadn't touched anything except the doorknob on the armoire, the zipper on the suitbag containing the *Star Trek* uniform, and the zipper on the flight bag. No sense leaving her prints all over the keys.

Jay closed her eyes, thinking hard, trying to recall the basic IRC logon command. Finally she remembered. She typed in / , then *List*. Instantly the screen cleared and reformed listing the number of people in the IRC chatroom. There was no one except SK-WIZ.

Who the hell are you?

There was one way to find out. On Internet you could use a program called Gopher to track down the real names, or at least the home terminal addresses of people you were talking to. Jay went through the commands but came up with a blank. SK was a 'blind' bulletin board, disguised as something else and unreadable by Gopher.

The Wiz, whoever he was, had obviously spotted her use of the identification program. As soon as she returned to the IRC chatroom, there was a query waiting.

***/.sk.Wiz   identify yourself [>:-<]

The image in brackets was 'smiley', one of hundreds of short-form codes made with punctuation marks to send a quick message. Most were faces turned on their sides. This one meant WIZ was angry.

Jay stared at the screen. What would Gaddis call himself? Not Spock, he wasn't a murderer. Then she remembered a smiley someone had shown her at the Bureau. He'd been a *Star Trek* fan himself. Her fingers hit the keys again.

***/.   [>:-I]

The smiley stood for net.startrek The WIZ answered immediately

***/.sk.Wiz   quit fooling around Speck.

Relieved, Jay nodded to herself. That made sense. Richard Speck was the Chicago man who'd killed eight student nurses in a single night. Speck equaled Spock. Spock equaled Gaddis.

***/.sk.Speck   sorry.

Jay desperately wanted a cigarette, but she didn't dare light one in the pine-scented atmosphere. Gaddis would smell it instantly. She looked at the screen. Now what was she supposed to do? Except for Gaddis, there was no proof that Special K had attracted real murderers. They could just as easily be like any other MUSE – a simulation, pathologically antisocial weirdoes trying to live out their grisly fantasies.

Shit shit shit.

***/.sk.Wiz	you don't sound like yourself. Problem?
***/.sk.Speck	cold [:̃(]
***/.sk.Wiz	Want to chat?
***/.sk.Speck	Maybe I'll just listen, okay? I'm all ears.
***/.sk.Wiz	Sure. [:-D]

The smiley for gales of laughter. At least she'd bought a little time with the ear joke.

But how the hell was she going to get out of it? This wasn't like a real conversation, one that ceased to exist the minute the words were spoken. She'd filled a screen with Q and As and there was no way to clear it off without alerting SK-WIZ. If she left the screen up, Gaddis would know someone had been in the house, pretending to be him. She looked at her watch and stood up. She'd been at it for almost five minutes.

Too long. Get out. Now!

Too late. She caught a flash of movement out of the corner of her eye and her hand instinctively went to the weapon holstered under her jacket. Before she had time to draw it out, the man was on top of her, pushing her to the floor. There was beer on his breath and the acid stink of sudden fear sweat was all over him. One of her arms was pinned under her; the other was forced down by the man's forearm, but her legs were free. She snapped up her right knee and caught him in the groin, hard. He screamed and rolled away, his grip loosening. Before he could pull himself up, Jay had the Browning out, the muzzle stuffed under his nose. Straddling him, Jay looked into the man's face. It was bizarre. Gaddis was a clone of what Nimoy had looked like ten or fifteen years ago, right down to the silly haircut. The only thing missing was the ears.

'Don't move a single muscle,' Jay ordered.

'Who are you?' Pained, but not frightened. Even with a gun in his face and an FBI agent kneeling on his chest, he was playing the role. Cool and logical.

'FBI.'

'Perhaps you'd like to tell me what you're doing in my house.'

'Searching it.'

'Presumably you have a warrant?' The eyes flickered, left to right. He was looking for her backup, half a dozen guys in body armor and dink hats with FBI across the front. It wasn't happening and he knew something was wrong.

Jay levered herself off the man's chest and stood back, the gun firmly held in both fists, aimed at the middle of his chest. 'Get up.'

Gaddis stood, wary eyes on Jay. He looked past her, toward the door. Still no US Cavalry. 'What's going on?'

'Shut up.' Jay motioned with the Browning. 'Sit in the chair.' Gaddis had to be put temporarily out of action so she could think. She was vaguely aware of the sound of screeching brakes somewhere in the distance. The faint light coming through the curtains was turning a dusky rose. The sun was setting.

'What if I don't want to?'

'I'll blow your fucking nuts off.'

Clear enough for you, jerk?

It was insane. A few blocks away people were pulling into the McDonald's drive through, scarfing burgers at Jack-in-the-Box, ordering popcorn shrimp at Red Lobster. And here she was ordering around a mass murderer. Threatening him. Where had they mentioned this in the brochure?

'I have rights.'

We're beyond that now, in case you hadn't noticed. This is the Twilight Zone, buddy.

'Not for the time being, Mr Gaddis.' She hauled back the hammer. 'Sit down.'

He looked nervous at the sound of his name. He shuffled back toward the chair and dropped into it. His eyes flickered again, watching the scrolling screen of the computer. There were little glistening beads of sweat visible under his eyes now. He blinked, staring up at her. He really did look like Mr Spock. She could see him in the *Star Trek* uniform, wandering around the Trekkie conventions.

Stalking.

Jay edged toward the desk, dipped her hand into the flight bag, and pulled out the roll of duct tape. She tossed it to Gaddis.

'Bind your legs. Tight.'

'What about Miranda? You have to Mirandize me.' He paused and swallowed. 'A real FBI agent would know that.'

'You've been watching too much television, Mr Gaddis. Miranda only applies after you've been placed under arrest. I haven't done that yet.'

'Then let me go.'

'Any time you want, Mr Gaddis.' She moved the barrel of the gun slightly upward.

He began wrapping the tape around his legs. He finished, then tore the strip from the roll.

'Now what?'

'Your right wrist. Tape it to the arm of the chair.'

He did as he was told. More sweat. Very frightened now. 'You won't get away with this, you know.'

Get away with what? What does he think I'm going to do?

'Just tape the hand and keep your mouth shut.'

What AM I going to do?

He finished taping the hand. Over his shoulder Jay could see that SK-WIZ was talking up a storm.

'You can't prove anything. This is illegal search and seizure.'

'What about those women? What was that?'

'I don't know what you're talking about.'

'Sure you do.' Jay kept her eyes on Gaddis and reached blindly into the flight bag. She took out the leather punch. 'They were Trekkies, or they just wandered into the conventions for a look. That's how you chose them. That's the link between the victims, isn't it?'

'What are you doing?' Real fear now, seeing the punch.

'Playing it by ear.'

Good thought, Jay. Give those poor women that much. Get something back, even if it's only a little.

She dropped the punch into the pocket of her jacket and took the roll of duct tape out of the man's free hand. She holstered the gun, then took the roll and quickly strapped down the left hand. She took the punch out of her pocket and gently tested the point with her index finger. A minute spot of blood appeared.

'You like sharp things, don't you, Mr Gaddis?'

'Please!'

Jay leaned forward and pressed the end of the punch against the fleshy part of his right earlobe.

'No!'

She pushed, feeling the punch pierce the ear easily. Gaddis screamed.

'You hurt me!' The logic was all gone. His voice was blubbering. Blood streamed down from his ear.

'Tell me about Special K,' she whispered. The man's eyes widened horribly. His streaming tears were leaving tracks and Jay realized for the first time that he was wearing some kind of make-up, liner or mascara.

'Leave me alone!'

'What are you going to do, call the police?'

'Please!' He was panting, breath coming in short, terrified gasps.

'Tell me. About the WIZ.'

'I don't know anything.' A stain spread out across his lap.

Jay stepped forward again, waving the punch like a wand. 'Yes, you do.' She moved her hand. Gaddis screamed again.

'I'm bleeding!'

'Did the women bleed?'

'Don't hurt me anymore!'

'You murdered them. You chopped each one up and then you masturbated into one of those Trojans, didn't you?' She moved the gleaming needle of the punch, stirring it over the spreading stain. 'Trojan large, but I bet you've got a teeny-weenie one, don't you, Mr Gaddis? Is that your problem?'

'Don't kill me!'

'I don't want to kill you, Mr Gaddis.'

Or do I?

She thrust gently forward with the needle, just enough to cut through the fabric of his shirt and into the small roll of fat around his waist. Blood began to soak the light cotton material. The man's entire body jerked back in the chair, desperate to get away from the punch. The sour scent of blood and urine began to mix with the pine-scented air freshener.

Too far. I'm going too far.

'How many, Mr Gaddis? Albuquerque Homicide has you down for nine. Were there more?'

'Ten, eleven. I don't know. I can't remember!'

'Yes, you can.' She moved her hand. Another scream.

'No more! Please, God no more!'

Wellee-wellee-well now. No more Mr Spock. Clockwork Orange time.

'What?! What?!' Full-scale panic. Christ! Had she spoken out loud?

I'm losing it.

'Tell me how many.'

'Fucking bitch!' He sprayed her with his spit, sobbing. 'Pig!'

Jay held up the punch, moving it back and forth in front of his eyes. 'Is that why you used this? To stick the pigs?' Her fist jerked forward. Hard. This time the scream seemed to go on for a very long time.

Stop it. Stop it now.

Blood was oozing out of the hole in his cheek. He was jerking back and forth in the chair now, rocking it, moaning.

Stop it. You can stop it if you want. You can leave it. Walk away.

'No.' A whisper. She looked past the squirming thing in the chair and stared at the computer screen. SK-WIZ was still talking and from the looks of it there were others on-line now. She went around the chair and leaned over the keyboard, reading the screen. She blinked, her vision suddenly intensely clear. There was a flush of liquid heat between her thighs, spreading like quicksilver into her belly, fisting up to clutch her heart. She drew in a gasping breath.

So strong.

She blinked again and let her fingers track over the

174

keys. Behind her, Gaddis was making small animal noises.

***/.sk.Unsub	Speck is logging off.
***/.sk.Berk.	?UNSUB?
***/.sk.Wiz	Unidentified Subject. Speck?
***/.sk.Unsub	No. Gaddis doesn't want to play any more.
***/.sk.Zod	I don't like this.
***/.sk.Berk	Ditto. no names, remember?
***/.sk.Wiz	Calm down, this isn't real.
***/.sk.Unsub	Wrong.
***/.sk.Zod	logoff
***/.sk.Wiz	Who are you? What are you doing?

Jay glanced back at the man writhing in the chair, then turned to the computer once again. Felt the slick damp. She typed out her answer in capital letters.

***/.sk.Unsub	WATCH ME.

CHAPTER THIRTEEN

If New York was America's intellect and Los Angeles its libido, then Las Vegas was the country's subconscious mind, a concrete, glass-and-neon cerebral cortex of yearning, of hopes desired and then dashed. A city of dreams where nightmares lived and walked the streets like ordinary men.

It was 5:15 a.m., and the Iceman was sitting alone at a window table in the dimly lit dining room of The Flame, finishing up his regular steak-and-egg breakfast while he leafed through last night's *Sun*, catching up on all the murder and mayhem fit to print. The Flame, with its trademark red-and-blue flickering sign on the roof, had been a Las Vegas landmark since 1961, and for the past ten years the Iceman had made the small, dingy restaurant his anchor, its flaming rooftop sign an icon marking the center of his universe.

Even with dawn no more than a faint purple smear behind the La Madre Mountains, the restaurant was doing a steady early-breakfast, late-dinner business, and the cramped room was more than half-filled with weary-looking junketeers, their fingers stained black from the dollar slots, and off-shift dealers having a meal before heading home. At this time of day the restaurant was one of the quietest places in the city – a pause, a place to rest between before and after.

A waitress filled his coffee cup and took away his plate. The Iceman folded his paper carefully, lit a cigarette, and looked out the window. There was a light stream of traffic moving along Desert Inn Road and turning on to the Strip. The huge sign on the Fashion Show Mall was offering a two-for-one special at Hot Dog On A Stick. Business as usual, except for the unwelcome visitor who'd briefly logged on to Special K.

The Iceman tapped his cigarette neatly on the edge of the ashtray. Unsub, using Gaddis's terminal in Albuquerque. Ten minutes after the false operator logged off the bulletin board, the Iceman had switched gateways on to the Internet and tried the number again, but there was no response. Gaddis, or Speck as he called himself, was gone, and something told the Iceman that he was gone for good. Something bad had happened; chaos was threatening to intrude upon order. His order.

Frowning, he fieldstripped his cigarette into the ashtray and gathered up his newspaper. He dropped two five-dollar bills on the table and left the restaurant. He'd walked from the little bungalow in Paradise Valley and he wanted to be back before it started to get hot. There was a great deal of work to be done before night fell again.

* * *

Goaded by restless frustration, Bill Hawkins paced through the maze of galleries in the National Museum of American History, vaguely aware that he had reached the third floor and the East Wing Military History display. He slumped down on to a bench and stared up at the massive, gloomy shape of the gunboat *Philadelphia*, sunk under the command of Benedict Arnold in 1776. Sitting in the shadow of a sunken ship captained by a failed traitor was as good a place as any to contemplate his own shortcomings.

After spending most of his adult life as a policeman of one kind or another, Hawkins had come to the conclusion that everyone on the planet, criminal or otherwise, had his or her own personal history, individually developed over time, just like the displays surrounding him. To solve a crime you had to be a human archaeologist, able to interpret and extrapolate the artifacts of each person's past. Which was why historians were more interested in ancient garbage dumps than they were in the Ramses Pyramid and the Parthenon. There was simply more to work with.

Except that the Iceman wasn't leaving behind any garbage.

To Hawkins' sure knowledge, the Iceman had repeated his ritual slaughter on fourteen separate occasions over the past ten years, with a total body count of thirty-seven victims. With certain, specific exceptions, the killer's protocol was invariably the same: a female victim, raped, murdered, and mutilated, and a male victim to provide him with a new identity as well as a short-term source of income.

If the female victim had a child, that child too would be killed. No attempt was made to cover up the murder of the woman, but the male victim was always put on ice – literally, giving the Iceman time to milk his bank accounts and credit cards before the victim was discovered in a freezer or refrigerator kept in a long-term storage facility or a vacant apartment with the rent paid up for several months.

By the time the body was discovered and the connection made to the female victim, the trail was stale and cold. Since the murder of Carol Prentice in 1968, the Iceman had never killed in the same state twice – hardly a comfort, since he still had more than thirty left to choose from.

And the Iceman had deviated from his routine only three times, once in 1974, again in 1984, and a third time last year. On those occasions there had been only a female victim. All Hawkins could do was to speculate that the killer had disposed of his male victim in a way that didn't fit the pattern, or that he had some basic, ongoing identity he maintained as a safety net.

It was a chilling thought; somewhere the longest-running serial killer in history was mowing his lawn, paying his taxes, and coaching a Little League team sponsored by the car dealership he owned, or his plumbing-supply company.

So how did you go about catching the son of a bitch?

Hawkins gazed up at the dark, worm-eaten flank of the *Philadelphia*.

History.

After returning from Denver, he'd assembled and printed out all 37 of the Iceman files, screw-binding the 435 pages into a single volume. Impressive, and utterly useless. The killer had left fingerprints with gay abandon, but none of them matched the main print indexes and databases available to the FBI. He'd left hair, skin and semen with equal carelessness, but no match could be found for any of it.

All of which made perfect sense, of course; the Iceman had begun his career with Carol Prentice in Berkeley. Prentice had been eighteen years old and it was likely that her killer had been roughly the same age. Too young to be printed by Selective Service and in 1968 you didn't need a thumbprint for your driver's license.

The only time he might have been printed was if he had a juvenile criminal record, and those files were invariably sealed. If he had a name, probable cause, and a very friendly judge, he might have a particular record opened – heavy on the *might*. That kind of fishing expedition was frowned upon in this era of political correctness.

Hawkins stood up and crossed the gallery to the looming hull of the gunboat. He reached out and let his fingers run across the two-hundred-year-old planking, trying to imagine the crash of salt spray breaking against the high, curved bow as she ploughed into battle, the smell of black powder from her cannon, the tang of freshly spilled blood, and the cries of her crew as she began to sink.

It was all there, dark and vivid and real, sealed into the ancient wood forever. In 1776 the ship had been a vessel of war, a thing of life and death. More than two hundred years later, she was a historical artifact sitting on the third floor of a museum in downtown Washington, D.C. How many stories had been bound up in her through all those years? How many beads on a string, notes on a timeline?

As far as the official record was concerned, the Iceman didn't exist, but that was an impossibility, no more than a bureaucratic perception: I have no number, therefore I am a cipher, a nonentity.

'Bullshit,' Hawkins whispered. The Iceman was flesh and blood, and once upon a time he'd had a name and an identity that was his alone. He'd begun his long journey of transformation after the murder of Carol Prentice, but once upon a time there had been a Before.

Hawkins stepped back from the gunboat and let it fill his field of vision. To see the forest, you had to find the trees. He'd have to go back to the beginning. Berkeley, 1968. History.

Det. Sgt Horace Sladky sucked in his belly and backed up against the wall, letting the morgue attendant wheel the bagged remains of George Gaddis down the hall and out the front door of the dingy Southside house. As the cart rattled down the front steps and into the harsh noontime sunlight, Sladky crossed the hall and went into the living room. His bald-headed partner, Marty Sugarman, was watching as the forensics types wandered around, taking photographs and dusting for prints.

'So?' asked Sladky.

'So we got Hand Job. No doubt about it.'

'Uh uh. Somebody else got him. Not us.'

'Does it matter?'

'Yeah, I think it matters.' Sladky nodded. He glanced through the open double doors leading into what had once been the dining room of the house. The chair they'd found Gaddis duct-taped to was still sitting in the middle of the room, surrounded by a snowstorm of paper. The computers looked as though someone had gone at them with a sledgehammer. 'It matters because we weren't the ones to run him down. It matters because someone else saw something we didn't.'

'Whoever he was, he did us a favor.' Sugarman grinned. 'Handed it to us on a silver platter.' The bald man moved to a small desk and pointed at a neat stack of papers. 'It all fits. Gaddis was doing his Mr Spock thing at Trekkie conventions that match the locales of the murdered women. The mutilated hands, even the messages.' He shook his head. 'Klingon, for Christ's sake!'

'Someone murdered him,' said Sladky. 'It's still homicide.'

'No, it's not,' said Sugarman. 'It was an execution. Whoever whacked him just saved the taxpayers of New Mexico a wad of money.'

'So what are we supposed to do?' Sladky asked. 'Put a

"Thanks to St Jude" notice in the paper and forget all about it?'

'You put one into St Jude and I'll put one into the B'nai B'rith.' Sugarman laughed. 'Cover all the bases.' He smiled at his partner. 'Come on, Horace, lighten up. The bastard murdered a whole lot of women. He won't be doing that anymore. Chalk one up for the good guys.'

'This isn't a Charles Bronson movie.'

'Maybe it should be.'

'You think he's going to do it again?' Sladky asked.

'Maybe. Unless you think this was a fluke. One way or the other, Horace, you got to figure this guy has access to some pretty good information. Better than us.'

'A cop?'

Sugarman shook his head. 'A cop wouldn't do this.'

'Who would?'

Somebody in the next room flushed a toilet and Jay Fletcher awoke. She rolled to the right and stared at the clock radio on the table beside the bed. Noon. She shifted slightly under the unfamiliar satiny sheet, felt the stickiness between her thighs, and blinked, remembering more than she wanted to.

She rolled to the left and stared at the figure lying beside her on the motel-room bed. He was naked. He was also young, eighteen if she remembered correctly, black, well endowed beyond any stereotypical fantasy, and uncircumcised, a unique, quadruple temptation that had been impossible to refuse at the time. She vaguely recalled that his name was Carl.

Late last night she'd come to her senses and found herself at the Monte Vista Fire Station, an upscale Art Deco restaurant with a singles club above it. Carl had been her busboy, removing the remains of her quail and wild mushrooms. She'd spotted him again in the bar an hour later and it hadn't taken much at all to seduce him. One thing rapidly led to another and after booking into the American Inn a few blocks away down Central Avenue, they got right down to business.

Blinking the sleep out of her eyes, Jay looked down at the sleeping boy. The dark, heavy tube of his penis lay across a hard-muscled thigh, the pinker, bulbous head now hidden by the shrouding foreskin. Last night it had stood up against his flat, coffee-brown belly like an enormous ebony club, so thick she couldn't wrap her fingers completely around it as she stroked and mouthed him toward the first of several astounding orgasms. She'd barely been able to get the first few inches of him into her mouth and later, not much more between her legs.

At first the sensation of having such a massive organ stuffed inside her had been exciting, but Carl's sexual sophistication turned out to be in inverse proportion to the size of his genitalia. After an hour or so of the young man's relentless thrusting, she felt as though she was being impaled on him, and the experience had left her dry and sore.

In the hot noon light filtering through the thin curtains over the window, Carl's ebony club of the night before looked more like something left for too long in the vegetable drawer of a refrigerator, but even limp it was still reminiscent of a length of firehose. He shifted on the bed beside her, his mouth working softly. She could see faint movement behind his smooth-skinned eyelids. His eyelashes were as long as a girl's. He was dreaming. Of what? Sex with an older woman, or a hip-hop video he'd see on MTV? Carl wasn't a man; he was just a well-hung boy.

And the sleeping boy was getting horny. Watching him, she saw his organ twitch on his thigh and begin to thicken. The thought of Carl jumping her bones again was more than she could take. Moving as quietly as she could, Jay slipped out from under the sheet and padded across to the bathroom, wincing slightly with each step. Her entire pelvic girdle was going to remember Carl for quite some time to come.

Jay climbed into the shower, closing her eyes against the hot, soothing spray, praying that it would somehow scour away her fear and confusion. After ten minutes all it had accomplished was to drain away the clotted remnants of her night with Carl.

Suddenly, standing there under the cascading water, the terrible reality of what she had done descended on her like a deadweight, leaden cloak. She sagged against the pale green tile wall of the shower enclosure and began to sob uncontrollably. She'd hoped that Carl would be some sort of phallic gris-gris she could put between herself and the events of yesterday afternoon, but it hadn't worked, at least not for long.

Sex might well be an affirmation of life, but in the end

it was poor camouflage for death. She'd extinguished George Gaddis as if snuffing a burning candle between thumb and forefinger and no amount of being rotisseried on Carl's enormous wang was going to make that go away. Not today, not tomorrow, not in a million years.

There were a hundred rationales for what she had done, ranging from 'taking back the night' for her 'sisters,' to simple, uncomplicated frontier justice, but the fact remained that she had killed a man, not in passion or self-defense, not even under the politically correct armor of temporary insanity. It was plain-as-day first-degree murder. And there wasn't a jury in the world that would convict her.

It took a few minutes, but eventually Jay pulled herself together, turned off the water, and threw back the shower curtain. She stepped out of the cubicle into the steamy bathroom, feeling a little better, but still weak-kneed from the post-trauma release of emotion. Using the plastic-wrapped, complimentary kit on the sink, she began to scrub at her teeth, trying to think it through.

It was true: if the case ever came to trial at all, there might be a conviction on some reduced charge, but it was unlikely that she'd ever see the inside of a prison. What was left of her career in law enforcement would be trashed, but she'd almost certainly have a long run as a celebrity. CNN would give her some variation on the O.J. Simpson treatment, Larry King would give her a whole program, and between the Movie of the Week contract and an exclusive book deal, she'd never have to work again.

They'd sell T-shirts outside the courthouse with a cartoon caricature of her giving the Vulcan salute and she'd probably get a *People* magazine cover. Her sister would be given a sidebar interview and she'd probably dig up some old family photographs of the two of them as kids. A pretty cynical view maybe, but probably not too far from the truth. She felt her stomach turn at the thought.

She spit a wad of toothpaste foam into the sink, then rinsed out her mouth. She didn't want to be Lorena Bobbitt or that woman who poured gasoline over her sleeping husband in Texas. She wanted to be herself, Janet Louise Fletcher, the FBI Special Agent with a knack for computer hacking and a weakness for good sex and Victorian children's books.

She used her palm to rub a circle of condensation off the mirror above the sink. Pink skin, flushed cheeks, hair slicked back against her skull, and wide eyes. 'No more Trekkies,' she whispered, and lonely frightened fifteen-year-old Janet Fletcher stared back at her and nodded, pleased.

CHAPTER FOURTEEN

From Oakland International, Hawkins took the Nimitz Freeway to 980, exited at Martin Luther King Jr Way, and drove his rental north into the heart of Berkeley. At sea level everything had been wrapped in a classic Bay Area shroud of soupy fog, but the university town was basking in pleasant, midafternoon sunlight when he pulled into the parking lot of Berkeley Police Department Headquarters, a four-story rectangle tucked in behind the Civic Center.

The building had the trademark, flat-faced plainness of a thirties WPA project and Hawkins was surprised to find that the large main-floor foyer sported an architecturally lavish, Edwardian split staircase that led up to the second floor. Beyond the staircase it could have been a medium-sized police station in any medium-sized city in the United States, an overcrowded maze of linoleum floors, narrow halls, grimy windows sealed shut by twenty or thirty semiannual coats of chipped paint in varying shades of institutional tan, and cubicles without air-conditioning.

Perry Goddard, the detective who'd caught the Carol Prentice case in 1968, was waiting for him in the departmental meeting room on the third floor. He was in his late sixties, Kojak-bald, trim, tanned, and healthy-looking. He was wearing a floral-print Hawaiian shirt, L. L. Bean hiking shorts, and Nike Airs. There was a dusty-looking records box on the scarred table in front of him.

Goddard stood, shook hands and introduced himself, then sat down again. Hawkins took a seat across from him.

'You want some coffee?' Goddard asked. 'I've still got a bit of clout around here.'

'No, thanks.' Hawkins smiled. On the far side of the meeting room the uniformed watch commander was watching them through the glass window of his little cubicle. 'How long have you been retired?'

'Better part of ten years,' Goddard answered. 'Started as a beat cop on University Avenue, went out as head of Homicide-Feloney Assault.' He glanced over his shoulder at the curious watch commander, then turned back to Hawkins, grinning. 'Werba over there was a rookie when I left; now he thinks he's God.'

'You look as though you're enjoying your retirement,' Hawkins commented. Goddard shrugged.

'Got a little bookstore on Telegraph Avenue. Dead Write. All crime stuff.' Goddard smiled. 'I've got all your books, by the way.'

'How am I doing?' Hawkins smiled back.

'Pretty good.' There was a pause. 'You going to write a book about Carol Prentice?'

'She's part of it.'

'Long time ago.'

'That's part of it, too.'

'The files were buried down in the basement,' said Goddard, putting out his hand and touching the record box possessively.

'I appreciate you digging the stuff up for me. Saves a lot of time.'

'You want to talk about this here, or someplace more comfortable?' asked Goddard. It was an invitation and the subtext was clear. Goddard wanted to be part of Hawkins' investigation. The last thing he needed was a retired cop with time on his hands, but the Prentice files were key to what he was doing.

'Up to you,' Hawkins said. 'This is your town.'

Goddard beamed.

Dead Write was a stucco-fronted hole in the wall just off Durant with a one-bedroom apartment above. The store itself was narrow and dark with aisles on either side of a single floor-to-ceiling bookcase that ran the length of the space. Classic rolling ladders were fitted to the center bookcase as well as to the ones on the side walls, and a coffee machine was sending out a sour, burnt odor that combined perfectly with the faint musty smell of ten thousand used paperbacks.

A middle-aged woman wearing a halter top and with her long gray hair in a thick braid was perched on a high stool behind a counter next to the door. She was reading a battered Mickey Spillane novel with a lurid cover, clucking critically as she flipped through the pages. Goddard introduced her as Grace, then led Hawkins to the rear of the store and up a flight of stairs to his apartment.

It was small, neat, and surprisingly bright compared to the gloomy store below. Tiny bedroom, galley kitchen, and a larger, high-ceilinged room with tall windows looking out on to Telegraph Avenue. It was furnished in bachelor anonymous – Naugahyde recliner, leather couch, slab-door coffee table, a replica rolltop desk piled high with paperwork, and two artificial ficus trees gathering dust on either side of the windows.

Goddard dropped the record case on to the coffee table. 'Beer?' he asked. Hawkins nodded.

'Sure.'

Goddard disappeared into the kitchen and returned a few moments later with a pair of tall-neck Coronas. He handed one to Hawkins, then flopped down into the recliner. Hawkins sat down on the couch. Outside he could hear the steady buzz of traffic on the busy street.

'So, you want to know about Carol Prentice.' Goddard took a long haul from his Corona and sighed.

'Whatever you can remember.'

'I went and dug out the files after you called. Had a look through most of it.' He shook his head. 'Took me right back. I'd just made detective when it went down. Crazy times.'

Hawkins nodded. The Beatles, Haight-Ashbury,

Vietnam, hippies, Woodstock still to come. 'Were you the first one on the scene?'

'No. Uniform. Can't remember his name. One of her friends came calling, found her, and called it in.' He took another swig from his bottle. 'I got it on rotation, after the prelim and the M.E. were done.'

'You never saw the body?'

'Not at the scene. I was at the autopsy, though.'

'Remember anything about that?'

'She looked like someone whacked her with a concrete block. Whole left side of her head was caved in. Flattened all the way down to her chin. That's when we started calling him Homer.'

'I don't get it.'

'As in home run.' Goddard made a bat-swinging motion from the squeaking depths of the recliner. Hawkins nodded. The Iceman, Homer ... nicknames to distance themselves from the terrible reality of what they were dealing with.

'There must have been a lot of kids like her around here back then,' he commented.

'Thousands.' Goddard made a snorting noise. 'Started in 'sixty-six as I recall. By 'sixty-eight it was a fucking invasion. Christ only knows why they made the sidewalks so wide in this town; it was like an invitation.'

'She was a registered student though, wasn't she?'

'Art history.' Goddard snorted again. 'I remember checking with some of her professors. Most of them never saw her. She maybe took ten percent of her classes.' He smiled. 'That's the way it was back then. All these kids in bare feet talking about the fucking peasants in Vietnam. Horseshit. It took cash to be poor back in those days. You should've seen them lining up at American Express to get their money orders from home. If you were really poor, you couldn't afford to be a hippie.'

'Her family had money?'

'Enough. Her old man was middle management with Kodak in Rochester. Paid her way at school. Expenses. Dope.'

'She used drugs?'

'Everyone was a druggie then.' He shrugged. 'We went through her apartment. Grass, hash, diet pills, blotter acid. Nothing major.'

'Was she dealing?'

'I'd guess so.' Goddard nodded. 'Not in a big way. Selling to her friends, like that.'

'No hard connections?'

'Nothing that would get her head caved in.' He shook his head. 'Naw. That Wheels character is the one who swacked her. Either him or the black boyfriend, but he didn't have the look. He was a mime, for Christ's sake! Who ever heard of a mime killing anyone. And he was right-handed.'

'You're sure the killer was left-handed?'

'You can check the pictures and diagrams if you want.' Goddard pointed his chin at the box on the coffee table. 'M.E. had it clocked as a southpaw right from the start. The killer swung left to right, from behind. Blood spatters on the wall and the bed were all to the right

194

side, and she fell to the right. Pretty awkward unless you were left-handed.'

'You checked on the black guy anyway, I suppose?'

'Sure.' Goddard nodded. He finished off his beer and set the empty bottle down on the floor. 'He had a rock-solid alibi. In San Francisco. Him and the whole mime troupe.'

'But he was having sex with her?'

'Yeah. He admitted that. Smart. Prentice had a foam slab instead of a mattress. Full of goodies for the lab boys. All sorts of pubic-hair samples. Plus the semen. He'd screwed her that morning, as a matter of fact.'

'There were two separate semen samples, weren't there?'

'That's right. The black guy's was fresher. She'd had sex with someone else the night before.'

'This Wheels character?'

'Maybe. We didn't have all the fancy DNA stuff you've got now. The blood type turned out to be the same as Lance Follett, the soldier boy they found in Tilden Park a few weeks later. Could have been him, I suppose.' Follett, Hawkins' first contact with the Iceman, half a lifetime ago.

'Any other evidence of that?'

Goddard shrugged, shifting in the chair. 'Some. She'd been seen on Telegraph with him. Sproul Plaza. Kind of stood out – hippie chick and a crew cut in uniform.'

'What about Wheels? Anyone ever see the three of them together? Or Wheels and the black guy?'

'Not that we could find out about. She was probably screwing them all, but separately'

'Anyone else figure in this?'

'Hard to say. We did some checking. It seems like she'd boinked just about everyone in the mime troupe. Even a couple of the women. I guess she wasn't too fussy.' He grinned. 'Not that anyone was too fussy back then. But the black guy, Wheels, and the soldier were at the top of the list.'

Hawkins thought for a moment. 'Did you meet the parents?'

Goddard nodded. 'Sure. When they came to collect the body.'

'What were they like?'

'Grieving. The father was trying to keep it together; the mother kept crying all the time. She lost it completely when she found out the daughter had been pregnant when she died.'

'She was pregnant?' Hawkins had never heard about that.

'Six or seven weeks gone. There was a note in her bag from one of the doctors at the Free Clinic. The mother was doing a lot of moaning about how Carol was their only chance for grandchildren.'

'The son. He was a priest or something?'

'That's right. Seattle, I think. It's in the file.'

'Ever talk to him?'

'No.'

'Did you ever develop any lead at all on the Wheels person?'

'He rode an Indian. Pretty rare bike, even then, but no one around here ever did any work on it for him. We even checked in San Francisco. Came up blank.'

'Did you run the bike through DMV?'

'You bet. Checked every plate Motor Vehicles issued for an Indian. Scratched.'

'Either you missed something or he didn't have a California plate.'

'We didn't miss anything.'

'She was a hippie kid. How hard would you work a case like that?'

'As hard as anyone else,' said Goddard. There was an irritated note in his voice. 'She was a homicide. She got what every homicide investigation gets.'

'How long did you keep the file open?'

'Almost two years. The soldier-boy connection added some heat to things for a while.'

'Maybe I should read through the files?' Hawkins suggested.

'Be my guest,' said Goddard.

The windowless chamber was no larger than a prison cell, silent except for the faint hum of the central air-conditioning, dark except for the glow of the three computer screens on a desk that took up more than half of the available space in the room.

To the Iceman, computers were more than just pieces of business or communications hardware, they were wonderfully complex musical instruments, able to capture and express the most subtle nuances of electronic tone and timbre. He'd purchased his first more than ten years before, his knowledge and skills keeping pace with each new generation of microchip and software.

A decade ago he'd been one of the earliest and one of the few; now personal computers were as ubiquitous as telephones. He didn't mind. Presented with a piano keyboard, almost anyone could tap out 'chopsticks' and most could play a simple tune. A few could stumble through the 'Wedding March' or an old Beatles tune, and fewer still could play one of Chopin's nocturnes. Following that analogy, he was the Glenn Gould or Vladimir Horowitz of computer operators. No concerto or symphony was beyond his reach. With a keyboard, enough RAM and a modem, he could create magic.

At the moment, that magic was letting him watch the continental peregrinations of William DeMille Hawkins. The Las Vegas casinos had their own electronic credit checking service, and so did the Citibank Credit Card Banking Center on West Sahara Avenue. By logging on to their globe-spanning network, the Iceman could track anyone who regularly used a credit card. According to the screen in front of him, the ex-FBI agent favored his American Express Gold Card for basic expenses, a Mastercard for airline tickets and hotels, and a Visa for car rentals.

Using the various card numbers, the Iceman had put a permanent flag on Hawkins' file, 'hooking' each transaction out of the databanks within seconds of the card being used. His entry into the networks was disguised with a systems operator password, so if there ever was an electronic audit, his computer would show up as a regular terminal within the system.

The Iceman was impressed. If he'd possessed normal human emotions, he might also have been nervous. Hawkins was getting closer – much closer than he'd expected, and much faster. In the past few days, the one-time cop had been to Phoenix, Denver, and now Berkeley, all names to conjure with for the Iceman.

Phoenix was Dr Saunders, Denver was obviously the Putnam woman and her daughter, and Berkeley had to be Carol Prentice. When he'd seen the Oakland car rental, he'd been intrigued. He'd assumed then that Hawkins was clutching at straws, digging back to the beginning with some faint hope of finding something he could use in the present. It had to be that black bastard Ritchie, the one he'd been sure would take the fall for Carol's murder. He was married now, still living in Berkeley after all these years. A stone unturned, gathering who knew what kind of moss. His only mistake. He should have killed him then, when he'd had the chance.

The Iceman smiled sadly and leaned back in his expensive, ergonomically designed computer chair. He stared at the screen and the list of Hawkins' credit card transactions. According to everything the Iceman had read on the subject – and he'd read a great deal – the average serial killer wanted to be caught and punished for his crimes, or at least have the opportunity to boast about them. He wasn't sure he agreed with that hypothesis, but even if it was true, it necessitated a hunter who was more intelligent than the hunted. In his case, that was highly unlikely.

He'd recognized the black, terrible depths of his psyche at an early stage in his career, and rather than be swallowed up by them like the lesser members of his breed, he'd turned the horror to his advantage, using his intelligence to understand himself, to recognize his weaknesses and his strengths. Wandering at will through the FBI databases had uncovered the nickname Hawkins had given him years ago, but he preferred his own description – he was The Alchemist, a transmuter of lead into gold, madness into power, hot, pulsing life into still, cold death.

Cruz was on the telephone when Jay walked into the office. Late-afternoon sun was sending slanting bars of dusty light across the long, narrow room as Jay sat down at her desk and flipped on the computer. Cruz scowled and went on with his conversation. A moment later he hung up and swung around in his chair.

'So where the hell have you been?' he asked.

'Working.'

'Is that right?' Cruz was angry, but there was something else in his voice as well. Worry? Jealousy? 'I called the house half a dozen times. I even went over there. The car was gone.'

'I told you, I was working.'

'On what?' said Cruz. 'Your tan?'

Keep cool, kiddo. He doesn't think you're a stone killer. He thinks you've been off screwing someone.

'I was in Albuquerque.' *Keep the lie as close to the truth as possible.*

'Doing what?'

'Like I said, working.'

'All night?'

'I booked into a hotel.' She paused. 'Is that a crime?'

'You didn't mention anything about Albuquerque to me.'

'I didn't think I had to ask your permission. I'm here to work up a computer system for you, remember? I had some things to do in Albuquerque.'

'Like what?'

'You want to tell me why I'm being interrogated, Cruz?'

The ex-fireman took a deep breath and let it out slowly. 'Sorry,' he said finally. 'I was worried, that's all.'

'Apology accepted,' Jay answered, smiling.

'So what were you doing in Albuquerque?'

'Digging.'

'Find anything?'

'Yes.'

'Such as?' The suspicion was still there in his voice. She forced herself to keep the smile on her face.

'I kissed ass with a bunch of people. City Hall, the Records Office. They agreed to let us hook into their databases.'

Not quite true, but close enough. After slipping out of the love nest on Central Avenue, she'd spent several hours establishing an official presence for herself in the city.

'You could have done that on the phone. The least you could have done was let me know what you were doing.'

Jay sighed. 'I'm used to working on my own, Cruz. I didn't think I had to check in with you every twenty minutes.'

'You don't.'

'Then get off my fucking back.'

There was a long silence. Finally Cruz spoke again. 'Sorry. Again.' He held up one hand, palm forward. 'Truce?'

'Truce.'

'So what did you find out?'

'Four victims, four fires. Bingham, MacDonald, Symington, and Lowenthal. Bingham works at Los Alamos and so does Lowenthal. Symington's a set designer for the Opera and MacDonald is a lawyer in Albuquerque.'

'We knew that already.'

'We didn't know that Symington had a roomie up until a year and a half ago. His name was Simon Kerzner. Ex-Hollywood type like Symington.'

'So he had a roommate.'

'Kerzner was gay. I think they were lovers.'

'*Was* gay?'

'Kerzner's dead. Suicide. He was HIV positive. So is Symington.'

'I still don't see the connection.'

'Kerzner was a model maker. He worked at the Los Alamos Museum. Bingham was his boss. Bingham also fired him, probably because he was HIV positive.'

'Oh shit.' Cruz whispered, sitting forward in his chair.

'Shit is right.' Jay nodded. 'How's that for motive? Rand Symington's boyfriend gets fired, then kills himself. To avenge his lover, Rand burns down Bingham's house.'

'And does the other fires as cover.'

'Hang on, Cruz; there's more.'

'Such as?'

'MacDonald, the lawyer. He's a partner in something called APMC, Armada Property Management Corporation.'

'Never heard of them.'

'APMC has a subsidiary – Spectrum Properties ... Ring a bell?'

'Spectrum is the owner of record for the tenement in Albuquerque. Jesus!'

'I can't quite put it together yet, but I'd say there's some connection between the tenement fire and the fires here. We just have to figure out what it is.'

Cruz grinned broadly. 'So who do we talk to first, hotshot? Bingham or MacDonald?'

'Bingham,' Jay answered. 'Los Alamos is closer.'

After politely declining the use of Goddard's couch for the night, Hawkins borrowed the file on the Prentice case, booked into the Travelodge on University Avenue, then went off in search of Thomas Ritchie, the murdered girl's one-time black lover, and the only one on Goddard's list who still lived in the area.

According to the retired cop, Ritchie had bailed out of the mime business a long time ago and had become a chartered accountant specializing in entertainment clients. He was married, had two teenage children, and lived in an upscale part of town in the hills overlooking the Berkeley Tennis Club.

Stephen's Way turned out to be a block-long street of cliff-hanger homes connecting two switchbacks on Gravatt Drive, a winding road that led even higher into the tree-shrouded hills. Both sides of the street were lined with cars, mostly Saabs, BMWs and Range Rovers. The colors of choice for the vehicles were all in the earth-tone range – lots of greens, dark blues, and slate grays. The only exception was a candy-apple-red '64 Mustang ragtop parked directly in front of Ritchie's house.

Hawkins had called Ritchie from the Travelodge, but even with half an hour's warning, the man looked nervous when he answered the door. The photograph in Goddard's file had shown a young man with a huge, light-bulb-shaped Afro and round, John Lennon–style sunglasses. Thin-faced and whip-skinny. The man standing in the open doorway of the concrete-and-glass house on Stephen's Way was balding, thick at the waist, and wearing tortoiseshell bifocals. Human geology at work; the inescapable erosion of youth.

'You're Hawkins?'

'Yes.'

Ritchie stood aside. 'I suppose you'd better come in.' The ex-mime led Hawkins down a wide, slate-floored hallway to a large rectangular room with a sliding glass wall that looked out over a leafy ravine to a Cinemascope view of the sun setting over San Francisco. The modern furniture was rattan with nubbly off-white upholstery. A slim woman in a knitted dress two shades darker than the upholstery fabric was sitting on a long boxy couch, with a coffee service on the glass-topped table in front of her. She was at least ten years younger than Ritchie and very attractive. Her hands were knitted together in her lap, knuckles pale with tension. The glorious view was the furthest thing from her mind.

'My wife, Claire,' said Ritchie, sitting beside her. He put out a hand, covering hers. 'This is Agent Hawkins, the man I told you about.'

Hawkins sat down in a large chair on the other side of the table. 'I'm not really with the Bureau anymore,' he said quietly. 'I'm a private citizen now. If you don't want to talk about this, that's your right.'

'Claire and I have no secrets,' Ritchie answered. 'You said you were helping the FBI with an ongoing investigation.'

'That's right.'

'Coffee?' asked Claire Ritchie.

'That would be nice. Cream and sugar, please.'

The woman poured and Hawkins took the bone china cup from her extended hand.

'I haven't thought about Carol Prentice for a long time,' said Ritchie. Beside him, his wife's lips thinned. The hands were back in her lap again. Hawkins sipped his coffee and waited.

'I didn't know anything about her until half an hour ago,' said Ritchie's wife.

'It didn't seem important. It was so long ago.'

'You were with the mime troupe then,' Hawkins supplied.

'Back in my hell-raising days,' said Ritchie, laughing. The sound was forced. Claire Ritchie glanced at him coldly. Hawkins wondered how hard she'd fought to sit in a room like this with the sun going down over the bay. There was as much fear in the look as there was anger.

'Carol Prentice was also with the troupe.'

'On and off,' said Ritchie. 'She never took it very seriously. The mime or the politics.'

'A groupie?'

'I wouldn't go that far.' Ritchie paused. 'She was young. Lost. Looking for something without knowing what it was.'

'I think that applied to a lot of people then,' said Hawkins. 'Myself included.'

'Claire was just a baby then.' Ritchie smiled. His hand moved toward his wife and then drew back.

'Something I've never regretted,' she said. 'It sounds like a horrible time.'

'What can you remember about the day Carol Prentice was murdered?'

'I've been thinking about that. Like I said, it was a long time ago.'

'According to the police file, the troupe was in San Francisco that day.'

'That's right. Some kind of protest thing in Golden Gate Park. I can't remember what for ... probably the war.'

'What time did you get there?'

'Early. Nine-thirty in the morning.'

'So you left Berkeley around nine?'

'We started gathering people together earlier than that. Eight, eight-fifteen.'

'You'd been with Carol?'

'I dropped in at her place. She didn't want to come along.'

'What time was that?'

'Around seven. She said she'd been up all night. Tripping.'

'She was on drugs?'

'Acid. She was just coming down.'

'What about you?'

'What do you mean?'

'Were you on acid, too?'

'No.'

'Carol was doing a little bit of dealing. Did you go over there to buy drugs?'

'No.' Ritchie frowned. 'I told you, I went over to ask her if she wanted to come along for the performance.'

'How long did you stay?'

Ritchie glanced at his wife. 'About forty-five minutes, maybe a little longer.'

'As I understand it, you had sex with her.'

'Yes.'

Claire Ritchie gave her husband a withering look. 'Oh, for Christ's sake,' she muttered.

'It was nothing,' said Ritchie. 'You don't understand, Claire. Things were different then.'

'Not so different,' his wife answered. Hawkins turned

to look out at the view, embarrassed. Claire Ritchie wasn't jealous of her husband screwing around more than twenty-five years ago. Her anger was much more recent than that.

Hawkins cleared his throat. 'There was ... evidence that she'd recently had sex with someone else as well.' Claire Ritchie looked even more disgusted.

'The guy with the Indian.'

'Wheels?'

'That's what he called himself.'

'There was a soldier, too. A man named Follett.'

'No. It was Wheels.'

'How can you be so sure?'

'She said so.'

'That's not in the file.'

Ritchie's voice was tense. 'I'm aware of that.'

'Why didn't you say anything at the time?'

'Because it was 1968 and I'm black.'

'I don't understand.'

'No, you wouldn't.' Ritchie wiped one hand across the thinning hair on the top of his head. 'Carol was murdered and Follett turned up dead a little while later. Follett was sleeping with her and so was I. Being in the middle of a love triangle like that and being black wasn't too healthy back then ... even in enlightened Berkeley.'

'So you're sure she'd been with Wheels the night before?'

'Positive. They dropped acid together and then they had a fight.'

'About what?'

'The fact that she was sleeping with me. He was jealous. Crazy jealous, if you believed her. That's what I told the police.'

Claire Ritchie stood up. 'I don't think I want to listen to any more of this.' She turned and left the room. Hawkins watched her go.

'Sorry if I've caused you any trouble.'

Ritchie shrugged. 'It's not your fault. It's been coming on for a long time. This just brought it to a head.'

'Did you ever meet Wheels? Face to face?'

'A couple of times. Once in a restaurant, another time at the university.'

'What was he like?'

'Quiet. Soft-spoken. Bright.'

'How could you tell he was bright?'

'It was just a feeling. He was a watcher, an observer.'

'You told the police he had a temper.'

'That's what Carol told me.'

'Violent?'

'Not physically, but he'd fly into rages. So she said.'

'Did he ever tell Carol anything about his background?'

'I can't remember very much. Except for the motor-cycle and the clothes on his back, he didn't have much in the way of personal possessions. Not that you needed much back then.'

'Was he Carol's drug connection?'

'He might have been.'

'Did she ever say anything about where he was from?'

'Not directly. He mentioned something to her about working for Osh-Kosh, though. In the warehouse.'

'The clothing company?'

'Yeah.'

'Oregon then.'

'Pacific Northwest anyway.' Ritchie pulled off his glasses and pinched the bridge of his nose. 'I remember seeing the bike parked in the alley around from her place once. I knew he was there, so I didn't go in. I think it had a Washington State plate.' He put his glasses back on. 'I couldn't swear to that, though.' He stared over Hawkins' shoulder at the sunset view, then nodded to himself. 'He was an orphan.' He paused, thinking, then nodded again. 'I think that's how he got into Carol's pants in the first place. Some sob story about how hard his life had been, how cool it was to come to the Haight and to Berkeley after what he'd gone through.'

'Where was the orphanage? Do you have any idea?'

'It wasn't really like that, I don't think. He and a bunch of other kids worked at some camp. On an island. Something to do with the church. He told her he'd rather be marooned on a real desert island than go back there.' Ritchie shook his head. 'Carol went for it hook, line and sinker, especially because of her brother.'

'It was a Catholic orphanage?'

'Yes. Father Crow and Sister Penguin. Carol thought it was funny, giving them names like that.'

'Did you know about the baby?' asked Hawkins. Ritchie looked away and nodded.

'Yeah.'

'Was it yours?'

'Who knows? She slept with a lot of people. She said it was mine, or at least that's what she told Wheels.'

'That's not in the file, either.'

'No, it's not.'

'Why did she tell Wheels about it?'

'To piss him off.'

'She was going to have an abortion?'

'The Free Clinic was only a few blocks away. Wheels told her she'd burn in hell if she had an abortion. Called her a murderer.' The black man sighed. 'Except he was the murderer, not her.'

CHAPTER FIFTEEN

The next morning Cruz and Jay took the Cherokee northwest into the foothills, hard on the heels of a grumbling summer storm. They reached Los Alamos just before noon. The sky overhead was boiling gray and black, the streets were deserted, and the air was restless with electricity.

'This is like the Twilight Zone,' said Jay, looking out through the windshield as they moved down Central Avenue. There were security gates and fences everywhere and the barracks-style buildings lining the streets were cold and oppressive. 'Spooky.'

'It's not all like this,' said Cruz. He turned off Central on to 19th Street, moving slowly north. The houses on either side were identical little postwar bungalows, their yards handkerchief-sized and laid out with scorched lawns drowning after the sudden downpour. Above the rooftops Jay could see the dark green of tree-clad foothills, but here there was nothing but gray on gray. 'This is the old part of town, built during the forties and fifties,' Cruz explained. 'The newer houses are a lot better.'

'According to the insurance report, Bingham's house was in some place called Urban Park.'

'Housing development on the west side, outside the old fence.'

'But now he lives around here?'

'Peach Street.' Cruz nodded, turning left. He drove on for a block, then turned right. 'This is it.'

'It's a Peach, all right,' said Jay. Peach Street was as dull and featureless as everything else she'd seen in old Los Alamos. Cruz pulled up in front of a bungalow and stopped.

'Looks like he's come down in the world.'

Jay glanced out the side window at the house. 'The insurance claim totaled a bit more than three hundred thousand, including contents. What do you think this place set him back?'

'Seventy at the outside.'

'Strange,' Jay murmured. They climbed out of the Cherokee and walked up a cracked cement walkway to the front door. The screen on the outer aluminum door was rusted and torn at the bottom left corner. Cruz knocked and they waited. A few seconds later, the inner door opened and Bingham appeared. He was on the short side, in his fifties, gray-haired with a neatly trimmed, dark brown spade beard shot through with streaks of white. He was wearing jeans, a pale green golf shirt, and a light blue cardigan. His eyes had the familiar, watery look of someone wearing contacts.

Bingham nodded to Cruz, ignored Jay, and ushered

them into the house. It was as bleak on the inside as it was on the exterior. Bedroom to the right, living room to the left, kitchen and bathroom at the rear. An alcove squeezed in between the living room and the kitchen masqueraded as an office. It was barely big enough for the student-sized desk and computer that took up almost all the space.

The furniture in the living room was battered and banal, clearly secondhand. There were no paintings or other decorations on the nicotine-colored walls. The whole place smelled faintly of cats.

'Can I get you anything?' asked Bingham. The offer was obviously a formality. Both Jay and Cruz declined. They sat on a low, brown leatherette couch. Bingham dropped down into a tartan-patterned upholstered chair. *What's a museum director doing in a place like this?*

'We'd like to talk to you about Simon Kerzner,' said Jay. She found herself frowning at Bingham's reaction.

He was waiting for it.

'I beg your pardon?'

'Simon Kerzner. He used to work for you.'

'Perhaps you'd better tell me who you are before I start answering questions,' Bingham answered coldly. According to the file Jay had read, the man had never been married. She could see why.

'This is Janet Fletcher,' Cruz answered. 'She's working with me.'

'In what capacity?'

215

'Any capacity I see fit,' said Cruz. 'Ms Fletcher is officially with the Federal Bureau of Investigation.'

'Oh,' said Bingham. He cleared his throat, the watery eyes darting back and forth between the two figures across from him. Cruz had been a cop once upon a time, and he still had the moves.

'Simon Kerzner,' repeated Jay.

'He worked for me, yes.'

'He committed suicide,' said Cruz.

'Really?'

'Just after you fired him,' said Jay.

'Are you trying to join those two facts together?' asked Bingham.

'We thought there might be a connection, yes.' Cruz nodded.

'I fail to see what this has to do with an arson investigation.'

'Motive,' said Jay. Bingham's lip curled.

'A dead man exacting his revenge?'

'The dead man's lover,' said Cruz.

Bingham shrugged. 'If you have a case against him, then arrest the man.'

'Who said it was a man?' Jay asked.

'Since Kerzner was a homosexual, I assumed his lover would be a man.' He pronounced the word *sexual* as though there was an extra S after the X.

'You knew Kerzner was gay?'

Bingham lifted his shoulders. The expression on his face was almost a smirk. 'He was HIV positive.'

'How do you know that?' asked Cruz. 'Did he tell you?'

'No. It showed up after his annual physical.'

'Is that why you fired him?' asked Jay. 'For having AIDS?'

'Certainly not,' said Bingham hotly. 'For one thing, that would have been wrongful dismissal.'

'Then why did you fire him?' asked Cruz.

'His work began to suffer after he was diagnosed.'

'But you didn't now he committed suicide?'

'No.'

'What did you know about his personal life?' said Jay.

'Virtually nothing,' Bingham responded. 'I knew he lived in Santa Fe and commuted every day. A number of my employees do.' He let out a long, irritated sigh. 'He was a technician. I barely knew him at all.'

'Just one of the little people, is that it?' Jay asked sourly.

'There are more than a hundred people employed by the museum, Ms Fletcher. I don't know them all personally.'

'Why did you choose this house to move into?' asked Cruz, gazing around the barren little room. 'Not exactly your style, is it?'

Bingham's voice was taut. 'It was available.'

'And cheap,' Jay commented. 'A lot cheaper than your other place.'

'My finances are no affair of yours,' Bingham snapped. 'And I still don't see what all of this has to do with your investigation. I told you before, if you have some idea that Simon Kerzner's lover was responsible for setting

217

fire to my house, then arrest him.' Bingham stood up. 'If there's nothing more...'

'Antiques,' Jay said quietly, staying where she was. 'Your insurance claim form mentioned a large number of antiques. Textiles. Navaho weaving in particular.'

'What of it?'

'Forty-two thousand dollars' worth.'

'You're doubting my claim, Ms Fletcher?'

'No. You've got all sorts of documentation to back it up. I've seen it.'

'So?'

'Just curious.'

'About what?'

'About why you haven't replaced any of it.' She waved her hand toward the bare wall behind Bingham's head.

'You don't replace material like that. What burned in the fire was priceless, unique. It took me ten years to collect it.'

'I would have thought you'd have made a stab at starting it up again,' said Jay.

'Perhaps my heart isn't in it any longer.'

'Perhaps not.' Jay stood up and Cruz joined her.

'You'll let me know when this is all resolved?' Bingham asked.

'You'll be the first to know,' said Jay, smiling. She and Cruz left the house and got back into the Cherokee.

'Bit hard on him, weren't you?' Cruz asked, starting the engine.

'He's an evil little shit,' Jay answered. She lit a

cigarette. 'He found out that Kerzner was HIV positive and he fired him. We both know that. The poor bastard gets a death warrant and his pink slip all in the same package.'

'Just remember, Bingham is the victim here, not the criminal.'

'Maybe,' Jay answered. 'It all depends on how you look at it.' She blew out a plume of smoke. 'I'd like to take a look at the place he used to live in.'

'No problem.' Cruz nodded. He put the Cherokee in gear and swung the wheel around, taking them back the way they'd come. A few minutes later, they were out of the grim core of Los Alamos and into a pleasant, tree-lined maze of suburban streets. The houses were mostly sixties and seventies rancher-splits, but they were a welcome relief after the miniature blockhouses in the middle of town. Automatic sprinklers kept the lawns green here and everyone's living-room window had a view.

Bingham's old address was on Ridgeway Drive, over-looking a steep canyon and a meandering, barely running creek. The lot was barren and looked recently graded. There was a Dumpster in the middle of the lot and a brand-new real estate sign next to the curb.

'Not bad,' said Jay as Cruz pulled to a stop in front of the vacant lot. 'He had full replacement insurance, so why move out of a neighborhood like this?'

'Like he said, the house on Peach Street was avail-able.' Cruz shrugged.

'It stinks,' said Jay.

'Bingham?'

'Yeah. He spends ten years and forty thousand dollars collecting Navaho rugs and then drops the hobby cold. He goes from an area like this to that coffin he's in now, with nothing on the walls and swap-meet furniture on the floor. It's not logical.'

'So what's your theory?'

'I don't have one ... yet,' she answered. 'But I sure would like to get a look at his last bank statement.'

William Hawkins drove his rental car through the town of Steilacoom on the southern edge of the city of Tacoma, Washington, eventually making his way to the ferry docks on Puget Sound, at the foot of Union Street. There were two separate landings, one for the penitentiary on McNeil Island, the other for the residential communities on Anderson Island, which lay slightly to the south, separated from its sinister neighbor by the chilly waters of Balch Passage. In the midafternoon sunlight, both islands could be seen, two miles offshore in the Sound.

Hawkins purchased a ticket, then drove the car on to the Anderson Island ferry. Ten minutes later, with only half a dozen vehicles on board, the ferry chugged out into Puget Sound. Hawkins left his car and went to stand by the rail for the twenty-minute ride. He yawned. The flight from Oakland that morning had been a bumpy one and he was getting tired of hopscotching across the country.

A quick call to one of his Jesuit friends at Georgetown

University the night before had given him everything he needed to know about the 'island' and the 'camp', Thomas Ritchie had mentioned. The island was Anderson Island and the camp was the St Vincent's Catholic Youth Training Facility on Amsterdam Bay. St Vincent's had been the next best thing to a reform school, and it had also served to staff the Diocesan Retreat House at Otter Bay, half a mile away down the coast.

According to his contact at the university, the Retreat House had been used by high-ranking members of the Church more for summertime R&R than for meditation. His contact wasn't quite sure about the details, but there had been a scandal surrounding St Vincent's in the mid-sixties, and it had been closed down completely in 1971. The Retreat House was still owned by the Church, but it had long ago been transformed into a bed-and-breakfast country inn and renamed Angel's Rest. Hawkins called from the Travelodge in Berkeley and made a reservation for the following day.

The little ferry announced its arrival with an ear-splitting blast of its horn, then disgorged its meager cargo. Hawkins found a crudely drawn map for sale at the general store and post office, then used it to make his way across the two-mile-wide island. The roads were narrow, but paved and well maintained, fringed on either side by thick stands of flowering dogwood and second-growth cedar and pine. The terrain was surprisingly hilly, dotted here and there with cleared slopes and tiny farms, like a miniature Ireland.

He turned off Yoman Street and drove up something

called the Ekenstam Johnson Road. At the top of the hill he could see two small bodies of water to the south. On the map they were marked as Florence Lake and Josephine Lake. They appeared to be connected by a narrow creek, and both of the oversized ponds had only a few cottages nestled among the screening trees. Florence Lake looked as though it had only one road down to the water. By all appearances the Anderson Island locals were very private people.

Hawkins continued on down the hill, reaching the center of the island. Following the map he turned right on to Sandberg Road and headed west toward the far side of the island and Otter Bay. Half a mile farther on was a turnoff to the right. A discreet sign told him he'd reached Angel's Rest Lane. He swung on to the graveled drive and a few seconds later he came to what had once been the Diocesan Retreat House.

Depending on personal taste, it was either a log cabin builder's ultimate fantasy or an architectural nightmare. The building was gigantic, three stories high with half a dozen different wings and cedar-shake rooflines jutting out in all directions. The foundation was made out of massive, irregular blocks of roughly quarried stone and three sides of the structure were surrounded by a broad, deeply shaded verandah supported by huge columns that looked like whitewashed telephone poles. Behind the building next to the parking lot was a high, chain-link fence surrounding a swimming pool and tennis courts. The pool was empty, its concrete walls cracked and stained a blotchy green.

Grass was growing up through the fissures that fanned out over the asphalt courts.

Hawkins got out of his car. The only other vehicle in the parking lot was a camper with a personalized license plate that said RETRD. He smiled; in his day it would have stood for *Retard* not *Retired*. Or maybe it meant *Retread*. The camper also told him that Angel's Rest wasn't doing a great deal of business these days.

Taking his overnight bag out of the trunk, he went around to the front of the hotel. Twenty feet away from the verandah, a short flight of concrete steps led down to a narrow pebble beach and a small floating dock. A mile or so to the west he could see the shoreline of the Olympic Peninsula. Even in the glittering sunlight, the pass between the island and the peninsula looked cold and dangerous, the water gray and choppy. Hawkins frowned, trying to imagine if Carol Prentice's killer had ever stood here, staring across the water, wondering if he could swim to freedom.

He turned away from the water, went up the wide verandah steps, and pushed through the double screen doors leading into the hotel. The foyer was wood-floored and gloomy, the only light coming from a tall, stained-glass window on the stairway landing. The leaded figure set into the glass was a haloed angel, huge white wings and succoring arms outspread. The angel's robes were pale rose glass, the eyes brown, the flowing hair silver and the halo sunflower-gold, all on a field of deep green and robin's-egg-blue. The overall effect made Hawkins feel as though he'd stepped into a tropical fish

223

aquarium or a colorized version of *Going My Way*. Resisting the urge to begin humming 'Too-ra-loo-ra-loo-ra,' he stepped up to the waist-high reception counter and gently tapped the old-fashioned bell. A moment later a man in his twenties appeared, wearing jeans, a Grateful Dead T-shirt, and plastic flip-flops.

'Mr Hawkins?' the man asked, stepping behind the counter.

'That's right.'

'I'm Byron Remocker.' He turned around the register book on the counter and offered Hawkins a ballpoint pen. 'Sign in and I'll take you up to your room.'

'Short-staffed?' asked Hawkins, scribbling his name below the only other signature on the page – *Mr and Mrs O. P. Casgrand*, almost certainly the people with the RETRD camper.

'Not really,' Remocker answered. 'My wife does the cooking and I do everything else. We're pretty much a two-person operation.' He came out from behind the counter, took Hawkins' bag, and led him up the stairs past the stained-glass angel.

His second-floor room was large and plainly furnished with a view out over the water. Remocker dropped Hawkins' bag on the dark-varnished, thirties-style bed, then opened the window to let in some fresh air.

'No bathroom?' asked Hawkins.

'Down the hall.' He smiled. 'You won't have to share, though; you've got the whole floor to yourself.'

'Business slow?'

'We get by. Not a lot of singles bother to come out here, but my wife knows a lot of New Age types. Groups. Three-day weekends stroking crystals and talking about the Great Goddess. Lots of hugging and kissing, that kind of thing. Pays the bills, and it's steady.'

'This wasn't always a hotel, was it?' asked Hawkins.

'No,' Remocker answered. 'It used to be a Catholic retreat house. The Church still owns the place; we just lease it.'

'How long have you had it?'

'Six years,' said Remocker. 'It's our version of going back to the land. I used to work at Boeing.'

'Why did the Church stop using it?'

'I'm not sure. It was empty for a long time before we took over. When we were cleaning up the place, Marnie – my wife – found a copy of *Time* magazine from 1970.'

'Odd.'

'You could ask the Swede about it if you're really interested.'

'The Swede?'

'Gunnar Gustavsen. Used to be the caretaker.'

'Where can I find him?'

'He's retired now. Has a little business collecting plants for herbal teas. Up at Higgins Cove.'

Gustavsen's house was located at the end of a dirt road a mile or so north of Angel's Rest. It was small, no more than a cabin, perched at the edge of a steep bluff leading down to the rocky shoreline. The house was surrounded

225

on three sides by heavy stands of dogwood, maple, and madrona pine, their branches rustling in the late-afternoon breeze blowing off the mile-wide strait separating the western coast of the island from the Olympic Peninsula.

Gustavsen was sitting on his porch in front of a rickety-looking card table. On the table there was a pile of bark and dried-leaf matter. He was using a battery-powered coffee grinder to turn handfuls of the leaves into an even finer powder, dumping successive loads into clear kitchen baggies. At first glance it looked like a cottage-industry drug operation. Watching the Swede work, Hawkins grinned. Gustavsen was an unlikely dope dealer. He was at least seventy, his broad, deeply tanned face seamed and cracked with time, his large nose battered by more physical forces, his thick hair bleached salt-white by a lifetime spent in sea air.

'Shittim,' he said, looking up as Hawkins stepped on to the porch.

'Pardon?'

'Shittim,' Gustavsen repeated. 'You want some?' He pointed a thick finger at the pile of leaves and bark on the table. 'Make you a tea of it.'

'I don't think so. Thanks anyway.'

'Look like you could use it,' Gustavsen grunted. His grinder whirred and he filled another baggie. 'Ark of the Covenant was made of it . . . and they shall make an Ark of Shittim wood': Exodus, twenty-five, ten.' Gustavsen let out a booming laugh. 'King James Version translates it as 'Acacia,' but it's still Shittim if you ask me.' He grinned at Hawkins. 'Latin name is *Cascara Sagrada*.' Somehow he'd expected the man to speak with a lilting Swedish accent, but Gustavsen's voice had the flat, deadpan tones of the Pacific Northwest.

'Cascara's a laxative, isn't it?'

'Like I said, looks like you could use some.'

'I've been doing a lot of traveling,' said Hawkins. 'I didn't think it showed.'

'Some people read books; I read faces. You look all plugged up, and not just your bowels.' He waved to a crude bench set against the wall of the house. 'Sit.'

Hawkins did as he was told. Gustavsen filled half a dozen more baggies, then put down the grinder. He turned to Hawkins, took a package of Marlboros out of the breast pocket of his workshirt, and lit a cigarette.

'Pretty,' said Hawkins, nodding toward the view.

'Wallpaper,' said Gustavsen. 'I've had it in front of my eyes for so long I don't see it anymore.' The Swede was an old man, but his gray-blue eyes were clear and intelligent. He took a deep drag on his cigarette, letting the smoke trail out through his ruined nose. 'You're with the police,' he said quietly.

'Was. My name is Hawkins.' He paused, faintly surprised at the old man's shrewd assessment. 'How did you know?'

'Not hard,' said Gustavsen. 'You said you've been traveling a lot. You didn't come all this way to sell me real estate in Florida and I've outlived all my relatives, so you're not a lawyer come to tell me I've inherited a fortune. And you look like a cop.'

227

'You'd have made a fair detective yourself, Mr Gustavsen.'

'Swede, or Gunnar.' The old man smiled. 'And I was a cop. MP at Pearl Harbor in 1941.' He leaned down and pulled up his right pant leg. An angry cicatrice of scar tissue ran up from his ankle, across his hairless, parchment calf, and ended at his bony knee. 'December seventh. Almost lost the leg. Gave me a purple heart and not much else.'

'You came back here?'

'That's right. No real jobs for cripples, so I went to work for Mother Church after the war.' He winked broadly at Hawkins. 'Probably started my Lutheran mother spinning in her grave, me toiling for the Papists.'

'You worked at St Vincent's?'

'That's right.' There was a long pause. Finally the Swede spoke again. 'Which is why you came all this way, I suppose.'

'What makes you say that, Swede?'

Gustavsen leaned back in his chair. 'Anderson Island isn't known for its high crime rate, Mr Hawkins. Unless you count littering by the summer people and stealing apples in season. If you're here, it's about the monsignor. About St Vincent's.'

Hawkins decided to play it straight with the old man. 'I'm a writer, Swede. I used to be with the FBI. I'm looking into a murder that took place in Berkeley in 1968. A few bits and pieces of information point to Anderson Island and St Vincent's. Other than that I'm flying blind.' He touched the patch over his eye. 'No pun intended.'

'I like a man who can laugh about himself,' the Swede answered. 'What's the connection between Berkeley and here?'

'I think the killer was an inmate at the training facility, or he worked at the retreat.'

'Same thing. They used boys from the facility as staff. Cooks, dishwashers, that kind of thing.'

'You were the handyman?'

'Handyman, plumber, carpenter, call it what you want. If it was broken, I fixed it. And the monsignor paid cash.' He smiled. 'Haven't paid income tax since they mustered me out of the Army.'

'That's the second time you mentioned the monsignor.'

'Monsignor Pozniak. Ran the facility and the retreat for the archdiocese. Combination warden and maitre 'd. Men hated him, women loved him, and he scared the shit right out of the boys.'

'There was a scandal,' said Hawkins. He waited.

'No,' said the Swede after a moment. 'There was a murder.'

'One of the boys?'

'The monsignor. They said it was an accidental drowning, but it was murder, believe me.'

'Why do you say that?'

Gustavsen nodded his head toward the bay and the waters beyond. 'No one goes swimming in Drayton Passage in the middle of January, Mr Hawkins. It's not healthy. Tide took him all the way up past McDermott

Point Lighthouse and up to Pitt Island. Barely enough left to bait a hook when they reeled him in. Identified him by his ring.'

'What about suicide?'

'Catholic priests don't commit suicide, Mr Hawkins, especially sons of bitches like his eminence Gregory by God Pozniak.'

'So who killed him? Did he have any enemies?'

'Hundreds. Every boy who ever went through the hell of St Vincent's under that sadistic bastard's charge.'

'Sadistic? You mean he physically abused the boys?'

'Abuse is one of those ten-dollar words you read in the magazines these days. I prefer torture.' Gustavsen paused for a moment, his face darkening. 'There were rumors of other things as well.'

'Sexual abuse?' It wouldn't be the first time. Gustavsen frowned, dropped the butt of his cigarette on to the porch, and ground it out with his heel.

'Call it by its real name, Mr Hawkins. Sodomy, buggery, forcing sex on innocent little boys, threatening them with hell and damnation if they didn't do exactly what they were told.'

'No one reported him?'

'I went to work for the retreat in 1946. Pozniak was just a priest then. He'd come and go like all the rest. He came to stay in 'fifty-six or 'fifty-seven, I can't remember which it was. He ran the training camp for twelve years. In that time there were more than twenty-five suicides. Before he came there hadn't been any.' Gustavsen lit another cigarette. 'No, Mr Hawkins, no one reported him. It was only after he died that a few of the boys came forward and put a word or two in the bishop's ear. They were grown up and gone and there was nothing to fear. The archdiocese ran its own investigation. That's when they decided to close the facility down. Swept it all under the rug.'

'It ended there? Nothing was ever made public?'

'They burned all the records. I saw them do it; great big bonfire on the beach. There was a lot at stake, and not just within the Church. St Vincent's was a Catholic facility, but it was supposed to be under the supervision of the State Youth Correctional Services Department.'

'And no one made any attempt to investigate the monsignor's death?'

'No. Rough justice, but at least justice was done. No one cried over his grave, I can tell you that.'

Hawkins waited. There was something else there, just under the surface. 'But you think he was murdered.'

'I do.'

'Did you ever talk to anyone about it?'

'We all talked about it.'

'Did you have anything concrete to go on?'

'No. Not really.'

'Not really, or a definite no?' Hawkins asked. Gustavsen was lost in thought for what seemed like a long time.

'I saw scores of boys go through St Vincent's, Mr Hawkins,' he said finally. 'But in all those years I only saw one of them stand up to the monsignor. He shamed me, because he had more courage in the face of that devil than I did.'

'Who was he?'

'Ricky Stiles. Richard Alexander Stiles. A foundling child. When he turned sixteen, they brought him down from the orphanage in Bellingham. One of the nuns had slapped him across the face for swearing. The next day he came into the classroom with a bicycle chain and almost beat her to death with it.'

'You think he had something to do with Pozniak's death?'

'The day after the monsignor drowned, Stiles stole a motorcycle from Pozniak's secretary at the retreat and disappeared.'

'A motorcycle?' asked Hawkins. He could feel his heart pounding. 'Do you remember what kind?'

'Sure.' Gustavsen nodded. 'Same kind I used on picket duty at Pearl.' He smiled. 'An Indian.'

Jay Fletcher sat in front of the laptop portable computer she'd set up on a small table in front of the living-room window and stared out into the night. On the far side of the ravine, she could see the lights of the Torreon Park subdivision. Beyond that, the Jemez Mountains were a ragged tear of blackness that blotted out the stars. She lit another cigarette, tucked one leg up underneath her, and turned her attention back to the screen.

The high speed 486 she'd picked up in Albuquerque, complete with its internal modem and CD-ROM, had almost snapped the mag-stripe spine of her Visa card, but it had been worth it. Using the passcodes from Cruz's office and the logs she'd taken from the Gaddis house, she'd finally figured out how Special K worked.

At first glance it was a Dungeons and Dragons-style role-playing game, one of a hundred thousand destinations on the Internet, accessible to more than a million personal computers that used the system on a regular basis simply by dialing it up on the telephone.

Once into the game environment, you found yourself in a world of cops, killers, and victims that wasn't much different from an average, if slightly more graphic hour of prime-time television. Victims could be avenged by friends and lovers, cops were given clues, and killers roamed the ethereal landscape wreaking havoc. Tasteless perhaps, but relatively innocent by Internet standards, and nothing compared to things like Filthnet, a pornography exchange, or Fetishlink with its seemingly endless list of subdirectories.

What was different about Special K were the trapdoors. Every role game Jay had ever heard of had all sorts of hidden pitfalls, but in the case of the game Gaddis had been playing, the trapdoors were just that — hidden exits that spirited you away from the game environment, spun you randomly through the twelve-city fiber-optic 'backbone' of the net, then cast you out through a gateway 'server' on to an anonymous network node that changed every time the game was played.

In simple terms, the trapdoors took you into another dimension, an electronic netherworld where maniacs

233

like Gaddis were accepted without question. If you knew where the trapdoors were, you could travel down to Special K's hidden levels, but you would be traveling blind. The only one who knew your final destination was SK-WIZ, presumably 'Wizard,' Special K's systems operator. The security value of the multilayered game was obvious.

The preliminary, role-playing level was there to filter out the amateurs – the people who thought that the game was only a game. Since the maze of electronic corridors connecting the trapdoors to the final 'chat' destination was randomly chosen, there was no way to backtrack and discover the originating modem number, thus protecting both the systems operator and anyone who logged on, slipped through a trapdoor, and eventually reached the node destination. Changing the node destination each day made the system doubly secure. Jay had almost laughed when she discovered the device. She'd seen a dozen variations of it in her favorite books. In the C. S. Lewis Narnia series, the trapdoor had once been a cupboard that led to another world in time and on another occasion it had been a painting on a wall. It was Alice's Rabbit Hole and Looking Glass, or the mechanism used by H. G. Wells in *The Time Machine*. The last time she'd seen it used was in the Schwarzenegger bomb about the kid who used a magic movie ticket to get sucked into an adventure movie.

The trapdoors were perfectly fail-safe. Except there was no such thing. SK-WIZ was good, but he was still constrained by the parameters of the Net. One way or the other, every bit and byte of information that zoomed up and down the Information Superhighway had to obey the rules of the road. The T3 'backbone' was a prime example and the fatal flaw in SK-Wizard's little scheme.

The Internet had begun as a way for scientists to exchange information over long distances and had originally been called Arpanet. As the system became more popular, it began to spread, putting more pressure on an already overloaded system of telephone lines.

By the early 1990s, traffic on the Net had become irritatingly sluggish and the T3 cabling system was introduced – fiber-optic cables connecting twelve main cities on the Net from Seattle, San Francisco, and Los Angeles in the West, to Hartford, New York, and Washington in the East, the other six cities spread out in between. Local area networks fed into the nearest gateway on normal telephone lines, which in turn shunted the messages on to the fiber-optic system. There was no way that the WIZ and his friends could avoid passing through one of those twelve cities on the way to their secret destination.

Gaddis, living in Albuquerque, would have been channeled to the T3 link in Houston, Texas. A person who went through a trapdoor in Kansas City would funnel through the St Louis access point, and someone from Salt Lake City would go through Denver. The process was called packet-switching, and without it the entire system would have collapsed years before under the sheer weight of information being transmitted.

To follow messages destined for the sublevels of Special K, she would have to lie in wait at each of those twelve packet-switching stations, identify the right packets, tag them, then trace backward through the system to the point of origin.

The programs she needed were already available, and after returning from Los Alamos, she'd simply downloaded them from CERT, the Computer Emergency Response Team at Carnegie-Mellon University in Pittsburgh. CERT, originally funded by the Department of Defense, had been responsible for tracking down Robert T. Morris, Jr, the Cornell graduate student who'd introduced the infamous Internet supervirus in 1988. Since then they'd worked closely with the FBI and had become known as the Internet Cybercops.

Jay was perfectly aware that what she was about to do was as illegal as using C-Bix to track down Gaddis, but she was well beyond that now. The killer's death had almost been an accident; when you got right down to it, she'd had very little choice. It was either him, or her. There was no use crying over spilt milk or a dead serial killer. If she didn't use what she knew to track down the other members of Special K, she'd never be able to forgive herself.

She sat forward, keystroked to the main menu on the hard drive, then called up her communications software. The downloaded programs from headquarters were already queued up in the Send box, the necessary numbers already waiting to be dialed. She took a deep breath, let it out slowly, then hit the Enter key. She sat back in her chair and stared at the screen, watching as her electronic bloodhounds were invisibly whisked out into the night. All she could do now was wait.

The Iceman passed between the huge bronze dolphins guarding the main entrance and stepped into the glass-domed lobby of the Mirage Hotel. Built in 1989, the triple-towered, three-thousand-room hotel and casino was still deemed to be the ultimate in Las Vegas over-kill and was the highest-ranking tourist destination in the city.

In any twenty-four-hour period, more than a hundred thousand people passed through the hotel, some to visit the dolphin aquarium in the back courtyard; others to see the famous white tigers used by Seigfried and Roy, the house magic act; still more to suck in the atmo-sphere of a hotel with dozens of indoor waterfalls, its own rain forest, and an outdoor volcano that erupted every half hour during the evening. Some even came to gamble.

Those who did were among the highest of the high rollers who came to Las Vegas. The Mirage boasted $500 slot machines, $100-a-bet video poker machines, and a casino that took in more money at its craps and baccarat tables in a month than some small countries saw in a year. If you were looking for a well-heeled visitor to Las Vegas, the odds were that you'd find him at the Mirage.

And after more than ten years in the city, the Iceman knew a great deal about odds. He could quote you the house percentages on faro, roulette, and blackjack; he could give you the odds on place bets, pass or come, don't pass, and don't come at the craps tables in most of the major casinos; and he could give you the probabilities and payoff ratios at Keno for everything from a three- to a fifteen-spot ticket. He could tell you about whipsaw bets at faro, where two bets were lost at one time; martingale systems for gambling, where the amount of the bet was doubled after a loss; and the chances of winning a box bet at craps.

He also knew the cardinal rule of living in Las Vegas: if you don't want to lose, don't play the game. In the end, if you played long enough, you would inevitably fail, since over the long haul, the percentages were always with the house. Still, sometimes a single bet, shrewdly placed, could make you a winner, and sometimes that single bet was necessary.

Navigating through the ebb and flow of people moving across the lobby, he made his way through the jungle of palms, plants, and white-washed cane-and-rattan furniture to the registration desk. Half a dozen clerks worked the lines of people booking in and booking out, backed by the hotel's trademark 57-foot-long, 200,000 gallon aquarium and its hundreds of tropical fish.

After waiting patiently in line for less than five minutes, he found himself facing one of the clerks. The Iceman then politely told the young woman that he was a special messenger from Los Angeles with some important documents for one of their guests. He gave the clerk the guest's name and, after a quick check, was informed that the person in question was not in his room. The Iceman thanked the hotel employee and walked away. Skirting the Lagoon Saloon, another oasis of palms and waterfalls, and ignoring the luring entrance to the casino, the Iceman made his way to the bank of elevators. At the core of the three slab towers making up the hotel, he rode up to the eighteenth floor.

Although he'd decided on his present course of action on the spur of the moment, he'd chosen his quarry with care, accessing both the Mirage reservation computer and the Credit Card Banking Center database to cull out a shortlist of possibilities. The best he could find on such short notice was Franz Schroeder, a businessman from Freiberg, Germany.

The Mirage computer had him listed as CEO of Elektrowerke A.G. with a five-day reservation; the casino had him cash-rated at $200,000 with a notation that he was a first-time visitor to Las Vegas. The Banking Center listed him as having seven major credit cards, both personal and corporate. Since Schroeder had reserved a single room, it was logical to assume that he was traveling alone.

Leaving the elevator, the Iceman walked down the long, silent hallway, then stopped in front of the door to Schroeder's room. He took out a handful of Smartcard electronic keys and began inserting them into the lock slot one by one.

Every room in every hotel was programmed with a different code, but the hotels had overriding superkeys that could open any room using a 'back door' four-number sequence that the Iceman retrieved from the appropriate security files in the hotel's computer. He had a collection of the cards and monitored the bi-monthly code changes, reprogramming the various cards when necessary. The lock released on the third try. He pocketed the other cards, opened the door, and stepped into the room.

Not lavish, but not cheap, either. The room was medium-sized and faced east, looking out over the hundred-foot-high glass reception dome; the front court-yard jungle of palms, ponds, and waterfalls; and across the Strip to the Imperial Palace. There was a queen-sized bed, rumpled and unmade, an open bottle of mineral water on the night table, a cupboard full of expensive-looking suits, thirty-eight regular, along with three pairs of handmade shoes. Bikini underwear and socks in the first drawer of the bureau, half a dozen neatly folded white silk shirts in the second drawer.

Schroeder's passport was hidden under the shirts. According to the document, Schroeder was fifty-two years old, blue-eyed, and brown-haired. The small photograph showed a pleasant-looking, smiling man with a narrow face, a graying mustache and goatee, and tinted, wire-frame aviator glasses. Not the face of a man with $200,000 to spend at the tables; but then again, the Iceman had realized many years ago that there was less in a face than there was in a name and little to be learned from either. He replaced the passport and crossed to the bathroom.

Schroeder's leather shaving kit stood open on the vanity. Braun electric razor, comb, a pair of military-style silver-backed hairbrushes with the initials *FS*, a small can of European talc, and a half-filled bottle of Lagerfeld cologne. The Iceman next checked the medicine chest. The only thing of interest was a prescription bottle from a pharmacy in Freiberg. It was for a generic form of chlorphentermine hydrochloride. Schroeder was apparently trying to lose a bit of weight the easy way. The fact that he was taking the appetite suppressant didn't really make a difference, but it might serve to obscure things at a later date if there were complications.

Returning to the bedroom, the Iceman went to the bar fridge and opened it. There were three bottles of mineral water, the same brand as the one on the night table. The Iceman picked up all three bottles, set them on the bureau, and unscrewed the caps. Taking a small yellow box from the pocket of his jacket, he removed a hundred extremely small white tablets, each one containing twenty milligrams of a drug known as hyoscine butyl-bromide. He poured an equal number of tablets into each bottle. The drug, even in the enormous doses he had just added to the bottles of mineral water, would not show up on any postmortem blood test, since hyoscine butyl-bromide was an 'orphan' drug that was normally unavailable in the United States. Scordin B or Stibron, as it was known in Japan, was an antispasmodic related to atropine, but up to twelve times more powerful. Even half a bottle of the dosed mineral water would send a very relaxed Herr Schroeder into eternity. The fatal sendoff would be hastened considerably if Schroeder had recently ingested even a small amount of alcohol. Given his age, the most likely postmortem finding would be simple congestive heart failure.

The Iceman screwed the tops back on the bottles, checked to make sure that the tablets had dissolved, then returned the bottles to the bar fridge He turned and looked around the room, making sure that everything was in order. The odds were good that within the next four or five hours, Franz Schroeder would return to his room. The odds were also good that he would have another bottle of his favorite mineral water. The Iceman checked his watch: seven-thirty. He'd return at midnight, hopefully to find his chosen victim dead and waiting. There was a red-eye L.A. shuttle out of McCarran at one; with any luck he would get into Berkeley before breakfast.

He frowned, wondering if all of this might actually be compounding the mistake he'd made in that half-forgotten past. He thought about it briefly, and then came to the conclusion that the odds really were in his favor. Odds, and a superior intelligence. The frown dissolved and then he smiled, anticipating the look on Tom Ritchie's face. Just what he needed – a trip down memory lane. The smile broadened into a delighted grin; on top of everything else, it was going to drive Hawkins right out of his tiny little mind.

CHAPTER SIXTEEN

The Iceman sat in the Berkeley Streets and Sewers van he'd appropriated, watching the entrance to the house on Stephen's Way. He'd been there for almost two hours now, and in that time he'd seen an aging Thomas Ritchie climb into his Mustang and drive off and a pink Home Maid Services Toyota arrive. The two Jamaican cleaning ladies were still in the house, and so presumably was Mrs Thomas Ritchie. Tommy had come a long way from the co-op house he'd lived in on Regent Street.

The nondescript Streets and Sewers van was the perfect cover. Someone sitting around in a rental car might have aroused suspicion and led to a roll by the Berkeley Police; a municipal truck with a man in coveralls dozing behind the wheel was next to invisible.

Tommy had looked healthy enough as he drove off in the Mustang, but the thinning hair and the little pot belly had been a bit of a shock. A long way from Regent Street, and a long way from the hard dancer's calves and the washboard-tight stomach. Time passing had worked on him like a stone, dulling his edge, blunting his sharpness.

Just like everything else in Berkeley, from what he'd seen so far. Crack dealers and the homeless in the dusty undergrowth that spotted People's Park. BMWs and Volvos replacing VW bugs and busses. Women joggers in skin-tight spandex with nylon fanny packs bobbing above their groins like bulging little codpieces. Middle-aged men with ponytails riding mountain bikes to work, with their briefcases strapped on to back carriers with bungee cords. Omelets made with free-range eggs and sun-dried tomatoes. The Revolution drowned in money. Woodstock II on pay-per-view. No causes left to fight for.

The Iceman smiled; when you got right down to it, he really had kept the faith all these years, refusing to lose his edge or have his sharpness blunted. He even looked pretty much the same – no pot belly, no sagging jowls, no gray hair or beard, except when it suited. Forever young, a lone warrior refusing to be co-opted. Like Hawkins. Still looking for justice after all these years. What a pair they made.

A buzzing sound disturbed his thoughts. He glanced at the digital watch on his right wrist and pressed the tiny button that reset the alarm. He took a small, brown leather pillbox out of his coveralls, removed two of the small black capsules, and swallowed them dry. He had enough left for only another twelve hours – an incentive for him not to stay in Berkeley too long, not to give in to temptation.

The two Jamaican women reappeared, lugging their

vacuum cleaners and sponge mops down the driveway to their car. They loaded up the Toyota and drove off. A moment later the garage door swung open and a bright yellow Mazda Miata backed out, turned, and came down the driveway. An attractive black woman in her thirties was behind the wheel of the little sports car, eyes covered with outsize sunglasses, her hair tied back with a bright green rag ribbon. Tommy's wife.

She drove past the van without a glance, heading toward Gravatt Drive. According to her Mastercard statement, she had a regular Thursday-morning appointment at the Berkeley Yoga Center on Ashby Street, which was probably her final destination. The Yoga Center was at least a fifteen-minute drive away and the session would last at least an hour. Plenty of time to settle in. To prepare.

He stayed in the van, giving her a few minutes, just in case she'd forgotten something. He glanced down at the seat beside him. On it there was an extra-long plumber's tool box. He reached out and flipped it open. It was empty except for one thing: a brand-new, three-quarter, children's size Louisville Slugger wooden baseball bat. The salesman at the sporting goods store in Oakland had suggested aluminum, but the Iceman had declined. Consistency was important. He closed the hasp on the tool box, grabbed the handle, and climbed out of the van. First he'd have his innings with the Ritchies, then he'd play ball with his old friend William DeMille Hawkins. Tie game, bottom of the ninth, two men out and a full count. One swing of the bat would change everything.

* * *

After leaving Anderson Island earlier that morning, Hawkins drove into Seattle on the I-5. He spent an hour with a bevy of bland-faced Child Welfare workers at the King County Courthouse, then traveled a few blocks to the sixties-style glass cube of the Public Safety Building. Citing departmental policy, no one at Child Welfare was willing to discuss any individual case, and the Seattle Police Department, though much more cooperative, couldn't tell him anything he didn't already know. Pozniak was long dead and no one had ever heard of Ricky Stiles.

By noon he was beginning to regret not taking up Gunnar Gustavsen's offer of a cup of Shittim tea. Intuitively, he knew that he was at a turning point in his search for the Iceman, but somehow he couldn't quite make it around that final corner. Investigative constipation. Eventually he found himself buried in the periodicals section of the public library, winding his way through the microfilmed archives of the *Seattle Post-Intelligencer*.

There were several references to Pozniak, mostly to do with his fund-raising activities on behalf of the archdiocese, his obituary, and a short running about his 'accidental' death that faded out after three days and five paragraphs. There was nothing at all on file about the St Vincent's Catholic Youth Training Facility on Anderson Island.

With nothing left to go on, he went up to the lobby, found a pay phone, and called the archdiocese office.

Cobbling together a story on the fly, he told the male secretary who took the call that he was on vacation and thought he'd look up his great-aunt, who'd been a nun, specifically a member of the Order of the Sisters of the Precious Blood. He wasn't sure, but he seemed to remember that she'd worked at an orphanage in Bellingham. The secretary put him on hold, then came back on the line a minute or two later. The orphanage had been closed for many years, but the facility was still in use, having been transformed into a rest home and hospice for elderly members of the Order. Hawkins took down the address, thanked the secretary, and hung up. He picked up coffee and a cinnamon roll at a nearby Starbuck's, climbed back into his rental car, and headed for Bellingham.

The small city at the northern end of Puget Sound was an hour's drive from Seattle, halfway to the Canadian border at Blaine. Once upon a time it had been a thriving coastal port; now its economy was rooted in the University of Western Washington and tourism. From a policeman's point of view, its greatest claim to fame was the fact that one of Ted Bundy's victims had come from the area.

Precious Blood Hospice was located on the wrong side of Chuckanutt Mountain in Bellingham's Fairhaven district. According to the brochure and road map Hawkins picked up at the Visitors' Information Center, the right side of Chuckanutt was a scenic, cliff-hugging drive along the coast, the hilly slopes above the road dotted here and there with six- and seven-figure chunks of prime real estate. The wrong side was covered with scrub pine and spruce, looked down on to the old Padden Reservoir, and stood over 'South', one of the oldest and poorest sections of Bellingham.

He eventually found the hospice at the end of a switchback halfway up California Street. The main building was a huge, four-storied Victorian pile made out of yellowed brick and capped with a mansard copper roof gone green with age. Somewhere along the line, two wood-frame dormitory wings had been added, and a drooping, rusted slab of chain-link fence marked off the spot where a minute, scruffy-looking baseball diamond had been carved out of the encroaching second-growth forest.

The grass was a two-foot-high swatch of hay in what had once passed for center field, and the pitcher's mound was covered in bracken. No one had played ball there in years. The closest neighbor to the hospice was an abandoned double-wide mobile home he'd seen on his way up the hill. Peace and quiet for the old dying nuns perhaps, but an isolated, segregated hell for the kids who'd lived here long ago. *Orphanage.* Even the word seemed old and out of date.

Hawkins climbed out of the car and stretched. A blue-robed fiberglass statue of the Virgin stood in a circular flowerbed directly in front of him. The Holy Mother was staring adoringly down at the reverently cupped object in her hands. The object was a fiberglass heart, wreathed in fiberglass thorns. The heart was a glossy scarlet, lurid against the pastel robin's-egg of the robes; drops of

blood had been lovingly painted dripping down on to the
enclosing hands. He squinted past the grotesque piece of
lawn art and stared up at the building. At dusk it would
look like a horribly magnified version of the Bates
house in *Psycho*.

'Coming, Mother,' he whispered. The building would
have been a perfect breeding ground for emotional
trauma, the ideal place to spawn a madman like the
Iceman. Skirting the statue, he went up the short flight
of steps to the main entrance and went inside.

There was a wooden table in the reception area just
inside the doors, but no one sat behind it. Several
hallways jutted out from the entrance area and a
wide staircase against one wall led to the upper floors.
The walls were wood-paneled to waist height, then
pale green stucco to the high, cracked plaster ceilings.
The floors were squeaking softwood plank covered
with brown linoleum. Hawkins tried not to breathe
too deeply; the stuffy air was heavy with the scent of
basement storerooms, night-stained sheets and old
age.

A heavyset woman in her sixties stepped out of a room
a short way down one of the narrow corridors. She was
wearing a tight-fitting nun's cowl and the white, bibbed
habit of a nursing sister. The black-and-silver crucifix
hanging from the belt around her spreading waist was
the size of a small hammer. She approached Hawkins,
the thick soles of her white shoes hissing across the
floor.

'Yes?' A strong voice, neutral for the moment.

'My name is Hawkins. I'm with the FBI.' Not a lie, but not quite the truth, either. He was glad he hadn't been raised a Catholic.

'My name is Sister Claude. How can I assist you?'

'I'm trying to locate someone who used to ... live here.'

'A sister?'

'No. An orphan.'

'The orphanage was shut down many years ago.'

'I thought there might be some records I could see.'

'The records were all transferred to the archdiocese office when the orphanage was closed.' And there wasn't much chance he'd get to see those, ex-FBI or not.

'Is there someone I could talk to, then? Someone who used to work here? Someone who might have known the person I'm trying to locate.'

'Why is the FBI interested in this boy?'

'I'm afraid I can't tell you that.'

'I see.' An impasse. There was a long pause. Finally the imposing woman spoke again. 'When was the boy here?'

'I'm not sure when he arrived. I do know he was transferred to the St Vincent's training facility in 1966.'

Sister Claude frowned. 'Monsignor Pozniak.' She paused. 'The boy was a criminal?'

'Not then,' Hawkins answered. 'He is now.'

'Such transfers were usually made only in extreme cases.' Her expression had hardened.

'You sound as though you worked here yourself.'

'I was administrative assistant to the Mother Superior.'
She gave Hawkins a long, searching look. 'What did
the young man do to warrant being sent to Monsignor
Pozniak's institution?'

'He struck a member of your order. A nun. He chain-
whipped her.'

Sister Claude stiffened and her pale blue eyes flashed
briefly. One hand went to the crucifix at her waist and
clutched it. There was something else behind the tight
expression on her aging face. Anger and, deeper still,
fear.

'The Stiles boy.' She whispered the name.

'That's right.' Hawkins tried to keep the elation out of
his voice. No need for Gunnar Gustavsen's cascara now.
He'd turned the corner.

'Tell me what he has done, Mr Hawkins.' There was a
nervous hitch in the old woman's voice.

'I'm afraid that's confidential, Sister Claude. I'm sorry.'

'Tell me.' It was an order. If he didn't tell her, the trail
would end here.

'He's killed. More than once,' Hawkins said. 'A great
many times, in fact.' Even now he wasn't sure of exactly
how many times. By his own count, the Iceman had
killed at least thirty-five times, and it was probably a lot
more than that.

The elderly nun nodded. 'Yes.' She didn't seem
surprised.

'Did you know him?' asked Hawkins quietly. Sister
Claude shook her head.

'Not well. I only knew what he did. Feared what he was capable of doing.' She released the crucifix. 'Come with me.'

She took Hawkins up four creaking flights of stairs to the top floor of the building, then led him to the end of a short, dimly lit hallway. She knocked once on the narrow, plain wood door, then turned the knob and stepped aside.

A woman dressed identically to Sister Claude was making up a simple iron bed, her back to Hawkins. The room was bare, except for the bed, a small chest of drawers, and a kitchen chair painted the same dusty shade of blue as the Virgin's robes outside. The only decoration on the white walls was a plain wooden crucifix over the bed. A small window looked out on the hillside and the city.

'Celandine, this is Mr Hawkins,' said Sister Claude, now standing at his back. 'He's with the FBI. He'd like to talk to you about Richard Stiles.' She paused. 'Would that be all right?'

'Of course,' said the woman, turning. She was smiling pleasantly. Sister Celandine was in her early fifties but looked much younger. The left side of her face had the smooth-cheeked, youthful look common to women who take up the religious life at an early age. As a child she had probably been close to beautiful.

The right side of her face was a ravaged mask of scar tissue, raised pink welts of shiny skin crossing and recrossing from her forehead to her chin, one scar cutting over her eye socket, pulling it half closed, another drawing down the right corner of her mouth. Hawkins stared, noticing that half of her right ear looked as though it had been torn away from her head. Standing there he felt a sudden wave of shame for ever having felt self-pity at the loss of his eye. Sister Celandine was a Janus-faced horror.

The woman sat down on the freshly made bed and let out a small, almost contented sigh. 'Dear me,' she said, still smiling, 'I haven't thought about Richard in years.' She looked up at Hawkins. 'What exactly would you like to know?'

Sister Claude put her hand on Hawkins' shoulder. 'I'll leave the two of you alone,' she said quietly. 'I have patients to attend to.' She turned away, her feet hissing off down the hall. Hawkins went to the window and looked out, then turned finally and faced the woman again.

'I knew he'd attacked you, but...'

'You didn't know the extent of the damage.' She smiled, the left side of her mouth lifting, the right remaining motionless. 'Don't be embarrassed, Mr Hawkins; I know how I look.' She gave a little laugh. 'Nuns don't have to look good, you know; it's not a prerequisite for the job and I'm reasonably sure that God doesn't care.'

'How old were you when it happened?' Hawkins asked.

'Twenty,' she answered. 'I was a novice. It was my first year as a teacher.'

'Not much older than Stiles,' Hawkins commented.

'No,' she answered. 'I didn't know people like that existed. Not then.'

'Why did he attack you?'

'He'd been teaching some of the younger children some foul words. Dirty jokes. I asked him to stop.'

'He didn't?'

'No.' She paused. 'Then he began making comments about me.'

'Physical comments?' said Hawkins, guessing. Sister Celandine nodded soberly.

'Yes. I was furious. I lost control of myself.'

'You slapped him.'

'Yes. It still bothers me when I think about it. I shouldn't have done that.' It was an incredible statement considering what he'd done to her in return.

'He came back the next day and assaulted you.'

'Yes.'

'How long after that was it before he was transferred to St Vincent's?'

'I'm not exactly sure,' she answered. 'I was in the hospital for quite some time. Several months. When I returned he was already gone. But I kept in touch.'

'Kept in touch?' With the boy who'd tried to kill her? The boy who maimed her for life?

'Not directly.' She flushed, the infusion of blood darkening the scars on her face into livid, coiling worms. 'I felt responsible. I wanted to know how he was getting along. I wrote letters.'

'To Monsignor Pozniak.'

'No. To his assistant, Father John. He took Richard under his wing.'

'Then Richard stole his motorcycle.'

'He didn't steal it,' said Sister Celandine, smiling again. 'Father John gave it to him.'

'How do you know that?'

'He told me,' she said simply. 'After he left.'

'St Vincent's?'

'Yes.'

'When was that?'

'Shortly after Monsignor Pozniak passed on.'

'Why did Father John leave? Because of Stiles?'

'No. John's faith was faltering. He'd become quite political. He helped start up the draft-dodger clinic in Seattle. Then he started taking draft evaders and deserters over the border into Canada. He was arrested twice. Finally he left the Church altogether.' She let out a brief sigh. 'I was sad about that for a very long time. He exiled himself to Canada. A political statement. He stayed there even after the amnesty. He's still there.'

'You hear from him?'

'Oh, yes,' she said. She stood up and went to the chest of drawers. 'John is my only contact with the outside world. He writes to me quite regularly. Tells me all about his trips.' She opened one of the drawers and took out a handful of brightly colored postcards. She handed one to Hawkins. The Eiffel Tower. He flipped it over and glanced at the message. It was standard; 'I'm fine wish you were here' material. Then he saw the signature at the bottom of the card.

'Jesus Christ!' he whispered.

'I beg your pardon?'

'The name,' he said, as the pieces of the jigsaw suddenly snapped together. 'The signature.'

'What's wrong with it?' said the woman with the ruined face.

'John Prentice.'

The priest from Seattle.

Carol Prentice's brother.

'This,' said Cruz, 'is going to take a lot of balls.'

'Maybe,' said Jay. 'But it might put out a few fires around town, not to mention saving lives.'

They crossed the lantern-lit courtyard of the Maria Teresa Restaurant, aiming for a table in the far corner. The table was backed by one of the high adobe walls of the hundred-year-old building. According to Cruz, the Maria Teresa was the best and most expensive restaurant in Albuquerque's Old Town district. Jay couldn't have cared less; food was the last thing on her mind.

'Just remember,' said Cruz softly. 'The son of a bitch is a lawyer, and he's connected.'

'Ask me if I care,' Jay answered.

'This is crazy,' muttered Cruz, hurrying to keep up with her as she threaded her way between the tables. 'Half of it's just theory. We don't have any proof.'

'If we scare him badly enough, he'll give us the proof,' Jay answered.

The man eating alone at the corner table was in his middle forties, tall, dark-haired, and expensively dressed. There was a wooden wine holder to the right of his chair and a fine leather attaché case was nudging the toe of his left shoe. There was a thick document on the table in front of his plate and he was leafing through it as he ate, a pair of tortoiseshell bifocals resting on the end of his nose.

He looked up as Jay and Cruz stopped in front of his table.

Eyes like a snake.

He swept off the bifocals with a practiced hand and offered them a blank smile. 'Can I do something for you?'

'Brian MacDonald?'

'Yes.'

'My name is Fletcher. I'm with the FBI. This is J. M. Cruz from the State Fire Investigation Service.'

MacDonald looked up at the two people standing in front of his table. The smile on his face remained blank. 'It's good to see affirmative action at work,' he said. 'If this is about the fire at my summer place, I'd prefer that you made an appointment during office hours.' He used his knife and fork to point down at his plate. 'As you can see, I'm having dinner.'

Jay looked at the plate. Dinner appeared to be some kind of chicken in a raspberry-colored sauce. 'We're not here to talk about your summer house. We're here to talk about the Armada Property Management Corporation.'

'I'm afraid I don't understand,' said MacDonald.

'Bullshit,' said Jay. She pulled a chair out from the table and sat down facing the lawyer. Cruz remained standing at her left shoulder. 'You're on the board of directors.'

'You make that sound like a crime, Miss Fletcher.'

'Special Agent Fletcher. And it might be.'

'Might be?' said MacDonald. He raised an eyebrow and put down his knife and fork. 'There are no "might be's" in law.'

'As a major shareholder in Armada Property Management, you *might* be aware that it also owns a company called Spectrum Properties. A tenement owned by Spectrum was destroyed by fire a few days ago. Arson.' Jay paused. 'You *might* also be interested to know that a number of people died in that fire. Most of them were children of illegal aliens.'

The lawyer looked directly at Cruz. 'Wetbacks, you mean.'

'Arson causing death is classified as homicide, Mr MacDonald. Murder. The fact that the victims were illegal immigrants makes it a federal case.' She smiled. 'But I'm sure you were already aware of that, weren't you, Brian?'

'I fail to see what any of this has to do with me,' he answered. 'Armada has a variety of interests in Albuquerque and elsewhere. If Spectrum Properties rented to illegal aliens, I assure you that they did so without knowing it.'

'Bullshit,' Jay said again.

'Are you saying that I had something to do with this tenement fire?' He smiled blandly. 'Because if you are, you'd better have some proof to back up your allegation. Not to mention something in the way of motive, Miss Fletcher.'

'Coyotes,' said Cruz, speaking for the first time. 'The tenement was a way station for a coyote operation.'

'Just what, pray tell, is a coyote operation?'

'Indentured labor,' said Jay. 'Cheap help on the farms. You take illegals, promise to get them into the country, and put them to work for your clients on this side of the border. You set up in places like that tenement twenty-four-hour day care so you can squeeze a few more shifts out of them. New Age slavery. From what the local police tell me, it's big business, Brian.'

'You're on dangerous ground, Miss Fletcher,' warned the lawyer. 'Another step and you might find yourself facing a lawsuit.'

No, asshole. You're the one on dangerous ground. You have no idea what I can do to you.

'You won't sue me, Brian, or anyone else. You know what I'm saying is the truth.'

The lawyer took a moment to pour himself a glass of wine from the bottle next to his chair. He sipped, then sat back in his chair. He hadn't lost one iota of his composure. 'Let's assume for one minute that what you say is true,' he said finally.

'Let's,' agreed Jay.

'I'm running this coyote operation you refer to. It's

making me large sums of money. Why would I burn it down?'

'You were getting ready to change locations anyway,' Cruz offered. 'And you had other things to worry about, didn't you?'

'Such as?'

'Hotplate Harry,' Cruz answered.

'Who?'

'Eleven people died in the fire,' said Jay. 'Nine infant children, the woman who was taking care of them, and a white male, midfifties, they found in the stairwell. It took a while, but they eventually identified him as Harry Radborne. A professional torch.'

'They called him Hotplate Harry because that was the way he preferred to set his fires,' Cruz put in. 'He'd put a tin can full of gasoline on a hotplate, then just walk away. Neat and clean.'

'So an arsonist dies in his own fire.' MacDonald shrugged. 'Poetic justice.'

'He was dead before the fire started,' said Cruz. 'Someone cracked him over the head with a hammer a few times. Crushed his skull. According to the medical examiner, it was done somewhere else. He was put in that stairwell.'

'And I was the one who dragged him there?' The lawyer shook his head. 'A fairy tale, Mr Cruz.' He picked up his knife and fork again. 'Come back when you've got some real evidence.' He went back to his meal.

Jay reached out, picked up the pepper shaker in front

of the lawyer, and unscrewed the top. She dumped the contents into the middle of the man's plate. MacDonald sighed and put down his knife and fork again.

'Now look what you've done. Gone and ruined a perfectly good plate of raspberry chicken.'

'And you've murdered eleven people.'

'Go fuck yourself, Miss Fletcher, you and your Chicano friend.' His tone didn't change. Beside her, Jay felt Cruz stiffen.

'From threats of litigation to swearing and racial slurs, all in two minutes.' She grinned broadly. 'Got you rattled, Brian?'

'Not at all.'

Bullshit.

'You're still here. Still talking.'

'Maybe I like the intellectual parry and thrust.'

'I thought you said there was no such thing as "maybe" in law?' It was Jay's turn to sit back in her chair. There was a long silence.

'Do you have some final point you'd like to make?' MacDonald asked. 'Before you leave?'

'One question.'

'By all means.'

Drop the hammer.

'What was Hotplate Harry blackmailing you about – the coyote operation or burning down your own house?'

The Cherokee's headlights burned a tunnel into the night

as Cruz and Jay drove toward Santa Fe. Albuquerque was far behind and there was nothing ahead of them except blackness. It was cold, even with the heater on, and Jay sat huddled against the passenger door, arms wrapped around herself.

'You really think it worked?' asked Cruz, turning to look at her. Jay's face was pale and ghostly in the dim light from the dashboard, but there was no mistaking the triumphant expression on her face, or the glitter in her eyes.

'Yes.' She nodded. 'That's the closest you'll ever come to seeing a lawyer expressing outright panic.'

'When we left he was pouring himself another glass of wine,' said Cruz. 'That didn't look like panic to me.'

'I accused him of murder,' Jay answered. 'You said it yourself. He's a lawyer, and he's connected. If he was even halfway innocent, he would have gone off the deep end and we'd be answering a lot of hard questions at the State Attorney's Office.'

'That could still happen.'

'Not a chance,' said Jay, shaking her head. 'Ten seconds after we left the restaurant, you can bet your ass he was using a cellular phone to scream for help. It's all falling down around his ears and he knows it. He's a slime-bucket racist bastard; he's not going to take the fall alone.'

'What do you think he'll do next?'

'Ask around, try to pull in some markers with whatever clout he's got. Then he'll sit on his hands and think about it for a day or two.'

'After that?'

'We'll get a call from him asking us what kind of deal we'll offer if he rolls over on his pals – including our friend Bingham in Los Alamos.'

'I still don't see how you made that connection,' said Cruz, shaking his head.

You don't want to know.

'It was your idea. Right from the start you said there had to be some connection between the four fires. Call it cop's intuition.'

And a slip-slide through a few confidential database files. Medical files, bank accounts, the personnel directory at Los Alamos – that one was a federal crime. One felony after another.

'So let's see ... Bingham and the other guy at Los Alamos – Lowenthal – invest in Armada. Their life savings.'

'And everything they could borrow,' Jay added. 'Lowenthal had three mortgages on his house. Bingham sold his rug collection – before the fire at his house.'

'MacDonald makes some bad investments, gets into trouble, Armada's about to go down the tubes, so he torches his summer place for the insurance.'

Jay nodded. 'He puts the bite on Lowenthal and Bingham. Either they come up with some more cash, or they're going down with him. He offers the services of Hotplate Harry and they take him up on it, except Hotplate gets greedy and puts the bite on MacDonald. Blackmails him.'

'Christ!' Cruz muttered. 'Talk about tangled webs.'

He thought for a moment. 'But it still doesn't explain Symington. How is he involved in all of this?'

'He's the patsy. All the HIV stuff was fluff and flummery. A happy accident as far as Bingham was concerned. In his position it would have been easy enough to find out about Symington's explosives ticket. He was perfect. Motive and opportunity; except he didn't have a motive at all. Los Alamos paid out of court for wrongful dismissal and that was that. They set him up to take the fall. Hotplate changes his MO for the Santa Fe fires and uses condoms. The finger points at Symington, and they walk away clean.' She shook her head. 'They even set it up so the fire at Symington's would only do minor damage. Makes him look even more guilty.'

'Why do I get the feeling you were snooping around in places you shouldn't?' Cruz asked. 'None of this sounds like it was on the public record.'

Smart boy.

Jay shrugged. 'None of it has to be used as direct evidence.' She smiled. 'And you probably won't need it anyway. We've got them running scared now; they'll trip all over themselves trying to see which one of them gets to roll over first.'

Cruz still looked worried. 'Still...'

'Come on, Cruz; this is one of those times when the end really does justify the means.'

The ex-fireman let it drop.

Twenty minutes later they reached Santa Fe and Cruz dropped off Jay at the house on the ravine. Exhausted by the hectic day, she started stripping off her clothes as soon as she was through the door and almost missed the blinking light on her computer announcing that there was an E-mail message waiting for her. Tossing her skirt and blouse over the back of the couch, she padded across the darkened living room and sat down at the computer in her bra and panties. She worked the keyboard and called up the message.

'Sweet Jesus!' she whispered. 'It works.' The message was a callback from the packet-switching trace she'd suckered on to the Special K bulletin board. From what she could see, the systems operator for the bulletin board was using security measures almost as sophisticated as the tracing program she'd downloaded from the CERT people at Carnegie-Mellon. Halfway through the trace, Special K's warning system was triggered and the bulletin board shut down automatically, ending the locator sequence and crashing the trace. The CERT program had failed to track down the complete phone number of the call coming into the bulletin board, but it had scooped the area code and the first three digits: (413) 637—

Switching to the CD-ROM, Jay inserted her American Business Information Phone Directory disk and typed in the numbers. That in turn gave her the Zip code for the location: 16057. She sat back in her chair and stared at the brightly glowing screen.

'Where the hell is Slippery Rock, Pennsylvania?' she said out loud.

And who's the killer hiding there?

CHAPTER SEVENTEEN

Just after nine o'clock the following morning, William Hawkins crossed the Canadian border at Blaine, Washington, and headed north toward Vancouver, British Columbia. The first thing he noticed was a complete lack of roadside billboards and the second was the fact that Canadians seemed completely to ignore the speed limit. Other than that the only difference he could detect between the two countries was that Canadian speeds and distances were shown in kilometers rather than miles.

After he'd driven for another twenty minutes or so across a flat delta landscape faintly reminiscent of some parts of coastal Louisiana, the six-lane turnpike suddenly narrowed and he funneled into the Deas Tunnel, which ran under the south arm of the Fraser River. He emerged in the sprawling bedroom community of Richmond, with Vancouver and the hump-backed coastal range of the Canadian Rockies shimmering like a vision of Oz in the sun-drenched distance.

According to his map book, Vancouver sat on a broad

tongue of land between the North Arm of the Fraser, which he had yet to cross, and something called Burrard Inlet, a narrow fjord that broadened as it fed out to the open sea. On the far side of the inlet were the mountains.

Instead of a tunnel, the North Arm of the Fraser was spanned by a dizzying array of bridges and cloverleafs, half of which led to Vancouver Airport, the other half offering various routes into the city itself. The address he had for John Prentice was in a neighborhood called Point Grey, just north of the University of British Columbia campus and only a few blocks from a beach on Burrard Inlet called Spanish Banks.

After a confusing battle with overhead road signs that didn't seem to make any sense, he managed to find the right exit ramp and slid on to South West Marine Drive, a narrow, winding parkway flanked by hedge and high-wall houses that wouldn't have been out of place in Beverly Hills. The homes on his left stood on a high bluff overlooking the Fraser and beyond the river he'd just crossed, Hawkins could see the flat expanse of the airport. According to his own, well-developed sense of direction, he was heading almost due north now, but he was rapidly learning that accurate directions and Vancouver street signs had very little to do with each other.

A mile or so farther on, the narrow road widened and the houses gave way to dense, well-groomed stands of cedar and pine. A few minutes later the road narrowed again as he drove around the perimeter of what was obviously the university campus. Eventually he found a turnoff that led down to the ocean; and after a brief stop in a beachside parking lot to consult his map book, he found the address given to him by Sister Celandine.

Prentice lived on a side street halfway up the steep hill that climbed away from the beach. The neighborhood was an oddball mix of tiny Victorian cottages, mid-sixties rancher split-levels and ultramodern glass-and-steel confections, their outer walls stuccoed in various shades of salmon and pale blue. Prentice's house was a standard split-level, its unassuming vinyl-sided front at street level with the rear of the house perched on stilts overlooking a narrow back alleyway.

Hawkins got out of his car, went to the door, and rang the bell. He'd been thinking all the way from Bellingham about what he was going to say to the man, and he still wasn't sure. Behind the door, the inside of the house was silent. Hawkins rang the bell a second time. A few seconds later, he heard shuffling footsteps and the door opened slowly. He found himself facing a boy of eighteen or nineteen. The boy was Vietnamese or Cambodian with a light olive complexion smooth enough to be a girl's. His hair was jet-black and very long. He was wearing skin-tight, white silk pants and a bright green silk shirt with a dragon motif that wound up over the right shoulder and crossed over the chest.

'I'm looking for John Prentice.'

'*Toi khong hieu.*' The boy lifted his shoulders and smiled. Hawkins recognized the phrase – it was one of

the first he'd learned as an MP in Saigon: 'I don't
understand.' He dug into his memory, trying to remember some rudimentary phrases in Vietnamese.

'*John Prentice dau?*'

The boy shook his head and started to close the door.
'*Khong day khong day.*' Not here.

'*Dau?*' said Hawkins. He put out one hand and kept
the door open. The boy looked frightened.

'Beach,' he said. 'On beach.' He held up his hands in
front of his face and mimed using a camera. '*Chup hinh.
Xi ne, xi ne.*'

Chup hinh was photograph, but what the hell was *Xi
ne*? Then he had it. *Xi ne* was the Vietnamization of the
French word *ciné*. Prentice was on the beach with a
video camera.

Hawkins smiled, took his hand off the door, and
thanked the boy. '*Cam on ong.*'

The boy bowed back and answered with equal politeness, but he was still nervous. '*Khong co gi.*' He closed
the door softly. Hawkins turned away, went down the
path to the sidewalk, and paused. He turned and
caught the flicker of a curtain moving at the edge of
the picture window. The kid was watching. Leaving
the car where it was, Hawkins walked to the end of
the side street, then turned left and headed down the
hill to the beach.

Crossing the road at the bottom of the hill, he walked
across the parking lot and bought a coffee from the
combination concession/lifeguard station. Sipping from
the Styrofoam cup, he followed the gravel bike path,

keeping his eye out for someone using a video camera. The beach wasn't crowded, but it wasn't empty, either.

An energetic squad of senior citizens in outrageously colored satin exercise suits was doing Tai Chi under the watchful eye of a wizened old Chinese man, a group of teenage boys and a tangle-footed Irish setter wearing a neckerchief were playing Frisbee up and down the tide line, and a score of men and women in bathing suits were sprinkled over the sand, playing Russian roulette with their sunscreens.

Out in the deep water of the inlet, a dozen freighters and tankers rode at anchor, with the tree-covered flanks of the mountains rising out of the sea behind them. At the far end of the inlet, Hawkins could see the spiked skyline of the city center. Lots of bronze-tinted glass and pastel concrete, a smaller, much prettier version of Los Angeles or Houston.

At regular intervals, huge driftwood cedar logs had been dragged up above the high-tide mark for use as back rests and windbreaks. A man with a video camera was perched on one of them, his lens trying to keep pace with the movement of the boys with their Frisbee. Hawkins paused in the shade of a tree beside the bicycle path and watched.

The man was in his early forties, wearing loose, dark blue sweatpants and a short-sleeved, white T-shirt that outlined the swell of his chest and the broad muscles of his shoulders. A body builder. The man's neck was thick and corded with muscle, supporting a large, leonine head. His hair was gray-blond, tied back in a long ponytail. Not Hawkins' image of the average defrocked priest; he looked more like an aging Ed 'Kookie' Byrnes from *77 Sunset Strip* – a beach bum jock with time on his hands.

Shooting video of teenage boys.

Hawkins came out from under the shadow of the tree and stepped on to the sand. He crossed to the cedar log and stood beside the man with the video camera. 'John Prentice?'

The man hit the Stop button on the camera trigger and looked up at Hawkins.

'Do I know you from somewhere?' Not suspicious, but not particularly friendly, either. Curious.

'No. You don't know me. My name is Bill Hawkins. I was at your house. Your . . . friend told me where I could find you.'

'Kim?' Prentice smiled. 'His English must be getting better. I'm surprised you found me.'

'I speak a little Vietnamese.'

'Oh?' Something went hard in the man's voice. There weren't too may reasons for a middle-aged white American male to know any Vietnamese at all. 'Army?'

'Military Police,' Hawkins answered. 'Tour and a half in Saigon.'

'Is that how you lost the eye?' Prentice asked. His mouth had turned up in a barely perceptible sneer.

'No,' said Hawkins, keeping his voice even. 'That was a Sears Gas Barbecue. I didn't read the instructions properly.'

272

'So what do you want with me, Mr Hawkins? The war's over. Amnesty for draft dodgers and deserters.'

'I didn't think you were either.'

'No. I wasn't.'

'You were a priest.'

'You seem to know quite a bit about me, Mr Hawkins.' Prentice put down the camera carefully on the water-smoothed surface of the log. He had biceps bigger than Hawkins' calves. 'I'm not sure I like that.'

'I was just in Bellingham. Visiting your old friend Sister Celandine. She sends her love, by the way.'

Hawkins watched as the color rose in Prentice's cheeks. Quick to anger. How quick to hold that anger in check?

'Why don't you get to the point, Mr Hawkins? You've clearly got some sort of hidden agenda.'

'Ricky Stiles,' said Hawkins flatly. The color drained out of Prentice's cheeks as quickly as it had risen. His hands clenched and the thick sinews in his neck stiffened. Then the hands flexed and flattened on his thighs.

'What about him?'

'You knew him at the St Vincent's facility on Anderson Island. Befriended him.'

'At St Vincent's you could use any help you could get. It wasn't the friendliest place in the world, Mr Hawkins.'

'So I gather. From what I understand, Monsignor Pozniak was responsible for the unpleasant environment.'

'Compassion wasn't his strong suit, no.' Prentice paused. 'Who exactly are you, Mr Hawkins? And why are you so interested in Ricky Stiles? All of that was a long time ago.'

'I'm a writer, Mr Prentice, and there's no statute of limitations on murder.'

'What's that supposed to mean?'

'Ricky Stiles murdered Monsignor Pozniak, then dumped his body in the ocean.'

'Pozniak drowned.'

Hawkins ignored the comment. 'The day after the murder, you allowed Stiles to take your motorcycle and let him out of St Vincent's. He disappeared.'

'He took it without asking.'

'That's not what you told Sister Celandine. And you never reported it stolen to the police in Steilacoom, the Pierce County Sheriff's Department, or the State Highway Patrol.'

Prentice hesitated. 'I didn't want to get him into trouble.'

'Some people might say that made you an accessory to murder.'

'The monsignor's death was never investigated as a homicide. He drowned.'

'I wasn't talking about Pozniak.'

The reply caught Prentice off guard and Hawkins had been a cop long enough to recognize genuine confusion when he saw it.

'I don't understand.'

'I meant your sister, Carol.'

Prentice looked stunned. 'What does Carol have to do with Ricky Stiles?' he asked. Once again the man both looked and sounded sincere.

'You never made the connection?'

'My sister was murdered by some boy she was sleeping with. They never found out who he was.'

'I did. It was Stiles.'

The expression on the body builder's face seemed to crumple before Hawkins eyes. 'Oh Jesus!' he murmured. 'Are you sure?'

Hawkins nodded. 'Positive,' he said. 'He was in Berkeley, driving your motorcycle and calling himself Wheels. It looks as though he was living off her for a while, and then he killed her.'

Prentice looked out over the water, across to the mountains on the distant shore. 'I was out of touch then,' he said quietly. 'I'd been up here and in Europe for almost a year before I even knew she'd been killed.' He turned and looked at Hawkins. All the hardness seemed to have drained out of him and his dark eyes were brimming with tears. He took a deep, shuddering breath. 'We weren't close, not then, but I always thought...' His voice trailed off.

'That there'd be time later?' Hawkins suggested quietly.

Prentice nodded. 'I suppose so.'

'I know that feeling.' It was true; he'd felt the same way about his own father, but by the time he recognized the emotion, it was too late; his father was dead.

The two men sat silently on the log for a moment. Down the beach the Frisbee players were moving out of sight, lost in the glare. Far away, at the head of the inlet, the boxy silhouette of a freighter was plowing slowly into view.

'What about Stiles?' said Hawkins finally.

'What about him?'

'What kind of relationship did you have with him? What reason could he have had for murdering your sister?'

'Is this important, or is this just something you're going to use in a story of some kind?' There was just a hint of the earlier coldness in his voice.

'It's important,' Hawkins answered. 'Pozniak and Carol were only the first.'

'Dear God,' said Prentice. 'I didn't know.'

'Stiles,' Hawkins prompted gently.

'He was incredibly intelligent,' Prentice said after a moment. 'Raw, untutored genius. Brilliant in the original sense of the word – he shone.' Prentice shook his head wearily. 'Just the kind of boy Monsignor Pozniak loathed. Someone who marched to a different drummer, who wouldn't be cowed.'

'The monsignor chose him as a whipping boy.'

'Yes. Almost from the first time he laid eyes on him. Ricky Stiles was a dream come true and his worst nightmare made manifest.'

'How so?'

'Brains and beauty both.'

'Stiles was handsome?' It was a startling thought; in

Hawkins' mind the Iceman had always been a shadowy, faceless creature. Now he was becoming real.

'As handsome as he was intelligent.'

'Pozniak wanted him?'

'Yes.'

'But Ricky wouldn't play along.'

'That's right. Worse than that, he defended the other boys. It drove Pozniak out of his mind.'

'So the rumors about Pozniak's abuse are true?'

'I'm afraid so.' Prentice's hands flexed into fists again, then splayed impotently across his thighs. 'The only thing that kept him from actually doing him harm was his own fear. He knew how violent Ricky could be. Knew what he could do if he was pushed too far.'

'Did you know about Pozniak at the time?'

'There was no direct evidence, but I suspected. Stiles came to me about one boy in particular. He asked for my help.'

'What did you tell him?'

Prentice shrugged. 'The truth. Reality, or at least how I perceived reality then. There was nothing I could do. I'd been ordained for only two years. I was just a priest. Pozniak was well known and well liked, at least outside the Church. He had a great deal of power.' He made a small hitching noise. 'Oh, Christ! I should have done something! Anything!'

'The boy Stiles was trying to protect?'

'Yes?'

'Was Stiles his lover?'

'It's possible, I suppose. There were usually between

one and two hundred boys at St Vincent's. Such things were inevitable.'

'Was Stiles gay?'

'I think Ricky was anything he wanted to be at any given moment. He had that quality; he was able to reflect his immediate circumstances like a mirror, show you whatever you wanted to see.'

'What about you?'

'I don't understand.'

'You and Stiles. Did you have a homosexual relationship?' It was a hard question to ask and probably harder still to answer. Prentice didn't hesitate.

His voice was firm. 'No.'

'Did you want one?'

'I won't lie,' said Prentice. 'It occurred to me.'

'But you never did anything about it?'

'No.'

'Or with any of the other boys?'

'No.' A deeply rooted pain there. St Vincent's had probably been a bittersweet hell of temptation for someone like Prentice, a young priest, as unsure of his faith as he was of his sexuality.

'Did Stiles know you were gay?'

Prentice laughed, the sound harsh and brittle, like the snapping of old bones. 'I wasn't even sure that I was gay back then, Mr Hawkins. I can give you the names of a string of therapists who'll attest to that.'

'Did you ever talk to him about Carol?'

'I might have mentioned her once or twice.'

'Told him that she was going to Berkeley?'

278

'It's possible.'

'What happened to the boy – Stiles' friend?'

'He committed suicide.' He paused. 'His name was Paul, like the apostle.'

'Could Stiles have held you responsible ... because you didn't do anything when he asked you for help?'

'I held myself responsible, Mr Hawkins. I still carry the guilt for that boy's death. It's the reason I let Ricky take that old Indian of mine. It's part of the reason I left the priesthood.' He lifted one hand to his chest as though he was feeling some faint, ghostly ache in his heart.

'So he took his revenge. Murdered your sister.' Hawkins paused. It was a reasonable hypothesis, the only one he could think of that fit the facts. 'You knew Ricky Stiles; was he capable of that?'

'Yes.'

There was nothing more to say. Hawkins reached out, put his hand on the man's shoulder for a moment, then turned and walked away. Prentice's voice stopped him.

'Do you have a car?'

'Yes. Why?'

'Where are you parked?'

'In front of your house.'

'I'll walk back with you.' Prentice picked up his camera and dropped down from the log. 'There's something I want to show you. It might help.'

'What?'

'A photograph. Of Ricky.'

The Iceman sat behind the wheel of his rental car and

watched as Bill Hawkins climbed into his own vehicle and drove down the hill. His old friend Brother Faggot stood at the curb for a few seconds, then turned and went back into the house. Finally the hunter and his quarry had been joined, but which was which? The Iceman's electronic stalking of Hawkins had led him back to Ritchie and the blissful, bloody charnel house he'd left behind in Berkeley, but the one-eyed bastard had also managed to put together Anderson Island and St Vincent's. The Iceman had been too late to catch Hawkins in Bellingham, but the trip to Vancouver and Queer John meant that he'd talked to Sister Celandine. He felt the old, precious pang in his chest as he thought of her, remembering the wonder of her face as it split and broke and tore at his hands. The rising joy of his new power. Long ago. His source. He blinked; that was then.

The Iceman had seen an envelope in Hawkins' hand as he left Prentice, and he intuitively knew what it contained. The old clipping, the picture from the *Berkeley Barb*. The Iceman had seen Hawkins, but it was tit for tat – now Hawkins had seen him as well. Something would have to be done about that, and soon.

But not yet.

The Iceman stared at the slightly down-at-heel house. If the little Viet houseboy he'd spotted was any indication, Brother John had come out of the closet at long last. He tried to imagine what the inside of the house would be like. White carpets and a round bed with black satin sheets? The houseboy in a frilly apron bringing his Dear John an aromatic cup of herb tea? Tight buns and tanned thighs, depilatory smooth. Little squeals of skinny-dick passion.

He felt himself begin to harden and quickly turned away from those thoughts, making himself remember St Vincent's. Squeaking floorboards in the middle of the night. Iron beds and the *swish swish swish* of Pozniak's robes shimmering through the dark dormitory, his big fat rubber-cased flashlight thumping into the palm of his hand. The whispers.

The Iceman gripped the steering wheel and tried to make himself forget everything. Forget who he was and where he'd come from. The only moment was now. He let himself feel the pain of it all, let it build within his head like a gathering storm cloud. Give them an hour or two. Let the darkness come and the rustling leaves bring on the night. Jabberwocky time. Snicker-snack. Feed the beast.

Just you wait.

The decision had come hard and Jay still wasn't sure it was the right one. She sat at Cruz's desk in the Fire Investigation Office, staring at the white envelope she'd propped up on the keyboard of his terminal. Cruz was down at the State Attorney's Office on South Capitol Street, organizing a criminal indictment against MacDonald and his cronies. He probably wouldn't come back to the office this late, but she didn't want to chance running into him, not now. It was time to go.

She stayed where she was and lit a cigarette. The question of Symington and his involvement in the string of fires had been resolved, at least in theory. Cruz and the army of suits down at the State Capitol would eventually grind the truth out of MacDonald. But that wasn't important now. She had bigger fish to fry. If she'd been the melodramatic type, she'd have said that destiny was calling.

Go. Now. Before you change your mind. Before you chicken out.

She took a long drag on the cigarette. She'd stayed up half the night, coming up with all sorts of schemes, including an involved scenario in which she faked her own death, pointing the finger at MacDonald. By the time the sun came up, she'd even figured out how to tap a vein in her arm for blood and then how to salt the interior of the car she'd been given. Drip and spray patterns, even one shoe left behind so the forensics types would have some proof that she was the one who'd been blown away in the car.

Crazy. And worse than that – final. You can come back from a holiday, but not from the dead. This way there was at least a chance. A diminishing escape route like the closing iris of a camera, getting smaller with every passing day. But still there, a faint hope.

The letter to Cruz was easy enough to understand and easy enough to believe under the circumstances. She'd established the basic computer system for the FIO, but the banishment from her job at the FBI had taken its toll. She was depressed. She was drained. She had to go away and think. Find herself. Figure out what she wanted to do with the rest of her life. All true. Sort of. She found herself thinking about the shrink she'd talked to back home. Maybe that was the way to go: dark office, nice plants, and heartfelt confessions. Soul cleansing. The easy way out.

Bullshit.

She had more than a month of accumulated sick leave and vacation, and she was going to take it, no matter what anyone else said. If Charlie Langford or anyone else back in D.C. didn't like it, well, that was just too goddamned bad. For a while at least, she was putting herself out of the loop. But she'd be in touch, she promised.

She stubbed out the cigarette. It really was time to go. Maybe the decision she'd made was illogical, but that was irrelevant. She looked up over the terminal and glanced through the window at the far end of the room. Sunset and faint traffic sounds. The real world. *A place where she didn't belong anymore.*

Jay reached out and flipped through the Rolodex on Cruz's desk until she found the number for Capital City Cab. She put her hand on the phone and dialed. Like a character in one of her children's books, she'd gone through a mirror, held fast to an amulet, found herself inside a wardrobe, and come out changed. And what had changed her? Maybe it was anger, maybe it was guilt. And after all, guilty she certainly must be. For if she'd been able to convince the good people of Tomahawk all those years ago, then Robby Robson would have been in

283

jail on the night of July 4, 1976, instead of celebrating the Bicentennial by choking Kimberly Sue Strzoda to death because she wouldn't let him go all the way.

CHAPTER EIGHTEEN

'You want to tell me just what the hell you think you're doing?' Lt Stanley Talman, head of Berkeley Homicide Felony-Assault, stared at Hawkins. The two men were sitting in Talman's tiny office on the second floor of Berkeley Police Department headquarters. The room was barely large enough for a desk, two chairs, and a bank of filing cabinets. There was a color photograph on the wall behind Talman's head. Talman in a bathing suit, sitting at the helm of a sailboat with a blonde in a bikini snuggled up beside him. Out of focus in the background was the Golden Gate Bridge. Glory days. In the photograph the haggard-looking policeman still had hair and his waistline hadn't started to spread.

Hawkins sighed. 'I told you. I've been looking into an old case. A murder in 1968. Perry Goddard was giving me a hand. It's that simple.'

'Nothing's that simple.' Talman growled. On the desk in front of him was a tall, insulated coffee mug with a plastic seal top, a bottle of dioval anti-ulcer liquid, and an overflowing ashtray. For the last twenty minutes, he'd been lighting a string of low-tar cigarettes and sipping alternately from the coffee mug and the dioval bottle.

'Until I talked to Carol Prentice's brother in Vancouver, I assumed that Thomas Ritchie was incidental, nothing more than a secondary witness.'

'Except now he's dead and so's his wife. Twenty-four hours after you talked to them.' Talman lit another cigarette. The room was already fogged with drifting threads of smoke. 'Same MO as the Prentice girl.' He shook his head. 'A fucking baseball bat.' He took the cigarette out of his mouth and took a noisy slurp of coffee from the mug. Hawkins winced. It must be bone-cold by now. The man's stomach had to be all ulcerating sewer.

'It's a message,' said Hawkins.

'To who?' asked Talman. 'You, me, Perry fucking Goddard? The Pope?'

'Does it matter?'

'It's insane.'

'I won't argue that.'

'This guy whacks Carol Prentice in 1968, then comes back more than twenty-five years later and snuffs Ritchie and his wife exactly the same way?'

'That's it.'

'Nuts.' The homicide detective squinted through the smoke at Hawkins. 'You think it's this guy Stiles?'

'I'm sure of it.'

'But you also say that I'm not going to find him on any computer, any list, any rap sheet, is that right?'

'Right.'

'He's a fucking magician, is that what you're telling me?'

'I'm not telling you anything, Lieutenant. You called me in here, remember?'

'You came back to Berkeley because of this picture, is that right?'

'Yes.'

'Let me see it again.'

Hawkins reached into the pocket of his jacket and took out the yellowed newspaper clipping he'd been given by John Prentice in Vancouver. It was from the April 12, 1968 issue of the *Berkeley Barb* and showed a picture of two young men running gleefully toward the camera. Behind them half a dozen policemen in riot gear were in hot pursuit. The caption read '*Outrunning the Pigs in the park.*' According to Prentice the boy on the left was Ricky Stiles. The boy on the right was a young Thomas Ritchie. Stiles had sent the clipping to Prentice care of the Draft Dodger Clinic in Vancouver, where he had received it sometime in May or early June. There had been a short note attached to the swatch of newsprint: '*Already famous, or should that be infamous?*'

Hawkins handed the clipping to Talman. The detective puffed on his cigarette, staring at it. 'This is the Wheels character from the Prentice case?'

'That's what her brother in Vancouver says.'

'I'll be fucked. Ritchie never said anything about knowing him.'

'He met Carol in June; this clipping is from April. Ritchie knew Stiles long before either one of them knew Carol Prentice. Ritchie lied.'

'Looks like the lie caught up with him,' said Talman. 'You mind if I take a photocopy of this?' He held up the clipping.

'Be my guest.'

Talman left the office. He came back a few minutes later with several copies of the clipping. He handed one to Hawkins. Talman had used the photocopy to enlarge the photograph to almost twice its original size. Any doubt about Ritchie's identity vanished.

'Thought you might like one.'

'Thanks.'

Talman looked carefully at Hawkins. 'You're sure there's no Bureau involvement in this? I'm not stepping into some kind of Fed intrigue?'

'No. I'm on my own.'

'Good,' said Talman, relaxing visibly. 'Life is fucking difficult enough.' He paused. 'You want to see where it went down?'

'It might help.'

'Come on.'

By the time they reached the house on Stephen's Way, the block-long street had been cleared of police cars, emergency vehicles, and the media. The only thing left to mark it as a crime scene were the loops and sagging lengths of yellow barrier ribbon, wrapping the house and grounds like some sad birthday package.

'Christ!' Hawkins muttered as Talman led him through the front door. The walls of the slate-floored hallway were speckled and blotched with brown. A huge spray of it arced along the left-hand wall, fine dots of dried blood going as high as the ceiling. One of Talman's forensics people had outlined an irregular stain on the slate with white tape and a tape arrow had been put in place beside a strip of blood that led down the hall.

'Follow the yellow brick road,' Talman grunted. They went down the hall to the living room. The strip of blood reached the white wall-to-wall carpeting and continued into the center of the room. There was a sticky puddle of red brown smeared on the glass top of the coffee table. 'Looks like he was waiting for her behind the front door,' Talman said, lighting a cigarette and looking down at the coffee table. 'Hit her once with the bat. M.E. said it split her skull like a melon. Then he dragged her by the heels into the living room and put her on the coffee table.'

'Organized,' Hawkins commented, referring to the difference between a murder where the victim is killed and left in place, and the one where the victim is arranged and put on display.

'Whatever,' Talman answered skeptically. Not a man who made too many distinctions when it came to violent crime.

'Was she mutilated?'

'You don't want to know,' said Talman.

'What about Ritchie?'

Talman hooked his finger and took Hawkins across the room to the sliding-glass doors leading out on to a narrow cedar deck. He pointed down. Hawkins could see nothing but treetops and the fresh scars of newly broken branches. 'Found him in the ravine. Knees were smashed; so were the arms and all the fingers on both hands. Teeth broken and the M.E. says there's evidence that he was choked, probably with a length of surgical hose, and then revived, maybe three or four times. Then he used the bat on him, one last time.'

'The other injuries were all ante mortem?'

'So the doc says.'

'Tortured.'

'Looks like it. When your boy Stiles was done, he went upstairs and took a shower. Might be some good stuff there for forensics. Take a while to find out.'

'Something spooked him,' said Hawkins, looking down into the ravine again. He turned and went back into the living room.

Talman followed him. 'Why do you say that?'

'Careless,' said Hawkins, looking around the room. 'Not like him at all.'

'Where do you get careless?' said Talman. 'He took them out and got away clean. You say he's untraceable. I don't call that careless. I call that getting away with murder.'

Hawkins shook his head. 'Stiles is crazy, but he's not a

fool. He didn't do this on a whim. He was worried. That's what brought him back here after all these years.'

'Worried about what?'

'Me. The fact that I was snooping around in the Carol Prentice case.'

'How the hell would he know that?'

'I'm not sure,' said Hawkins. 'But he knew.' He swept a hand around the room. 'This is a cover-up. Stiles came back to clean house.'

'Cover up what? Jesus man, its been almost thirty years.'

'I found out that Thomas Ritchie was lying. He knew Stiles, was friends with him. Maybe he was lying about something else as well. Something that worried our killer.'

'Like what?'

Hawkins shrugged. 'I don't know, but it was important. So important it brought Stiles out of the woodwork.'

'I can't see it,' said Talman.

'Neither can I. Yet,' Hawkins answered. 'Where's Perry Goddard?'

Talman grinned coldly. 'At his bookstore. Keeping a low profile and wondering if I'm going to bust his fucking chops for letting you see the Prentice stuff. He thinks I'm going to try and get his pension cut off.'

'You want me clear of all of this? Out of the picture?'

'Fuck no!' breathed Talman. 'That photograph you showed me is the only lead I've got.' He paused, hesitating for a few seconds. 'Just so long as I don't wind up with egg all over my face, Hawkins.'

'No egg. I'm going to need Goddard, and I'm going to need the Prentice file again.'

'You really think you're going to find anything in all that old shit?'

'Yes. Something that was overlooked back in 1968. Something that scared the hell out of Ricky Stiles.'

Jay flew in to Pittsburgh and then drove right out again. According to the brochures, it was a cosmopolitan hub of culture second only to Paris, or Philadelphia at the very least, but she'd seen the truth as they cut through the iron-gray smog above Greater Pittsburgh International Airport. The city was a dark stain on the landscape, and no cultural cosmetics were going to change the fact that it was rooted in puddled steel and petroleum byproducts and had been for more than a hundred years. Pittsburgh was the city that Hollywood had chosen for movies about being born on the wrong side of the tracks. At night the furnaces and mills and refineries probably glowed like the fires of hell.

She rented a car, found the Airport Parkway, and went south to Interstate 79. Then she turned due north. Somewhere between Albuquerque and the Appalachians, any second thoughts she'd had about what she was doing seemed to slip away into some hidden corner of her mind. She was perfectly aware that what she was contemplating had more than a hint of madness to it, but it just didn't seem to matter. Her course was set, the decision made. Like skydiving for the first time; once you jumped out of the plane there was no way to change your mind. One way or the other, like it or not, the next stop was ground zero.

Forty minutes later she slid off the interstate, turned on to State Highway 108, and rolled into the town of Slippery Rock, Pennsylvania. According to the sign it had a population of twenty-two thousand and was proud to be home to about a dozen service organizations. She found a motel on the edge of town, checked in, and then had a look at the telephone directory; it was less than a hundred pages, White and Yellow pages combined.

From what she could tell, most of the business district was on South Main Street, with the rest of it strung out along route 108. According to the brochure from the Slippery Rock Heritage Society she found in her night table, the town had once been a bustling steel and oil center, but now its economy depended largely on the state college on the western outskirts. There was a police department, a courthouse, and a fire hall on East Water Street, at least ten automotive-parts stores, and a rape/pregnancy crisis center. All the modern conveniences. The map in the front of the phone book showed two rivers, a flying club, a drag strip, and a shopping center. Unfortunately, it didn't show her where she could find the local serial killer.

Putting aside the phone book, Jay showered, changed

into jeans and a T-shirt, then went on a walking tour. Zoning in the town was obviously fairly slack. Old wooden houses stood beside cinderblock machine shops, setbacks from the streets didn't follow any strict pattern, sidewalks came and went, and there were trees everywhere. The overall effect was surprisingly agreeable. In the midaftenoon sun, Slippery Rock gave the impression of being a pleasant, slightly down-at-heel Anytown, USA, nestled in a shallow river valley, surrounded by low rolling hills.

The town center was formed by the intersection of 108 and South Main. Three sides of the crossroads were built up, but the southern side was still open field, cut through at an angle by a meandering creek. Four or five blocks down South Main, the street became State Highway 258 again, and off to the left Jay could see the large, sprawling campus of Slippery Rock State College. To the left of the campus, in the slanting shadow cast by an old-fashioned water tank on stilts, Jay could also see a chain-link enclosure and a set of squat cinderblock buildings that was almost certainly a low-security prison of some kind.

Jay turned around and headed back for the center of town. The trace she'd put on Special K had been specific – the call she'd trapped with it had come from here; but how did a killer keep from giving himself away in a place as small as this? Living in Slippery Rock would be a glass-house existence; most of your friends were also your cousins and everyone knew the state of your bank account and your marriage. If you wanted to have an affair with your neighbor, you probably had to do it in a motel across the county line.

The direct approach – going to the police station – was out of the question. Proper channels and due process, all the short cuts and perquisites of an FBI agent, were denied to her now; it was just the hunter and the hunted. Thinking that, she shivered even though the sun was still warm on her shoulders as she made her way back to the motel.

Which is which?

Back in her room she went through the phone book again, jotting down names and numbers that might come in handy. For a town of its size, Slippery Rock was thick with state and federal agencies, all of which would be computerized. Get into one and she could probably get into them all, even if it meant using the bypass codes from Cruz and playing electronic hopscotch across the country.

If necessary, she could also use her own access codes to get into VICAP and the other Bureau databases, although that was a much riskier proposition; entry into the huge mainframes in Washington and Quantico would leave footprints no matter how carefully she tiptoed through them. On the other hand, those mainframes were accessed legitimately ten thousand times a day; the chances of anyone noticing a single, errant peek through the keyhole was remote. If she was lucky, the monolithic bureaucracy she'd hated so much would be her best defense.

Luckily, the telephone in her room didn't run through

a switchboard. She unplugged it from the jack in the wall, replaced it with a line from her laptop, and used the built-in modem to 'phreak' her way out on to an unregistered line. Unregistered lines were normally used by the phone company to check their equipment and were numberless as far as the computers were concerned. Phone phreaks had discovered the invisible lines years ago and used them to place unrecorded long-distance calls.

Jay set the necessary parameters on the modem and started up the program. It would take a while, but eventually it would log any telephone line in the Slippery Rock area that used a computer modem. That, hopefully, would narrow things down a bit. She checked her watch; it was just after three. There was no local newspaper in Slippery Rock, which meant she'd have to drive into Butler, twenty miles away.

In comparison to Slippery Rock, Butler, the county seat, was a thriving metropolis, complete with a large courthouse and a jail in the middle of town and its own bus line. The buildings downtown were predominantly brick and locally quarried stone, with a sprinkling of glass-and-concrete blockhouses rising ten or twelve stories, appearing to prove that the bustling little city of a hundred thousand had a future as well as a past. From what Jay could see on the way into town, its economy depended on Pullman-Standard, America's Largest Manufacturer of Freight Cars, and the sprawling Armco steelworks just outside the western city limits.

The Butler *Eagle* occupied a low brick building on

West Diamond Street, tucked in behind the neo-Gothic courthouse with its church spire clock tower and the grim-looking jail building. The 'murder' folder in the newspaper's archives was depressingly thin. In the last ten years, the majority of homicides were domestic and usually involved alcohol at one level or another. During the same period, there had been only four killings in Slippery Rock. Two were husband-and-wife disputes, one later turned out to be a suicide, and the fourth was an accidental murder that took place during a gas-station holdup. There were even fewer missing-persons cases in the archives, and none at all in Slippery Rock.

Which meant one of two things – either her quarry lived in Slippery Rock but chose his victims elsewhere, or he was fabricating the killings completely, making up stories to boast about on the Special K bulletin board. Of the two alternatives, the first seemed the most likely to Jay. She knew intuitively that SK-WIZ would have picked off an impostor almost immediately; Special K was no place for amateurs or liars. She grimaced as she closed the file folder; God only knew what the initiation rites were to become a member of the Wiz's select little group of demons.

So, unless the computer in her hotel room came up with something, she was at a dead end. She thought for a moment, then on a hunch reopened the murder file. More than half of the clippings had the same byline – Christy Skeed. She returned the file folders to the archive librarian and went upstairs to the editorial offices, but the *Eagle*'s lady crime reporter was out on assignment and no one knew when she'd be back. Acting on a second hunch, Jay left the building and went back out on to West Diamond. Leaving her car where it was, she walked the short block up on to Main Street and found what she was looking for less than a hundred feet from the Courthouse – a greasy spoon cafe called Phil's.

The little restaurant was a hole in the wall between a shoe store and Butler Smokes, a combination newsstand and tobacco shop. It was late afternoon now and Phil's was empty except for an immensely fat man in a dirty apron who was scraping a day's worth of bacon grease and hamburger cinders off the grill behind the counter – probably Phil himself.

Jay sat down on one of the red leatherette stools. Places like Phil's didn't exist in Washington or Santa Fe anymore, miniature jukeboxes like a row of chrome-and-plastic tombstones on a Formica countertop, the mouthwatering stench of ancient french fry grease soaked eternally into the pale green walls, five small booths opposite the counter, and a huge brass cash register at the front showing NO SALE. There was a spike beside the cash register almost completely filled with Thank You, Call Again receipts.

Phil's was doing a land office business and Jay was pretty sure the receipts were only the tip of the iceberg. She was willing to bet that good old Phil rang up only every second or third meal tab on the register to keep the IRS happy and slipped the rest into some cavernous pocket underneath that apron. Most of it probably came from an assortment of cops, lawyers, and newshounds, since Phil's was the closest eatery to both the courthouse and the *Eagle* offices.

The fat man behind the counter continued his scraping for a moment longer, then turned, wiping his shovel-sized hands on the apron. He was in his fifties with a broad, Slavic face creased with the kind of lines you get from smiling a lot.

'Help you, lady?'

'You're Phil?'

'In the flesh, and lots of it.' The smile switched on and the creases vanished. 'Phil Kowalchuk.'

'Jennifer Smith.'

'Pleased to meet you. What can I get you, breakfast, lunch or dinner?'

'Christy Skeed.'

'What about her?' The smile lost a bit of its intensity, but not much.

'She come in here very much?'

'Every day.'

Two points for intuition.

Jay put on her own best smile. 'Breakfast, lunch or dinner?'

'Sometimes all three. Why?'

'I'd like to talk to her.'

'Police?'

'Statistician,' she answered. The wide expanse of Phil's sweat-shiny forehead wrinkled.

'That's a new one.'

'We're putting together a statistical database on

regional crime,' said Jay. 'I thought Ms Skeed could help me out.'

'You try the *Eagle*?'

'Not there.'

'She'll be along,' said Phil. 'Find a booth and I'll get you some coffee. I'll send Christy over when she comes in.'

'Okay.' Jay stood up. She glanced appreciatively around the room. 'When I was a kid, we had a place like this in my hometown. The owner baked all kinds of pies. I don't suppose you do that kind of thing?'

The smile blossomed hugely. 'Apple, blueberry, peach cobbler, rhubarb, pumpkin in season, and lemon meringue all year round.'

Jay put the back of her hand up to her forehead and pretended to swoon. 'Are you married?'

'Thirty-two years.' Phil beamed. 'Who do you think does the baking and how do you think I got this way?' He slapped his belly with a meaty hand.

'Too bad.' Jay sighed. 'Lemon meringue.'

Half an hour and two slices of pie later, Christy Skeed slid into the booth across from Jay. She was in her midtwenties and had a shaggy cap of red-blond hair, a round, freckled face, and the strangest eyes Jay had ever seen. One was blue, the other brown, and both seemed touched by tiny flecks of gold.

'My grade-two teacher thought I was possessed by the Devil,' said the woman. 'The evil eye or the mark of Cain or something. There's a scientific name for it, but I can't remember what it is.'

Jay flushed with embarrassment. 'I didn't mean to stare.'

The reporter shrugged. 'Feel free. Everybody does. I don't mind.'

Phil brought her a cup of coffee and a slice of apple pie with cheese and ice cream. She took a sip of the coffee, sighed with contentment, and began attacking the pie. Jay started to put out her cigarette, but the woman shook her head. 'Keep smoking. Everybody at the office does. Only public building in Butler County where you can still get lung cancer without guilt.' Phil returned with the coffeepot, topped up Jay's mug, beamed at Christy, and went away again.

'You're the crime reporter for the *Eagle*.'

'Right. Phil says you wanted to talk to me about crime statistics?'

'That's part of it.'

Christy took another sip of coffee, gave Jay a quick assessing look, then went back to her pie. 'What's the rest of it?' she asked around a mouthful of apple and ice cream.

'Slippery Rock.'

'A small town in western Pennsylvania. Home of Slippery Rock State College, of which I am a graduate, and not very much else. What about it?'

Jay finished her cigarette and took a sip of the fresh coffee. 'Let me put it this way,' she said, putting down her cup. 'We've taken a special interest in Slippery Rock.'

'You're a Fed, aren't you?' said Christy. She licked her

fork and used the flat of it to pick up the last few crumbs of pie crust on her plate.

'I work with them.'

Not really a lie.

'I don't even know your name.'

'My name's Jennifer Smith.'

'This is about the letters, isn't it?' The reporter reached out, took a cigarette from Jay's pack, and lit it. She leaned back in her seat, puffing thoughtfully. The different colored eyes had an almost hypnotic effect.

'It might be,' Jay answered carefully.

What letters?

Christy shrugged. 'We haven't had one for a year. Old news now, if it was ever news at all. I'm surprised you guys are interested.'

'Why don't you tell me what you know?'

Christy took another puff on her cigarette and made a small snorting sound. 'That's supposed to be my question.'

'If there's anything in it, you'll get the scoop first, how's that?'

'All right. How much have you got on this already?'

'Pretend I don't know anything.'

That was true enough.

'Six letters spread out over two years, about one every four months.'

'Sent to the *Eagle*?'

'Yes. The first two went to Bernie Lane. Then he took a job with a paper in Boston. After I took over the crime beat, the letters started coming directly to me. Actually it was the same letter, four times.'

'Photocopies?'

'No. Printed by hand. Different colored pen each time.' She closed her eyes. 'Blue, green, red, then a sort of purple shade.'

'What did the letters say?'

'Like I said, it was always the same: "The bad seed must be rooted out and the soil of the sinner made barren. Thus we shall be redeemed." Crank stuff.'

'Signature?'

'No. But there were always a few hairs taped to the bottom of the page.'

'Hairs? What kind of hairs?'

'Human hairs. Very fine, like a baby or an old man.'

'Did you give the letters to the police?'

'Tried,' said Christy, taking a swallow of coffee. 'State Police said there was no evidence of a crime so they didn't want to touch it. The cops in Slippery Rock weren't interested either.'

'Why did you try and give the letters to the Slippery Rock Police?'

'The letters were postmarked Slippery Rock. Mailed at the post office.'

'What did you do then?'

Christy shrugged. 'Checked it out the best I could.'

'No missing old men? No missing babies?'

'No. Closest thing was an old lady with Alzheimer's who wandered off at Slippery Rock Park. Fell into Glade Run Creek and drowned.'

'You never had the hairs examined by a forensics lab?'

'I've got Ebenezer Scrooge for a boss.' Christy laughed. 'No budget for that kind of thing.'

'And then the letters just stopped coming?'

'Yes.' She nodded. 'About a year ago.'

'Nothing since?'

'No. I figure he moved away, or got bored.' She shrugged again. 'Anyway, there was no story in it.'

Jay thought for a moment. 'Was there anything strange about the letters, other than the hairs and the colored ink?'

'The printing was very neat, very precise. Like an architect, or a draftsman.'

'No spelling errors, no screwy grammar?'

'No.'

'The paper?'

'Ordinary typewriter paper.'

'Envelope?'

'The same.' She paused, frowning. 'Wait. There was one other thing.'

'Yes?'

'Whoever sent those letters smoked a pipe. I remember thinking that when I opened the first one. It was the same for the other three.'

'Why a pipe?'

'My dad smokes one. Has for as long as I can remember. My mom still complains about the stink on his clothes. The same smell was on the paper and inside the envelope.'

'Any particular kind of smell?' Jay asked.

'Sweet,' the reporter answered. 'Like cherries.'

The Iceman sat in the darkened room, face lit by the glow of the screens, playing the game, again and again, refining, changing, his deft fingers spinning over the keys like fire. The game was the lure, and the bait had to be kept fresh at all times. In the beginning the landscape of the game had been an ethereal thing of words and concepts, attracting only the most sophisticated players, like Christie, his first, the psychiatrist in Baltimore who liked little girls so much. The technology had changed, though, and using a dozen different sources, from Flight Simulator to complex fractal imaging systems, he'd built up a real world of mountains, lakes, deserts, and valleys, of castles and dungeons, of mansions and hidden chambers, all of them so real that even players like Billy Ray, the AIDS freak from Taladega, Alabama, could enjoy them.

There was a score of players actively engaged in the game and for most of them the world he'd created was far more real than the one in which they lived and breathed and killed. On the Net, each one of them was free to be himself, to tell his story, to act out his dreams without restraint or fear. He'd even had a few joking, private on-line chats with Christie about the therapeutic value of the game and Special K in general. The psychiatrist made a fair case for the game as a viable assimilation tool, removing the social stigma of deviant behavior in an environment where deviance was a norm.

It was inevitable, at least to Christie, that their shared avocation for sudden death would eventually be accepted by the outside world as nothing more than a fact of daily life, with no more moral weight put upon it than the predatory habits of a swooping owl or any other animal that hunted in darkness. As Christie put it, in a world gone mad, who was there to call any one of them insane?

He sat back in his chair and watched the room he'd just created take shape on the screen directly in front of him. He'd built the chamber for Seefeld, the latest member to be accepted into Special K. In it, the German could re-create his hammer-wielding rituals for all of them to enjoy.

The room was a graduation gift. Seefeld was the first member from a foreign country and for a long time the Iceman had watched him meandering around the upper levels of the game, logging on and logging off erratically. Initially, he appeared to be an ordinary hacker with a penchant for violent Multi-user Dungeons and Dragons gaming, but eventually he found the trapdoors and demanded entrance into the real Special K.

All the players had been nervous about accepting someone from another country, if only because satellite transatlantic use of the Internet was more vulnerable to surveillance, but the Iceman had been intrigued. He asked Seefeld for his bona fides and was presented with a string of child kidnappings, killings, and mutilations going back for three years. After consulting with Christie, the Iceman put a trace on Seefeld the next time he came through the upper level trapdoors and followed him back to the Austrian city of Linz, Adolf Hitler's home town, which seemed appropriate enough.

From Linz, the Iceman tracked Seefeld through the EUnet to Munich. From there he accessed three different news agency databases, where he checked Seefeld's story. Dates, times and events matched perfectly, but the Iceman wasn't satisfied. He asked Seefeld for detailed information about his crimes not available to the press, then checked those against the computerized police files. Once again the details matched. As a final test, the Iceman asked Seefeld for the date and location of his next crime. The German did so willingly, and this morning, right on schedule, news of another child kidnapping appeared on the German wire services.

The Iceman nodded approvingly at the finished image on the screen. When he booted up the game and the bulletin board that evening, he'd import the new file and leave a double {[:> smiley message for Seefeld to show that he'd been accepted into the group. He smiled happily in the darkness. The chamber he'd designed for Seefeld bore a remarkable resemblance to Father John's little den of iniquity in Vancouver. He was particularly proud of how he'd handled the white marble fireplace and the sprays of blood across the pale mottled surface. The sooty remains of the houseboy forced up the chimney was a nice touch as well.

He laughed softly and began to hum a Leonard Cohen song. It was one of his favorites: 'First We Take Manhattan, Then We Take Berlin.'

CHAPTER NINETEEN

The Carol Prentice files were spread out all over Perry Goddard's apartment above the bookstore. Some of it was pinned to the easels they'd borrowed from Felony Homicide, some was piled on the coffee table in front of the leather couch, and the rest was scattered across the living-room floor. The two men had been working on it since late the previous afternoon and both of them looked haggard and tired.

Goddard was sprawled in his reclining chair, a Corona in his hand. Hawkins sat on the couch, staring at the easels set up on the far side of the coffee table.

'Nothing,' said Goddard. He belched noisily and sat forward, the recliner squeaking as it moved with him. 'It was all done by the book. We didn't miss a trick.' He shook his head. 'This is all bullshit. We're chasing after a ghost.'

'A ghost didn't crush Claire Ritchie's skull with a baseball bat which he then used to rape her; Ricky Stiles did.'

'And you say he did it because of something from the original murder?'

'Yes. I'm sure of it.'

'Why?' asked Goddard. 'The guy's a nutbar. Maybe he just came back for old times' sake; maybe he just wanted to finish up what he started.'

'No,' said Hawkins, shaking his head.

'Why not?'

'Because it doesn't fit the pattern. It's not the way Stiles does it.' He shook his head again. 'No. He came back because we were getting too close.'

'Too close to what?' said Goddard, exasperated. 'If it's something we didn't pick up on back in 'sixty-eight, why would we see it now?'

'I don't know.'

'Yeah?' grunted Goddard. 'Well, neither do I.' He waved a hand at the mess surrounding them. 'I don't see anything except a bunch of paper that doesn't add up to a goddamned thing.'

'It's here,' said Hawkins.

Goddard snorted. 'You're just as crazy as Stiles. He's worried about something that isn't there, and you're on a wild goose chase looking for the same thing.'

'You missed the fact that Thomas Ritchie knew Stiles before either one of them hooked up with Carol Prentice. If you missed that, maybe you missed something else.'

'Oh Christ!' moaned Goddard.

'Go through it again,' said Hawkins. 'Step by step.'

'All right.' Goddard let out a long, sighing breath and flopped back into the arms of the reclining chair. 'One more time.'

'Who called it in?' Hawkins prompted.

'A girl named Maureen Donegan. Just an acquaintance. They were supposed to be going shopping. The Donegan girl finds the front door of the apartment open, goes in, and finds Prentice. She freaks out, but she makes the call. We roll the closest unit and that's how it goes down.'

'Then what?'

'The unit calls for Felony Homicide. My partner Eddie Cochran catches it. He goes out for a look and calls for the meat wagon and the ID boys. I was in court giving evidence in another case. By the time I got there, they'd already taken away the stiff.'

'What was going on when you got to the apartment?'

'They were still taking pictures. Eddie was having a fight with one of the guys from Narcotics.'

'About the drugs that were found on the premises?'

'Yeah. The Narc wanted the stuff, but Eddie insisted that it was evidence for Felony Homicide.'

'How was it resolved?'

'I told the Narc to take a flying fuck at himself.'

'That was that?'

'That was that.'

'Then what?'

'Then nothing,' said Goddard. 'Eddie went off to talk to the neighbors and to round up Ritchie.'

'How did you know about Ritchie?'

'The Donegan girl.'

'Did she know Stiles as well?'

'Only as Wheels.'

'What happened then?'

'It's in my notes. I helped the ID guys bag the drugs and do the evidence inventory. We put a seal on the door, took the evidence to the Property Room, and that was it.'

'Everything from then on took place away from the apartment? The interviews with the Donegan girl, Ritchie, the Prentice girl's other friends?'

'Yeah.'

Hawkins chewed on his lower lip. 'Which put Stiles out of the loop, even if he had stuck around.'

'I don't get you.'

'Stiles came back after almost thirty years because he was frightened. He killed Ritchie because of something Ritchie knew.'

'How about the fact that the two of them knew each other?'

'That's not enough. It was something from the past that could hurt him now, in the present.'

'Like what, for Christ sake!? We've been over this a dozen times already.'

'Ritchie knew something about Stiles. Something that Ritchie might not even have remembered.'

Goddard nodded slowly. 'Until you came along to refresh his memory?'

'Maybe.'

'Something personal?' offered Goddard. 'It had to be

312

something no one else would know.' He shrugged. 'Maybe Ritchie was a fag or something. From what you tell me, it sounds as though Stiles goes both ways, or at least he did.'

'That wouldn't do it.'

'Then what?'

'Something personal,' said Hawkins softly. He shuffled through the file folders and stacks of papers on the coffee table. 'You said you did an evidence inventory?'

'The folder with the blue tab,' said Goddard, pointing. Hawkins picked up the file and began going through the pages. There didn't seem to be anything out of the ordinary. Beyond the physical evidence such as bloodstains, the file was mostly concerned with the drugs and drug paraphernalia that had been discovered on the premises. Various bongs and pipes, rolling papers, perfume vials with hashish oil residue, a four-pipe hookah. Standard hippie utensils for the era.

The inventory also included a list of Carol Prentice's cosmetics and other private effects, mostly taken from the bathroom in the apartment. Seen in the light of her known sexual history, the list told an interesting tale. Pink clamshell Ortho diaphragm case; a rolled-up, partially used tube of Blue Ointment, which meant crab lice in the recent past; K-Y lubricating jelly; and an unopened box of Tampax.

According to the investigative report done by Goddard and his partner, a check with the Berkeley Free Clinic showed that Carol Prentice had been two and a half months pregnant at the time of her death. The Free

Clinic also had a record of her bout with crabs, a cured case of gonorrhea, an ongoing problem with nonspecific urethritis, and her original prescription for a diaphragm during her first week at UC Berkeley the previous year. In other words, the young woman had been quite promiscuous. There was also a note in the Free Clinic file indicating that Carol had been *virgo intacta* at the time of the fitting for the contraceptive device. Pure and innocent out of Rochester, Carol Prentice had obviously joined the Free Love Generation with enthusiasm.

Hawkins went back to the evidence inventory. In addition to the sex-related goodies there was a medicine chest full of over-the-counter remedies and four different prescription drugs, including one for belladonna and another for a high-octane inhalant.

'She had some kind of bronchial trouble?'

'Asthma.' Goddard nodded from his chair. 'We even checked with her doctor in Rochester. She also had a major hay fever problem.'

Along with the drugs for her asthma there was a listing for a pill bottle found beside the bed. No prescription label. There were six capsules in the plastic container, all the same – white with a red stripe through the middle and a code on either side of the stripe, P.D. 387.

'There were some pills beside the bed,' said Hawkins.

'There were pills everywhere, for Christ's sake.'

'These didn't have a prescription label.'

Goddard shrugged his shoulders. 'Doesn't ring a bell.'

'Which way did the mattress face, can you remember?'

Goddard struggled with the question for a moment. 'North,' he said finally. 'Foot toward the door.'

'If you were standing at the end of the mattress, which side was Carol found on?'

'The right, lying on her side. He whacked her left-handed, remember?'

'But from the head of the mattress, it would be reversed. As far as Carol was concerned, she slept on the right side.'

Goddard pictured it in his head, then nodded. 'Check.' He frowned. 'So what?'

'My first question. Which side of the mattress were the pills found on?'

'There should be a diagram at the end of the report.'

Hawkins flipped to the last page. He nodded to himself. The ID code for the pill bottle in the inventory matched the circled number on the left-hand side of the mattress. 'The left.'

'Like I said, so what?' said Goddard.

'Men tend to sleep on the side of the bed that leaves their writing hand free,' Hawkins answered. 'The hand they use to caress with when they're having sex.'

'I wouldn't know,' Goddard said. 'It's been so goddamn long I don't remember. But I still don't see what difference it makes.'

'Relative to the person in the bed, the pills were found on the left side. Which means they probably belonged to a left-handed person.'

'Shit!' breathed Goddard, sitting forward in the chair again. 'Stiles.'

'You never checked to see what the pills were for?'

'Give me a break.' Goddard snorted. 'Berkeley was drug city back then, and it wasn't a narcotics case anyway.'

'True enough,' said Hawkins.

'So how do we find out what they were? All the evidence will have been tossed years ago.'

'It shouldn't be too hard,' said Hawkins. He went to the phone, used a Bureau calling code, and connected with the FBI Laboratory Division in Washington. He read off the pill numbers from the evidence inventory and waited. He had his answer within five minutes.

'Well?' asked Goddard as Hawkins returned to the couch.

'P.D. 387 and the white-and-red capsule is the old designation for a drug named phenacemide. Its active ingredient is a chemical called phenurone.'

'Sounds like an antibiotic. Maybe he had the clap, too.'

'It's an anticonvulsant,' murmured Hawkins.

'Seizures, fits, that kind of thing?'

'Yes,' said Hawkins. 'It was introduced back in the sixties to replace phenobarbital.'

'For what?'

'Epilepsy.' There was a note of triumph in Hawkins' voice. 'That's why Stiles came back. Thomas Ritchie knew that Ricky was an epileptic.'

* * *

Jay Fletcher had come awake in her motel room just after sunrise with drying tears on her cheeks and no memory of her dreams. For some reason she felt over-whelmed by a tremendous sadness that went far beyond herself. Her heart ached for the world, and that, of course, was ridiculous. She tried to shake off the feeling by going for a run through Slippery Rock's dozing streets and wound up at a bakery on South Main that was just opening for business. She bought a still-warm muffin and a cup of scalding coffee and went back to the motel. While the coffee cooled, she took a quick shower, then she sat down at the computer.

Returning from Butler the previous evening, she'd found that her search program had snagged twenty phones in the calling area that were connected to modems. A quick check with her CD-ROM phone directory showed that twelve of those lines were con-nected to Slippery Rock State College, eight to the library, and four to individual offices.

Another modem was located at the District Magis-trate's Office on Franklin Street, the fourteenth at the police station on East Water Street, the fifteenth at the Slippery Rock Area School District Office on Kiester Road, and the sixteenth at the rape/pregnancy clinic, located in the same building as the District Magistrate.

The only commercial modem in use was one at the Slippery Rock Giant Eagle store in the plaza on the northern edge of town. That left three modems being used by private individuals. Using the CD-ROM again, she backtracked the numbers and found the names, jotting them down on a piece of motel stationary:

Dr Evelyn Kushinski, Grove City Road
John Gordon, P. Eng., Maltby Street
Elias M. Telfer, Elm Street

Jay chewed on the edge of her Styrofoam coffee cup and peered down at the sheet of paper. She could rule out Dr Kushinski, since women serial killers were virtually nonexistent, and John Gordon, the Engineer on Maltby Street was probably a poor choice, too; serial killers in the professions were rare, and especially in the practical ones like accountancy, the physical sciences, or engineering. That left her with Elias Telfer, whoever he was.

On the other hand, she couldn't really rule out the commercial and institutional modem lines. It was possible that her man was using a line at the college library, the District School Office, or even the Giant Eagle. She exchanged the coffee cup for a cigarette, trying to imagine a clerk at the Giant Eagle slipping into the store after-hours to chat with SK-WIZ. Somehow it didn't seem very likely.

'Shit,' she muttered. The predatory optimism she'd felt the previous day was fading fast, and she was irritated with herself for thinking it was going to be easy. Her ability to use the computer without the normal constraints concerning the rules of evidence was a definite advantage, but it wasn't a magic wand.

She waited until nine o'clock, then put in a call to Christy Skeed at the Butler *Eagle*. The crime reporter hadn't yet come in to work, so Jay left a message, asking her to check the three names on her list. With that done she packed away the computer, left her room, and drove to the state college campus.

The college was located on what had once been the gentle slopes of an Indian gathering place called Kus Kuskuski, or the Sugar Maples. A stand of the maples was still there, but most of the meadowlike hillside was covered in a patchwork of modern buildings bound together by a web of walkways and roads.

For Jay it was like going into the past, and she found herself feeling slightly disoriented by a sense of emotional vertigo – Slippery Rock State College wasn't too far removed from her own alma mater at the University of Ohio. Fresh-faced girls in kilts and white blouses, clutching piles of books against their chests, boys slouching beer-eyed out of high-rise dorm units with bags of laundry over their shoulders.

The bicycles of her era had been replaced by Rollerblades, the old VW bugs changed into neon-tinted Honda Civics proudly displaying the requisite Grateful Dead decals. Piss and vinegar days, as her father used to call them. Days when you thought you knew everything even though you'd barely tasted life at all. She felt the dawn sadness well up in her again as she drove along Campus Drive toward the library and had to blink away the rising tears, fighting them off with a burst of anger at herself for being such a sentimental jerk. She found

319

an angled slot in front of the seventies-style concrete building, parked, and then went up the broad flight of steps to the main entrance.

The Slippery Rock State College Library facility was like a thousand other facilities of its kind from coast to coast. An educational Holiday Inn with standard dirt-colored industrial carpeting, infinite ranks of blond oak, and second-year library science students, all girls, all wearing glasses and frayed jeans, all trying to look very serious and self-important. Jay smiled as she went through the subway-style turnstile into the library proper. She was willing to bet she'd find exactly the same kind of kids in the college bookstore, the only difference being that they'd be second-year English instead of library science students.

The research computers were located in the rear of the brightly lit building, a dozen of them fitted into small, individual work carrels that were little more than booths separated by head-high partitions. From what she could see, about half of them were multimedia terminals with stacked CD-ROM units. Three of the carrels were occupied.

Jay chose a vacant booth, sat down, and switched on the machine. She went through the straightforward main menu and accessed the Windows Program Manager; as she'd thought, the computers were equipped to ride the Internet, but there was also a logon-logoff meter and a code request for a user account number. It was beginning to look as though she could scratch the library off her list.

Jay took the terminal back to the main menu, switched it off, and went in search of someone who could answer a few questions. She found a particularly snotty-looking girl with dark hair in a bun, and flagged her down.

'Yes?'

'What are the hours here?'

'I beg your pardon?'

'The hours, dear; how long are you open?'

'Eight to eight, seven days a week.'

'Who gets in after-hours?'

'No one.'

'No special passes?'

'Some of the professors and TAs do research at night.' The girl frowned and put on her best official look. 'Can I ask why you want to know?'

'I'm from the State College Ways and Means Committee,' Jay snapped, making the name up out of thin air.

It worked. The girl paled. 'I'm sorry. Is there anything else I can help you with?'

'Are there any other computers in the building?'

'Three, but they're not for use by the students.'

'Who uses them?'

'We do. The library staff.'

'Are they actual computers or just terminals to the college Administration mainframe.'

'I don't think I understand.'

'What do you use them for?'

'Keeping track of the books. Managing the stacks, tracking overdues.'

'Can you do anything else with them?'

'I don't know what you mean.' She was pulling on the braid hard now, her eyes darting back and forth behind the big-lensed glasses she wore.

'Could you type a letter to your Aunt Minnie on one of them? Draw a picture? Add up a column of figures?'

'No.'

Terminals. Useless. The son of a bitch isn't here.

'All right. Thank you, Miss . . . ?'

'Albright. Candice Albright.'

'Thank you, Miss Albright.'

'If there's anything else . . .'

'You could do one thing for me?'

'Yes?' Eager as a cocker spaniel puppy. Jay used a slip of paper from one of the carrels and wrote down the three names she'd culled from her list. She handed the paper to the young woman.

'I'd like you to check these names for me. Find out if they've ever taken books out of the library. Or if they've ever used the computers.'

'Of course.'

'Good. Are you here during the day?'

'Yes. I'm on the mentor program this semester, under Eugene.' She flushed bright pink. 'Mr Kyle that is.'

In your dreams, sweetie.

'Good. I'll call you this afternoon.'

'I'll have the information ready for you.'

'Wonderful.' She rewarded the young woman with a smile. 'You've been a great help.'

322

'Thank you.'

'Good. You can go.'

The girl scuttled off. Jay watched her vanish into the sea of books. Trying not to laugh, Jay turned and left the library.

When she got back to the motel, the flashing message light was blinking on her telephone. The message was from Christy Skeed. Jay called the *Eagle* and the crime reporter came on the line.

'Find anything?' asked Jay.

'Not much.' Christy answered. 'But like they say in journalism school, even negative information can be useful.'

'Such as?'

'Nothing at all about this Dr Kushinski or John Gordon. Telfer's the only one with any file at all.'

'What kind of file?'

'Complaints.'

'What kind?'

The reporter laughed. 'You name it. Everything from by-law changes to charges of conspiracy against the police.'

'Conspiracy about what?'

'Cat murders.'

'What?'

'There was a rash of animal mutilations a few years ago. Mostly cats. They'd be found sliced in half. Almost surgically. Telfer's a cat freak. He insisted that the police were in league with the college science department. You know, providing animals for dissection.'

Christy laughed again. 'The only trouble is, the college doesn't use cats; it never did. Frogs only.'

'Sounds like a nut case.'

'Eccentric anyway.'

'Could he have written the letters?'

'I suppose it's possible. He's weird enough.'

'Okay, thanks.'

'No problem. Let me know if anything else comes up.'

'Absolutely.' Jay hung up the phone. Animal mutilations were a common feature in serial killer case histories, but the mutilations usually took place in adolescence. Still, it was better than nothing, and Telfer's phone line was connected to a modem. A visit to the complaining cat freak was definitely in order.

Elias Telfer's house on Elm Street turned out to be a scrappy-looking clapboard bungalow on a junk-filled lot backed by a sloping stand of trees and uncleared brush. The windows were covered in stapled, loose-fitting sheets of thick plastic; there was moss on the shingled roof and the front stoop had vanished entirely, replaced by a stepped arrangement of concrete blocks and boards. Directly across from the house was a large construction site that appeared to have been abandoned years ago. Telfer definitely lived on the wrong side of the tracks or, in this case, South Main Street.

Jay parked the rental in Telfer's cluttered driveway and stared at the squalid little house. As well as several rusting cars and trucks up on blocks, doorless refrigerators, and scattered piles of used and mismatched

324

lumber, there were chicken-wire enclosures every-where; by the time she climbed out of the car, she was surrounded by a horde of curious cats, including an enormous, bright orange creature the size of a small dog, with one eye gone and half an ear chewed off. She found herself wondering if she should have brought the pistol buried in the bottom of her suitcase; Telfer's domain was a cross between the Bates Motel and *The Texas Chainsaw Massacre*. Except you couldn't get rabies going to a cult horror film.

It was all wrong, of course; Telfer was a possible suspect in a multiple-murder investigation. You didn't just go up to his front door and knock, you got fifty guys in Kevlar vests, tapped his phone, and never came closer than bullhorn distance. If he didn't come out in five minutes, you dropped a dozen rounds of tear gas through the windows. She didn't even have a purse-size can of pepper spray.

She didn't have anything.

Escorted by a trotting phalanx of felines, Jay did exactly what she knew you weren't supposed to do in a case like this: she went up to the front door and knocked. She felt something against her leg and almost jumped off the rickety steps. It was the bright orange, half-eared, half-blind monster, rubbing against her ankle and purring like a well-tuned outboard motor. She heard muffled footsteps and then the battered-looking front door opened.

'Hey, man, what's happening?'

Elias Telfer was not at all what she'd expected.

Visions of the Bates Motel faded. The man standing in front of her was in his early forties, short and trim, wearing a Phillies baseball cap over long gray hair neatly tied back in a ponytail. He was also wearing an ancient, heel-worn pair of cowboy boots, flared denim jeans so old that the blue had faded almost to white, and a Che Guevara T-shirt. He had round cheeks and laughing blue eyes, and he was wearing bifocals.

'Elias Telfer?'

'*C'est moi.*' He grinned. He used the toe of one boot to poke gently at the huge cat winding itself around Jay's legs. 'And that's Motorhead. He likes you. Want a beer or something?' The cat lover's voice was soft and pleasant, not far removed from Motorhead's purring.

'My name is Jennifer Smith. I'd like to talk,' said Jay.

'Sure thing,' said Telfer. He stood aside and waved Jay into the house. 'C'mon inside.'

The house was small, well organized, and neat as a pin, even if it did reek of cats. There was a small kitchen, a living room/dining room combination, and another room at the back. The furniture was secondhand and none of it matched, but it all looked comfortable. In one corner of the living room there was an old school desk topped by a reasonably new-looking computer setup.

'Make you some tea?' the man asked.

'No, thanks.'

'Back in a sec.' Telfer disappeared into the kitchen and came back with a short-necked brown beer bottle without a label. 'Make it myself,' he said, holding up the bottle. 'Organic. Weaker than ferret piss, but I like it.'

He dropped down into a sagging upholstered chair across from Jay. 'You look like a cop,' he said pleasantly. 'Back in the old doper days you would have made me nervous.'

'I'm interested in your letters to the Butler *Eagle*.' She leaned hard on the word *letters*, watching his response carefully. He grinned and took a swallow of his home brew.

'Which ones? I give them shit about everything I can think of.'

'You sound like you've made a career out of it.'

'I have.' Telfer jerked a thumb over his shoulder at the computer. 'I do a broadsheet called "Bad News". Get it printed in Butler every two weeks. Five, six hundred hard-core subscribers, Honolulu to Anchorage. And I write stuff for *Harrowsmith, Whole Earth, Mother Jones*. Not much of a living, but it's a life.'

That explains the modem. This guy's no killer.

Motorhead jumped up into Jay's lap, curled into a furry ball, and started to purr again. Jay reached out and stroked the massive head. The purring sound got even louder.

'The cat killings,' she said. Telfer's expression darkened.

'You heard about those?'

'Yes.'

'Fuckin' A evil, pardon my French.'

'You really think the police were involved?'

'No. I just wanted them to get off their asses.' He nodded toward the computer again. 'Animal Rights has

327

an electronic wire service; you read about that kind of thing all the time, local shelters selling black market animals to schools, brokering exotics, that kind of thing. I knew it wasn't that. There was some creep out there killing for the fun of it. A real freak.'

'Cutting them in half.'

'Worse. I saw a few of them. Eyes poked out, heads smashed, legs amputated ... then they were cut in half. Sometimes with the heads missing. Fuckin' gross, pardon my *Français*.'

'And then it just stopped?' Jay asked.

'Seems so.' Telfer shrugged. 'Not that I got any help trying to figure out who it was.' He shook his head. 'Even Kushinski wouldn't get with the program. He didn't want anything to do with it. Asshole.'

'Dr Kushinski?' asked Jay.

'You know him?'

'You said "he". I thought Evelyn Kushinski was a woman.'

'Definitely male. The local vet. He's got a place out on Grove City Road in Harrisville, three, four miles from here.'

'He's a veterinarian and he didn't take any interest in the animal killings?'

'Naw,' said Telfer, curling his lip scornfully. '*Pardonnez moi*, but the guy's a Fuckin' A creep. If he wasn't a vet, I'd say he was the one tortured those cats himself.'

Cruz sat in the small municipal courtroom on the fifth floor of the Albuquerque Public Safety Building and watched as Brian MacDonald's arraignment proceedings came to an end. Cruz had already given his evidence, but he'd decided to stick around for the satisfaction of watching the slimy bastard being dragged off to jail. The only thing missing to make it perfect was the presence of Jay Fletcher.

Cruz frowned, vaguely aware of MacDonald's lawyer as he made a last-ditch attempt at getting bail set for his client. Jay's sudden disappearance had been nagging at him since he found her 'resignation' letter propped up on his computer keyboard. He was angry at her for leaving him swinging in the breeze with the Safe Sex investigation still unfinished, but he was also worried.

He hadn't known Jay for very long, but her abrupt decision to leave seemed out of character. She just wasn't the type to leave a colleague in the lurch, or to abandon a job half done. She'd been acting a little hyper ever since her unscheduled, solitary trip to Albuquerque and the brief confrontation they'd had, but Cruz put that down to his own mixed feelings about their relationship. For some reason he'd been positive that she'd slept with someone while she was away from Santa Fe, and he'd been shocked by his reaction to the possibility of her having had a sexual encounter: he'd been jealous as a jilted lover. He wouldn't mention that part of it when he called Langford in Washington to report Jay's unexpected departure, a call he couldn't put off much longer, even if it did wind up landing her in deep shit.

His thoughts were interrupted by a light tap on his

shoulder. He turned and found himself looking at a basset-faced man sitting on the bench behind him. The man had a cop's sad smile, sincere as a lump of coal.

'Cruz, isn't it? FIO in Santa Fe?'

'That's right. Do I know you?'

'Horace Sladky, APD Homicide.' He lifted his jowled chin in MacDonald's direction. 'I heard you got your man. Came down for a look.' He grinned. 'Nice to see a lawyer getting what he deserves. Fucking coyotes.' He paused. 'You plead him down?'

'No,' Cruz answered, faintly proud of the fact. Between his own investigation and the information Jay had pulled out of her magic box, they had more than enough evidence. 'Second-degree murder, eleven separate counts. One for each person who died in the fire. Conspiracy on top of that. We're still not finished. He's not the only one who's going to take the fall for this.'

'Looks good on him,' said Sladky. The judge denied MacDonald bail pending a preliminary hearing and the lawyer was taken away. MacDonald's own lawyer watched him go, then began packing up his briefcase. People in the courtroom began straggling off. Sladky eyed them casually, then turned back to Cruz. 'So where's your partner? The Feeb?'

'Out of town.' How did an Albuquerque Homicide dick know Jay?

'Too bad,' said Sladky.

'You know her?'

Sladky shrugged his broad shoulders. 'Met her after the fire. She took a wrong turn looking for coffee and wound up in my Task Force Room. She was pretty interested in the case I was on. Thought she'd like to know we wrapped it up.' He paused. 'Had it wrapped up for us, actually.'

'Which case was that?'

'Serial killer. We kept it out of the press. Never made a splash.' He grinned bleakly. 'So to speak.'

'That's the kind of thing she was doing for the Bureau,' said Cruz. 'Computer profiles, helping out guys like you.'

'Yeah. So she mentioned.' Sladky nodded, then smiled. The detective's small, searching eyes were expressionless as glass. 'She out of town for long?'

'I'm not sure,' said Cruz. 'She's on personal leave.'

'Really?' said Sladky. 'Death in the family, that sort of thing?'

'Something like that. Why? Did you get the man?'

Sladky lifted his shoulders again. 'Someone else beat us to it,' he said quietly. 'Very nasty. Very neat.' The homicide detective stood up. 'Just thought she'd like to know.'

Cruz nodded. 'I'll tell her next time I see her.'

'Yeah,' said Sladky. 'Do that.'

CHAPTER TWENTY

The San Francisco Epilepsy Foundation was located on the South Embarcadero in SoMa, or the South of Market area, not far from the old China Basin Channel and the approaches to the Bay Bridge. In Hawkins' day as a young MP based at the Presidio, South of Market had been a dingy industrial district servicing the wharfs of the Embarcadero, filled with narrow streets, gloomy warehouses and the cheapest hookers you could find in the city.

Times had changed. The Moscone Convention Center now occupied an eleven-acre block in the middle of the district and had acted as a hub for a general revival in the area. Now the warehouses were full of fern bars, tattoo parlors, and upscale boutiques, with the lofts above rented out to artists, dancers, and musicians.

The previous afternoon Hawkins had called the Epilepsy Foundation and made an appointment with their resident research physician, an earnest, nervous-looking man in his thirties named Shelburne. He had a corner office on the third floor of a renovated factory building that looked out over the South Bay. Instead of a stethoscope, Shelburne had glasses he kept around his neck on a black silk tether and he was wearing a white lab coat over his dark, chalk-stripe suit. For the last few minutes Hawkins had been trying to soothe the doctor's apprehensions about connecting Ricky Stiles to his professional specialty. The Iceman was hardly an appropriate poster boy for fund raising.

Shelburne was frowning. 'I hope you're not under the impression that epilepsy is a root cause of psychosis,' he said.

'I'm not saying anything at all, Doctor. I don't know anything at all about epilepsy. That's why I'm here.'

Shelburne nodded, but he still had a worried expression on his face. 'Epilepsy is a disease that's been terribly misunderstood over the centuries.' He flashed a brief smile 'A bad rap, you might say.'

Hawkins nodded. 'Falling Sickness.'

'The Great Trouble, The Sacred Disease. It's had a great many names. The word comes from the Greek, meaning to take hold of, to seize.'

'As in seizure.'

'Yes.'

'How common is it?'

'Overall, about five people in a thousand, worldwide.'

'In the US?' asked Hawkins.

'Somewhat less. Perhaps three in a thousand.'

'Less than half a percent.'

'Something like that.'

Hawkins nodded. It didn't sound like much, but it was still 140,000 people. A big crowd for the Iceman to hide in. 'I asked you about a drug when I called. You said you hadn't heard of it.'

'Yes,' said Shelburne. He flipped through a notebook on his desk. 'Phenacemide, or phenurone.'

'That's it.'

'I had to look it up,' said Shelburne. 'It's not used in epileptic drug therapy anymore.'

'But you did find it?'

'Oh, yes. It was taken off the standard list in the mid-seventies. The FDA proscribed it three years later.'

'You mean it's no longer available?'

'Not in the United States.' Shelburne smiled. 'It's what we refer to as an "orphan drug."'

'You'll have to explain that.'

'An orphan drug is a drug that is usually only effective for rare diseases. It's either not cost-effective or too toxic for general use. The point is, the drugs aren't available in the United States because they haven't received FDA approval, or that approval has been withdrawn.'

'What category does phenacemide fall into?' Hawkins asked.

'The latter,' Shelburne answered. 'Even when it was available, it was only used as a last resort.'

'Why?'

'As I said, high levels of toxicity. The side effects are appalling, at least from what I've been reading.'

'What kinds of side effects?'

'It's a long list.'

'I'm not in any hurry.'

'Suicidal depression, liver damage, loss of potassium, bone marrow depression, rashes, chronic headaches, weight loss, anorexia nervosa, nausea, vomiting, abdominal pain, photosensitivity.'

'Photosensitivity?'

'It's common to a lot of drugs used for epilepsy and to the disease itself. In severe cases, a patient has to wear very dark sunglasses into the late evening.' Shelburne sighed wearily and shook his head. 'That's part of the mythology, too. A great many epileptics shun daylight entirely and prefer the night.'

'Like a vampire.'

'I'm afraid so, yes.'

'But you say the drug was only given in extreme cases?'

'Grand mal seizures, type two, and especially psychomotor epilepsy.'

Hawkins was starting to get lost in the terminology. 'How many different kinds of epilepsy are there?'

'Quite a few.' Shelburne smiled again, his nervousness receding as he warmed to his expertise. 'Have you ever been about to fall asleep and been jerked awake by an involuntary muscle spasm? They usually occur in the legs, sometimes the arms.'

'Sure. It happens to everybody. An anthropology professor I had said it was a holdover from caveman days. The kind of twitching dogs do when they're going to sleep. A survival instinct.'

'Your professor was wrong' said Shelburne. 'What you experienced is called myoclonus. It usually lasts about ten milliseconds. It's actually a form of what we call akinetic epilepsy. Most of us can control it, but in severe cases it can be fatal. In children, unrestricted myoclonus is called West's Syndrome. Children who manifest the disease have something called Salaam Attacks, uncontrolled bending forward at the waist. Eventually it causes anoxia, brain damage, and death.'

'So everyone has epilepsy?'

Shelburne nodded. 'To a greater or lesser degree, yes. Epilepsy is an electro-chemical phenomenon within the brain. Normally messages are sent over the neural pathways in pulsed sequences. In an epileptic the electrical signals come in uncontrolled bursts. In the most severe cases, the entire brain-electrical system is triggered at once.'

'A short circuit.'

'More like a massive surge. The result is just what happens when the circuits in a house overload.'

'The breakers trip,' said Hawkins.

'Exactly. In an epileptic the system shuts down, which results in a seizure. Some epileptics have fewer, some more. Some seizures are more intense, some less so. It's all relative.'

'But phenacemide would only be prescribed for someone with severe epilepsy, is that right?'

'Yes. As I said before, particularly in the case of someone with psycho-motor epilepsy.'

'Which is?'

Shelburne sat back in his chair and twiddled with the silk string on his glasses. 'Did you ever read a book, or see a film called *The Terminal Man*?'

Hawkins nodded. 'Michael Crichton, the same guy who wrote *The Andromeda Strain, Jurassic Park*.'

'That's the one. The disease the lead character in the book had was psycho-motor epilepsy. Most forms of epilepsy seem to be genetic; psycho-motor is usually caused by some serious trauma – blow to the head, a fall, a long-term illness with a high fever: When the book was written, electrode therapy was all the rage as a cure for it.'

Hawkins nodded. He had a vague recollection of cutting up a *Life* magazine for a school project. Pictures of cats with wires dangling out of their skulls. Depending on which button you pushed the cats would either hiss and spit, or curl up and purr. 'I remember reading something about it,' he said.

'The rage didn't last,' said Shelburne.

'It didn't work?'

'It worked, but only on some patients, and only to a certain degree. It was also very invasive – you had to attach dozens of electrodes at various places in the brain, a major surgical procedure. It didn't work at all on people with temporal lobe epilepsy, or patients with deep-seated lesions.'

'So everyone went back to drugs.'

'Yes.' Shelburne pursed his lips and twiddled with his glasses again. 'I expect to see a resurgence of direct mechanical procedures, though. The technology has changed a great deal since Mr Crichton wrote his book. Microchips and all of that. I can't say that I'm looking forward to it.'

Hawkins tried to steer Shelburne back to the subject at hand. 'What proportion of epileptics have the psychomotor type of the disease?'

'Ten percent, roughly.'

Hawkins nodded. Much better; they were down to about fourteen thousand people now. 'Of those, how many would have been taking a drug like phenacemide?'

'Not many. As I said, it was only used in the severest cases. Perhaps ten percent again.'

Down to fourteen hundred. The Iceman was being pushed into a steadily closing net. 'I don't suppose there's any list of patients like that.'

'I'm afraid not,' said Shelburne, shaking his head.

'If patients like that couldn't take phenacemide, what kind of drugs would they be taking?'

'A combination of regular anticonvulsants. Dilantin and phenobarbital, for instance. Not anything like as effective, though. Life expectancy would be poor.'

'Why?'

'Dilantin/phenobarbital wouldn't completely control the incidence of the seizures. Every seizure that did occur would cause some brain damage. Eventually the patient would succumb, probably die in status epilepticus.'

More terminology. 'What's that?'

'SE is the accumulated effect of a number of seizures

over a long period of time. It causes gliosis – deterioration of the brain itself. Eventually it brings on a condition in which the patient has a number of grand mal fits without regaining consciousness in between. Every cell in the brain begins to fire at once.'

'What happens?'

'Functional exhaustion of the cerebral cortex. Heart failure, respiratory failure, inhalational asphyxia, total dehydration, massive brain damage. Any or all of those. In the end the brain becomes totally starved for oxygen.'

'And the patient dies.'

'Yes. Patients with the type of condition requiring a drug like phenacemide probably wouldn't have a very extensive adult life.'

'The patient I'm concerned with is probably in his midforties,' said Hawkins.

Shelburne raised an eyebrow. 'I see.'

'How is he surviving?'

'There's only one way,' Shelburne answered. 'It means he's found some source for the phenacemide.'

'Even though it's banned by the FDA? Is that possible?' There was a long pause.

'Yes.' The answer came out with some difficulty, but Shelburne wasn't about to lie. 'There are ways.'

'Tell me,' said Hawkins.

The Slippery Rock Rape/Crisis Center was located in a large wood-frame house on Franklin Street in the middle of town. The offices were on the main floor with a dormitory for runaways, rape victims, and battered women. The director of the center was a woman named Astrid Kee, a grown-up version of Candice Albright, the library student at the State college.

In Astrid's case the braid was streaked with gray and she had the tight, bitter mouth of someone who has endured more than enough of her own and other people's pain and suffering. Her office had the requisite 'Take Back the Night' and 'I am Proud, I Am Woman' posters, a dying rubber plant in one corner and a trio of industrial-strength filing cabinets.

There was a small cardboard sign on Astrid Kee's battered old desk announcing 'This is a Smoke-Free Environment'. On her way into the clinic, Jay had seen a small room off to one side equipped with a sophisticated computer set-up, a small screen press, and a collating photocopier.

'Just who did you say you were with?' asked Kee, sitting behind her desk. Jay caught a touch of Back Bay Boston in the woman's voice. Astrid was a long way from the comforts of home.

'CERT,' Jay answered, 'Computer Emergency Response Team.'

'Never heard of it,' said Kee. She sat back in her squeaky wooden swivel chair. Jay struggled to keep her expression blank. Astrid Kee was a pain in the ass from the 'All women are sisters' school. Except all women weren't sisters any more than all men were brothers. Jay managed to keep her feelings in check. 'We trouble-shoot the Internet,' she said, trying to keep her tone as pleasant as possible.

'What does that have to do with us?'

'Your clinic on-lines. RAPE from time to time. You also subscribe to SASH-L.' The first was an ongoing discussion about rape; the second was a newsletter/ discussion bulletin board for discussion on forming policy and organizing against sexual harassment of all kinds.

'You have some problem with that, Ms Smith?'

'Not at all.'

'Good,' said Kee. 'Because we're trying to do a job here. We don't get any government grants either, and we don't like government intrusion.'

'CERT isn't a government operation,' said Jay.

'Bull,' replied Kee. 'You're funded by them, I'll bet.'

'That's not the point, Ms Kee.'

'Then what is?'

Someone's tapping into your computer and swacking the victims you're supposed to be helping.

'We think someone is accessing your computer every time you go on the Net.'

'That's ludicrous.'

'No, that's a fact.' It wasn't really, but Jay was fairly sure of it. After getting back from her meeting with Elias Telfer, she'd plugged in her laptop and run a diagnostic on every one of the modem lines except for the ones at the college. The crisis center line was the only one that showed any backdoor intrusion. The common term for it was 'bagging.' When the crisis center opened its electronic 'door' to connect with the Internet, someone was sneaking in.

'How did you find out about it?'

'It's what CERT does, Ms Kee.' She turned her smile up a notch. 'We weren't snooping, believe me.'

'Why would anyone want to get into our computer?'

'Hackers do it for fun,' Jay answered. 'But usually they choose to hack into a system that presents a challenge.'

'So who's doing it?'

'We're not sure. What sort of files do you keep in the computer?'

'Case records, correspondence, that sort of thing.'

'Names and addresses of the women you help?'

'Yes.' Hesitant.

'Follow-ups?'

'Sometimes.' Astrid Kee's brows knitted together. Jay was on thin ice again. 'Why?'

'There are some people out there who think that being raped, or getting pregnant is an open invitation.'

'You mean there's some deviant out there, cruising for victims?'

Jesus! You have no idea.

'It's a possibility.'

'I can't believe it.'

'Really?' said Jay. 'There are hundreds of sex groups on the Net. They're advertising Virtual Reality Sex in magazines. Why not this?'

The crisis center director sat forward abruptly. 'This is incredible. I'll have to tell...'

Jay interrupted quickly. 'I'd appreciate it if you didn't say anything about this for the moment.'

'We have to stop it!'

'Of course. That's our objective. But we don't want to spook him. He'll just move on, worm his way into some other group like yours.'

Astrid Kee stared at Jay from the far side of the desk. This was something outside her experience and she knew it. Some of her earlier belligerence faded.

'What do you want me to do?'

'Tell me something about how the center works.'

'We counsel woman who've been violated and abused.'

'How long have you kept your case files on the computer?'

'Since we opened up. Three years. Originally we were headquartered at the college. Women Against Violence Against Women.'

WAVAW, not the best acronym I've ever heard.

'Did you use the college computers?'

'Yes.'

'But not here.'

'No.' More hesitation. 'We don't have any affiliation with the college.' Some kind of political split? Too fundamentalist for the school?

'Who has access to the machine?'

'I do. Kelly Quarrington, my executive assistant. Our accountant.'

'The accountant is a woman presumably?'

'Yes. Hilda Jovanavich. She has an office on South Main.'

'Anyone else from outside?'

'No.'

'How often does Hilda come in to work on your books?'

'Once every two weeks.'

And I'll bet she does the same thing for Dr Evelyn Kushinski at his veterinary hospital.

Throw a back door program on to Hilda's program disk and it would be planted invisibly in the crisis center computer the next time the accountant made her rounds. Simple, but very efficient.

Something he learned from SK-WIZ maybe?

'Are most of your clients local?'

'Some. A lot of the battered women.'

'A lot of date rapes from the college?'

The woman's eyes flashed. 'Rape is rape. Dating has nothing to do with it.'

'Sorry. What I meant to say . . .'

'I know what you meant,' Kee answered. 'And the answer is yes. The majority of the rapes we deal with are from the college. So are the pregnancies.'

'What happens to them?'

'I don't understand.'

'Your clients. After they've come through here. Do they go back to school, go home, disappear?'

'It varies.'

'Do you tell the pregnant ones to have abortions?'

'We don't *tell* them anything,' snapped Kee. 'We counsel them.'

'But you do suggest abortions.'

Kee stared at Jay, her expression icy. 'I don't see what any of this has to do with someone stealing our files.' The director paused. 'Frankly, I don't like the way this conversation is going at all.'

Don't lose her. Blind her with bafflegab.

'I'm not making any value judgments,' Jay soothed. 'But I have to know your procedures if I'm going to be of any use. If you're counseling young women to have abortions, you might be triggering deviant behavior of some kind. Abortion is just the kind of issue that sets some people off.'

'I'm aware of that,' Kee answered dryly. She paused. 'Yes. We do counsel women to have abortions in some cases.'

'You recommend specific abortionists?'

'I hope you're not going to ask me for names.'

'Of course not.'

'We send our clients to specific abortion clinics. We make the appointments, provide transportation. Sometimes we even pay for them.'

'Out of state.'

'Not necessarily. Out of Butler County, though.' Her nostrils flared angrily and two spots of color appeared on her cheeks. 'The good people of Butler don't take kindly to our presence, let alone an abortion clinic.'

'You follow up the cases you send out?'

'If we can. Some of the girls ... women, don't come back to school.'

'You lose track of them?'

'In some cases.'

That has to be it. It's the only thing that fits.

Jay could feel the panic rising in her again. She'd spoken to too many people, left too obvious a trail. It was time to fade out of the picture. If she made much more of an impression, the whole thing was going to fall apart.

'Ms Smith?'

Jay blinked at the sound of Astrid Kee's voice. She'd been staring off into space.

Christ! I'm losing it.

'Sorry. I was just trying to evaluate the situation.' Panic. And something else. The heat. She was close; she could feel it.

'Should we suspend our use of the computer until you've . . . done whatever it is you're going to do?'

'No.' Jay shook her head. 'Don't do anything out of the ordinary. I'll have to go back and make my report before we do anything concrete.' She decided to throw in something to keep the clinic director at bay.

'I'm afraid we might have to bring the Bureau in on this.'

'The Bureau?'

'The FBI.' Jay nodded.

The woman on the other side of the desk stiffened. 'I'm not sure my board would approve of something like that.'

'There might not be a choice. This is beyond CERT's mandate.'

'So is involving the FBI without cause.' The Kee woman was clearly very nervous now. In the past few years, there'd been a number of lawsuits and criminal proceedings revolving around places like Astrid's operation coercing minors to have abortions.

If Kee had ever condoned such an act, and it had

involved crossing a state line, it would become a federal crime, kidnapping and unlawful confinement to be precise.

Jay stood up. 'Why don't we do it this way? I'll work up my report, but before I do anything; I'll call you with my recommendations. Wait until then before you consult your board.'

Kee nodded, the relief visible on her face. 'That sounds reasonable.' She extended a hand and Jay shook it. The grip was dry and bony. Jay tried to imagine Astrid consoling an eighteen-year-old who'd just been assaulted by her new 'boyfriend.' Somehow it didn't compute.

'I'll be in touch.'

Don't hold your breath, Ms Kee. Once I'm done, I won't be coming back this way again.

It was evening, and darkness was falling on the Strip. This was the Iceman's favorite time; in the blasting light and heat of day, Las Vegas had no substance; her colors were washed out, her cracks and breaks and flaws too obvious. It was only with the coming of night that the city truly came alive; fantasy became reality, the flaws were hidden behind raging strips of brilliant neon and flashing, trip-switch incandescent rainbows.

At night he could breathe.

He was restless after having spent the daylight hours in his special dark and hidden room, fused to the screens and keyboards, feeding on their power in a vain attempt to stave off what he knew was coming. The symptoms were clear; he'd watched them approach like huge black crows, winging their way across the mountains to cast their shadows over him.

He reached the Strip on foot, and turned up toward O'Sheas. He walked, forcing himself to concentrate, letting his nostrils fill with the street smells of overheated asphalt, food from a hundred restaurants, perfume and body odor, cold blasts of metal air from the casinos. Sometimes if he concentrated hard enough, he could put off the inevitable for a little while longer, pretend that he was just like everyone else until pretense became impossible.

He knew there was very little time. All day he'd felt the alternating waves of lethargy and euphoria, drowsiness and stunning, overwhelming depression. Thirst that could not be quenched. How often? How many times had he been through this, fought against it, then finally embraced it?

Even with his lightly tinted photo-optic contact lenses, the popping lights surrounding him seemed to bore directly into his senses; colors became sounds, touch became taste. Soon all of it would focus down a single tunnel track of feeling like the pounding wheels of a racing freight train thundering toward him.

Without thinking, he continued to walk steadily forward, his hands coming together in a complex knitting movement that lacked only the clicking of needles. He stopped, leaning against a newspaper coin box for a moment, bracing his elbows on it, forcing the fingers to stop moving. But the knitting went on and now it felt as though his tongue were swelling, filling his dry mouth, pressing against teeth and palate, choking off his airway.

He made a tiny cry that no one heard. The plastic of the lenses in his eyes was burning the delicate membranes and fluids. He was vaguely aware of a couple pausing a few feet away. The man and woman were dressed in matching T-shirts from The Dunes.

'Hey, man, you all right?'

The Iceman gritted his teeth and made the small, growling cry again. The woman tugged the man's arm. The Iceman willed the couple to turn and leave before he did something they would all regret.

'He's drunk.'

'No. I think he's sick. Christ, honey, look at his face!'

Not sick. Changing, right in front of their eyes. He had to hurry. Coming out had been a mistake.

'Let's go.' The woman tugged the man's arm again. Reluctantly the man abandoned his role as Good Samaritan.

Saving his life. No hot blood arcing into the cooling air. No slash and cut. Not now. Not yet. Swift slice of whispering sound from Louis De Ville. What a slugger.

The couple moved away. The Iceman abandoned the safety of the coin box and turned back the way he'd come. The lights were alive now, thousands of flashing snakes writhing above his sight line. The only thing keeping him going was the knowledge that this had all happened before, just this way, in just this sequence. If he followed the pattern, traced the maze of memory, he'd find his way home again.

He began hearing the music just as he reached the corner again. The soft singing of small birds gathering on a wire or in the branches of a tree. Cicada bright, a single note, buzzing from the flashing lights, offset by the symphony from the walls of humanity that pressed fleshily around him. What song? How long? 'Ding Dong'?

Ding, dong, the witch is dead.

The Wizard would sleep soon. The pills would help, a little. The others would just have to get along without him tonight. He found the corner, blindly saw the trail of breadcrumbs he and Gretel had left behind, followed them into the darkness, hearing far above him the terrible sound of monstrous, flapping wings.

Not sick. Becoming.

Cruz sat in the task force conference room at Albuquerque Police Headquarters, sipping Horace Sladky's godawful coffee and watching the grizzled-looking detective paw his way through a file folder of witness reports. The cop's summons earlier that day had been blunt and unequivocal: if Cruz wanted to avoid getting his ass put through the wringer, he'd better get it down to APD Headquarters on the double.

'You couldn't have told me what the problem was on the phone?' Cruz asked.

'No,' said Sladky. He found what he was looking for

and pulled a sheet of paper out of the folder. 'We gotta keep this low-profile or we're both going to get burned.'

'So tell me now.'

Sladky glanced down at the sheet of paper in his hand. 'Hand Job,' he said.

'The killer you found?'

'Himself.'

'I'm an arson investigator, Sladky, not a homicide dick.'

'Your Feeb associate. The one who wandered in here after that big fire, remember?'

'Jay Fletcher. You were asking about her at the MacDonald arraignment.'

'That's the one.'

'What about her?'

'Did some checking. According to my information, she was using a Department of Highways vehicle while she worked with you in Santa Fe. A green Ford Escort. GTJ 946.'

'It was an Escort,' said Cruz. 'I don't remember the tags.' He frowned. 'Get to the point, why don't you?'

'The point is, we canvassed the neighborhood a few blocks around the place Hand Job got whacked. Somebody remembered the car.'

'When?'

'An hour and a half before we got our anonymous call.'

'This somebody remembered the license plate number?' Cruz snorted. 'Bit of a stretch, don't you think?'

'Maybe. Except the person who picked up on the car

has the same initials, GTJ. That's why she remembered the tags.'

'Is that why you were asking about her at the arraignment?'

'No. That was a hunch. This is fact.'

Cruz shrugged. 'Pretty circumstantial.'

'What are you, her fucking lawyer? She's a cop. We can place her car within a block of the crime scene at the time the crime took place. She's a computer nut and so was Hand Job. Whoever took the slimy son of a bitch out had good information. Cop's information.'

'She's a suspect?'

'A prime one. Unless you can tell me otherwise.'

'Shit.'

'Yeah, that about sums it up.' Sladky nodded. 'You still haven't heard from her?'

'No.'

'What about her people in Washington?'

'Not that I know of.'

Sladky pushed the report back into his file folder and stared across the table at Cruz. 'How do we handle this?'

The implication was clear. Sladky had allowed Jay access to information about the killer and Cruz was supposedly responsible for her actions while she was in Santa Fe. If she was the one who'd nailed the Hand Job killer, both he and Sladky were going to be in very hot water.

'We handle it carefully,' said Cruz after a moment. 'I'll ask around.' He paused. 'How long can you keep the thing about the car under wraps?'

'A couple of days,' Sladky answered. 'Week at the most. Much longer than that, it comes out, people are going to start talking cover-up.'

'I'll work as fast as I can.'

'Find her quick,' said Sladky. 'And I think you'd better get on to her people in D.C. I don't think Hand Job was the only one on her wish list. I think this is just the beginning.'

Jay kept down her speed as she drove along the dark country highway. In daylight the landscape of Butler County was a pleasant enough mix of low hills and rolling moors. At night, now, knowing what she knew, it was a secret, alien soil of shapes and shadows waiting to swallow her alive.

Hands gripping the wheel, she shifted on the seat, feeling the comforting weight of the 9mm nudging at the small of her back. It had all come together in the last few hours and she wasn't sure she was ready. With more time she could have thought it out, planned her strategy, examined options.

Chickened out.

Too late for that now.

It had taken no time at all to check on Hilda Jovanovich and discover that she was also the veterinarian's accountant, and the call from Candice Albright at the college library had put the cap on it. Kushinski was a regular visitor to the library, both via modem and in person. From what the Albright girl could tell, he seemed to have a particular interest in *Roe* v. *Wade* and

354

anything else that had to with abortion. His secondary choice of reading material concerned the local history of the Slippery Rock School Board, especially information about the old Crocker Consolidated School on the outskirts of town.

A quick run to the Slippery Rock Municipal Offices on West Cooper Street confirmed his interest. The Crocker School, a combined elementary and junior high built in 1937, had been abandoned in the mid-seventies after a fire gutted the auditorium and gymnasium. The cost of refurbishing the building was prohibitive and the School Board decided to build two new schools instead. The Crocker property, beyond the city limits, between Mulberry Street and Dickey Road, was abandoned.

Three years ago, feeling the economic pinch, the Slippery Rock School Board put the property up for auction. No one was willing to come up with the minimum bid at the time, so the property was withdrawn. A year later, less than two months before the first letters began arriving at the Butler *Eagle*, the School Board tried again. This time there was one bidder – Dr Evelyn Kushinski, the veterinarian from Harrisville. According to his bid application, on file at the Municipal Office, he intended to have the existing building razed and a game farm and wildlife sanctuary put in its place. So far he'd done nothing with the property at all.

Game Farm, Jesus!

She'd spent the balance of the day in Harrisville,

355

sitting in her car, smoking cigarettes, and keeping an eye on Kushinski's clinic. He'd done a steady trade in ailing puppies, sick budgies, and pregnant hamsters all afternoon, but Jay hadn't seen one cat go into the low, red brick building. At six, with dusk settling over the surrounding hills, the lights in the clinic went off, and the ones in the upstairs apartment went on. There was only one vehicle left in the small paved lot in front of the clinic – a black-and-white zebra-striped Land Rover that looked as though it had come out of a safari movie. Jay had checked on that, too – the vehicle was owned by Kushinski.

At nine, with night almost completely fallen, she got her first glimpse of the vet as he came out of the clinic, locked the door behind him, and headed for the Land Rover. She was surprised at how ordinary he looked. A small man, not much over five feet, in his late thirties or early forties, round-faced, clean-shaven, wearing a dark blue windbreaker and an Ivy League cap against the early evening chill. A nobody. Anybody. A little man who took too much interest in abortion, drove a zebra-striped four-wheel drive, and played killing games with monsters on the Internet.

What ever happened to *Leave it to Beaver* and *Father Knows Best*?

Canceled. Killed in the ratings.

Consigned to cable lingo, syndicated ghosts endlessly repeating episodes showing a world that didn't exist anymore, maybe didn't exist then. No murders in Mayberry, and Jane Wyatt never had to explain the facts of life to Princess. Not Kushinski's life, nor hers for that matter.

The animal doctor climbed into the Land Rover, started the engine, and pulled out of the parking lot. He turned east on Grove City Road, heading into the center of the village, then turned south on State Highway 8. Jay stayed well back, she had a fair idea of where the cat-hating bastard was going. Kushinski with his rage-filled letters, searching for a wider 'audience' for his crimes. Kushinski who could make young, desperate girls disappear.

But that had been the easy part, of course. On the face of it, the disappearance of that many girls should have rung an alarm somewhere, but from long experience Jay knew that a name without a body to go with it was just a missing person, and missing persons were at the bottom of every police department's list, right next to the Bigfoot and UFO sightings.

Kushinski was well out of sight as Jay drove through Slippery Rock on 108. On the right, two streets back and up the rise, she could see the mercury vapor splotch of livid yellow marking the police station. A chief, three constables, and two cars on revolving shifts. No backup there, even if she had been in a position to call for help.

It wasn't even ten o'clock, but most of Slippery Rock was shut down for the night. In the distance to the east she could see the lights of the college buildings, but the town in between was a puddle of darkness. She drove through the flashing yellow at the intersection of South Main and the highway, then kept going, passing the motel, continuing southwest. The houses on the right began to thin out and half a mile later there was nothing but scrub brush and treelots on either side of the road.

Her headlights picked out the Mulberry Street turnoff and she slowed. There was no traffic ahead and nothing behind. Slowing even more she switched off her lights and drove on in complete darkness. Without her lights the low black shapes of the hills around her seemed to leap forward, pressing in on either side of the car. Jay had a brief, terrifying image that almost sent her off the road: the Headless Horseman on his fire-eyed horse, chasing Ichabod Crane through the desperate landscape of Sleepy Hollow. She'd wet her bed for a week after seeing that on *Walt Disney Presents*. Her sister, Mikey, had teased her mercilessly about it.

Why all this stuff from when I was a kid? What's wrong with me?

Oh, nothing, just another boring evening without a date.

She regained control of the car. Fifty yards ahead she saw the turnoff through the trees. She slowed to a crawl, then turned without signaling. Suddenly she could hear the crunch of gravel under the tires. She kept going, leaning forward, peering through the windshield. No sense in tempting fate; she had to park well out of sight of the highway just in case a curious policeman came cruising by.

She parked, two wheels leaning into the shallow ditch, and climbed out of the car. She took a long, slow breath, tasting the night air. Cedar, pine, the faint, sweet-rot scent of old hay, moldy leaves. Far above her, invisible, she heard the boom and screech of a diving nighthawk. A small breeze shuddered through the boughs of the trees on both sides of the gravel drive, setting up a dry, steady whisper.

She thought briefly about having a cigarette to calm her nerves, decided against it, and checked the weight of the gun again. Still there. She moved forward carefully, keeping to the slight, leaf-filled depression to avoid the sound of her feet on the gravel. Less than a minute later, she reached the end of the trees, and the remains of the old Crocker Consolidated School stood before her, a hundred feet away across what had once been an open lawn. The school was larger than she'd expected, a two-story red brick colonial, eight windows wide on either side of a tall, fan-vault doorway. Jay paused in the last shadows to let her eyes adjust and forced herself not to think about smoking.

The driveway continued around the lawn, curving in front of the main entrance. A bare flagpole stood in the middle of a raised mound in front of the front steps. There was no sign of the Land Rover; Kushinski had probably parked around the back. Jay closed her eyes, trying to visualize the plans of the building she'd seen at the Municipal Offices.

The school was built in the shape of an amputated H, the long arm facing her, the short wing behind it connected by the ruins of the auditorium and the gym. Both floors of the front section contained the classrooms used by the junior high; the back section was for the elementary school. As well as the main entrance, there were at least half a dozen other doors leading in and out of the school. Too many escape routes.

No lights. Either Kushinski did his work in darkness or he was using one of the classrooms that faced away from her. She tried to remember the arrangement of the rooms. Two classrooms and an office on either side of the main doors with a long corridor running behind. To the far right, added on at the rear, was the Junior High Library. Above it on the second floor, the science lab.

That's it. That's where he is.

She pelted across the open space, bending low, losing her footing on the damp high grass, recovering, racing forward until she was into the shadows again. She went up the broad steps. The double doors, split and ruined by the firemen's axes, were hanging from their hinges. A scattering of windblown leaves and twigs pointed like an arrow through the gap. Jay slipped inside.

She stood stock-still beside the doors, listening hard, waiting again while her eyes adjusted to the denser darkness within the building. More smells, mostly sour. She reached out and touched the nubbled surface of the wall nearest to her. Paint over heavy cloth, probably asbestos. Fifty years spent teaching the four food groups and all the time they were giving kids lung disease.

The floor was ancient linoleum, laid out in squares of black and white like a chessboard, time turning the white to a fainter tint of black. Her lips pulled back in a tense grin; it was all so fucking familiar. She'd been here before – so had every other kid in the world. Nine months a year of purgatory. She could walk the halls of Crocker blindfolded.

Up a second flight of steps, worn in the middle. The faint outlines of doorways in the gloom. Offices, one for the principal, one for the vice principal. If you were a kid, being sent here was a death sentence. To use the main entrance except for fire drills or accompanied by a parent was tantamount to suicide.

At the top of the steps she was faced with a wide hallway, left and right. Directly in front of her was a huge, floor-to-ceiling display case, the glass smashed into a million pieces. They'd saved the football trophies, the plaques, and the honor roll of students who'd died in World War II. Where there had once been a pair of heavy fire doors, there was nothing but a charred, gaping hole. Beyond that must be the auditorium and the gym. Remembering the floor plans at the Municipal Offices, she turned right, following the long hall down to the far stairway. To left and right, metal locker doors hung open like broken teeth.

There was another smell in the air now, something horrible. She paused, reaching to the small of her back and taking out the pistol. She knew what the smell was. Rotting meat, rich and pungent. The only thing missing was the buzz of feeding flies.

And there was a sound, utterly at odds with the terrible stench. Faint, coming from a long way off.

Vivaldi. Swallowing hard, she turned the corner, put one foot on the stairs, and almost screamed as something brushed against her face. She reared back, bringing up her weapon, sucking in her breath as she prepared to fire.

Oh God.

Hanging on dangling lengths of twine that stretched up into the darkness of the stairwell like some enormous wind chime were the remains of at least a hundred cats – heads, hindquarters, torsos and tails, legs and paws. Some had fresh, glazed eyes filling sockets, open mouths still pink, while others were obviously much older, fur lifeless, matted with dark clots, eyes sunken, exposed flesh black and leathery.

Totems.

Like skulls on bamboo stakes in Borneo to keep enemies at bay. A signal to the sane. Madness lies ahead. Turn back, turn back.

No way, no way. Too late, too late.

Jay stepped forward and went up the stairs, edging around the small horrors, fighting back the surge of sour bile that was filling her throat, holding her breath against the smell. Thankfully, at the top of the first landing, the charnel maze of animal parts came to an end. At the bottom of the second landing only one length of string ran up to the ceiling high above, lit softly by the faint moonlight pouring in through the single, tall window. Jay stopped again and stared. No more cats.

A human hand, string neatly knotted around the exposed wristbone, fingers pointing toward the floor. A girl's hand. There was a ring on the baby finger, a hair-thin band of gold and a tiny heart-shaped stone, pale blue. The hand was fresh, the skin taut and pink, the wrist bone white, the yellow, cheesy marrow clearly visible poking up from the ragged stump of the splintered radius and ulna.

Don't lose it now. This is going to get worse.

She eased around the hanging hand and continued up the stairs. The movement of air set the hand spinning slowly, the little ring with its inset stone catching the light from the window as it turned. Jay kept close to the wall, forcing herself to go on. The music was louder now, *The Four Seasons*. 'Winter' if she remembered correctly, which was ironic, because she could feel the salt sweat running down the creases of her neck and pooling at the base of her spine.

She reached the top of the stairs. Peeking around the corner, she could see a spill of light coming through a doorway at the end of the hall, no more than twenty or thirty feet away. The science lab. The brittle strains of the music gathered strength and under the sound Jay could hear a humming whistle that kept roughly in tune. Straining her eyes she could see a plain chair against the wall close to the door. There was something piled on it. Clothes?

Jay stepped out into the hall. She stood there, waiting, until the music reached its climax, then eased the slide of the pistol forward and back, pushing a shell into the chamber. Not the standard full-metal jacket loads the manual called for; these were hollow points. If she had to shoot, she wanted a hole in him the size of a dinner plate.

There was a short silence and then the music began again. 'Spring' now, the music richer, lighter, full of life. Jay knew Vivaldi was never going to be the same for her again. She eased forward, back against the wall, taking one step at a time, placing each sneakered foot carefully, pausing every few feet to listen again.

Another smell now, even worse than the stench of the dangling chunks of desiccating meat in the stairwell. Thick acid fumes that seared the inside of her nostrils and made her eyes water. Using her free hand, she wiped away the burning tears and began breathing through her mouth in quick, short pants. She tried to tell herself it was just the smell, but she knew better. It was the closeness.

Jesus loves me, this I know.

Another step. Stop again. She was standing no more than a yard away from the chair outside the door to the Crocker science lab. They were clothes: thin, dark socks; pale silk boxer shorts, folded; linen trousers, folded; light blue oxford cloth shirt, folded, and a dark blue poplin windbreaker. Sitting on top of the windbreaker was the Ivy League cap, and on top of that, a wallet and a heavy bunch of keys.

For the Bible tells me so. He's in there, naked. Oh God!

She reached out and touched the keys. Even through the acid reek, she could pick off the smell of too much after-shave on the clothes. Jade East? Did they make that anymore, or was it just her imagination?

Gordie Saybrook was wearing Jade East the first time he stuck his hand down my pants in the backseat of his mother's brand-new Buick Riviera. I was wearing White Shoulders.

By the book she took a deep breath, exhaled, and swung around the chair, stepping forward into the doorway, the pistol aimed, right hand braced in the palm of her left.

The room was large, rectangular, and high-ceilinged, lit from above by half a dozen banks of fluorescents. Somehow he'd managed to run power into the room. The tall windows were blacked out with thick felt held in place with silvery strips of duct tape.

The old science lab had been transformed into an embalming chamber. Sheets of plywood had been laid out over the lab tables, covered in heavy plastic. From where she stood, Jay could see the remains of a woman decomposing on one of the tables. Her head was gone and so were her hands and feet. On the floor, several huge cooking pots full of some tarry, bubbling liquid had been set on to hotplates.

Four chairs had been set out beside the cauldrons. On one there was a small, expensive-looking boom box; on the other three, facing the music, were three seated figures, all young women, all fully clothed. They sat rigidly, their faces blank and lifeless. A blonde and two brunettes. The blonde's right eye was missing, the hole filled with cotton waste. Her right hand was gone as well, snapped off at the wrist.

Taxidermy.

Dear Lord, he's stuffing them.
Trophies, like moose heads on the wall.

At the front of the room, the teacher's desk had been replaced by an immense, zinc-covered table. On it there was another body, skin pulled off in a single piece and dangling from a last attaching point at the scalp. Kushinski, naked, his own skin oily with sweat in the glare of the lights, was bent over the flayed figure on the table, carefully removing the eyes from their sockets. He had a Sherlock Holmes–style pipe in his mouth and Jay could just catch a whiff of the sweet, cherry-flavored tobacco he was smoking.

There was a tray of instruments by his right hand – large hooked knives, broad needles, sail maker's twine, and several saws. Behind him, only partially visible was a tall, skeletal construction of plastic tube and chicken wire complete with hinged armatures and a roughed-in plaster skull. Two large, brown, artificial eyes were already in place.

Jay must have made some sound because Kushinski looked up from his work and stared at her. He looked confused for a moment, and then he smiled. He raised his small right hand and used it to wipe away the sweat from his forehead. His left hand was between his legs, hidden by the table. When he spoke his voice was soft and pleasant with a faintly British accent. Seeing the direction of her glance, he beamed brightly.

'I always do the eyes first. I like them to watch, don't you?'

CHAPTER TWENTY-ONE

'I'm impressed,' said Charles Langford, seated behind his desk in the basement of the Hoover Building. 'At least now we have a name for the bastard.'

'Maybe you're impressed,' said Hawkins, sitting across from him. 'I'm not. Stiles has always managed to stay at least one step ahead of me. That hasn't changed.' He shook his head. 'He knows every move I make.'

'You're convinced he's working through some kind of computer access?'

'Positive. It's the only thing that makes any sense. It's too much of a coincidence that Ritchie and his wife are bludgeoned to death twenty-four hours after I interviewed them. Stiles isn't following me around personally; he's doing it electronically. Credit cards.'

'So he's a hacker?'

'Looks that way.'

'If he's checking up on your credit card use, then he's pretty sophisticated,' Langford answered. 'Maybe a professional. If he's tapped into the credit card databases, there's not much you can do to protect yourself except stop using the cards. Pay cash.'

'Hard to do these days; and I'm not sure I want to protect myself.'

'If you don't cover your ass, he'll know you're coming.'

'He knows anyway. If I keep on using the cards, maybe I can draw him out into the open. I can't let something like the Ritchies happen again,' said Hawkins. 'If I hadn't gone to see them, they might still be alive.'

'You don't know that for certain. It might have been a coincidence.'

'Bullshit, Charlie. But thanks anyway.' Hawkins turned in his chair and stared at the big wall map of the United States. 'If I could play his game, I could pin him down; I know it.'

'Play his game?'

'Like I said, turn the tables on him. Do some hacking on my own.'

'The epilepsy thing?'

'Yes. I spent a lot of time with the guy at the Epilepsy Foundation in San Francisco and an hour on the phone this morning with the National Epilepsy Foundation here in D.C. If Stiles has this psycho-motor version of the disease, there are only four drugs he could be taking – dilantin, carbamazepine, valproic acid, or any combination of phenobarbitals; that's the official line.'

'Unofficially?'

'An orphan drug. Phenacemide. You can't get it in the

States. Stiles was using it back in the sixties, when it was still on the approved list.'

'Check on who's bringing in the drug from outside the country and you narrow the field?'

'Exactly.'

'Who makes the drug?'

'A bunch of companies. One in Sweden, one in France, another one in Canada. I'm betting he's getting the stuff in Canada. It's closest and its easiest. From what the doctor in San Francisco told me, Stiles is probably ordering it over the phone and getting it mailed to him.'

'Is that legal?'

'It's a gray area. Lots of people are doing it, especially AIDS patients and their doctors.'

'How many people are we talking about? Possible buyers for the drug?'

'If I could get into the Epilepsy Foundation files, I could give you a pretty good idea.'

'They won't give you access?'

'Not without a warrant.'

'Which we're not going to get, I'm afraid.'

'Unless we make this whole investigation official,' said Hawkins.

'Forget it,' Langford answered. 'Some serious shit has just been thrown into the Bureau fan, and I think there's more coming.' He reached into the pocket of his jacket and tossed a curling piece of waxy fax paper on to the desk.

'What's this?'

'Read it; I'll weep quietly here in the corner.'

The fax was a photocopy of a tear sheet from the Independent News Service wire. It was slugged as having originated from the Butler *Eagle* in Butler, Pennsylvania. The byline was attributed to someone named Christy Skeed:

INS/Butler Eagle/dateline: Slippery Rock/Skeed
Acting on an anonymous tip, local police in this small Pennsylvania community discovered the body of local veterinarian Dr Evelyn Kushinski in the science laboratory of the abandoned Crocker Consolidated School on State Highway 108. A preliminary investigation suggests that Dr Kushinski had himself been involved in a murder spree going back several years.

The remains of at least nine female victims, all between the ages of eighteen and twenty, have been discovered at the school, which has been empty for almost fifteen years.

Police Chief Eric Sommers refused to comment on the Slippery Rock serial killer, except to indicate that the rash of animal mutilations in the Butler-Slippery Rock area over the past two years can probably be attributed to Dr Kushinski as well.

This reporter has also learned that a woman identifying herself as 'Jennifer Smith' had been asking questions about Dr Kushinski as well as several other people in the area. Smith, representing herself as being a member of CERT, the Computer Emergency Response Team, is also known to have talked to the Slippery Rock Rape/Crisis Center. Astrid Kee, Director of the Center, refused to comment.

The investigation continues.

'Some vigilante took out a serial killer?' asked Hawkins, tossing the fax back on to the desk. 'That's a new wrinkle.' The FBI computer expert nodded.

'This Jennifer Smith woman. The Skeed woman sent me that story about an hour before Sommers, the Slippery Rock Police Chief, called in the State Police. The Penn State boys called us. We're officially involved.'

'I'd have thought it would be handed to Behavioral Sciences.'

'There are computers involved. The police went through Kushinski's residence. He was fully equipped, except everything had been smashed. They're sending us what's left of his hard drive to see if we can recover anything.'

'So what's the problem?'

'I think I know who Jennifer Smith is,' said Langford flatly.

Hawkins smiled. 'So you'll be a hero.'

Langford shook his head. 'I think she's one of ours.'

Hawkins stared. 'A Bureau agent?'

The older man expelled a long sighing breath. 'Remember when I first asked you to pick up the Iceman thing, run with it outside channels? I mentioned one of my people, a woman named Jay Fletcher. She got herself into some hot water in California, dug into a database without authorization, compromised an indictment. I sent her to Santa Fe to cool her heels. She was supposed to be setting up a computer system for an arson investigator named Cruz.'

'I remember you saying something,' Hawkins answered. 'You were upset about it, as I recall.'

'I still am.'

'So?'

'She's disappeared. Left Cruz a letter saying she was taking some personal leave time. She had quite a bit coming.'

Hawkins frowned. 'I don't see the connection.'

'A few days before she took off, the police in Albuquerque wrapped up a string of killings. Called the guy the Hand Job killer. Never made it into the media. They got an anonymous call. Found the guy dead. He was into computers too, all smashed.'

'The same MO.'

'Right.'

'Any other evidence that it was this Fletcher woman?'

'Not yet. We're working on it.'

'Internally.'

'You bet your ass.' He tilted his chin toward the fax lying on the desk. 'That went out on the wire this morning. How long do you think it's going to be before the tabloids pick it up?'

'Not long,' said Hawkins. 'But there's still no real link between this Jennifer Smith and the Bureau.'

'The reporter who sent me that story is already suspicious. Give it another day or two and they'll be beating down my door.'

'It's pretty thin, Charlie. Maybe you're just being paranoid.' He smiled fondly. 'You do have a reputation for being a bit of a Nervous Nellie.'

'I'm not being paranoid; I'm being careful. Fletcher is a computer expert with a questionable ethics record; at the very least, she's someone who's willing to bend the rules to suit her own objectives. Two psychopaths get zapped and they're both computer freaks.'

'Don't you think that's a bit farfetched?'

'What? Computer psychos?' He shook his head. 'The Internet's just another environment and it doesn't have a police force. Not yet. Right now it's Wild West time out there in the ozone. Christ, Bill, you said it yourself – even the Iceman, this Ricky Stiles character, is a hacker.' The FBI man paused. 'Jesus! There's a thought.'

'What?'

'Fletcher. She developed a program for us called the Criminal Behaviors Index, C-Bix. Given access to enough databases, she was sure that it could be used to track down repeat offenders – like serial killers. If I'm right, she's snuffed two of them already. Maybe there's a connection between what she's doing and Ricky Stiles.'

Hawkins shook his head. 'Coincidence,' he said. 'It has to be.'

'There's no such thing in our line of work, and you know it.'

'You're talking about a lady Charles Bronson. A female *Death Wish*. A revenge vigilante who's ridding the world of murderers and rapists. She's a pipe dream, Charlie, a New Age feminist fantasy. I'm talking about a real-life sociopath who's been slaughtering people at will for the past twenty-odd years.'

'Maybe they're part of the same nightmare,' said Langford.

'Maybe.' Hawkins sighed. 'But in the meantime I need some of your expertise.' He picked up the *Berkeley Barb* clipping from Langford's desk. 'Does Jack Prine still work for you guys?'

Langford nodded. 'Sure. He ages well.'

'Cute,' said Hawkins. 'You think he could add twenty-five years to our friend Stiles?' He handed the clipping to Langford.

The older man looked at the picture and bobbed his head. 'I think we can manage that. Anything else?'

'Stiles' epilepsy medication. If I can track it down, I can nail him, Charlie. Once and for all.' He paused, staring closely at his old friend. 'If you're right about this woman Fletcher, maybe we should take a page from her book. Maybe it's time we stepped into their world, fought them on their own ground, by their own rules, not ours.'

Langford shrugged. 'I'm an old dog, Bill; I don't know

any other rules than the ones I've been playing by for a
lot of years.'

'Then maybe it's time you learned.'

Langford turned and flipped through the Rolodex by
his phone. He found what he was looking for and
scrawled a number on a piece of notepaper. He handed it
across the desk. 'Call this number. His name, believe it
or not, is Wacker. Tell him I gave you the number and
tell him what you need.'

'He's private?'

'Very.'

There was a knock and Charles Langford looked up. A
short, dark-haired man was standing in the doorway.

'I'm looking for Charles Langford's office.'

'You found it. What can I do for you?'

'My name is Cruz. I've got some information about
Jay Fletcher you might be interested in.'

Jay Fletcher stood at the window of her hotel room and
looked out over the Chicago skyline. From where she
stood, she could see the Navy Pier and the lakeshore
campus of the University of Illinois. Beyond that, Lake
Michigan itself was alive with the white-flag sails of
scores of small boats from the yacht club, taking
advantage of the stiff onshore breeze. The midafternoon
sun was shining brightly and there wasn't a cloud in the
perfect blue sky.

She'd asked for a room with a view of the John
Hancock Building and the hotel had been glad to oblige.
It stood like a towering Egyptian obelisk a mile to the

south. Built in the late sixties, the gigantic building was still impressive. Broad at the base, it rose, strapped with its massive trademark X-beams, narrowing slightly, for exactly one hundred stories, the roof topped with the soaring needle spires of twin microwave antennae that added another hundred feet to its overall height.

She'd done her homework earlier that morning. She knew that the first five floors of the John Hancock were given over to a retail concourse and that the next six floors contained parking for the offices above. The sixteenth and seventeenth floors held the lower mechanical service areas, including air-conditioning, heat, and electricity.

Floors eighteen to forty-one were offices, forty-two and forty-three were mechanical floors, and forty-four was the supermarket, fitness club, and swimming pool. Forty-five to ninety-two were residential, with a total of seven hundred and fifty apartments of various sizes. Originally they'd all been condominium residences, but over the years more and more had been rented out to leased tenants by their owners. Floors ninety-two through one hundred contained more mechanical areas, a restaurant and bar, several television stations, radio stations, and an observation deck.

On any given day, there were more than five thousand people living and working in the building, consuming a total of 600,000 gallons of water, creating fifteen tons of garbage, and using enough electricity to power six thousand suburban homes. The building had twelve hundred miles of wire and cable, and utilized fifty separate elevators. The express elevators took more than half a million nonresident visitors to the observation deck and restaurant each year. Even after more than twenty-five years, it still qualified as the largest mixed-use building in the world.

Of the five thousand people who lived and worked there each day, Jay Fletcher was only interested in one. According to her information, his name was Homer Ellis Dunton, and by his own testimony he had savagely murdered eleven people over the last six and a half years. Sometime tomorrow, she was going to kill him.

Jay dragged the heavy curtains across the view and turned away from the window. The headache that had been tapping at her temples since she'd arrived in Chicago was now hammering at her skull like a kettle drum, and the Xanax prescription she'd lifted from Kushinski's apartment in Harrisville didn't seem to be doing anything at all. Jay was reasonably sure that there wasn't a pill on earth that would change how she was feeling right now.

Murderer.

She crossed the semidarkened room and stood beside the enormous bed. She toed off her sneakers, pulled her T-shirt up and off, then unclasped her jeans. She sat down on the bed, peeled off her jeans, and lay down, back against three of the four pillows.

The television was on, but she'd muted the sound. The only noise in the room was the almost subliminal hum of the air-conditioner. It was turned up high, the cold air bringing up goose bumps on her bare skin.

After spending half the night driving across country and most of the morning finding out what she needed to know about Homer Ellis Dunton, she was exhausted, but she knew there was no way that she was going to sleep. Cold-blooded murder was better than half a dozen Cafe Cubanos when it came to keeping you awake.

She closed her eyes and felt a sudden rush of vertigo as the veterinarian slithered into her consciousness and she remembered what she'd seen. How many women had lain, eyes half-open in a half-dark room, as they waited for him to practice his terrible skill on them? He'd stepped away from the table, one hand extended to greet her, the other wrapped around the small pink spike of his penis. She'd lifted the gun then, aimed it directly at his head, but it didn't seem to bother him; his smile and the rapid movement of his hand continued as he came toward her.

Intimate friends who shared the same secret, enjoying the moment together.

Say hello to your new neighbor.

She hesitated only for a split second, any thoughts of questionable morality erased by the utter depravity of the man approaching her, and the evidence of his madness that lay all around the terrible room. Jay shot him once, the soft-nosed bullet entering the orbit of his right eye and tearing through the optic canal into his brain. The pipe flew out of his mouth and up into the air, ash and hot coals dropping down on to the sinewy corpse in front of him. The back of his head blew out all over the old-fashioned blackboard behind him, spraying bone and blood on the chalk-dusty slate. Jay had bent over and vomited.

The whole thing had taken place in an instant, less time than it took her to flip from one television channel to the other. A moment that she'd replayed in her head a thousand times over the past few hours. She pushed the image out of her head, trying to replace it with the flickering scenes on the screen at the foot of the bed.

Eventually she found the pay-per-view channels and slowed down. Stallone, Jackie Chan, and Bridget Fonda. A choice of four different pornos: two straight, one lesbian, and a mixed gender called *Cheating Wives*. The porn flicks allowed you three minutes of preview each so she began flipping back and forth between them; it was a game she'd played in hotel rooms before, always in search of the elusive answer to the simple question, Why? Who wants to see other people screwing?

Lonely people.

On the glowing screen she watched as a blonde in her thirties stretched her legs apart and smiled as a beefy football player type with zits on his rump inserted himself into her with clinical precision. The blonde still had her shoes on. The video cut to a grittily realistic close shot of his organ as it moved in and out of her with the precise timing of a metronome. The shot jumped to a wide shot, showing her spike heels drumming into his pimpled ass.

Did Kushinski see something like this when he killed them?

Or did he see cats?

What did a normal man think about, watching this? Less lonely times? Did a normal man think about movies like this when he was with his wife or girlfriend?

Two women were attacking each other with vibrators on the next channel up, grunting and growling at each other as they slid around on a circular bed covered with black satin sheets. Jay could see the shadow of the boom mike over their heads. Maybe that was it; when you watched a Stallone movie, no one was really dying or bleeding, or even getting laid. What she was seeing now was utterly real. The perfect candid camera. No faking, no morphing, no special effects.

The third channel was a reprise of number one except the football player was black and the woman was a redhead. He was copulating with her from the rear, rhythmically slapping her buttocks with every second or third stroke.

With the flame patch of her pubic hair and the pink meat between her legs, it looked like a black bone knife slicing into an open wound. He was almost as well-endowed as Carl, the Albuquerque busboy. The woman looked as if she was watching clothes go around in a Laundromat dryer.

Remember how it felt? Right after you blew his brains out? Like flying or doing acid or falling down a deep black velvet well. Like the first time you ever went skinny-dipping on that little private lake, in the middle of the night, and you lay on the raft with the moon over your head and the water lapping. Letting the entire universe have its way with you.

Like sex. Maybe better.

On the last channel a woman was copulating with three men simultaneously, every orifice filled to over-flowing while another woman watched, chewing gum and pretending to masturbate with a huge, jelly-slick dildo.

Jay's preview time ran out and the screen went black, flickered, and came back on with a message telling her how much it would cost for her to see more of the same. She stared at the screen for a moment, then used the channel changer to turn off the television.

Rolling over on to her side, she reached out and pulled the telephone from the night table on to the bed. She punched an outside line, then called the number in Washington she'd repeated to herself like an incantation all the way from Harrisville. Her friend Nadine's psychiatrist, the one she'd seen just before she went to Santa Fe.

All she got was a recorded message; there was a beep and then a blank tape hiss. Jay listened for a moment and then hung up. What was the point in leaving a message of her own? She put the phone back on the night table, picked up the channel changer, and switched on the TV again.

CHAPTER TWENTY-TWO

Charles Langford sat in the squeaky, wicker basket chair, shifting his weight uncomfortably, realizing just how far he was from being politically correct. His preliminary investigative dip into Jay Fletcher's personal life had uncovered Nadine Wilson, Jay's neighbor, and from Nadine it was only a single step to Dr Sarina Chisolm, the psychiatrist from Capitol Hill Hospital. It was a step he was beginning to wish he hadn't taken. The whole thing was coming apart right in front of him; Cruz was cooperating, acting as a 'friend of the Bureau' by giving Hawkins a hand, but Horace Sladky, the Albuquerque cop, was a wild card. Sarina Chisolm was another one.

The shrink on the other side of the antique table looked like a chubby version of Candice Bergen with gray hair and a shawl. The office itself was a magpie's nest of cultural icons ranging from a stoneware bowl of eagle feathers on the table to Mexican rugs on the floor, with macramés everywhere and a framed original poster for *Hair*, the rock musical, beside the door.

Langford was willing to bet that Dr Chisolm wasn't really a Sarina either; the name was probably as after-market as the decor. Given her midforties appearance, she was more likely to be a Patricia or a Barbara. Regardless of what her name was, the doctor was a royal pain in the ass.

'Why are you so concerned about Jay's mental state?'

'She's been having problems.'

'You said she tendered a letter of resignation?'

'Not exactly. She said she was taking a leave of absence.'

'That sounds reasonable enough to me, Agent Langford.' She made his official title sound like ashes in her mouth. Probably called all policemen 'pigs' back in the sixties and still wasn't far from it.

'Under ordinary circumstances, I'd agree with you, Dr Chisolm.'

'You haven't told me anything extraordinary. Yet.'

'Jay's been under a great deal of stress.'

'Yes.' The nod was telling, the cautious frown profound. Hints of the Wisdom of the Ages. 'I gathered that from my brief meeting with her.'

'Did she mention any feelings of serious depression?'

'You know better than that, Agent Langford. That's confidential information. Doctor/patient privilege.'

'Did she talk about suicide?'

'Again, confidential.'

'Look, Dr Chisolm, I'm trying to help Jay, not hurt her. I think she's in trouble.'

'What makes you think that? She decided to take a

vacation. In my opinion she sounded as though she needed one.'

'The Bureau has that effect on a lot of us,' Langford said dryly. 'But that's not the point.'

'What is?'

'I need to find Jay Fletcher. Now.'

'I'm afraid I can't help you, then. I have no idea where she might be.'

'She hasn't been in touch?'

'I saw her once, and that was only for one session.'

Langford nodded. Chisolm wasn't being evasive, but he'd caught a flicker of something in her voice. Worry? No. He watched her plump hand reach out to adjust the bowl of eagle feathers. Not worry. She's figuring out the odds. She knows something.

'How about a professional opinion, then,' he said finally.

'An opinion on what?'

'A hypothetical situation.'

'A hypothetical situation regarding a female FBI agent perhaps?'

'Perhaps.'

'It would depend on the hypothesis, I suppose. As long as there was no abuse of trust.'

'What if I told you an FBI agent had gone over the edge?'

'What edge, and how far?'

'Cracked up. Lost it. A complete mental breakdown.'

Sarina Chisolm laughed. 'Those are mental health chestnut,' she said. 'You'll have to be more specific.

What has this hypothetical FBI agent done to suggest that he or she has "gone over the edge," as you call it?'

'What if she killed someone?'

The psychiatrist stared at Langford, then looked away, apparently studying one of the macramés hanging on the far side of the room. Then she turned back to him.

'Killing is part of what an FBI agent does, isn't it?'

'Not really. I've been a member of the Bureau for almost twenty-five years and I've never fired my gun off the practice range.'

'But you are trained for it. The possibility is there.'

'Of course. In real terms, though, you could just as easily say we're trained *not* to kill people.'

'A last resort.'

'Yes.'

'But presumably the FBI wouldn't hire someone who was fundamentally unable to take another life.'

'Like a conscientious objector?' Langford asked. He shrugged. 'I suppose not.'

'So your hypothetical FBI agent is capable of killing?'

'Yes.'

'In the line of duty?'

'No.'

Chisolm was silent again. She'd assumed that Langford was using a roundabout way of telling her that Jay had killed a criminal and had cracked up afterward, then disappeared.

'Murder?'

'Let's call it justifiable homicide,' Langford answered, trying to soften it.

'In the legal sense?'

'No, morally justifiable, at least in the agent's mind.'

The psychiatrist frowned. 'I find it difficult to imagine such a hypothetical context.'

'Then I'll suggest one,' said Langford. 'An agent who feels that the system is not functioning properly, who has been frustrated by it, who decides to expedite justice by her own hand.'

'Vigilantism.' Chisolm nodded sagely. 'The justification for violence used by groups like the KKK.' They were back to political correctness.

'Not quite,' said Langford, shaking his head. He was dying to smoke a cigarette, but he knew it was out of the question.

'Then you'll have to explain it more fully.'

'A rapist who is emasculated by his victim. Is that a crime?'

'Of course. The rape and the emasculation are two different acts.'

'But one leads to the other.'

'Which is why we have people like you, Agent Langford.' Chisolm pursed her lips. Her hands came together like a tent of fingers beneath her chin. 'You're supposed to catch and convict rapists so women don't have to take the law into their own hands. You're talking about the essence of civilized behavior.'

'And if the system doesn't work?' Langford asked. 'What does the hypothetical agent do then? Only one rape in ten is reported, Dr Chisolm, I'm sure you're aware of that. What about the other nine? Where is the justice for them?'

'Somewhere in the future,' said Chisolm, smiling and leaning back in her chair. It was one of the most idiotic things Langford had ever heard. 'Change takes time,' she added. 'Women have been waiting for equality for the last two hundred thousand years or so, we can wait a little longer.'

He stared at her. Sarina Chisolm clearly lived in a fantasy world of pompous twaddle. The New Age would be ushered in any minute now and everything would be wonderful. It was the old 'If Richard Nixon smoked a joint, the world would change overnight' theory. Nixon hadn't taken a toke, but Bill Clinton had, and it didn't make one iota of difference. Neither the President nor Sarina Chisolm had ever seen what the Iceman did to his victims. Last night the pictures had come in from Slippery Rock, Pennsylvania. What would Chisolm think of those?

'Do you have a cat?' Langford asked.

'No, why?' asked the psychiatrist, confused at the oddball question.

'Just wondering,' Langford answered. 'It doesn't matter.' There was a short silence. 'What about the hypothesis?' he said eventually.

Chisolm sighed. 'Anyone, given the motivation, is capable of violence, even murder, especially if they feel they've been wronged,' she said. 'It's simple human nature.'

'What about multiple murder?'

'You're saying that your hypothetical agent has killed more than once?' Again there was the faint, shocked look, and the secret guilty glance away from him. She did know something.

'Twice.'

'And will do so again?'

'Possible. Even likely.'

There was a pause. 'Oh dear,' said Chisolm. 'You're putting me in a difficult situation, Agent Langford.'

'I'm not putting you in any situation, Doctor. I'm just telling you what I know.' He grimaced. 'Which isn't much at this point.'

'We're not talking hypothetically now, are we?'

'I'm afraid not.'

'Oh dear,' she said again. Langford waited. Chisolm's face moved through several different expressions.

'Have you heard from Jay?' he asked quietly.

'No.' She paused, mouth open, on the verge of adding something. Then her mouth snapped shut. 'No,' she repeated. Talking to herself. He let her twist in the breeze for as long as he dared, then made his play. Interrogation of a potentially hostile witness, page thirty-two in the manual. He sat forward in the wicker chair and spread his hands out in front of him, palms up.

'Look, Doctor, I'm on Jay's side here. I don't know what your philosophical stance is on the police, or the Bureau, or the state of the world in general, for Christ's sake, all I know is that she's in trouble, bad trouble. I want us to get to her before someone else does. If she has been in contact with you, I'd like to hear about it now, not later. Later may be too late. For all of us.' The last of it was a subtle threat.

If it comes out later that she got in touch with you and you didn't do anything, your airy-fairy reputation's going to go down the fucking toilet, Doc.

'Have you heard from her?' He tried to keep the tension out of his voice. Soft and gentle.

'No. I haven't heard from her,' Chisolm answered. 'Not directly anyway.'

'What does that mean, not directly?'

'When I came in this morning, there was a message on my answering machine.'

'From Jay?'

'I'm not sure. Possibly.'

'What was the message?'

'There wasn't one. Just someone breathing. A sub-audible.'

'What's that?'

'People under extreme stress sometimes speak aloud without realizing that they're doing so. We all do it, actually, some more than others. Usually the sound is below normal hearing range, what they used to call thoughts in the throat. The more stress, the more audible. Usually.'

'Could it have been Jay?'

'It's possible. It was definitely a woman's voice. There was a hollowness to it . . .'

'Long distance?' If it was, the telephone company would have a record of where the call originated.

Chisolm nodded, pulling her shawl more closely

around her shoulders. 'I thought so when I played it back.'

'Do you get a lot of that?' asked Langford. 'People calling up without leaving messages?'

'No. Not really. I don't have that kind of practice. Most of my clients are in long-term analysis.' She smiled sadly. 'Many of them have become my friends.' She collected cures like medals and called them friends, but there hadn't been enough time for that with Jay.

'Do you still have the tape?'

'Yes,' said the psychiatrist. Langford nodded to himself; the lab boys could pull it up, perhaps even identify the voice.

'Could you hear what she was saying?'

'I think so. It was just a whisper. She repeated it twice and then hung up.'

'What did she say?'

'*What's the point? What's the point?*'

Bill Hawkins and Cruz sat on either side of Jack Prine in the basement of FBI Headquarters and watched as the computer-graphics specialist scanned the newspaper clipping from the 1968 *Berkeley Barb*. Almost magically, an enlargement of the yellowed, half-tone photograph began to take shape on the big double-page computer screen in front of them.

'Black guy or the white guy?' asked Prine.

'White,' Hawkins answered.

Prine made a snorting sound under his breath. 'The

black guy looks like a skinny version of that actor on *Mod Squad*, remember him?'

'I think his name was Luke.' offered Cruz.

'That's the one,' nodded Prine. 'Big hair, just like this character. All he ever said was "solid."'

Prine fiddled with the computer mouse and the image of Thomas Ritchie as a young man slid off to the right. Prine tapped the keyboard and Ricky Stiles' face filled the screen.

'Solid,' said Prine, and snorted again. He sat back in his chair and scratched his jaw. 'Interesting face. How old is he in this picture?'

'Eighteen, nineteen. The photograph was taken in 1968.'

Prine nodded, eyes fixed on the screen. 'So he's mid-forties now.' He rummaged around in the pocket of his grimy lab coat and took out a tube of mints. He popped one into his mouth, sucking loudly.

'Anything special you can tell me about him? Not his rap sheet. Personal information.'

'He's epileptic. Charming. Extremely intelligent. Probably a computer specialist.' Hawkins smiled. 'Like you,' he added.

'A smart, good-looking hacker with epilepsy.' Prine laughed. 'Except for the epilepsy we've got a lot in common.'

'Not as much as you think,' Hawkins answered.

'Okay, let's see what we can do.' He used the mouse pointer to click on the image's eyes. 'If he's like the rest of us, his lamps are going bad. How about glasses?'

'His looks are too important to him. More likely he'd be wearing contacts.' Hawkins thought for a moment, remembering what the doctor in San Francisco had told him. 'Make them tinted. Epileptics are photosensitive.'

Prine nodded absently. 'Hard to say here, but I'd guess his eyes are blue. We'll tint them brown.' He clicked the mouse and the eyes on the screen darkened. 'Add a few crow's feet for good measure.' The eyes aged visibly, looking strangely wise in the youthful face.

'Eerie,' said Cruz. 'All this stuff is like voodoo to me.'

'Join the club,' said Hawkins.

'Always start with the eyes,' said Prine, ignoring them. 'Windows on the soul and all that crap. But it's true. Get the eyes right and you can work from the middle to the outside.' The computer expert hit another sequence of keys and the picture of Ricky Stiles suddenly vanished.

'What happened?' asked Hawkins, startled.

'Relax,' Prine murmured. 'I'm just adding thirty years of experience.'

'How does that work?' Cruz asked.

'You want the technical explanation, or the quicky layman's version?'

'Quicky layman's,' said Hawkins.

'There's a bunch of standard parameters for human aging we program in. Skin resiliency, skeletal shrinking, that kind of thing. By the looks of it, your man here's an ectomorph – medium height, and wiry. Maybe he'll get a bit of a gut between eighteen and fifty, but

it won't be much more than that, the face will stay thin.'
Prine plucked at his lower lip. 'He sedentary or active,
do you think?'

'Active,' Hawkins answered. 'And you really don't
want to know how he gets his exercise.'

'Booze?'

'No. Bad drug reactions.'

'What about the drugs? Any physical side effects from
whatever it is he's taking for the epilepsy?'

'Maybe a bit of water retention. Nothing obvious.
What he's got sometimes causes liver damage. He might
be a little jaundiced.'

'Cigarettes?'

'No idea. Maybe.'

'Okay.' Prine nodded. 'That should give us a place to
start.' He tapped at the keyboard for a moment, then hit
the Enter button. Stiles' face began to appear on the
screen again, forming quickly in lines drawn from left to
right. Less than a minute later, the image was complete. Stiles, but not Stiles. A good-looking man in
middle age with dark, expressionless eyes. The hair had
drawn back slightly, giving him the hint of a widow's
peak, and the high cheekbones had become more
accentuated. There were faint lines drawing down the
mouth and the narrow chin had broadened slightly.

'Strange,' Hawkins murmured, looking at the screen.
The enemy had a face at last.

'He looks familiar,' said Cruz, staring curiously at the
screen. 'An actor maybe?'

Hawkins snapped his fingers. 'Reminds me a little of

the guy who played Charles Manson in that TV movie, years ago.'

'Steve Railsback.' Prine nodded. 'He was in a movie with Peter O'Toole called *The Stunt Man*.' Prine gestured at the screen. 'This is what he looks like now. Close, anyway.' He glanced back at Hawkins. 'A killer, right?'

'How did you guess?' asked Hawkins.

Prine shrugged. 'I've been doing this for a long time; you get a feel for it. He's got the look. It's what he does. A pro. And I can tell you something else.'

'What?'

'He loves his work.'

The Iceman knew that curiosity hadn't killed the cat; it was arrogance that did the feline in. He sat in the half-dark Tijuana hotel room and contemplated the prostitute sprawled on the narrow bed a few feet away. She was grotesque, of course, but that was part of her charm. Fifteen or sixteen years old at most, already running to fat, her buttocks sprinkled with adolescent pimples, her pudenda thick and dangling from overuse, a misplaced adult slash. Her fish-belly stomach sagged like a fleshy apron over the joining of her thighs, and her breasts flopped like half-filled bags of sugar. Her face was round as a pie plate with little pig eyes, a wide nose, and a small but very expert cupid's-bow mouth. Tiny stained teeth. Hair like old black rope.

What had he been thinking about? He smiled to himself. Curiosity, that was it. Curiosity and dead cats.

He glanced at the folded copy of the *L.A. Times* in his naked lap. The story was small, three paragraphs at the bottom of page six. First Gaddis and now the veterinarian from Slippery Rock, Pennsylvania, the one who'd called himself Dr Cream. Someone out there had been curious enough to find Gaddis and now it had happened again. The one who signed off 'Watch Me.' It had to be.

What was it that Monsignor Pig used to say? Once is happenstance, twice is coincidence, three times is ... who? The story in the *Times* suggested that the killer might be a rogue cop. Was that a coincidence too, with Hawkins so close? The Iceman thought about that for a moment, staring blankly at the sleeping whore. Eventually he dismissed the idea. Watch Me was a hacker and Hawkins wasn't. Somebody else, then. Call him Ted, then, for Bundy, who was long past caring.

So who was next on Watch-Me Ted's list? He closed his eyes and called up a mental image of a map of the United States. It was a long jump from Albuquerque to Slippery Rock, but there had been a fair bit of time between them, too. Time for Ted to get the Hunger? Gaddis might have been chance, a first taste, but dear, sick Dr Cream was definitely a sign that Ted was going to continue snacking, with the Special K bulletin board as his menu.

The Iceman closed his eyes again, feeling a light, saline sting. When he went to pick up his pills, he'd get some lens solution as well. He tried to concentrate on Ted and the death of the man in Slippery Rock. Dr Cream had been truly mad, a late addition to the group, and one whom both the Iceman and his friend Christie had discussed at length. His animal fetish was an interesting element, but both he and the Baltimore psychiatrist agreed that he was unstable. The chances were good that he wasn't very careful, either. Gaddis had led Ted to Dr Cream, so it followed that Cream would almost certainly lead Ted to someone else on the list. If the Watch Me killer really was a hacker cop, there was a good chance he'd be coplike in his thinking. Like Hawkins, he'd be methodical.

The Iceman conjured up his mental map again. Which players were closest to Slippery Rock? There was Christie in Baltimore, of course, but he was far too well hidden; even the Iceman had never been able fully to trace or identify him. There was Landru in Cleveland, which was close enough, but the Iceman hadn't seen him log on in months. The next closest was Gecht in Columbus, the strange one who was always quoting from the *Tibetan Book of the Dead*.

Assuming that it was Gecht, what was he supposed to do about it? He could go to Ohio and warn him in person, but there was no way of knowing when Ted was going to strike, or if he was going to strike at all. It would also break one of the Iceman's own rules – since establishing Special K, he'd scrupulously avoided actually coming face to face with any of those who played the game, even though it had been suggested more than once.

After long and careful study, the Iceman had come to the conclusion that the players, with the exception of himself and Christie, all lived lives delicately balanced on the edge of madness, and despite the fact that their ability to discover the bulletin board hidden beneath the game in the first place effectively winnowed out true maniacs like Jeffrey Dahmer and his ilk, the chances were good that most of them would eventually be caught. To come face to face with any one of them was a risk he wasn't willing to take. He had no intention of being put into a mental institution for the rest of his life, or living out an endless sentence like Charlie Manson. He'd had enough of that at St Vincent's.

He glanced at his watch – not quite ten in the morning. He'd be done here in another hour and back in San Diego just after lunch. From there, home was only an hour away by air; he'd be back in Las Vegas by mid-afternoon. He'd post a message for Gecht on the board and hope for the best. He would also keep a close watch on things when the game began this evening, just in case Watch-Me Ted was lurking in the bushes somewhere.

He stood up, yawning, the newspaper sliding off his lap. He glanced down at himself. Not hard, but that didn't matter, especially in a place like this. He crossed to the bed. The fat girl had been doing some mending when he bought her for the night and there was needle, thread, and scissors still on the night table.

The Iceman reached down and shook the girl's shoulder. He grimaced; her skin was waxy with sebum and felt faintly oily. Beneath the greasy sausage skin she was probably alive with half a dozen different sexually transmitted diseases, including AIDS. Not that it really mattered to him; after all, he wasn't about to have sex with her. He sniffed lightly and for a moment he thought he could smell the pine-and-sea scent of Anderson Island, far away.

The girl on the bed opened her eyes and saw him standing less than a foot away. She sighed, yawned, then struggled into a sitting position, swinging her fat legs on to the floor. She yawned again, then took him into her mouth, bending over, the hugely false sounds of her small, smacking lips almost laughable.

Her filthy hair parted with its own weight and he could see the soft dimple between the base of her skull and the Atlas vertebra of her spine. From there it would only be a short poke into the pons and fornix in the center of the girl's brain. An easy, simple transition from one zone of being to the next, a useless life given some meaning by its sudden winking out at his hands.

She continued to snuffle loudly between his thighs. He felt the old pains and the distant whispers. A favor to her. A pleasure to him. Fair exchange. As good a description of love as he'd ever heard. What more could a girl like this want, or hope for?

He reached out for the scissors.

It cost Jay Fletcher twenty dollars to identify Homer Ellis Dunton; that was how much she bribed the ornately uniformed doorman standing guard at the banks of residential elevators at the John Hancock Center. She told the beak-nosed old man she was from *People* magazine and was doing some background on famous residents in the building and that she wanted to

do her research without them knowing. The doorman
looked as though he couldn't have cared less.

He told Jay that Dunton was a lousy Christmas tipper
and informed her that on most days Dunton left the
building around ten and came back shortly after lunch.
He always left alone, but every now and again he'd come
back to the John Hancock with a good-looking girl on
his arm – not a pro, according to the doorman. He didn't
know what Dunton did for a living, if anything.

Folding the twenty neatly and slipping it into the
pocket of his jacket, the doorman told Jay he'd give her a
wink and a nod when Dunton appeared. Jay found a
comfortable chair screened by a few plants and sat down
to wait. At ten-fifteen a well-dressed man in his
midtwenties stepped out of one of the elevators and
headed for the North Michigan Avenue entrance. The
doorman waved at Jay and pointed one white-gloved
hand at the receding figure.

Dunton ignored the row of American United cabs and
turned south along the wide, busy street. The souvenir
guide book in Jay's hotel room said that this was the
beginning of the Magnificent Mile, a gauntlet of the
best shopping in Chicago. Jay wasn't interested in
shopping and neither was Dunton. Walking at a brisk,
steady pace, he kept on moving south, ignoring the
displays in the windows of Tiffany's, Gucci, and
Hammacher Schlemmer.

Jay couldn't tell much about him from the back. Her
brief look in the main lobby of the John Hancock had
given her the fleeting impression of dark, youthful good

looks, and the suit he was wearing was obviously made to measure, but that was about it. She could have increased her own pace and followed him more closely to get a better look, but for the moment she decided to stay in the background.

Dunton kept walking along Michigan Avenue, crossing the Chicago River just beyond the Tribune Tower. They'd gone more than a mile and Jay began wondering if following Dunton was a waste of time; the two- or three-hour window of opportunity created by his daily sojourn might have been put to better use by getting into his apartment at the John Hancock.

A quarter of the way down the broad greenery of Grant Park, Dunton turned and went up the wide steps of the Chicago Art Institute's imposing entrance. Jay followed, still keeping well back, almost losing Dunton in the crowds of schoolchildren milling around the huge stone lions guarding the front doors. She purchased a ticket, picked up a map at the information desk and headed into the maze of galleries.

For half an hour she tracked Dunton through the collections: Medieval, Renaissance, Impressionist, Post-Impressionist, Asian, and Contemporary Photography. She barely noticed the artwork around her; all of her attention was on Dunton. He didn't seem all that interested in the collections, either. He moved from painting to painting, room to room, with slow familiarity; he'd obviously been to the Art Institute many times before. His real interest seemed to be the other people around him, his eyes sliding over the drifting groups and individuals as though he was looking for someone in particular. He seemed especially interested in women between the ages of twenty and thirty-five, glancing idly at the ones traveling in pairs or groups, paying more attention to any woman traveling alone. At one point he sat down on a low, leather bench in one of the galleries and started up a conversation with a woman in her late teens or early twenties who was making a sketch in an open pad on her lap. From the other side of the large room, Jay watched as they talked for a moment. Finally the girl with the sketchpad smiled and shook her head. Dunton made some comment that made the young woman laugh briefly, and then he moved off again.

He's trolling. Looking for a pretty little minnow.

Bait and hook. Dahmer offered money, Gacy promised work, and Bundy used a phony cast on his arm for sympathy. What shining lure was Dunton using on the end of his line? She frowned as something floated up out of childhood memory. That was happening a lot these days. What was it? Something about fish.

Big fish have bigger fish, upon their backs to bite 'em.

That was how she'd do it. Be a bigger fish. Keeping her eyes carefully turned away, she walked behind Dunton and headed into the next gallery, praying that he wouldn't turn around and go back the way he'd come. The room was intimately small, mostly dark with dramatic halogen pin lighting over half a dozen large glass cases. According to the sign, this was the Rubloff Paperweight Collection. Rubloff had apparently been a

Chicago real-estate magnate with a penchant for the shimmering glass objects and had donated them all to the Art Institute. Jay went to the cases and gazed down at the glittering displays, trying to look consumed with interest. For the moment she was the only one in the gallery.

A few minutes later she became aware of a presence off to one side and slightly behind her. Her mouth went dry and she had to swallow hard before she dared to look up. Dunton was standing a little back from the display case. He glanced at her, then turned back to the paperweights.

What? Not pretty enough for you?

Dunton moved closer to the case, resting his hands on the edge of it. Jay noticed the ring on his third finger. An Egyptian scarab carved from black stone, set into a thick, gold bezel. He turned to Jay and smiled pleasantly.

'Beautiful, aren't they?' His voice was a cool baritone, oddly masculine.

'Yes,' said Jay. 'But paperweights seem like an odd thing to collect.'

'Collectors are odd people,' Dunton answered, smiling. Jay smiled back. At close quarters Dunton was still handsome, but Jay thought she could sense something weak about him. The chin was a little too broad, the long patrician nose too smooth, the lips too full. Suddenly startled, she realized what she was seeing.

Jesus! Not even thirty and he's already had a facelift.

'Are you a collector?' she asked.

'I like to think so.'

403

'Which means you must be odd.' She smiled.

Careful!

'I'm pretty boring, actually. So people tell me.'

'You don't look boring.'

'How do I look to you?' he asked.

'You want the polite answer or the honest one?'

'The honest one,' Dunton answered, looking her full in the face. His eyes were calf-brown and large, a good match for the slightly pouting lower lip.

'You look rich,' said Jay. Which was no lie. Both the shirt and tie were silk. The shoes looked handmade and Italian. 'You're dressed beautifully and only someone with money hangs around museums in the middle of the day.'

'I am rich.' He smiled back. 'I think that's why people find me boring.'

'I thought you said you were a collector.'

'I am.'

'What do you collect?'

Girls? Cats, maybe?

'Different things,' he replied. 'My parents were collectors; I guess it runs in the family.'

'They don't collect anymore?'

'They're dead.'

'I'm sorry.'

'Don't be.' He shrugged. 'It was a long time ago.' He paused, continuing to stare. 'What about you? You're wandering around the Art Institute in the middle of the day; are you rich, too?'

'Vacation.'

'By yourself?' he asked pleasantly. Jay let her smile twitch down a notch; the average single woman in this situation would start getting suspicious after a question like that. She had to play the part.

'Why do you ask?' she said.

Dunton broadened his own smile. 'Because I was going to ask you if you'd like lunch,' he explained. 'I don't ask out married women.'

'Do I look married?'

'No. You look interesting.'

Like a trussed-up turkey on a spit.

She left it for two heartbeats, then smiled coyly. 'Are you trying to pick me up?'

'No.' The perfect look of shocked surprise. Who, me? 'I'm asking you out to lunch, that's all.' It was all so ordinary, a good-looking man picking up a woman in a museum. The kind of thing that happened every day, a thousand times over. Much smoother than a singles bar, and fewer witnesses.

Another two beats. A normal person would think about it. 'Okay,' she said finally. 'It's your town, where should we go?'

Please, God, don't say 'my place'; I'm not ready. Not yet.

'The Ninety-Fifth,' Dunton said promptly. 'The food's quite good and it has the best view in Chicago. As long as you don't mind heights.'

'Where is it?' Jay asked.

As if I didn't know.

'On top of Big John,' Dunton said.

405

Wide-eyed and innocent.
'Big John?'
'The John Hancock Center.'

At noon, Langford met with Hawkins and Cruz at Hawkins' Georgetown University office to compare notes.

'I don't know why we do this shit,' said Langford, dropping down into the big chair across from Hawkins. 'You meet the worst people in the world, and that's not counting the criminals.'

Hawkins smiled. 'The shrink got to you?'

'Big time.' Langford groaned. 'Born to be an inter-fering, down-the-nose condescending pain in the ass.'

'It's hard to imagine Jay going to see a psychiatrist,' said Cruz, turning away from the big map on the office wall. 'Not her style.'

'Grasping at straws, maybe.' Langford shrugged. 'I thought sending her down to you would give her a break, take her out of the stress loop.' He made a snorting sound. 'That sure as hell backfired.' He glanced carefully at the arson investigator. 'You two didn't have any ... problem, did you? Something that might have sent her off the deep end?'

'No.' Cruz answered flatly. 'I think ...' He paused.

'What?' asked Hawkins, sensing something behind the hesitation.

'I think maybe there was something there between us, or there could have been. It was pretty undefined.'

'Some kind of romantic involvement?' asked Langford.

406

'Maybe. I didn't push it. Right from the start I figured she had some complicated stuff to get through.'

'Like going crazy,' Langford said. There was a long pause.

'I don't think she's crazy,' Cruz said finally. 'There's more to it than that.'

'Like what?' asked Hawkins. 'You've been closer to her than anyone else recently; that's why you're here, to give us some kind of insight.'

'We need a hook,' Langford agreed. 'Something to go on.'

'I think she was fed up. I think she'd had enough. Ten years of dealing with the freaks and the crazies. It got to her. She snapped.' He frowned. 'And I think she was lonely. Desperately lonely.'

The telephone rang and Hawkins picked it up. He listened for a moment, then handed the receiver to Langford. 'Technical Services at Quantico.'

The old man took the phone. He listened, nodding, for the better part of five minutes, jotting down a few notes on a pad in front of him. Finally he hung up and sat back in his chair, groaning.

'Anything useful?' Hawkins asked.

'It's Fletcher.' Langford sighed. 'We had a recording of her from when we were doing work on that Stress Analysis Detector last year. Perfect match with the answering-machine tape from the psychiatrist's office. We've got her.'

'Where?' Cruz asked.

'Confirmed off the shrink's billing file. Chicago Hilton. She's using the Slippery Rock vet's credit card. Eh-ve-lyn,

Eve-Eh-lin, it's all the same to American Express. She's in the glue, dead bang.' He shook his head wearily. 'Son of a bitch! How am I supposed to explain this to the suits upstairs? Another year and I could have taken early retirement. Gone to sponge off my kids in California.'

'Maybe that'll happen sooner than you think,' said Hawkins. He grinned 'You'll get a book deal out of this, maybe even a movie.'

'Yeah.' Langford snorted. 'What actor's going to want to play the part of the boob who hired a loose cannon like Fletcher? Red Skelton's dead and Tom Hanks is too skinny. Shit!'

'How are you going to handle it?' asked Hawkins.

'Not a whisper of this to the Chicago Field Office. I'll send a Ghost Squad on the next flight out.' Ghost Squads had officially died out with Hoover, but there were still times when a few trusted, handpicked agents who could keep their mouths shut were used to good effect. Langford glanced at Cruz. 'None of this leaves the room, Cruz. You got that?'

'Mum's the word.' The arson investigator nodded. 'I just don't want to see her hurt, that's all.'

'None of us do,' said Langford. 'Believe me.'

'A watch on the hotel?' Hawkins asked.

Langford nodded. 'For now. They'll call in when she turns up. If she makes a move to leave town, they'll bag her and bring her in.'

'You're not going to be able to keep this quiet for long,' said Hawkins.

'Tell me about it,' said Langford. 'I'm not trying to

Watergate this thing, I just need some time to get my shit together.' He ran a hand over the thinning hair on the top of his head and let out a long, noisy breath. 'What about you? Wacker any help?'

'So far, so good.' Wacker the Hacker was an Ex-FBI technician who specialized in cleaning up people's pasts and inventing new ones for them. Wacker didn't come right out and say it, but he implied that he also worked for the CIA from time to time. Hawkins had given him his wish list the night before and Wacker had called him back within two hours.

'You've narrowed things down?' asked Langford.

Hawkins nodded, glancing at the computer fax print-out Wacker had modemed to him from his loft head-quarters in New York. 'According to your friend Wacker, there are four thousand registered cases of psycho-motor epilepsy in the United States. By cutting out people who are too young, too old, or female, you get that number down to less than five hundred. Of those, fewer than two hundred take phenacemide.'

'The drug Stiles uses.'

'Yes.' Hawkins flipped the page of his printout. 'Like I told you before, there are several companies that manufacture it, but the Canadian one has complied with the FDA ruling about direct-mailing some pro-scribed drugs. If an American wants the drug from them, they have to get a prescription from a Canadian doctor, then smuggle the stuff across.' He shook his head. 'I can't see the Iceman taking that kind of risk.'

'What does that leave us with?' asked Langford.

'Most of the people on Wacker's list use a brand made by Recklerpharm, a German company. Ninety percent of them, in fact.'

'Stiles is getting his drugs from Germany?'

'Recklerpharm has a plant that makes phenacemide in Mexico. Juarez. They won't mail-order either, but they've got a big outlet that sells the stuff over the counter in Tijuana. According to the Recklerpharm representative I talked to this morning, there are only nine people they deal with who use a dose as high as Ricky Stiles.'

'You're getting close,' said Langford.

'Close isn't good enough,' Hawkins answered. There was a long pause. Finally Cruz spoke.

'Okay, now what do we do?'

'I'm still not convinced there's a connection between Stiles and the lady agent.' Hawkins frowned. 'I'll concentrate on Stiles for the moment, see what I can find out in Tijuana. You two can handle Fletcher.' He glanced at Langford. 'I presume this is still off the record, at least for the time being.'

'Yes.'

'Okay. I should be back within twenty-four hours. Meet me at my place tomorrow night. Maybe we'll know more then.'

CHAPTER TWENTY-THREE

'Well,' said Dunton expectantly. 'What do you think?'

Jay Fletcher stood just inside the front door of Dunton's apartment on the ninetieth floor of the John Hancock Center and stared. 'It's magnificent,' she whispered. And it was.

The huge open space had been created by joining two studio apartments together and removing most of the dividing walls. The loftlike environment was on the northeast corner of the building and the reflected light from the setting sun had turned the distant ruffled water of Lake Michigan into a sheet of hammered gold. She and Dunton had spent the whole day together; in less than an hour, it would be fully dark.

'My mother collected the Greek and Egyptian artifacts. The Mayan collections were my father's.' He paused. 'The contemporary paintings and photographs are mine.'

The main room was filled with art of every kind. Chunks of Greek columns supported exquisite Egyptian figurines, Mayan sacrificial bowls stared gloomily from

411

glass shelves lit by tiny spotlights in the ceiling, and the white walls were hung with paintings large and small from almost every period Jay could name. The floors were covered in neutral gray carpeting. The furniture, what little there was of it, was modern, pale and leather.

According to Dunton, both his parents had been born wealthy and after joining their fortunes, they spent most of their lives traveling all over the world, collecting. There had been a cold edge to the explanation; while his mother and father roamed the world, their only son had spent the better part of his youth and adolescence in a succession of expensive boarding schools.

His intellect hadn't come up to his parents' expectations and in the end the best he could manage was a mediocre degree in art history from a small Midwestern university. When his parents were in Chicago, they lived in the family house in the near-in suburb of Oak Park, a rambling, early-Frank Lloyd Wright mansion. Their son had been exiled to the lavish eyrie in the John Hancock.

Out of the corner of her eye, Jay caught a flicker of movement. Turning, she saw that the wall separating the main room from the kitchen area was almost completely filled with a gigantic inset television screen that was showing a reverse-angle view of herself standing at the door. Dunton saw her look of surprise. He pointed up at the ceiling a few feet in front of her, and Jay saw the lens of a minuscule security camera staring down at her.

'I've got them all over the place,' he said. 'They're connected to the motion sensors in the security system; they turn on automatically when you move in front of them.'

'Worried about thieves in the night?' asked Jay.

Dunton shook his head. He shrugged off his jacket and dropped it across the lap of a seated Egyptian figure to the right of the door. 'Not really. Just an eccentricity.' His expression soured slightly, his smile becoming almost a sneer. 'Mummy and Daddy wanted me to become an art historian.'

Mummy and Daddy?

The sneer deepened. 'It was their fondest dream. You might say I fulfilled it for them posthumously.' He gestured toward the giant television screen. 'Passing time is history, and art is whatever you want it to be. Ergo, art history. I record everything.'

'Everything?' said Jay, trying to keep it light.

Everything has a hidden meaning when you know your date's a psychopath.

'Pretty much,' Dunton answered. 'Would you like a drink?'

'No, thanks.'

No booze tonight; gotta keep your wits about you, Janet Louise.

Dunton nodded, then walked across the large room and disappeared behind the dividing wall. She heard the clinking of ice cubes in a glass and the *snap-hiss* of a can being opened. She reached down to the small of her back and touched the comforting bulk of the Browning.

413

Secure that she could defend herself, she crossed to the television screen and examined it, noticing that as she moved, the image changed.

According to the discreet nameplate, the television was a Stewart Filmscreen Opta90, presumably meaning it was ninety inches. There was a small inset keypad controller to one side, as well as an inset rack of other equipment including a VCR, a videodisc player, a JVC 100 CD changer, and a massive Yamaha tuner. Below this was a second area given over to security, including a separate slow-speed video recorder, camera controls, and the controls for the motion sensors. Beneath the second rack of equipment was a storage area for CDs and videotapes. Hundreds of them.

Jay reached out and let her hand run across the brushed chrome and flat black faceplates of the electronics. Everything was art, and Dunton said he recorded all of it.

You tape the women, don't you, Homer? Tape them and kill them, and watch them die, again and again.

Dunton's voice came out of nowhere. 'Please don't touch anything!' Jay almost jumped out of her skin. She jerked upright. He was standing behind her, less than a foot away, a cut-crystal glass of some dark liquid in his hand. She hadn't heard a thing.

He could have killed me.

'Jesus! You scared me!'

'I'm sorry. The equipment is very sensitive, that's all.' He held out the glass. 'Sure I can't get you something? It's just Coke.' His smile flickered.

414

She shook her head and smiled. 'No thanks.' Not a chance; Christ only knew what'd he'd put into it. She kept smiling. Chloral hydrate to knock his victims out before he killed them? Or did he like them alive and kicking? She wasn't sure yet, but she wasn't going to risk anything stupid.

Dunton dropped down on to a low sofa set at an angle to the viewing screen. He crossed his legs, resting his glass on his knee. He looked like an ad in *The New Yorker*. Jay offered him a small nervous smile, then wandered around the room slowly, examining the various artwork at close hand. She stopped in front of a large, roughly framed canvas against the far wall. Two figures, both male, wrestling together on a dark background, some sort of frame or cage sketched around them in faint white lines The figures were dark and brutal, features only barely signified. Were they fighting in their strange, amorphous landscape, or having sex? Were they real or were they someone else's dream? It was impossible to tell.

'Francis Bacon,' said Dunton from across the room. 'One of my favorites.' He stood up, moving smoothly, like oil on water. Like a snake. Jay could feel her heart begin to pump harder and her mouth go suddenly dry. How long did he wait? How far did he string it out?

What does he do with the bodies?

Dunton joined her in front of the painting. He put one hand on her elbow and leaned toward her ear.

'Let me show you around,' he said.

415

He led her through the various collections, giving their individual histories and the stories of how they'd come to be collected by his parents or himself. He stayed on her right side, his hand never leaving her elbow. If she had to get to the Browning quickly, she was going to be in trouble.

On the other side of the kitchen area there were three more rooms. The doors of two of them were ajar. One door opened on to a large, glass-tiled bathroom; the other gave her a glimpse of Dunton's bedroom, all done in black and white and gray. There was a desk set up under the bedroom window, most of its surface covered by an array of computer equipment.

'What's the computer for?' asked Jay.

'It's how I keep track of the things I collect,' Dunton explained. 'And I play games with it. It feeds to the screen in the main room.'

'You like computer games?' asked Jay.

Hidden meanings.

Dunton nodded. The smile flickered again. He was becoming increasingly nervous. Eager. The dark clouds would be gathering in his head as the moment came closer.

'I love them. Especially the role-playing ones. I can be anyone I want for as long as I want.'

'Any favorites?' She'd seen fragments of the game on Special K, both on Gaddis' computer and Kushinski's. Serious stuff, with fractal imagery that was right up there with the best you could buy commercially.

'All the Dungeons and Dragons ones. Myst. I haven't

been playing long, so I'm still learning.' He paused. 'Would you like to see?'

I'd love to, but not quite yet.

'Maybe later.'

They reached the door to the last room. There were large clay figures set into custom niches in the wall, two on either side of the door. The statues were painted brightly, and very old.

'They're Egyptian,' said Dunton. He ran a perfectly manicured hand down a row of hieroglyphics on one of them.

'They look like big wine jars,' said Jay.

Look at the lock on that door! It's like a bank vault.

'Close.' Dunton smiled. 'They're canopic jars, used for storing the body organs while a person was being mummified.' He touched the top of the one on the far left; it was an animal head, blue and green with huge ears like a bat. 'This one is Duamutef, the Jackal. He guarded the stomach. The baboon-headed one beside it is Hapy, guardian of the lungs. The other two are Imesty, which held the liver, and Qebehsenuef, the falcon, who cared for the intestines.'

Jay smiled weakly. 'I hope they aren't still in there.'

Dunton's voice was flat and expressionless. Jay could see the hard muscle of his jaw twitching slightly. 'Not anymore,' he answered. She put her hand on the knob of the door standing between the figures.

'What's in here?'

Dunton took his hand away from her elbow, reached

out, and gently gripped her wrist. He removed her hand from the knob. 'My private collection,' he said.

'Can I see it?'

Are you out of your fucking mind?!

Dunton stared at her. The brown eyes were huge and empty, dark holes bored into the middle of his head. The hand on her wrist was cold and clammy. 'Not right now,' he said. He took her by the elbow again and led her back to the main room.

Do it now!

Her nerves were screaming. Through the picture windows at the far corner of the room, she could see that the darkness was complete. Chicago was a pool of winking lights below her, a million miles away. Beyond that the lake was a flat black hole in the world.

Do him before he does you!

Not yet. Not until I'm sure. I can't just kill him.

Yes, you can.

'Why don't you sit down?' said Dunton, pushing her gently toward the couch. 'I'll show you one of the games I really like.'

Jay did as she was told, seating herself on the couch as Dunton crossed to the screen and squatted in front of the storage racks. He chose a tape, slipped it into the VCR, then picked up a complicated-looking remote control unit. Jay tucked one hand slightly behind her back, gripping the reassuring butt of the Browning.

She thumbed off the safety as Dunton joined her on the couch. He kept a foot or so away from her and

pointed the remote control unit at the screen. The
television snapped on instantly. On the screen Jay could
see a vividly realistic, computer-generated image of a
desert scene. Against a cloudless blue sky a thousand
rolling sand dunes led down to a distant oasis surrounded by emerald palms. Through the trees she could
make out the spires and minarets of a lavish palace. She
was horribly aware of Dunton seated next to her, the
razor edge of his yearning coming off him in desperate
waves, but she was riveted by the image on the screen. A
programmer, even a brilliant one, would have worked
for weeks to obtain this kind of surreal detail even if he
was using scanned images from real photographs.

'It's beautiful,' she said.

'It gets better,' said Dunton.

The image shimmered like a heat mirage on hot
asphalt, then congealed again, reforming to show a
close shot of the palace she'd seen a few seconds before.
Spires, towers, battlements, and two huge wooden
doors. At ninety inches the picture on the screen should
have broken down into a million jagged pixels of blurred
light, but it held together perfectly. Jay had played
around with computer graphics programs in her spare
time and she knew what people like Jack Prine could do,
but this was beyond anything she'd ever seen. Genius.

Madness. She had seen it before, a fleeting glimpse on
Kushinski's screen in Pennsylvania.

Her mouth tasted like hot metal. She cleared her
throat. 'What's this called?' she asked.

'The Wizard's Kingdom,' Dunton answered.

419

No it's not.

Dunton's voice seemed to be coming from far away. 'Would you like to play?'

She blinked. The beautiful palace in the desert was gone. In its place the screen now showed the interior of Dunton's apartment. The camera was somewhere behind her. There was a figure on the couch and at first she thought it was her. Then she realized that on the television, Dunton wasn't sitting beside her. The shot changed again. The woman on the couch – much younger; streaked blonde hair; glasses across a freckled nose; short, rust-colored skirt; white blouse; long tanned legs; and sandals. Looking up, an expectant smile. Sudden, terrible fear and her mouth opening to scream and then something long, like a hooked needle, shattering the lens of her glasses and thrusting into her eye. The screen went red, then blank.

All in a single blink of time Jay heard Dunton's whispered shaking voice: 'I am Horus.'

God of the Dead.

And then there was no thought, only a fierce and overwhelming joy that gripped her somewhere below her stomach and rose upward like a furious driving piston forcing the air out of her lungs in a single bursting roar. Her hand slipped out from behind her back, the Browning feather light, and then it was Dunton's fear and widening eyes.

'But Mummy always lets me win.' A spoiled child's voice.

'Not this time.'

'You fucking cunt!'

He lurched toward her, hand up in front of his face, like a claw. Something gleaming in it, long and hooked. The room filled with his rattling scream.

'CUNT!'

Freak.

She found herself standing by the window, staring out into the night. Far behind her Dunton was sprawled across the spattered couch. The big television hummed quietly. Her eyes were half closed and she could feel a sweeping lethargy creeping through her bones and muscles. She still had the Browning held loosely in her right hand. There was something in her left hand as well, closed in a spasm fist, her knuckles white. She opened her hand. Dunton's scarab ring, the one she'd first noticed at the Art Institute. The thick gold band was slick with blood. Drying, sticky, gluing the ring to her hand.

A souvenir.

At the Behavioral Sciences Unit, they'd call it something else.

Totem.

What a madman takes from the body of his victim to remind him of the moment, to remind him of what he has become.

She.

'No. I'm not like them,' she moaned and leaned her forehead against the cool glass of the window. Closed her hand into a fist again. Closed her eyes. 'I'm not.'

What else do you call someone who's killed three times?

Different.

How?

They want to do it. Need to. Death is their life, their meaning.

And you?

She turned away from the window. Looked across the room at what was left of Homer Ellis Dunton. Saw herself on the giant screen and understood what she had to do. Understood the future.

I do it because it's necessary. Someone must. Before it's too late.

The 911 call was logged on to the Chicago Police Department's blotter at 11:05 p.m. Since the Chicago 911 system is equipped with an automatic backtrace function showing the number being called from, it was easy enough to track its source – a public booth at O'Hare International Airport.

Following up on the initial call, two members of the CPD Homicide Division went to the John Hancock Center, arriving at Homer Dunton's apartment at exactly midnight. On their discovery of Dunton's body, a full investigative team was called in. Around one o'clock in the morning, the locked door next to Dunton's bedroom was opened by a CPD Technical Division locksmith. Shortly after this the locksmith was taken to Northwestern Memorial Hospital to be treated for severe shock.

Less than an hour later, news of the horrifying discovery at the John Hancock Center leaked to the local media. Several newspeople made the connection to the killing in Slippery Rock and by 3:00 a.m. the story was out on all the national wire services. By 4:00 a.m. the Chicago Police Department also noticed the similarities between the John Hancock killing and the advisory they'd received on the murder of Kushinski, the Slippery Rock veterinarian.

By 5:00 a.m. the Chicago Field Office of the FBI had been notified and by 6:30 the day-shift doorman at the John Hancock was happily telling his story about the woman who had followed Homer Dunton the previous morning. He gave paid interviews to three different syndicated tabloid news shows before he was officially interrogated by Chicago Homicide. By 7:00 a.m. he was talking to CNN in Atlanta and by 7:30 the news finally trickled down to Charles Langford in Washington D.C.

At 9:15 Langford and J. Cruz were at Washington National boarding a Continental Airlines flight to Chicago.

CHAPTER TWENTY-FOUR

'Jesus!' muttered Cruz, stepping out of the room that Homer Dunton had used to store his 'private' collection. He kept the after-shave-soaked handkerchief over his mouth and nose until he'd reached the relative safety of the main room at the far end of the apartment. Eight of the eleven bodies in the collection had already been removed, but the three remaining were among the worst. The forensics crew from CPD was going through the room in shifts, and all of them were wearing firemen's respirators.

Langford was standing at the corner window talking to one of the people from the Chicago Medical Examiner's Office. Dr Elson, the Deputy M.E., was a woman in her midfifties, gray-brown hair back in a bun, a lean, ferret face with slightly bulging eyes; and an overbite. She had a surgical mask dangling around her neck and a cigarette in her hands. As Cruz approached he could see the shiny smear of Vicks VapoRub under her nose.

'Dr Elson here was telling me how our boy went about his business,' said Langford.

'You've seen the room?' the woman asked.

Cruz nodded. 'Just now.' He'd seen worse at arson scenes, but not by much.

'Interesting,' said Elson. She took a drag on the cigarette and blew it out through her nose in little trickles. 'From the looks of this place, he took a few hints from the Egyptians. Removed a piece of the ceiling, revented the outside hot air return, and let nature do the rest.'

'Natural mummification,' said Cruz. The three bodies still in the room were already beginning to desiccate, drawing up in their heavy plastic shrouds as sinews dried and shortened, pulling the limbs into a mockery of the fetal position. The same thing happened to bodies in the furnace heat of a fire. The room was perfectly sealed, bone-dry, and at least 120 degrees Fahrenheit. Any telltale odors were flushed through Big John's complex system of filters and catalytic converters, the hot air eventually spewing out through the roof stacks.

Elson barked out a smoky laugh. 'As natural as you get on the ninetieth floor of a building.' She pursed her lips judiciously. 'I suppose Big John is Chicago's version of a pyramid.'

'Any signs of sexual assault?' asked Langford.

'The external genitalia were sliced off on all of them,' said Elson calmly. 'I'd say it's a good bet.'

'They look eviscerated,' put in Cruz. He'd seen a row of pastel-colored plastic buckets in the room, all of them stained and crusted.

'All the tools in there look like his own idea of Egyptian embalming equipment,' said Elson. 'Took a course in it, premed. Flint knife, brain hooks to mush things up before he flushed out the skull, strips of linen.' She shook her head. 'Pretty efficient really, when you think about it. He kills his victims, guts them, then grinds up their innards in the garburetor – we've already found traces – then he packs up what's left and leaves it in the room to dry out. He could have done another twenty or thirty before he had to think about putting them somewhere else.'

'How long has he been at it?' Langford asked.

'Hard to tell.' The doctor shrugged and dragged on her cigarette again. Behind them another bagged body was being removed. 'The last two in there are the oldest. Five or six years at a guess. They're different from the others, too.'

'How so?'

'Age and sex. One of them's male, in his sixties, maybe older. The only man in the group. The other is female, about the same age.'

'His parents?' Langford suggested.

Elson nodded. 'That's what I figure.' She glanced at her watch. 'Time's up, break's over.' She smiled. 'Anything else I can tell you?'

'No. Thanks,' said Langford. The doctor smiled again, pulled up her mask, and headed back toward the terrible room.

The FBI man watched her go. 'You saw the computer?' he said to Cruz.

'Yes. Smashed. According to Sladky the computers in Hand Job's house had been treated the same way.'

'Albuquerque, Slippery Rock, and now here. Way too much for coincidence. I don't care what Hawkins thinks, there's a connection between all of this and Ricky Stiles. There has to be.'

'Not much to go on,' said Cruz. He looked around the lavish room. 'Jay's long gone and we don't know where.'

'If Hawkins can get a lead on Stiles in Mexico, it might give us Fletcher at the same time. I can't think of anything else.'

'So let's hope he comes up with something,' said Cruz.

'Yeah. Soon,' agreed Langford.

By the time Langford and Cruz reached the John Hancock Center, Jay Fletcher had already been in Los Angeles for half a day. Homer Dunton had fifteen different credit cards and kept a neat list of Personal Identification Numbers for them in the desk in his bedroom. Acting on the faint possibility that her spur-of-the-moment call to Dr Chisolm might have been traced the night before, she didn't return to the hotel, even though it meant leaving the laptop computer and her spare clothes behind. Instead she took a cab directly to the airport.

Using a number of Automatic Teller Machines at O'Hare, she cash-advanced all of them to the limit, then tossed away the cards. There were several domestic flights she could have taken, but she eventually decided on the red-eye to Los Angeles. The imagery she'd seen on the Wizard's Kingdom game suggested somewhere hot and dry, which ruled out the eastern part of the country.

She slept like a stone through the entire flight and booked into a small, Italianesque hotel on Pacific Boulevard suggested by her cab driver. The hotel was halfway between Long Beach and L.A. proper, and they were happy to accept a three-night cash deposit in lieu of a major credit card. Just as importantly, some of the rooms were equipped with VCRs. Reasonably sure that she'd covered her electronic tracks, at least for the moment, she ordered a room-service breakfast with a double order of coffee and then settled down with the tapes she'd removed from Dunton's apartment, going over them again and again.

One of them was particularly interesting because it showed Homer Dunton playing through several levels of Wizard's Kingdom, which, she now realized, was the Dungeons and Dragons-style role-playing game that 'covered' the Special K bulletin board. Presumably SK-WIZ was the 'Wizard' who had designed the Kingdom as well as the electronic bulletin board it shrouded. Nothing in the documentation she'd found at Gaddis' house in Albuquerque, at Kushinski's in Harrisville, or Dunton's apartment gave any clue to the location of the Special K systems operator; all she had to go on was the game.

From what she could see on the tape, there were at least five basic levels to the game and at least twenty different scenarios. The first level was called Ripper and was really nothing more than a historic re-creation of the Whitechapel murders, complete with spooky London streets, a cloaked and mysterious killer, and his assorted prostitute victims. Apparently the object of the first level was to kill the victims without being caught and without leaving an assortment of clues behind. The only thing that differentiated the first level from any game you could buy at a software store was the lurid violence of the murders, which included a choice of organs that could be removed from each corpse.

By successfully completing the first level, you were automatically taken through a creaking doorway and down a flight of stone steps to the second level – Blood Doctor. Blood Doctor was loosely based on the exploits of Dr Marcel Petiot, the French physician who murdered scores of people, mostly fleeing Jews, during World War II. There were a number of roles to choose from on the Blood Doctor level, including an assortment of Gestapo officials.

Level Three magically brought the game back to the United States with The Migrant. Here the leading role was that of Juan Corona, the Yuba County labor contractor convicted of sexually assaulting, robbing, and murdering more than twenty-five migrant workers during the mid- to late sixties. Level Three was different from the preceding two; it included Corona's trial, a role for his mysteriously deceased brother Natividad, and a special maze section in which you had to dig in a number of spots to discover the hacked and headless bodies of the victims. To take on the lead role of Corona required the player first to discover the machete used to murder the victims; there was also a choice of sexual options for all the players, including the Yuba County sheriff. Level Three was even more violent than the two previous ones, almost to the point of obscenity. Another rampart established to ward off all but the most serious players.

Level Four, Death Team, was a bizarre mix of themes that used a broad spectrum of North American serial killers for its cast of roles including the L.A. Zodiac, Berkowitz, the Green River Killer, the Boston Strangler, Ted Bundy, and John Wayne Gacy. There seemed to be few rules beyond slaughtering the greatest number of people in the least amount of time. On Level Four the details of the killings seemed the most important, with points awarded for things like choice of killing instrument, method of body disposal, and totems taken.

Eventually, a player with enough determination reached Wizard's Kingdom itself – the level Jay had seen briefly the previous night in Chicago. On the tape, Dunton roamed the various levels at will, but he kept on coming back to that one. After the opening sequences of the oasis palace, the player went through the main doors into a succession of rooms, each more grotesque than the last. The imagery of the fifth level seemed less complex than the preceding ones, details barely roughed in. Halfway through Dunton's play on the tape, Jay realized why.

The fifth layer had been designed specifically for players who had already discovered how to get from the game to the bulletin board below. Dunton used his skills to open doors into half a dozen rooms, and one of them showed a killer mutilating his victims' hands, splitting them between the second and third fingers. The Hand Job killer from Albuquerque. Gaddis.

A 'room' within the game for each player to graphically describe his exploits. There was already one for Dunton, reached by going down a long stone corridor that had walls decorated with a hideous string of Egyptian hieroglyphics.

Jay wound and rewound her way through the tape a dozen times, but there was nothing on the tape that seemed to lead anywhere. She'd checked Dunton's computer files in Chicago, but there'd been nothing there, either; unlike Gaddis and Kushinski, Dunton kept no logs or records. After dealing with the youthful collector, she'd managed to access the bulletin board by tracking calls on Dunton's communications software, but even after half an hour of hacking, she hadn't been able to get anywhere. The bulletin board was blank, with no on-line chats in progress, and the only thing of interest was a brief posted warning advising anyone reaching Special K that there was the possibility of an intruder on the Net. Presumably that meant her.

Stumped for the moment, Jay left the hotel, went to a nearby strip mall, and bought herself some basic necessities including new clothes. That done, she returned to the hotel, showered, and changed. Struggling into a fresh pair of jeans, it suddenly occurred to her that her period was almost a week overdue. Stress, or, God help her, pregnancy. She counted back the days and heaved a sigh of relief; unless her system was severely out of whack, her chances of being pregnant by the black busboy were minimal.

She switched on the tape again, running it up to the Level Five opening, and freezing it there. Was the Wizard's Kingdom where he lived, or just his not-so-imaginary underworld of horror? The only thing she could think of was the quality of the image itself. If the WIZ was doing this in his spare time, maybe he was doing the same thing for a living.

Checking through the Yellow Pages, she made a list of half a dozen stores in L.A. that specialized in role-playing computer games. List in hand she pulled the tape out of the VCR and left the hotel. Three hours and over a hundred dollars in taxi rides later, she found what she was looking for just off the I-5 turnpike south of Anaheim, in Orange, California.

CHAPTER TWENTY-FIVE

More than twenty years before, the SAC of the San
Diego FBI Field Office had described Tijuana to Hawkins
as 'a hemorrhoid on the asshole of America.' In those
twenty years, the population of the Mexican border
town had swollen to more than a million souls and no
amount of diplomatic ointment was going to ease the
painful itch of a people being paid less than 30 percent of
what the same job offered a few miles to the north.

Hawkins spent more than an hour at the border,
sweltering in the midafternoon heat as the line of cars,
trucks, vans, and campers ahead of him moved slowly
forward. Eventually he got his Tourist Card and windshield sticker, paid a few dollars *mordida* to the
uniformed inspector, and drove his un-air-conditioned
rental into Mexico. In the two decades since his last
visit, nothing very much seemed to have changed except
that there was simply more of everything, spread out
over a greater distance.

The streets were narrow, noisy, and jammed with
traffic; everyone seemed to be selling something to

everyone else, and a hundred thousand signs screamed out their messages in English, Spanish, and Spanglish, a bizarre combination of both languages. In Spanglish a boat was a *canoa*, a taxi stand was a *sit-io*, and a taxi driver was a *chofer*.

There was dust everywhere, along with a brown pall of engine exhaust that was worse than anything he'd ever seen in Los Angeles. Driving through the center of Tijuana, he could barely see more than a hundred yards ahead. Hawkins wondered if there was a Spanglish word for catalytic converter. Somehow he doubted it; most of the cars he saw with Mexican plates were mid-seventies or earlier.

He eventually found the address he was looking for on the ragged outskirts of the city along the Tijuana-Ensenada Highway. The Farmacia Enfermo was located between a massive automobile junkyard and a window-less building crested by a huge neon sign that said HITACHI. The farmacia was a one-story concrete-block bunker about as big as a medium-sized supermarket. According to Hawkins' information, it was the largest outlet for the phenacemide compound manufactured by Recklerpharm.

Thankfully the interior of the huge drugstore was air-conditioned. Hawkins stood just inside the doors for a few moments, enjoying the cool air and trying to get his bearings. He'd been warned by the Recklerpharm repre-sentative in San Diego that a Mexican drugstore had little or nothing in common with its counterpart in the United States. Real prescriptions were almost unknown, drugs were doled out in single pills or by the crate, and most large farmacias had little booths where you could inject yourself with everything from antibiotics to morphine.

The Farmacia Enfermo was laid out in a complicated series of aisles and islands, with no signage anywhere. Bins full of Band-Aids stood cheek by jowl with toothpaste displays piled to the ceiling, and there was a Medusa-like assortment of brightly colored enema bags lurking beside a long table stacked with generic vitamin C bottles.

As far as Hawkins could see, everyone in the drugstore was Mexican. Here and there white-coated men and women wandered around checking things off on clipboards and answering the odd question in loud, machine-gun Spanish, raising their voices over the rattle, thump and scratch of the music blaring over the loudspeakers. Hawkins recognized it as the same rhythm-heavy, twanging stuff he'd been listening to all the way from San Diego; Mexican *ranchera*, or country music, bellowing out from Radio XEG in Monterrey, the largest station in Mexico.

He went through four of the white-coated attendants before he found one who could speak English. The young woman directed him to a distant counter at the far end of the building. Reaching the counter, Hawkins caught the attention of another white-coated figure, this one white-haired and wearing glasses.

'Excuse me, but do you speak English?'

'Of course,' he answered mildly.

'You're a pharmacist?'

The man smiled. 'We are all pharmacists here.'

Hawkins nodded. This was worse than he'd expected. The girl who'd directed him to the counter couldn't have been more than sixteen; it was doubtful she'd even finished high school, let alone completed university training as a pharmacist.

'I'm looking for a particular drug,' said Hawkins.

'We have many drugs here,' said the man, gesturing broadly with one hand. 'We are, after all, a farmacia.'

'This is an anticonvulsant.'

'We have several.'

'Phenacemide,' said Hawkins. The man thought for a moment, then nodded.

'Yes.'

'You carry it?'

'Yes.'

'Where would I find it?'

The man smiled again. 'I would have to look.' He stayed where he was.

'I'm actually interested in someone who purchases a prescription for it,' said Hawkins.

'Ah,' said the man. The smile didn't change, but his eyes brightened behind the glasses. 'Then you don't want this drug for yourself.'

'No.'

'Ah,' said the man a second time. He seemed to be enjoying himself.

Hawkins pulled the computer-enhanced picture of

Stiles out of his pocket and unfolded it on the counter. The man glanced at it.

'Have you ever seen this man?' Hawkins asked.

'You are with the American police?'

'Yes,' Hawkins answered flatly. He waited for the pharmacist to say something, but the man simply stared at him balefully, his vague, smiling expression still unchanged.

'Have you seen him?' Hawkins asked again.

The pharmacist shrugged. 'It is difficult to say.' He looked down at the picture, then up at Hawkins. 'We don't get very many *gabacho* here.'

'*Gabacho*?'

'White.' The man's smile increased slightly. 'Like you.'

'This *gabacho* buys phenacemide. He's an epileptic.'

'Ah,' said the man a third time. Hawkins resisted the urge to reach out and throttle him with his own narrow little tie. Instead he reached into his pocket and pulled out his wallet. He extracted a five-dollar bill and put it on the counter beside the picture. The man's expression shifted to one of concentrated thought.

'Well?' Hawkins asked.

'He is a little familiar, yes.'

Hawkins put down another five.

'How familiar?'

'I think he comes in from time to time.'

'You think?' Hawkins added a third five-dollar bill. The man nodded.

'Yes. He comes here.'

'And buys phenacemide?'

'Yes.'

'Does he use a prescription?' asked Hawkins. 'From an American doctor?' It was a long shot.

'Prescriptions are not necessary for an anticonvulsant,' said the pharmacist. He smiled broadly. 'Who would take such a thing if they did not have convulsions? It would be very foolish, don't you think?'

'Yes.' Hawkins had run out of fives. He put down a ten instead.

'That is not necessary,' said the pharmacist.

'I need a name,' said Hawkins.

'Perhaps I could remember it.' The pharmacist waited. Hawkins dropped a twenty down on the counter. The pharmacist took it, then handed back the ten. Change back from his *mordida*, just like buying a Big Mac. 'Just a moment,' he said. He disappeared behind a pile of cardboard boxes containing powdered baby formula and reappeared a few moments later holding a credit card slip in his hand. 'This is the person you want.' He handed the slip to Hawkins, then scooped up the rest of the money on the counter. The carbon-stained flimsy was from a Citibank Visa.

'I can't read the name,' said Hawkins. The flimsy was from the bottom of the carbon set. The only thing he could make out was a vague, two-letter blur at the bottom of the address square. Me, Ne, Mo ... it was impossible to tell. Maine, Nevada, or Missouri. Quite a geographical spread. 'This is no use at all.'

'There is no name,' agreed the pharmacist, 'but the number is clear enough.'

'Can you get me a name to match?' asked Hawkins.

The pharmacist shrugged. 'Perhaps. It would take some time. If you have a number where I could reach you...' The man let it dangle. Hawkins thought quickly. He was supposed to be back in Washington that evening. He took an old business card out of his wallet, scribbled down his home phone number, and handed it to the pharmacist.

'If I'm not there, leave a message on my machine.'

'I might incur some expenses in finding out the name for you, señor.'

Hawkins sighed. 'I'm out of cash.'

'That is no problem at all,' said the pharmacist, beaming brightly. 'As you see, we take all major credit cards.'

In the end it turned out to be remarkably simple. The young, extremely knowledgeable clerk at the GameMaster outlet in Orange took one look at the Wizard's Kingdom tape and immediately identified the style of the imaging as being the work of Softimage Creations, a games company headquartered in Carson City, Nevada.

Paying cash again, Jay bought a new, high-powered laptop to replace the one she'd left behind in Chicago, and picked up half a dozen Softimage games as well. Returning to the hotel in Long Beach, she loaded the Wizard's Kingdom tape into the VCR, booted up the laptop, and began running the games, one after the other.

Most of them were standard Dungeons and Dragons scenarios, but even so, Jay could see the similarities to Wizard's Kingdom. The equivalent game software that the clerk had shown her at GameMaster was comic book stuff by comparison – drooling, overdrawn, ghouls and goblins, flashy colors, and childish sound effects. The Softimage games used color much more subtly, the imaging itself was sharper, and the games had a sophisticated, adult edge that was missing in the others.

Of the six games she purchased, four had the same artist credited in the opening frames: Merlin Ambrose. One of Jay's favorite books as a child had been T. H. White's *The Once and Future King* and she picked up the reference immediately. In White's book the famous magician, who helped King Arthur establish Camelot was given the Latin name Merlin Ambrosius. Merlin the Wizard. SK-WIZ wouldn't be the first killer of his kind who'd foundered on the rocks of excessive ego. It was the last game that pulled the noose taut around the psychopath's neck.

According to the clerk at GameMaster, Hold 'em-Fold 'em, while not a role-playing game, was the most popular piece of software ever produced by Softimage. Reading the credits as the game opened, Jay saw that it had been first copyrighted in 1980, and the listed artist was Merlin Ambrose. He was also given the 'created by' credit, which meant he probably got an ongoing royalty from Softimage for his work.

Hold 'em-Fold 'em was an old-fashioned arcade-style game with a full spread of gambling options, including craps, roulette, keno, stud poker, blackjack, and several different slot machines. There was even a subgame that let you bet on major sporting events, complete with a big board run by a swashbuckling one-eyed tout named Rick the Geek.

The artwork within the game was rougher and less sophisticated than the other games designed by Merlin Ambrose, but the opening sequences were a dead giveaway. Hold 'em-Fold 'em opened with a desert scene that was identical to the one in Wizard's Kingdom. He'd simply transposed the complex imaging from the software program to the bottom level of his game on the Internet.

Staring at the screen of her laptop, then comparing it to the image frozen on the television screen behind her, Jay finally saw the joke. Rolling sand dunes, pink flamingos standing in a magical oasis with a gleaming palace behind them, all set against a star-dusted night sky that vanished like a shimmering mirage as you began the game.

Dunes

Oasis

Flamingo

Palace

Stardust

Mirage

They were all names of casinos in Las Vegas.

Got you.

443

She shut down the computer, packed her few belongings, and called a cab. It was late afternoon by the time her flight took off from L.A.X. When she landed at McCarran International Airport in Las Vegas, darkness was already beginning to fall. She booked herself into the Best Western close to the airport on Paradise Road and set up the laptop again. There was still more work to be done before she made her final move.

The Iceman sat in his dark, secret room, surrounded by a thousand images of the world he'd spent so much time and effort creating for himself. In front of him two screens were glowing, one showing the on-line Associated Press news service, the other hooked into the Citibank Credit Services Center.

AP was putting out the Homer Dunton story with a three-star flash and repeating it every hour. There was also a byline sidebar attached to the story datelined Butler, Pennsylvania. The murders of Kushinski and Dunton were being connected, although no one had put together the link with Gaddis yet, but he knew that would come eventually. Both the AP story out of Chicago and the sidebar from Butler mentioned a woman named Jennifer Smith as being a suspect, and he'd seen a promo for *Hard Copy*, the TV tabloid, which also mentioned a woman as the probable murderer.

Based on an interview with the reporter from the Butler *Eagle* and the doorman at the John Hancock Center, AP even managed to come up with a rough sketch of what she looked like: a dark-haired woman in her mid- to late thirties, pretty enough if you liked the aging pixie type, but with an edge of something sad and dangerous around the eyes and mouth. They were calling her the Ladykiller. He had to smile at the ambiguity of that; if anyone could be called a ladykiller, it was him.

Of more interest and concern to him was the electronic spoor being left behind by Bill Hawkins. Berkeley, back to Washington, a brief hiatus there, and then a sudden trip to San Diego. Now Tijuana; a purchase made at the Farmacia Enfermo in midafternoon. The only reason the one-eyed shitfucker would go to that particular farmacia in Tijuana was because he'd managed to figure out the nature of his real power. In front of him, one of the screens stuttered, and a new line traced across it. Hawkins was on the move again; an airline ticket purchase in San Diego again. He was booked on a flight into Dulles. Back to Washington.

Sitting in the dark room, the Iceman suddenly felt the world begin to fall away around him, and the perfectly filtered air was abruptly filled with the choking, overwhelming scent of lavender. He froze in his chair, feeling his muscles begin to constrict, aware in some part of his mind that he was going into seizure. Not that he minded; after nearly an entire lifetime with his sacred affliction, he'd become almost friendly with its symptoms and effects. Knowing that increasing stress often triggered his fugues, he'd taken a double dose of the phenacemide less than two hours ago, and he was

445

secure in the knowledge that he'd be able to control any seizure that threatened to cause him harm.

Shitfucker.

He could hear someone whispering the word. Pozniak? *You really think you can threaten me, you little shitfucker? Who's going to believe you after what you did to that nun at the orphanage? Shitfucker.*

He wished he'd had a baseball bat for the penguin with her hidden breasts and the soft pink flush of her cheeks. Instead of chain. Still, you used what was at hand; you did what you could with what you had. He'd learned that. Secrets.

Pozniak's body turned to cold wax in the waters of Puget Sound.

The hard thunder of Father John's Indian between his legs.

The soft wet smack of Father John's sister's skull imploding in the sunrise Berkeley morning.

The first time. Twelve. When he thought that he was dying, and heard the one true voice of God, ringing like the massed bells of St Peter's in his ears. When the blackness descended and the birds flew up with the dark sound of dry leaves rustling in dead trees.

Shitfucker motherdeath.

The feel of himself in Ellen Putnam's toothless mouth while her daughter watched, trying to scream without her tongue, and the snot ran out of the mother's nose like water.

Kill them all.

He blinked and stared at the computers. The monitors

had gone blank except for their moving starfield screen-
savers. He glanced at the glowing dial of his wristwatch,
knowing what to expect. Almost an hour had gone,
flashing by in a few quick seconds. In seizure there was
no such thing as time; sometimes he thought he could
live in those blank spaces forever, live within its elastic
universe where he would be left alone.

Kill them all. The voice was right.

*It's the only way. Hawkins first, then the Ladykiller.
Don't watch her.*

Watch Me.

CHAPTER TWENTY-SIX

Charles Langford sat in his basement office at FBI
Headquarters in Washington D.C. and contemplated a
future that was rapidly closing in on him. So far he'd
had three meetings with the suits upstairs, none of
them positive, and if it hadn't been for the fact that the
director was on holiday white-water rafting in the
Grand Canyon, Langford knew he would have been
called on to that particular carpet as well.

Everything had begun to unravel the night before
when *Hard Copy* went on the air with its story. Through
the reporter in Butler, Pennsylvania, a vague associa-
tion had been made with the Bureau, and from that
point on the shit really began to hit the fan. Within
hours a leak connected the Hand Job killing in
Albuquerque with both Kushinski and Dunton, and it
didn't take the local press long to trace things back to
Nadine, Fletcher's neighbor. That in turn led to the
good psychiatrist Dr Chisolm and a quick and dirty
interview on *Good Morning, America*. Apparently she
invoked doctor-patient privilege only if she wasn't

being paid to talk about her clients. She spent a lot of time covering herself by referring to 'hypotheticals' of one kind or another, and she never called Jay by name, but to Langford it was still a clear breach of ethics. Anything for a news bite.

On Network Television Chisolm specifically stated that 'Jennifer Smith' was an FBI Special Agent and also mentioned that the agent had recently been involved with a dubious court case in which she'd been made the scapegoat. The implication was that the Bureau was ultimately responsible for her actions.

The TV research people had done their homework and the interview was chock-full of statistics about how few female Special Agents there were, incidents of sexual harassment, and the high rate of suicide among ex-FBI employees.

They somehow failed to mention that Jennifer Smith had been transferred away from Bureau Headquarters because she'd obtained evidence illegally and had prejudiced a case being made against a maniac who liked to hack off women's heads and jerk off into the hole.

According to office gossip, half the nation's Talk Radio programs were running with the story, including Howard Stern in New York. Public sympathy seemed to be on the Ladykiller's side. A woman driven over the edge by her bosses, turned into a latter-day version of Bonnie without Clyde. *Thelma and Louise* was brought up regularly as an analogy, and so were Charles Bronson and the *Death Wish* films. Everyone had picked up the Ladykiller nickname and Langford knew it was going to stick to her, and to him, like Crazy Glue.

Several major women's organizations had started Ladykiller Defense Funds in the event that she was caught and indicted for the three murders so far, and Langford knew that it wouldn't be long before the first Ladykiller jokes started on the cocktail-lounge circuit. Leno would probably go with it tonight if Letterman didn't beat him to the punch.

In other words, it was an unmitigated public relations disaster, even worse than when the rumors first started floating around that J. Edgar liked to put on pretty dresses and wear silk lingerie. The only positive thing was that no one had figured out Bill Hawkins' role in all of this.

If the ex-FBI man managed to track down Fletcher and Stiles both, it might just be enough to pull the fat out of the fire, but Langford didn't believe in miracles. It was time to call in the troops, muddy the trail, and cover as many asses as he could, including his own. Feeling the first queasy twinges of an incipient bout with his ulcer, Langford picked up the phone and began to place a series of strategic calls.

The Iceman squatted Indian-style, hidden in the dappled tree shadows fifty yards from William DeMille Hawkins' front door. He held a pair of high-powered binoculars up to his eyes, scanning the old farmhouse and the grounds around it. By his calculations Hawkins had been six hours ahead of him getting into Washington.

There was no car parked on the circular drive that ran by the front door and for the last two hours there had been no sign of any activity within the house.

He let the binoculars drop around his neck and closed his eyes. Sometimes – most times – his own senses were more acute than anything else. Little things – tiny sounds, vague scents in the air, movements in the air itself. Ghost vibrations. Magic.

Hawkins wasn't here. Hadn't been for a while. Would be soon. Tiny jeweled shoes and a child swept up in a tornado. Wizard of Oz. The Iceman swallowed, tasted himself. Tornadoes. Maelstroms, chasms opening beneath his feet. Top of the World, Ma! End of the world. It was finishing now, the long dark walk, all of it coming to an end, but not here, not yet. Still a little more to do, a little more to feel before the final transformation.

The Iceman could smell the rich dark soil at his feet, and the richer perfume of the wisteria. The corner of his eye began to pulse and twitch. He reached down and patted the pocket of his windbreaker. The pills. But it wasn't that. The tic in his eye was Hawkins.

He's not in the cycle, out of the circle. The Other.
He doesn't belong.

Coming here he'd toyed with the thought of letting himself become Hawkins, even if it was only for a little while. Take his life and live it, become the other hunter. But that would have been madness, of course. Mixing oil and water, fusing fire to air. Taking Hawkins within him would be death, and the Iceman knew it. Two sides of the same coin could not occupy a single face. He could take, but he could not Be.

Too close.

The woman who answered the phone at Softimage Systems of Carson City, Nevada, wouldn't give Jay Fletcher the time of day, let alone a telephone number or an address for Merlin Ambrose. Jay eventually managed to reach the Company President, a man named Lyle Keefer, but he was equally firm; under no circumstances would he tell Jay, or anyone else, any personal information about Softimage employees or freelance designers.

With the front door slammed in her face, Jay went around the back. By means of the on-line Help number printed on the Softimage game boxes, she used her newly purchased computer to hack her way into their system. She could have done it in a matter of minutes using the programming she'd left behind in Chicago, but even without it she managed to work her way past the various 'firewalls' Softimage had erected to protect itself. By lunchtime she was wandering around through their Unix mainframe system, searching for anything with a tag referencing Merlin Ambrose. By midafternoon she had it; Merlin billed his services through a company called ByteMe Inc., with a listing in New York and a local post office box in Las Vegas.

The New York listing was a phoney. She knew the standard ITT/ATT line check codes by heart and using them she discovered that the ByteMe number was what phone phreaks called a wishing well. The line was permanently open and could be used to jump from one switching network to another without leaving any trace. For Jay it was a dead end.

Working her way back into the Softimage system, she used the ByteMe billing code numbers to run through their entire database. It took a while, and twice she was almost sure that someone at Softimage was aware of an intruder in their system, but eventually she found a match. SK-WIZ, aka Merlin Ambrose, aka ByteMe Inc., was also using the name Lance Follett, c/o Redi-Mail Inc., on East Flamingo Road. Redi-Mail turned out to be a combination mailing service, E-mail address, and desktop publishing company.

It was now late afternoon and Jay realized that she hadn't eaten anything since the sandwich she'd had on the flight in from San Diego the night before. She jotted down some notes, including the trapdoor code she'd left in the Softimage Unix system, then bailed out and shut down the laptop.

According to the map on the inside cover of the Las Vegas telephone directory, East Flamingo Road was only a few long blocks north of her hotel. SK-WIZ, or Lance Follett, was so close now she could almost feel his cold breath on the back of her neck. She shivered slightly in the flat, air-conditioned air blowing through the room and felt a pleasant, vaguely erotic tension in the pit of her stomach.

The odd sensation brought her up short. Fear perhaps, anxiety or simple fright, but not this. If things went the way she'd planned, she'd be confronting a homicidal killer within the next twenty-four hours. That shouldn't...

Turn me on.

She slammed shut the phone book and stood up. She wouldn't think about that. Not now. Not yet. She gathered up her room key and went out the door.

It was fully dark by the time Cruz and Charles Langford reached Hawkins' house on the Potomac Palisades. Langford pulled the Saab to a halt behind Hawkins' car on the driveway and stared at the dark house.

'No lights,' said Cruz, sitting in the passenger seat. 'I thought he told you ten o'clock.'

'He did,' said Langford. He still made no move to leave the Saab. 'Called me from his office at the university.'

'Car's here,' said Cruz. 'Maybe he's taking a nap.'

'Hawkins doesn't nap,' said Langford. 'He was expecting us. Something's wrong.' He reached down and picked up the cell phone from its clip under the dash. He hit the buttons, then held the phone up to his ear.

'Nobody home?'

'Answering machine.' He hung up the phone.

'Does he have another car?'

'No. He's there, but he's not answering.' He paused. 'He doesn't know about the Prentice murder in Vancouver yet. Christ! I let this spin out too long. Stiles is too close.'

Langford took his keys out of the ignition, leaned

over, and unlocked the glove compartment. 'There's a thirty-eight in there. Get it.' He eased open the driver's-side door of the Saab and stepped out into the darkness. Cruz found the gun in the glove compartment and took it out. He checked the load, left on the safety, and slipped the weapon into his jacket pocket. He got out of the car and joined Langford on the gravel drive. Off to his right, the wind was rustling through the trees along the clifftop. To his left, the screening wall of forest between the road and the house was a flat, black mass of shadow. Cruz watched as Langford pulled his own weapon out of a shoulder holster. It was enormous, finished in dull silver. By comparison, the thirty-eight Cruz held was a pea-shooter.

'It's a four fifty-four Casull,' Langford said quietly, seeing the younger man's glance. 'Freedom Arms makes them for myopic old farts like me. Take out a pickup truck at a hundred yards, blindfolded.'

'How do you want to do this?' Cruz asked.

'No back and front,' said Langford. 'We'll wind up killing each other, or Hawkins will kill us first.' He stared at the house a few yards in front of them. Dead quiet. 'Stay on my left. I'll go in and move right, you follow, move left.'

'You know the house?'

'Yes. Long hall. Hawkins' study is on the right, living room and dining room on the left. Kitchen at the back.'

'Any other exits?'

'Back door from the kitchen, French doors off the study into the garden.'

'Security?'

'Pretty basic. Motion detector floods by the door and a silent alarm. If the automatic lights don't go on when we hit the door, that means the system's disabled.' He paused. 'You okay with this?'

'No problem.'

'Sure? You can back out now if you want.'

'I'm sure.'

'All right.'

Langford moved forward, easing up the broad wooden steps that led to the front door. The security lights stayed dark. He pointed to his left with the gigantic weapon and Cruz nodded. The younger man took up his position and Langford tried the doorknob. He jerked it back quickly, as though he'd been burned.

'What?' Cruz whispered. Langford held the hand out. 'Smell.'

Cruz did as he was told. Langford's palm was smeared with something dark. The odor was unmistakable.

'Blood.'

'Christ!' Langford whispered. He used two fingers and turned the doorknob. The door opened easily. He stepped inside, moving to the right with two quick steps. Cruz followed, moving left, his weapon held in the approved, two-handed grip. The interior of the house was dark and silent, but Cruz could taste the familiar tang of blood everywhere. Out of the corner of his eye he saw Langford sag visibly.

'No one here,' Cruz said softly. Langford nodded.

'No one alive.' He reached out with his free hand,

sweeping blindly across the wall until he felt the protruding nub of a light switch. He flipped it on and the hallway was suddenly flooded with light.

'Jesus!' said Cruz. Directly in front of him, less than an inch from the toe of his boot was a lake of blood, long spiking rivers of it following the crevices between the hardwood floorboards. The light switch under Langford's hand was smeared with more blood and two narrow tracks of it led down the hall beyond the bloody pool in front of him.

'Stay behind me,' Langford ordered. Cruz could hear a dry, frightened hitch in the older man's voice. He nodded. Langford stepped over the glistening pool and kept close to the wall, avoiding the blood tracks leading down the hall. Cruz followed.

The trail led into Hawkins' den.

'Oh, shit.'

William DeMille Hawkins was seated in front of his computer, head lolling against the back of his chair. His throat was split by a broad gash cut so deeply that the yellow-white of his spine was clearly visible and a bone-handled carving knife had been slammed through the socket of his good eye. Cruz felt bile rise into the back of his mouth and it took everything he had to keep from vomiting. Beside him, Langford was frozen to the spot, staring. Cruz noticed that the twin trails of blood came through the doorway behind him, ending at the computer workstation. Hawkins had been killed in the front hall, then dragged into the den and arranged in the chair.

Langford's face was twisted with anguish as he stared at his friend. 'Oh, Jesus, Bill. I'm sorry.'

The FBI man moved and Cruz followed. They crossed to the computer. It was up and running, the screen bursting with small exploding balls of color like a fireworks display, backlighting a single word scrawled across the glass in red. Blood red.

'Ladykiller,' Cruz read from the screen. Beside him, Langford reached out a tentative hand toward the bone handle of the knife in Hawkins' eye. He hesitated, then drew back.

'Bullshit,' he said. 'Jay Fletcher didn't do this.'

'Unless she caught him by surprise.'

'She didn't do it,' repeated Langford. 'It doesn't fit the pattern.'

'Stiles?'

'Yes,' said Langford, stepping back. 'It has to be. Bill was getting too close.' He shook his head. 'I think he knew.'

'That Stiles was after him?'

'Yes. He knew Stiles was tracking him through his credit cards. Following him electronically.'

'And now Stiles leaves a message about Jay.'

'A challenge. Throwing down the gauntlet. To us. To Fletcher.' He groaned. 'Goddamn! This makes it a thousand times worse.'

'What do you mean?'

'Ladykiller,' said Langford, pointing at the screen. 'Everybody knows about her, but no one knows about Stiles. He's set it up so she'll take the fall.' He stared down at the corpse in the chair, the gaping wound in Hawkins' throat grinning up at him in a bloody parable of a smile. 'We can't go public with this. If the press gets hold of it, there's going to be a fucking panic.'

'So what do we do?'

'Find her. Find them both. Now.'

The phone beside the computer twittered musically and Cruz felt his heart leap into his chest. Langford reached out, hesitated, then hit the speakerphone button on the console.

'Yes?'

The bland, bored voice of a telephone operator droned into the room. 'Collect call for Mr William Hawkins from Tijuana, Mexico. Will you accept the charges?'

'Yes.'

'Go ahead.'

'Mr Hawkins?' The voice had an accent, making the name sound like *Ho-keens*.

'Yes?'

'I am the Farmacia Enfermo in Tijuana. You remember?'

Langford barely hesitated. 'Yes.'

'I have the name for you.'

'The name.' Langford said it flatly, praying that an explanation would be forthcoming.

'*Si*. The man who takes his medication from us.'

'Medication.'

'*Si*.' The voice was sounding a little frustrated now. 'For the falling sickness. *Epilepsia*, you remember?'

'Oh, yes. Of course.'

'On the credit card slip it was invisible, but I have the number and I call the good people at Visa, yes?'

'Yes.'

'*Si*. And they give us what we want, señor.'

'The name.' Stiles.

'*Si*. And the address, as you wished.'

'Yes.'

'The man you want, his name is Lance Follett.' His second victim. Third, if you counted the bastard priest Hawkins had told them about.

'Can you spell that?' asked Langford. The man from the farmacia did so. 'And the address?'

'*Si*. The credit card address is Post Office Box 22483, Las Vegas, Nevada 89119.'

CHAPTER TWENTY-SEVEN

Reaching Las Vegas shortly after breakfast, Cruz found a motel on the outskirts of town willing to take cash instead of a credit card, did some spadework on his own, then drove to the police station on Stewart Avenue. He didn't have much time. Langford had enough muscle to keep the murder of William Hawkins quiet for a little while, but eventually he was going to have to go public.

His own mandate from Langford was clear. He was the last card in the FBI man's deck. Cruz had a recent personal relationship with Jay Fletcher, and there might even be some kind of emotional bond between them. His job was to find her and hopefully reel her in, using that personal relationship. If that wasn't possible, he was to call Langford for immediate and official backup and then bail out completely. He had no official status, and any official contact with Jay Fletcher, or, God help him, Ricky Stiles, was verboten. Once the murder of Hawkins was revealed, there would be no turning back, and eventually, everything would come out into the open.

Cruz found the Metro Police building tucked in behind City Hall, only a few hundred feet away from North Las Vegas Boulevard and the Strip. There was no FBI field office in Las Vegas, and even if there had been, Langford had made it clear that Cruz was on his own. Cruz knew he was going to be relying on the local police and the old boys' network for assistance.

They didn't offer much. His background as an ex-cop held a little water, but it didn't take him very far. The fact that he was being purposely vague about why he wanted Lance Follett didn't help.

He was passed around from division to division until he wound up in the Records Department, sitting across a desk from a good-looking sergeant named Raybolt, who looked more like an aging showgirl than a police officer. She was in her late thirties and trying hard to stay there, hard-bodied and green-eyed with flaming red hair knotted up in a complex skein at the base of her neck. She fitted her blue-and-black uniform like a glove and she had a voice like rusty nails. There was a fan-powered, smoke-eating ashtray to the left of her computer and a stack of red-and-white Marlboro packages on the right.

'You're a cop?'

'Was a cop. Arson investigator now. Santa Fe.'

'And you want to track this guy down, using our database?'

'If that's possible.'

Sergeant Raybolt coughed and lit another cigarette.

The fan in her ashtray whirred. 'You try looking in the telephone book?'

'There's no listing for a Lance Follett.'

'Maybe he's unlisted.'

'Nope. Tried that too.' The Nevada Bell operator had been pleasantly cooperative after he explained that he was with the FBI, but there was no record of any kind for Follett, listed or unlisted, in Las Vegas or anywhere else in the state. Another name to trace.

'So all you have is the Post Office Box number?' Raybolt asked.

Cruz nodded. 'It's the post office on Swenson, at the corner of East Flamingo Road.' The building was huge, one long wall filled with hundreds of private boxes. Given enough time and people, he could have put it under surveillance, but he had neither.

'Neither rain nor sleet...' said Raybolt, her face cracking open in a brief grin. 'No way they're going to let you into that box, right?'

'Not even with a warrant,' said Cruz, shaking his head. 'It would take me a week of filling out forms just to get a maybe.'

'How bad do you want this guy?' asked Raybolt.

'Bad-bad.'

'That bad?' Raybolt smiled bleakly. She swiveled in her chair and stared at the blank screen of her computer. 'Maybe we'll just take a quick tiptoe through the tulips here.' She booted up, then glanced at Cruz. 'You married?'

'Nope.'

'Good. I pull this off, you take me to dinner, how's that?'

Cruz smiled. The direct approach. 'After I put him away.'

'John Byner's at The Dunes.'

'Who?'

'He's a comedian.'

'You can name the place,' said Cruz. 'Just so long as you find the man I'm looking for.'

'We looking for anything special?'

'He's an epileptic.' Unless the whole epilepsy thing was a blind. Unless Hawkins had been wrong all along.

'I hate to tell you this, but that's not a crime in Nevada.'

'Subject to fits and seizures,' quoted Cruz. 'He might have a restriction on his driver's license.'

'Or he might just lie.' Raybolt shrugged. 'But let's give it a shot.' She tapped away at the keyboard, sat back, and waited. A few seconds later the screen hiccuped, then filled with data.

'Anything?' Cruz asked.

Raybolt scanned the screen, then shook her head. 'No. Some people with Parkinson's.' She looked at Cruz and lit another cigarette. 'What else?'

He tried to think. Killers were like firebugs; no matter how hard they tried, there was always a trace of their presence at the crime scene. So what had Ricky Stiles left behind, somewhere, somehow?

'How about murder?' he asked eventually. Sergeant Raybolt lifted one heavily eyelinered brow.

'You've got to be kidding. We get half a dozen a week.'

Ricky was smart; he wouldn't foul his own nest. If he lived in Las Vegas, he lived here clean as a whistle, Mr Joe Average.

'How about out of towners with a local connection?' said Cruz, trying to think it through. 'Recent ones.' According to Langford, Ricky had panicked and killed Thomas Ritchie and his wife. The murders in Canada and Hawkins' execution were also outside of Stiles normal pattern. If Langford's profiles were right, that could mean that Stiles was breaking down. Maybe he'd made another mistake, closer to home.

'Hang on,' said Raybolt. She addressed the computer again. Another wait. 'Only one in the past little while,' she said finally. 'Hooker in Tijuana. The guy who ran the hotel says he was sure the suspect had Nevada plates.' She made a little clucking noise. 'Put a pair of scissors into the back of her head. Jeez!'

Scissors in the head. The butcher's knife in Hawkins' eye. 'How long ago?' asked Cruz.

'Wednesday,' said Raybolt, checking her screen. The dates matched. Ricky Stiles had been in Tijuana buying phenacemide the same day the Mexican prostitute was killed.

'Did anyone run the license plate tag?'

Raybolt nodded. 'Sure. Me. Says so right here, so I must have.'

'Who owned the car?'

'Rental. Avis from the Airport. Paid for with a credit

card belonging to a Mr Franz Schroeder of Freiberg, Germany.'

'Stolen?'

'Probably. Schroeder was DOA at Desert Springs Hospital a few days before that.'

Cruz sat back in his chair, stunned. 'Murder?'

'Heart attack or stroke, it says here. No sign of foul play. The guy who killed the hooker probably stole the card. Or maybe he bought it on the street.' She shrugged. 'Either way it's a dead end.' She tapped the screen. 'It's got zero priority.'

You should have looked harder, thought Cruz. Hawkins and Langford had told him enough about Stiles' patterns for him to make the connection. He was willing to bet Stiles killed the man in Las Vegas, then used the card to finance his trip to Berkeley.

'The guy exists,' said Cruz. 'I'm almost sure he lives in Las Vegas, or somewhere close by – close enough to make use of that PO Box. I don't have time to stake it out. There has to be some other way.'

Sergeant Raybolt shook her head, sighing wearily. She stubbed out one cigarette and lit another. 'Listen up, I'm going to give you a lecture. You're living in the past. It's not like it used to be, ten, even five years ago. Look at me. I'm thirty-nine years old. When I went to school, an adding machine was a big gray thing with a handle my dad dragged up out of the basement come tax time. Now you can get one that straps on to your wrist, does formulas for rocket fuel, and gives you your pulse rate at the same time it's adding up your checkbook and telling you the time of day. Computers used to be big as a Nash Rambler, now you can launch missiles with a laptop. It's all numbers now, pass codes, Internet, and cash machines.'

Cruz slumped back in his chair. 'You're right,' he said quietly.

Raybolt reached across the desk and patted his arm. 'Nice try, but I think this guy has you beat.' She smiled. 'If you want, I'll take *you* out to dinner. I've still got a little room on the old Visa.'

Cruz sat forward suddenly. The message on Hawkins' machine from the pharmacist in Tijuana. Langford tracking Fletcher, Ricky Stiles tracking Hawkins. Credit cards.

'Cash,' he said quietly. 'She'll be using cash now.'

'She?' said Raybolt. 'I thought we were looking for a man.'

'We are,' said Cruz, sure now that he had the answer. 'And she's going to lead me to him.'

Jay Fletcher sat at one of the courtesy desks in the post office on Swenson, blindly filling out change-of-address cards, trying to keep one eye on Follett's box at the same time. She'd been sitting at the desk for the better part of an hour now, and if she stayed much longer, people were going to get suspicious. By coincidence, the courtesy desk was positioned less than six feet away from the bulletin board where the FBI Ten Most Wanted posters were tacked up. Give it another day or so and she'd be up there with all the others.

Staking out the Wizard's PO Box was obviously nothing more than a frustrating waste of time, but she didn't see what else she could do, given the dead end at Redi-Mail. She filled out another card, added it to her pile, and turned slightly in her chair. The postal station was a long rectangle, the side walls loaded with hundreds of brushed-steel boxes. At the far end of the high-ceilinged public area was a long counter manned by three or four postal workers. Behind the counter area, masked by a dividing wall, was the postal station itself. From what she'd been able to tell, the boxes were filled from the rear; small glass inserts in each door allowed the box holders to see if there was any mail waiting without actually opening the box itself. She'd already checked the Wizard's box number. It was empty except for a small postal service card. Checking at the front counter, Jay discovered that the card in the box was an advisory telling the Wizard that he had a parcel waiting.

According to the mail clerk she talked to, it was likely that the Wizard had already had an identical card sent to his home address, telling him that the package was at the post office. In other words, if he did come in, it was unlikely that he'd check his box at all, he'd simply present his card at the counter and get his package along with any other mail he might have. If he did that, it was going to be another dead end, since she had no way of knowing what the man looked like. She thought briefly about telling the clerk she was with the Bureau, but that would have meant presenting ID in her own name and it probably wouldn't have worked anyway; the US Postal Service was unlikely to give her any information without a blinding array of bureaucratic bullshit.

So give up, stupid. Turn yourself in.

Not a chance. Maybe if she managed to bring the Wizard down, maybe then. But not yet. There had to be a way. One more kick at the can. She tapped her change of address cards into a neat pile, scooped them up, and joined the line at the parcel counter. It was noon now, and there were half a dozen people ahead of her in line. As they all moved forward slowly, she practiced a line of bullshit for the clerk. Somehow she had to know when Follett came for the parcel.

Three people ahead of her now. A guy in a hard hat right in front of her, ahead of him a woman with a baby in her arms and another in a stroller, both squalling. She put a hand down to her belly, tried to imagine a child growing there, day by day. Banished the thought.

The line moved forward again. A dark-haired, medium-height man at the counter now. Wearing a bright red, nylon windbreaker, some company name embroidered obscurely across the back in electric blue. The clerk drifted off into the back. The line ahead of her waited. The baby in the woman's arms was staring back over its mother's shoulder, eyes wide and full of tears, snot dripping down to its chin. The child shuddered, sucking in a long, wet breath, lips pouting. So much for biological clocks, she prayed hers came with a silent alarm.

The name on the back of the windbreaker.

Softimage.

The company that made the Wizard's Kingdom.

Oh shit.

The clerk came back with a parcel, gave it to the man in the windbreaker, and whacked something with a rubber stamp. Jay froze. The man in the windbreaker turned, walked down the line, glanced briefly at the woman with the squalling children.

Eyes met with hers. Deep, black eyes in a pale face. Locked. He stopped, staring right at her, and all she could see was the eyes. Curve of lips as he smiled.

It's him! He knows!

He began to move quickly toward the door. Jay stood where she was for a single, mind-numbed moment, then turned, reaching under her jacket, clutching at the butt of the Browning tucked into the waistband of her jeans. The baby in the line began to bawl again She saw the red and blue of the jacket slipping through a swarm of people coming through the doors. No chance to fire. A miss would mean an innocent death. In a place like this, even a ricochet could be fatal. He was getting away and there was nothing she could do about it.

Go after him.

She ran, dodging an old woman with a walker who'd trudged up behind her in the line, pushing through a clutch of chattering young women in Holiday Inn uniforms, finally reaching the door and slamming through it just in time to see a flash of red and blue getting into a taxi at the curb. Checker. Vision blurring

472

in the sun. No time to get the tags, but enough to read off the hack license: 4772. It headed east, toward the Strip.

'Son of a bitch!'

She stood there, watching her quarry vanish into the heavy traffic moving along Flamingo Road. Right in the palm of her hand and he'd slipped through her fingers. She spotted another Checker cab heading in the same direction as the car used by the Wizard, jumped out into the street, and flagged it down, ignoring the screech of brakes and the horn blasts as she zigged and zagged her way to the other side of the avenue. She wrenched open the door of the cab and threw herself into the back seat.

'You out of your mind, dear?' The woman behind the wheel of the taxi was in her fifties, huge breasts ballooning out over her pale blue terrycloth halter top.

Jay tried to catch her breath. 'A guy just got picked up by one of your cabs. Heading east toward the Strip.'

'You're not giving me one of those "follow that car" routines, are you?'

'I want to know where he's going.'

'No way.'

Jay reached into the pocket of her jeans and pulled out a wad of bills. 'Fifty do it?'

'I'd need the car number.'

Jay passed the money forward. '4772,' she said.

'Hang on.' The woman punched a set of numbers into the keyboard of her trip computer. 'Just take a second,' she said, looking back over her shoulder. Jay nodded, still breathing hard. Words began to scroll across the liquid crystal display unit: Mirage.

'What's that?'

'You'll see.' The woman pulled abruptly out into the traffic and headed for the Strip.

The Mirage was something right out of the Wizard's game. Waterfalls, lagoons, a thousand palm trees in gigantic pots. Bengal tigers and an erupting volcano looming in front of the gilded dolphins spouting water by the main doors. No sign of Follett. She headed into the rain forest lobby and let her eyes roam over the crowds of milling people. Nothing.

A flash of red. She focused on it, picking off the line of blue lettering as Follett slipped through the crowds and went through the entrance to the casino.

He was waiting for me.

She threaded her way through the crowds, walking as quickly as she could without attracting too much attention, and headed into the casino. It was enormous but strangely informal. More tropical plants and Jimmy Buffett music wafting over the rows of video-poker consoles and slot machines. Acres of craps. Soft lights and blackjack. Once again, the distant flash of red and blue, moving quickly toward another exit.

He was waiting for me.

Through the rows of slots, following the taunting jacket. From the casino on to a moving sidewalk that hummed and bumped along, heavy with tourists toting cameras. At least half of them were Japanese. The gun on her back was like a lead weight against her spine. Too many people. The bastard knew she wouldn't do anything here.

She stepped off the moving sidewalk and blinked, wondering if she'd slipped into some kind of dreamworld – Follett's madness. She found herself standing in broad daylight, clouds gently drifting in a blue sky, a pleasant breeze blowing in her face as she stared down a long, stone-floored causeway flanked by dozens of small stone buildings with terracotta tile roofs. Ancient Rome. Women in togas and a fountain in front of her with marble statues. Not statues at all. The fountain was spurting water and the statues were playing musical instruments. Laser beams danced across their blank, plastic faces. Electronic birds twittered somewhere. A young man walked by in a pale yellow Roman tunic, wearing a sandwich board over his chest, advertising something called Boogies.

The Twilight Zone.

On her left, a directory. The Forum Shops. Now she saw it. Theme shopping in a Roman Market. Vuitton luggage in the window of one shop, Gucci in the window of another. The fountain figures were Disney-style robots and the sky was a back-projected trompe l'oeil illusion on a huge arched ceiling high overhead.

Where is he?

There. The windbreaker again, turning into a space between two shops a hundred yards down the time travel arcade. Virtual reality made almost real. Follett in his element.

Waiting for me. How?

He knew I'd come.

Go to the post office.

475

'Tricky bastard.'

He'd put a flag on his files at Softimage and she'd tripped some kind of an alarm. An early warning system. She pelted down the street and turned in between the shops, hand on her weapon.

Got you now.

Gone. A bored man with a plastic laurel crown standing beside a rack of keys. The sign above the door said VALET PARKING EXIT. Furious, she brushed past the parking attendant and pushed through the door. She stopped, blinking in the sudden, blinding sunlight. In front of her a paved lot the size of a football field shimmered in the early-afternoon heat. A thousand cars baked on an asphalt griddle.

No flash of red and blue. She'd lost him.

CHAPTER TWENTY-EIGHT

Janet Louise Fletcher, known as Jay to her friends, if she still had any, and now as the Ladykiller to everyone else in the world, stood in front of the bathroom mirror in her hotel room and surveyed the damage. A slightly less than anorexic version of Sinead O'Connor approaching forty. She'd seen her face splashed over half a dozen newspapers in the hotel newsstand and, coming back to her room, she'd seen the head shot they were carrying on CNN every half-hour.

With four fast coats of self-tanning lotion on her face and a whole lot of eye shadow and mascara, she wasn't anything like the pictures they were running and she prayed the taxi driver and the mail clerk at the post office didn't make the connection. The rough buzzcut she'd given herself and the scalp massage of Lady Clairol Silvertip were the best part, but the plain lens glasses and the bicycle pants and skintight T-shirt outfit she'd picked up did their bit as well.

Arch-fiend on vacation.

Somewhere between Albuquerque and here, Jay
Fletcher had disappeared. Jay Fletcher couldn't exist in
the same world with people like Homer Dunton or Dr
Kushinski with his ridiculous little pink Willie and his
cherry tobacco. You couldn't be Jay Fletcher anymore;
you just couldn't. Mom was a tattoo on Jeffrey Dahmer's
arm and Apple Pie was something you used as a sex aid.
Nothing worked now; the world was running on empty.
A line of poetry drifted up out of her past, something
she'd learned in school, dimly remembered. Betrayed by
the bitch psychiatrist in Washington. Betrayed by
herself. Again.

The center cannot hold.

And here she was, right at that center, a stranger.

The center cannot hold.

She turned away from the mirror, afraid that she
would have to give herself a name. Give what she was
doing a name. It felt as though she was spinning off into
space, everything that she had been, was, or ever could
be falling away like the scraps of her own hair on the
cold tiles of the bathroom floor. When the chambermaid
came in tomorrow, would she know what she was
sweeping up – evidence of the Ladykiller? More likely
she'd mutter something in Spanish under her breath
about pig-tourists. Tomorrow. Once upon a time she'd
known what that would bring: coffee and a doughnut,
eagerness for work, peace of mind, later in the day a jog
along the Canal with Nadine, puff-puff, hey, wouldn't it
be nice to live in Georgetown?

She stumbled out of the bathroom, lay naked on the

bed, trying to slow the desperate beating of her heart. The tears that were forming in her eyes.

'Big Girls Don't Cry.' She remembered the first time she'd ever heard that song. An old, scratched 45 in the counter juke at Fernie's, a block away from school. She'd played it over and over again all that summer of 1976. 'Big Girls Don't Cry.'

Outside it was getting dark again and the planes were roaring over the hotel with the whole city beginning to burn and flicker like a giant neon beacon in the middle of the desert. She'd almost had him, but she'd let him get away. This time she was going to nail him.

Just this last one, I promise.

What do you mean, promise? You think he's the last serial killer in the world? He's not even the last serial killer in the state.

And that was it, wasn't it? We should have expected all this death and killing; it had to come because we all grew up. We were born into a world where little girls wore frilly dresses and looked either like Veronica in the *Archie* comics or Margaret in *Dennis the Menace*. Fat girls and plain girls were the only ones who knew about sex because they were the only ones who needed it; the pretty ones got by on promises. The dolls we coveted had smooth plastic bodies and breasts without nipples. Barbie never got her period or worried about her mother finding cum stains in her panties. Skipper grew up by lifting her arm. The only ones who died on television were the guest stars.

There was no rape in America; there was only

laughter and sunshine. Murder was a mystery to be
solved by the end of a thin paperback. Stephen King was
a worried schoolteacher with a pregnant wife, living in
a trailer somewhere in the backwoods of Maine, desperately tapping out dirty stories for *Men Only* magazine in the middle of the night, only dreaming about the
horrors in his future. Everything was going to be just
fine.

Nobody shot presidents.

Nobody carved their initials in the belly of a pregnant
actress, then wrote *Helter Skelter* on the walls in
blood.

She'd had a friend when she was five, a little boy
named Arnie Arthur Bellecamp whose parents still
hadn't bought a television. One day they did, and
Annie thought it was a dream come true. The voices
came from behind the fabric covering the swivel base
and the music was provided by a tiny orchestra of
musicians no larger than toy soldiers. The screen
was a window into some other universe sponsored by
Palmolive and Eno Fruit Salts, and when you wanted to
go out and play, you simply switched off the set and left
the room, secure in the knowledge that when you
returned, you could turn it on again and pick up where
you'd left off.

We all believed.

Not anymore.

Jay Fletcher lay in the gathering gloom, cold air
across her body, the air filled with the jet scream of the
descending planes, her heart slowing carefully, the

tears drying. She smiled up at the ceiling, letting it all come out of her in a single wave of nothingness that left her soul empty, clear, and pure.

It was all memory and what you did with it. Like a computer with its hard drive overloading. From time to time, you had to purge, delete that which was no longer needed. Take out the dark spots, clean up the viruses, and worms, rid the past and future of those black sucking things surrounding you, give yourself a fresh start. You could remember only so much before it destroyed you, and the center finally collapsed.

Years ago she'd taken two weeks of a summer between degrees, bought a cheap charter to Europe, and hitchhiked around. Standing by the side of a highway in Belgium, it suddenly occurred to her that two world wars had been fought across the ground where she stood, and the fields of grain around her and the dark forest in the distance had once echoed to the screams of half a million dying men.

The history, the memory, was all around her, invisible unless you allowed yourself to see it. She'd bent down, picked up a handful of dirt and held it to her nose, trying to smell the past. She couldn't. Standing up and sticking out her thumb again, she wondered if she was crazy, then told herself that everyone gets a little crazy sometimes.

A little crazy for a little while longer. If I don't stay down the rabbit hole for too long, I'll be able to find my way back up to the surface. I'll wake up beside my sister with my little dog asleep in my lap and the rabbit will

*just be a rabbit, no pocket watch or waistcoat and gloves.
I'll be back on the banks of the Thames with Lewis
Carroll.*

*Remember him? The pedophile who liked taking
pictures of naked little girls.*

Dear God, leave me alone.

She climbed out of bed and began to dress.

The episode at the post office had been a fiasco, but
getting into Redi-Mail's innards had been a snap, and
she cursed herself for not figuring it out sooner. She'd
dropped into Redi-Mail after losing Follett at the
Mirage and after she told the nerd behind the counter
about her own interest in computers, he'd been only too
pleased to give her a tour. She'd stood beside him,
shoulder-surfing as he showed her his chops on the
incoming fax computer, and two minutes later she'd
memorized his SysOps entry code into the whole local
area network that ran Redi-Mail's computers.

Back at the hotel, she'd used the code to piggyback on
the next incoming call to the little business and everything after that was easy. Lance Follett had an open
account with Redi-Mail; a lot of his long-distance time
racked up with Softimage in Carson City, with the
remainder logged to an unfamiliar number in Boulder,
which was probably his gateway account into the Net. It
was all she needed.

In the end, that was the ultimate weakness – one way
or the other SK-WIZ had to have an ordinary telephone
line, with an ordinary number, if he was going to reach
the big bad world out there. His billing address was the

482

post office box, but the phone number was local. Leaving the hotel again, she took a cab to the Clark County Library on Escondido Avenue and consulted a commercial three-way directory. According to the book, the telephone number was for an address on Caliente Street. The big municipal map in the library, showed her that Caliente Street was no more than a mile or so away, east of the university complex and south of the Liberace Museum. Simple as one, two, three.

Wearing her T-shirt and spandex outfit, she looked at herself in the mirror again.

You can stop yourself. You don't have to do this.

'Yes, I do.'

She tucked her Browning into her shoulder bag, took a last look at the stranger she'd become, then turned and left the room. It had come full circle now, like a novel by James Joyce. The end was about to begin.

The Ladykiller reached Lance Follett's house on Caliente Street just after 10 p.m. She'd called the number several times, the last from a pay phone at the 7-Eleven, where she'd picked up her camouflaging bag of groceries. No answer. Maybe he was out, or maybe he was waiting. In the dark. He would have seen the pictures in the newspaper by now, or seen the sketch on television. Nadine had lots of pictures of her; in a day or so they'd have her photograph, not just a drawing, wouldn't matter then.

The house was a plain, fifties-style rancher just like the ones on either side of it. One-storied, covered in a yellow stucco parched and windblown down to a pale, jaundiced cream. The grass on the lawn was almost exactly the same color. She'd gone around the block twice, picking up as much detail as she could each time. A third time would look suspicious. She'd spun it out long enough. The Ladykiller went up the cracked concrete walkway to the front door. No vehicle in the carport. Lots on the street. Middle-class or lower, Chevs and Fords. No shadowed figures waiting, or at least none that she could see. The house had its own transformer box to the right of the front steps. She could see a heavy-duty cable running through the glass chamber of the meter.

220 current. All that computer equipment.

Reaching the door she shifted the groceries. She'd kept the Browning in her shoulder bag, then transferred it to the 7-Eleven bag on her way down to Caliente Street. Now it was in her hand, hidden in her armpit, a spare clip tucked into the waistband of her bicycle pants. All she had to do was drop the grocery bag, aim, and fire. No discussion, no explanation, no games this time. No time to think for either one of them.

He's an animal. Put him down.

She knocked.

The door shifted under her knuckles. It was unlocked and ajar.

This is an invitation.

Step into my parlor, said the spider to the fly.

Who's the spider?

Who's the fly?

She stepped into the house, put down the bag of groceries in the narrow hall, and brought up the Browning in her hand. No smells like at Kushinski's. Clean, maybe a hint of pine air freshener. But whispers. Sounds coming from the other rooms.

The hall was dark, the only light spilling in from the open door. She closed it behind her, then paused, letting her eyes adjust, the Browning now raised in the ready position at her cheek. No surprises. Whispers. The sound of a humming air-conditioner riding over everything. She nodded to herself. The door was open and the compressor was working overtime as the cool air it produced was being sucked out into the hot desert night.

This isn't like the others.

The T-shirt and the spandex bicycle pants had been a good idea. Nothing to catch and pull, nothing to slow her down. She was a smooth, sure thing, aerodynamic as a bullet striking home. Nothing to stop her. She moved slowly down the hallway, silently slipping the bag off her shoulder with one hand and easing it to the floor. Nothing in it that she needed.

She could feel every part of her body, every inch of sinew and bone and muscle. Every nerve ending. The bicycle pants were molded against her hips and groin like another skin, hot and tight and powerful, so terribly, awfully, wonderfully strong.

All those lectures about the organized and the disorganized, the rituals of it all, the deep psychological roots of serial death. She could feel the loose touch of Dunton's scarab on the index finger of her left hand.

Totems. All a crock. There was nothing very hard to understand about it. Some people were addicted to cigarettes, others to booze or pills. Some, a few, were simply addicted to killing, and like any other vice, the need grew with passing time as tolerances to the drug increased. A bigger fix. They did it because it felt good, gave them pleasure. And it hurt so many other people, not just the victims, but their families, too. The killers didn't care, why should they?

I care.

She reached the end of the hallway and paused again, listening to the whispers muttering behind the deep hum of the air-conditioner. The air was freezing cold and she had to fight off the urge to shiver. She gripped the butt of the Browning hard, slipped into the room beyond, rustling through the long beaded curtain.

Don't look!

She stood in the Wizard's living room and surveyed his kingdom. It was fifteen feet on a side, one wall taken up by a large picture window, covered by dark drapery that blocked out the street beyond. Crammed with furniture. One couch, dozens of little mismatched knick-knack shelves, end tables, card tables, occasional tables. A single rocking chair in the corner.

On the tables and the shelves, five hundred candles lit and flickering. On the other walls ten thousand photographs, large and small, torn and bent and crumpled into a mosaic of insanity that paced across the nation from one coast to another. On the floor, a dozen cheap cassette decks, each one playing a different whispering symphony of agony. A dozen television sets on more tables, black and white, color, old and new, all linked to a single videotape recorder, all playing the same thing, a portfolio of madness, a hundred times worse than Sladky's wall of pictures showing the Hand Job victims, a thousand times worse than Dr Kushinski's cats. Résumé for an executive position in hell.

Oh, Jesus, how many has he killed?

Hundreds?

In the twisting shadows cast by the candles, she could see it all. Torn faces stripped down to blood and bone, eyeless faces, faces that had no face at all. Children, men, and women, dozens of them, scores of them, and everywhere around her, the barely heard sounds of crunching bone and moans and incoherent rattling screams of terror.

I want him.

How do you want him?

Dead.

Behind her a section of the wall burst open silently on its hidden hinges and out of the corner of her eye she caught a glimpse of the whistling baseball bat as it swung through an arc that missed the back of her head only because she had instinctively jerked away from the falling blow almost before she was aware of it. The bat caught her on the shoulder and she felt the shuddering pain slice across her chest and neck. She fell, rolling to one side, sending tables and candles scattering across the room.

The batter screamed. 'Watch *me*! Shitfucker!'

Face up, half blinded with pain, she lifted her gun hand and fired as the looming figure leapt forward, raising the bat again. She kept her finger down on the trigger, a fraction of her mind aware that she was emptying the clip without aiming. The figure hurtled backward and more tables crashed as he struck the far wall, tumbling to one side, the bat still in his hand.

Her finger came off the trigger and the firing stopped. Six, seven, eight? How many left?

Dead. He has to be dead. I fired point-blank.

She felt a searing pain on her cheek, then felt it again. Cut? Bleeding? No. Hot wax, dripping down on her from somewhere. On the far side of the room the dark figure groaned, then rose up from the floor, using the baseball bat as a lever. The shape of him was wrong, boxy and hard-edged, and his legs rubbing together swished like plastic. Some kind of suit.

Oh shit, he's wearing Courage. Kevlar body armor, the fucking Policeman's Friend.

Off to one side, the hidden door sagged open and she could see into the little room beyond, choked with computer equipment. Center of the Wizard's Kingdom. The figure stumbled against one of the overturned tables and almost fell again.

'Shitfucker.' The word came as a whisper and she heard him repeat it with each step he took toward her.

All around the room the candles licked at the photographs, starting little fires. The man stamped them out as he came forward, still leaning on the bat. Something dark was leaking down one plastic-covered leg.

I got him.

She kicked hard, sending one of the tables spinning toward the man, knocking over another group of candles. He responded by lifting the bat, smashing it one-handed across his chest, demolishing one of the television sets and sending up a spray of sparks. She forced herself on to her side, screaming again as she put pressure on her ruined shoulder.

Someone must have heard the shots. They'll call for help.

Don't be an idiot. No one's coming.

She scuttled back, kicking at more tables, reaching out with her gun hand to swipe at a skein of cables, sending a pair of television sets crashing down on to the floor. The man continued to come forward, lifting the bat high now, ready for the killing blow. She could see him clearly now, his smiling face above the ribbed carapace of body armor protecting his chest.

'Shitfucker!'

He's pretty.

That's why he smiled at me.

She lifted the Browning, letting her arm aim itself like a pointing finger, just like the Academy instructor had told her. Point and kill. She'd worn body armor once or twice herself, remembered the crotch flap and the little dip for your throat.

Her brain told her finger to squeeze the trigger, but nothing happened. Her arm and hand were still numb from the blow he'd struck. Nerve paralysis. From six feet away, he swung the terrible bat again, crashing his way toward her through the flickering light from the candles. All around her the tapes whispered and moaned, his victims dying again and again. She scrabbled backward, pushing a table down in front of him, delaying him for another second. Again the bat swung and wood splintered.

'Shitfucker!'

She got her feet under her and rolled away to the right, bringing down a shower of candles, more hot wax splashing down on to her. Even trying to lift the right arm was impossible now. She used her left hand to reach over for the gun, but he swung again, coming in behind her now. Directly in front of her was the open door to the secret room. A few feet. A yard. Lashing out with one leg she managed to bring down the big bookcase, scattering its contents into the middle of the room, the heavy piece of furniture toppling down behind her. Bouncing off the wall, she veered into the secret room with its massed racks of computer equipment.

He's got you cornered. This is what he wanted.

Bizarrely she found herself staring at a twenty-gallon aquarium filled with tropical fish that were swimming around benignly in blue-lit water. Computer hard drive below it, modems and switching equipment above. Sound of a little air pump and streams of bubbles. Still no feeling in her arm.

'You can't go in there!' The voice was a banshee scream. Behind her was the whistling sound of the bat cutting through the air. The aquarium smashed and water, fish, and shards of shattered glass rained down on to the floor. She hurled a chair behind her, then threw herself down, ducking under a large, metal desk. Twisting, she saw Follett's legs and the frenzied bat as it swung again. Her arm was a single burning ache now, but at least she could move her fingers.

Another minute, that's all I ask, please, God!

She crabbed back even farther, reaching into the small of her back for the spare clip. Follett swung the bat again and again, filling the air with the sound of ruptured plastic and grinding metal, his breath coming now in heaving, choking gasps.

Thirty seconds.

She brought her knees up as the bat sliced down under the desk, tip glancing off her shin and making her scream aloud. She slammed the butt of the gun down on to the tight flesh of her thigh, popping out the empty clip. In front of her in the dim light, she could make out Follett's sneakered feet splashing through the broadening pool of water on the linoleum-tile floor.

He's not wearing any socks.

Jay forced herself back even more into the corner, still protected by the surface of the desk above her. Her hand caught in the tangle of cables running down behind the desk, frustrating her attempt to get at the spare clip.

Please, just a little more time!

Fingers found the clip, pulled it from the gripping spandex waistband.

Dropped it.

Oh shit.

Silence. Dripping water. Follett standing back now, visible up to the knees, bat swinging softly back and forth. The sound of his breathing less ragged. A soft moan. Again she noticed the dark stain on his leg, running down into his right sneaker. Blood. She'd managed to wound him anyway. Slow him down. But not enough.

He's got me now.

He bent down, staring under the table, balancing himself with the bat. She stared back at him and saw that the light in his eyes was fiercely bright as though he'd recognized something wonderful a thousand miles beyond her in the twisting light of the guttering candles in the room behind him. The huge eyes slid into her, filling her completely, taking away her breath.

'Almost.' He smiled. 'You almost did it.'

She felt the clip behind her on the cool floor, brushing it with the tips of her fingers. Not nearly enough time. She brought the arm forward, felt it tangle in the cables again, and paused, glancing down at the puddle of water on the floor between them.

A chance?

'I guess you outsmarted me,' she said. He smiled.

'Playing for time?' The smile broadened. The eyes were like holes in the world. Dead. 'Why bother?'

'Never say die,' she managed weakly. Felt the thicker weight of a power cable. Tugged, making sure she pulled at the connected end, not the wall socket. Felt something give. Tugged again.

'I could never figure that one out.' He shook his head,

still smiling with his mouth, but with pain in the hard muscles of his jaw. The blood was over his shoe-top now, mixing with the spreading puddle of aquarium water. 'Never say die,' he repeated. 'Doesn't make sense. If you're dead, you can't say anything anyway.'

'I'm not dead yet.'

'You will be. Soon.'

'You think I came here alone, Mr Follett. Wizard Man?' A weak bluff, but she needed time. Tugged on the cable again, prayed it would be long enough. Felt more give.

'I know you did. And your weapon is out of bullets.'

'You counted?'

'If you could fire, you would have by now.'

'Smart boy.'

That beautiful face. How many times? A hundred, two, three?

'Smart enough.' He paused. She kept staring, maintaining eye contact, trying to keep him talking. Tugged again, felt the cable give, slip, and snake down behind her. Let her fingers touch. Plug end. Power cord for at least one of the computers, maybe the main power cord.

Pray for me.

'What's your name, Miss Watch Me? I collect names, you know.'

Keep him talking.

'Jay.'

Two killers, having a conversation.

'That's a bird, not a name.' She let the Browning fall out of her right hand, watched as his eyes flickered to it.

Gripped the plug end harder in her left hand, bent the thicker, ground prong with her thumb. Felt it snap.

'Janet,' she said. 'Janet Louise.'

'I don't like it,' he answered. She grimaced.

'Never been a favorite of mine, either.' She shifted her weight slightly, getting ready. One slim chance.

'I think I'll call you Celandine,' he said softly.

Who?

He rose, groaning, pushing himself up with the bat. Time had run out for one of them.

What did they call it at the Academy? That first-session course in first aid?

Instantaneous Ventricular Fibrillation.

'Come on, Janet Louise, come on.' Voice soft as an angel's wing. Angel of Death. 'Love is never having to say you're sorry.'

Cardiac arrhythmia.

She flipped the ungrounded power cable out from behind her back and into the puddle two feet in front of her. Squeezed her eyes shut with the sizzling flash of brilliant pulsing light.

Fatal.

You should have watched me.

She opened her eyes and watched as the body twitched and heaved, lips pulling back over gleaming teeth, ripples of current skating across the puddle of water like ribbons of St Elmo's Fire. Heels drummed on the floor. Her fingers gripped the cable and she pulled hard, dragging the plug end out of the wall socket behind her. There was a sharp snapping sound and the crackling current vanished. The body sagged and then was still. Fall of the Wizard's Kingdom. His reign was over.

The King is dead.

Long live the Queen.

When Cruz walked up to the house on Caliente Street, the door was standing slightly open and he could smell the distinctive odor of burning candles. He pushed open the door with one finger. Distantly he could hear the faint shuffling sounds of someone moving around. Stepping inside he left the door wide open behind him.

'Jay?' he called out. 'Jay Fletcher?' He slipped Langford's .38 short barrel out of his belt. No answer, but the shuffling sounds had stopped abruptly. Fletcher, or Stiles? He called out again. 'Fletcher? It's Cruz.'

Still no answer. He stepped forward down the short hall. Ahead he could see flickering light and the shadows of someone moving. 'Fletcher?'

Silence. He reached the end of the hall, lifted the handgun, and took two steps forward into the room, sweeping the gun around in a wide circle. Dozens of smashed television sets, the littered remains of a score of cassette-tape machines. He turned at a moving shadow behind him. Another room. He stepped into the doorway, gun at the ready. He stopped, rooted to the spot as his adapting vision picked her out. She was standing over the smoking ruins of Ricky Stiles, using a baseball bat like a crutch. She was favoring her left side and her face was screwed up in pain. There was a Browning automatic stuffed into the waistband of her skin-tight bicycle pants, bulging out the fabric in phallic parody.

There was something else there as well. Even in the half-light Cruz could see her diaphragm rise and fall in jerks and the panting, open mouth. Her breasts were moving quickly with the short, sharp breathing. Sex, or something even more potent, was coming off her in waves. He glanced down at the bat in her hands and then at Ricky Stiles. He was wearing body armor. There was some kind of wound high on his hip, but the face was unmarked. There was a faint scent of ozone in the air. Beyond the body, Cruz could see a small room filled with smashed computer equipment. There were tiny, smouldering fires everywhere, flames spurting and dying, wisps of smoke trailing into the air.

'Cruz?' She looked up blearily, blinking in the guttering light. She was hyperventilating, her voice gasping.

'Yes.'

'Why?' Her hand went to the butt of the Browning. There was something almost brutally erotic in the gesture and Cruz had to look away, not trusting his own expression.

'Him,' he said, ducking his head in the body's direction. 'Follett's dead.'

'His name wasn't Follett; that was one of his victims, a long time ago. His real name was Ricky Stiles.'

'How do you know that?'

'I've been talking to Charlie Langford.'

'He sent you after me?'

496

'I sent myself.'

'Why?'

'Because this has to stop. Stiles is the end of it, Jay. You can't go on.'

The woman looked down at the body and shook her head. 'I don't think Ricky Stiles was his name, either,' she said quietly, her breath evening out. 'Not that it matters.' She looked up at Cruz again. She was calm now, but her hand still rested on the butt of her weapon. She looked terribly tired, but he reminded himself quickly of what she had proved capable of doing. She stepped over the smoldering body, dropping the baseball bat as she went. Cruz followed her into the main room of the house. She turned to him, frowning. 'How did you find me?' she asked.

He shrugged. 'You started paying in cash. These days that makes you stand out like a sore thumb. It didn't take long to run you down once I figured that out.'

'How did you get here, to this house?'

'You were the computer expert. I figured you'd do what I couldn't. Lead me to Stiles.'

'So you followed me?'

'Yes.'

'And just waited around? You must have known what was going to happen.' She stared at him coldly. 'What if he'd killed me instead of the other way around?'

He shrugged. He'd already thought about that. To hell with Langford. He had his own personal agenda here, just like Jay. 'Then I would have had a perfect reason for blowing him away, wouldn't I?' He looked down at what was left of Ricky Stiles. 'This was your game, Jay. It was yours to finish, not mine. Win or lose.'

'Fairly unethical, don't you think?' she said. Her eyes were sagging closed with fatigue. 'Not to mention immoral.'

'You're hardly in a position to talk about morality.'

'This is ridiculous,' she muttered. 'I'm leaving.' She took a step forward, but Cruz blocked her path.

'I can't let you do that,' he said, raising his weapon slightly.

'Why not?'

'Because you're a killer. Because you'll kill again if I let you go. Because you broke the rules, Jay.'

The woman sighed wearily. Her breathing and her voice were almost back to normal. 'You don't get it, do you? There are no rules anymore. We make them up as we go along. I'm not a killer; I'm just someone trying to fill a hole or two in the dike.' She tilted her head back toward the body in the hidden room. 'These aren't human beings. They're not even animals. They don't have hearts, or souls or feelings. They do what they do because they want to do it. Nothing more complex than that. Machines that eat and breathe and shit and kill.' She paused. 'You would have let me die in here, you said so yourself. That puts you and me on the same level. So who are you to judge me, Cruz?'

She gestured toward the room filled with computer equipment hidden behind the hinged false wall. 'Take a look for yourself. I have. There's enough evidence in there to track down a dozen others just like Stiles, but

Charlie Langford won't use it because it's tainted – fruit of the poisonous tree or whatever the hell the law says.' She was breathing harder again, her hand clenching and unclenching on the Browning. 'Well, screw the law,' she said furiously. 'If I don't stop them, nobody else will.'

'What are you looking for?' asked Cruz.

'Call it whatever you want,' she answered. 'But get out of my way.'

'And if I don't?'

'What are you going to do?' she asked, smiling now. 'Shoot me?'

He looked at the gun in his hand then back at the haggard woman standing a few feet away. He shook his head and tucked the .38 back into his belt.

'No. I can't do that.' And that was a lie. He could, but he wouldn't. She knew it was all a matter of choice, and he'd made his just as surely as she'd made hers.

She nodded, then came forward, brushing past him, heading down the hall, her left shoulder visibly sagging. As she went by him, he wanted to reach out, to touch her, to say something.

'Jay?'

'What?' she asked, turning as she reached the front door.

'It's not going to be easy.'

'You could make it easier,' she answered.

'How?'

'Give me some time. An hour. The night. A day. Anything.'

'I'll think about it.'

'Do that, please.' She smiled, letting it light her face this time. 'I'm not crazy, you know.' The smile soured wryly. 'A little strange maybe, but not crazy.'

A different kind of animal.

'I know that,' he said quietly. He paused, then spoke again. 'Where will you go?'

She looked beyond him, staring back toward the terrible room, thinking even further, remembering what she'd read on the only computer screen still working. The printout she'd found and stuffed down the back of her bicycle shorts. The horror lying ahead.

'Germany,' she said, lying, remembering the other name she'd seen on the crazy veterinarian's database in Slippery Rock.

Baltimore. A doctor's appointment.

'What will you do there?' Through all the pain and weakness and fatigue written across her face, he could see something deep within her, yearning and almost sad. For the second time, he wanted to reach out and comfort her, touch her, hold her close. He didn't move. She smiled, remembering a few moments between them in Santa Fe. Thinking about what could have been. Would have been if she had stayed. Could be even now perhaps.

Really? Can I still have that kind of life?

All he has to do is ask.

No. Too late for that now. Too late for anything except what lies ahead.

She gave him a little wave, then stepped out through the door, into the warm night, the sky above her filled with stars just like the dreaming night oasis of the Wizard's Kingdom. Far more exciting and beautiful than anything offered by the glittering city that lay all around her. She thought about Cruz, and almost turned again, back to a world that might have been, could have been. He spoke to her from the doorway. One last time.

'You can't go on with this, Jay.' He paused. It was a plea. 'You can't.'

She answered him softly, without turning, looking up at the endless sky and the stars. 'Really?'

Walked away.

Watch me.

More Compelling Fiction from Headline Feature

JOHN T. LESCROART

HARD EVIDENCE

'A GRIPPING COURTROOM DRAMA ...
COMPELLING, CREDIBLE' *Publishers Weekly*

'Compulsively readable, a dense and involving saga of big-city crime and punishment' *San Francisco Chronicle*

Assistant D.A. Dismas Hardy has seen too much of life outside a courtroom to know that the truth isn't always as simple as it should be. Which is why some of his ultra-ambitious colleagues don't rate his prosecuting instincts as highly as their own. So when he finds himself on the trail of a murdered Silicon Valley billionaire he seizes the opportunity to emerge from beneath a mountain of minor cases and make the case his own. Before long he is prosecuting San Francisco's biggest murder trial, the accused a quiet, self-contained Japanese call girl with an impressive list of prominent clients. A woman Hardy has a sneaking, sinking suspicion might just be innocent ...

'Turowesque, with the plot bouncing effortlessly between the courtroom and the intraoffice battle among prosecutors ... The writing is excellent and the dialogue crackles' *Booklist*

'A blockbuster courtroom drama ... As in *Presumed Innocent*, the courtroom battles are so keen that you almost forget there's a mystery, too. But Lescroart's laid-back, soft-shoe approach to legal intrigue is all his own' *Kirkus*

'John Lescroart is a terrific writer and this is one terrific book' Jonathan Kellerman

'An intricate plot, a great locale, wonderfully colourful characters and taut courtroom drama ... Highly recommended' *Library Journal*

'Breathtaking' *Los Angeles Times*

FICTION / THRILLER 0 7472 4332 8

STEVE MARTINI

PRIME WITNESS

'MR MARTINI WRITES WITH THE AGILE EPISODIC
STYLE OF A LAWYER QUICK ON HIS FEET' John Grisham

'Steve Martini seems to have hit the nail right on the head'
Irish Times

'A real page turner' *Sunday Telegraph*

PRIME WITNESS

In the space of five days the rural college town of Davenport
is rocked by four brutal murders: two couples –
undergraduates – whose bodies are found tied and staked out
on the banks of Putah Creek. Then two more bodies are
discovered. This time the victims are Abbott Scofield, a
distinguished member of the university faculty, and his
former wife Karen.

The police suspect Andre Iganovich, a Russian immigrant and
part-time security guard, but Paul Madriani, hot-shot Capitol
City lawyer, thinks there is more to the case than meets the eye.

Forensic reports on the physical evidence suggest lingering
questions about the Russian's involvement in the Scofield
killings, and Paul becomes increasingly convinced that the
second murders are the product of some copy-cat killer – a
cold and calculating murderer who has taken the lives of the
Scofields for reasons that Paul is determined to uncover . . .

'Prime is indeed the word for this involving read'
Publishers Weekly

'Nice insider touches, and a hard-punching climax'
The Times

FICTION / THRILLER 0 7472 4164 3

A selection of bestsellers from Headline

BODY OF A CRIME	Michael C. Eberhardt	£5.99	☐
TESTIMONY	Craig A. Lewis	£5.99	☐
LIFE PENALTY	Joy Fielding	£5.99	☐
SLAYGROUND	Philip Caveney	£5.99	☐
BURN OUT	Alan Scholefield	£4.99	☐
SPECIAL VICTIMS	Nick Gaitano	£4.99	☐
DESPERATE MEASURES	David Morrell	£5.99	☐
JUDGMENT HOUR	Stephen Smoke	£5.99	☐
DEEP PURSUIT	Geoffrey Norman	£4.99	☐
THE CHIMNEY SWEEPER	John Peyton Cooke	£4.99	☐
TRAP DOOR	Deanie Francis Mills	£5.99	☐
VANISHING ACT	Thomas Perry	£4.99	☐

All Headline books are available at your local bookshop or newsagent, or can be ordered direct from the publisher. Just tick the titles you want and fill in the form below. Prices and availability subject to change without notice.

Headline Book Publishing, Cash Sales Department, Bookpoint, 39 Milton Park, Abingdon, OXON, OX14 4TD, UK. If you have a credit card you may order by telephone – 01235 400400.

Please enclose a cheque or postal order made payable to Bookpoint Ltd to the value of the cover price and allow the following for postage and packing:

UK & BFPO: £1.00 for the first book, 50p for the second book and 30p for each additional book ordered up to a maximum charge of £3.00.
OVERSEAS & EIRE: £2.00 for the first book, £1.00 for the second book and 50p for each additional book.

Name ....

Address ....

....

....

If you would prefer to pay by credit card, please complete:
Please debit my Visa/Access/Diner's Card/American Express (delete as applicable) card no:

Signature .... Expiry Date ....